MW00526835

A
CERTAIN KIND
OF
STARLIGHT

HEATHER WEBBER

TOR PUBLISHING GROUP
New York

A CERTAIN KIND OF STARLIGHT

A Forge Book
Published by Tom Doherty Associates / Tor Publishing Group
120 Broadway
New York, NY 10271

www.torpublishinggroup.com

Forge® is a registered trademark of Macmillan Publishing Group, LLC.

The Library of Congress Cataloging-in-Publication Data
is available upon request.

ISBN 978-1-250-86729-2 (hardcover)
ISBN 978-1-250-86731-5 (ebook)

Our books may be purchased in bulk for promotional,
educational, or business use. Please contact your local bookseller
or the Macmillan Corporate and Premium Sales Department
at 1-800-221-7945, extension 5442, or by email at
MacmillanSpecialMarkets@macmillan.com.

First Edition: 2024

Printed in the United States of America

10 9 8 7 6 5 4 3 2 1

This one is for my dad
and his big, patched-up heart.

A CERTAIN KIND
OF STARLIGHT

CHAPTER ONE

Addie

Rooted deep within a woman's complex DNA was the right to pick and choose the traditions and societal conventions she followed. This was especially true for matriarchs, the backbones, the older women who had seen it all, heard it all, *dealt* with it all, and no longer gave a flying fig what others thought. After years of living, of giving, of conforming, she now played by a set of rules carefully crafted from experience.

I personally believed southern women took this notion to a whole other level and kept that in mind as I studied my daddy's older sister, Verbena Fullbright, fondly known by those closest to her as Bean.

Sitting primly, properly, on a stool pulled up to a stainless steel counter, Aunt Bean had her rounded shoulders drawn back, her head held high. Earlier today she'd been to see her lawyer, old Mr. Stubblefield, so she wore a long-sleeved leopard-print maxi dress and leather slingbacks instead of her usual baking attire. Her hairstyle was a cross between a pixie cut and a pompadour, the color of merlot. Her fingernails were painted black, a polish that would surely raise eyebrows around town if the people here didn't know her and her funky style so well.

It was clear that even while feeling puny, Aunt Bean had stuck to her own particular notions of what was right and proper. She'd never attend a business meeting without wearing heels, even if her swollen feet had to be wedged into the shoes.

"Lordy mercy, those pearly gates are in for a mighty reckoning when I come calling. The heavens will be shaking," Bean said theatrically, humor vibrating in her loud voice.

Her spirited statement was punctuated by two quick thumps of her wooden walking stick on the cement floor, the dramatic effect unfortunately mellowed by the stick's thick rubber tip.

"Quaking, even," Delilah Nash Peebles said as she removed a cake pan from an oven and slid it onto a multi-level stainless steel cooling rack that was taller than she was. She glanced at me, the crow's feet at the corners of her eyes crinkling. "We all know Bean won't be knocking politely. She'll thunder on in and try to take over running the place."

Mid-January sunshine poured in through the glass front door and tall windows of the converted big red barn on Aunt Bean's vast property. It was the temporary home of the Starling Cake Company while the bakery's Market Street location underwent a massive renovation.

I'd arrived a half hour ago and had been feeling a sense of déjà vu since—because this space had previously housed the bakery when it had been a home-based business. The air was once again scented with Aunt Bean's homemade vanilla extract—along with a hint of chocolate and coffee from the mocha cakes currently baking—and everything looked the same as it used to when I was a little and practically glued to her apron strings. Three double ovens on one wall. Two stainless steel workstations. Four stand mixers. The decorating corner. An old range. Two massive refrigerators. A large bakery case.

And just like old times, I fell straight into helping where help was needed. Currently, I was dusting greased cake pans with cocoa powder while trying not to flat-out panic about my aunt's health issues.

"Plus," Bean sniffed loudly, indignantly, "I have a few

grievances that need airing. Saint Peter's going to get himself a right earful."

Delilah added two more pans to the rack. "It's no secret that you have a knack for speaking your mind. If I had a dollar for every time you've fussed about fondant, I'd be a rich woman. Poor Petal was fixin' to pitch a hissy fit when you told her you wouldn't use it for her wedding cake."

"Petal Pottinger?" I asked. "She's getting married?"

I felt a deep ache, one I had become familiar with since moving away from Starlight, from home, twelve years ago. It came from feeling like I was missing out. Mostly because I was.

"Sure enough. She's getting hitched to Dare Fife next weekend in the ballroom at the Celestial Hotel," Delilah said. "I'm convinced he's the only good apple to fall from his crooked family tree. He's almost twenty-two and hasn't been thrown in jail yet, unlike the rest of the men in his family. Has himself a good job, too, at the flour mill."

Dare *Buckley* Fife. My stomach rolled with worry for Petal, because around here, the Buckley name was synonymous with danger, with dishonor, with *damage*.

Bean shifted on the stool. "That Dare's a good boy, so Petal might be all right at picking men, but God love her, she ain't got the sense God gave a goose when it comes to cake. I call it *fondon't* for a reason. And I'll keep on saying it until my very last breath."

"Can we *not*?" I asked, releasing a pent-up sigh. "We don't need to be talking like you're standing on death's door, Aunt Bean."

Because she wasn't. She *wasn't*.

"Now, Addie, it's just talk," she said. "But you know how I feel about dyin'. I'm not the least bit scared of it, though I hope it'll hold off a good while. I've still got some livin' to do."

She might not be scared, but I sure was.

I'd known Bean hadn't been feeling well for months now. After a bout with the flu last November, she'd started having trouble standing for long periods of time and walking distances without feeling out of breath and woozy—which was why she'd gotten the walking stick. I'd chalked up her slow healing simply to getting older. She was closing in on sixty-four, an age when most would be thinking about retiring. But not Aunt Bean.

Like generations of Fullbright women before her, she'd devoted her life to baking. To sharing with others, through cake, the ability to see the bright side of life and its possibilities.

When people tasted one of her confections, they were flooded with pleasant sparks of warmth and happiness as glimmers of hope and optimism, comfort and contentment filled emotional cracks created by life's trials and stresses. Her cakes healed the *soul* and enhanced the inner light that helped guide people through hard times and enabled them to find silver linings in even the toughest situations.

For the bakery's customers, the effects of the cakes lasted a good long while. Weeks. Sometimes months.

For the women in our family, the ability to see a bright side and all that came with it was a near constant in our lives, first appearing almost two hundred years ago after a star fell from the sky onto family land. Legend was that somehow the fallen star with its special glow had given us the gift, and we felt honor bound to use it to bring light and hope and *brightness* to others.

But beyond the glimmers, our bright sides also included the ability to see the good *in* a person, something that was revealed when we looked deeply into someone's eyes. The glow of an inner light showed us the people who were kind, decent. And warned of those who were not.

Right now, though, as I sat in the barn kitchen, I was struggling to see any kind of light. There was no silver lining to be had.

When Bean had called this morning, telling me to get myself immediately back to Starlight for an emergency family meeting about her future plans, I'd felt an ominous chill that couldn't possibly be related to *retirement*. A dark cloud descended.

Gloom followed me as I made the hour and forty-five–minute trip southeast from my apartment in Birmingham to the property that had been in our family for generations. The cloud had lifted only slightly when I'd found Aunt Bean waiting to welcome me with open arms.

Like always.

Immediately I'd noticed the physical changes in her. She'd puffed up a bit since I'd last seen her at Christmastime. Swelling. *Edema*. Then she told me she'd been to see a cardiologist in Montgomery earlier this week and he'd run a test that was worrisome.

I didn't know how to process the information. Not the shock of it and certainly not the sprightly tone Bean and Delilah were using in talking about her possible death, of all things.

I lifted a cake pan, holding it carefully as I turned it this way and that, coating the surface in cocoa powder while I tried to think of something to say. Anything. But all the questions, all the love I had for my beloved aunt, were tangled up in a painful lump in my throat.

Currently, Delilah worked at my side, scooping dark batter from a stainless steel bowl into the pans I'd already set aside. Aunt Bean's Moonlight Mocha cake was my favorite, rich and fudgy with a decadent mocha filling and frosting.

The massive kitchen, which took up the whole ground floor of the barn, was quiet this afternoon, a rarity for a Friday. I was surprised the other two Sugarbirds—the collective nickname of the bakery's employees, not including Aunt Bean—weren't here working. Then I realized Aunt Bean had planned it that way. So she could have this talk with me without *everyone* butting in.

"I need your help, Addie." Aunt Bean's gaze leveled on me, light yet serious. "With my plans for the future, now that I'm dealing with this heart dropsy."

Heart dropsy. Such a cutesy term for heart failure.

It's what the preliminary test suggested. The doctor had prescribed medications, but a more aggressive treatment plan wouldn't be decided until other tests were completed.

Delilah flashed me a sympathetic look as Aunt Bean said, "You know I'm a planner at heart."

She always had been. She was a list maker, an organizer, a get-it-done and do-it-right kind of woman.

"In light of my current health issues," she said, "I thought it best to do some *advanced* planning for the family businesses. Just in case."

Just in case.

Wrapped tightly in sweet vanilla, the words whirled around as I pieced together what she truly meant: *Just in case* her prognosis was poor. Her heart incurable. Her condition terminal.

Pulling over a stool, I sat down before my knees gave way.

While there were two family businesses, the Starling Cake Company and Starlight Field, the bakery had always been my happy place growing up. Working alongside Aunt Bean and the Sugarbirds and my best friend Ree had been a joy. It was a place filled with love and happiness. A place to create and share. It was where I started to heal after my daddy's death. Where possibilities seemed endless. Where hope was always in the air, along with the scent of vanilla.

One of the hardest things I'd ever done was walk away from it.

From this whole town, really.

"Though I've had plans in place for a long time now," Bean said, "it's been a minute since they've been updated. They weren't nearly as detailed as I'd have liked them to be with itemization and whatnot."

"Sure am glad I'm not George Stubblefield today." Delilah let out a small laugh as she referred to our family's lawyer, but I noticed mournfulness now glistened in her dark gaze, nearly hidden behind a pair of hot-pink cat-eye glasses.

I was relieved to see the sadness, consoled by the fact that

I wasn't the only one devastated by Bean's health troubles. Delilah had just been putting on a brave face.

I suspected Aunt Bean was doing the same. There was no way, none at all, that she was taking this situation blithely. Aunt Bean was simply trying to find the light in this darkness, something that came as naturally to her as breathing.

But sometimes there was no bright side to life's most painful moments.

I knew that better than most anyone.

"Hush now." Aunt Bean waved her off. "There are still directives that need to be fine-tuned, but for now I'm satisfied with the progress."

Plans. Directives. She was talking about her *will*.

"Oh lordy." Delilah filled another cake pan. Her silvery-black hair sat atop her head in a braided crown, and there was a smudge of flour on her dark nose. "No doubt there are spreadsheets."

Aunt Bean said, "*Of course* there are spreadsheets."

She rested her hands atop the walking stick. On her wrist was a simple gold watch that had a tiny blue sapphire set into its face. It was a throwback to another time with its narrow shape and crown and needed winding every day. Some of the links were shinier than others—recent additions, I realized, most likely to accommodate the swelling.

Trying to distract myself, I grabbed another stack of pans to grease and flour. I knew from experience that tonight the baked cake layers would be crumb coated and refrigerated. Tomorrow morning, they would then be fully frosted and decorated. The take-out window would open at ten A.M. and because the cakes were sold first come, first served, without a doubt, by nine thirty there would be a line of cars flowing down the driveway and along the county road, hazard lights flashing as people patiently waited to for a taste of magic to heal their souls.

Aunt Bean went on, saying, "I'm not worried about the fate of the bakery. It's the field that concerns me."

At the mention of the field I vehemently shook my head and

reached for the star-shaped sapphire pendant that hung from a long chain around my neck. It had been a gift from Aunt Bean when I was little, and holding it had always brought a small measure of comfort—something I needed desperately right now.

"All right, punkin. We won't talk about it right now, but it *has* to be discussed soon." Her voice was steady, strong. "We must plan ahead to ensure that Winchester Wingrove does not gain possession of the starlight field."

The field was the site where a star had fallen in 1833 during a massive meteor shower, creating a shallow crater, a star wound. On days when the sun shone brightly, come nighttime in that grassy, bowl-shaped field, glowed a certain kind of starlight. It rose from the ground, a shimmery curtain of blue and yellow and silver and green that danced across the earth like aurora. In that magical light, those in need of guidance received the gift of clarity.

"Winchester, the greedy, self-serving money-grubber, will do everything in his power to get his hands on the field." Bean's walking stick once again banged the floor, two quick bursts, the sound still disappointingly muffled in comparison with her vehemence. "Particularly since Constance Jane has passed on, God bless her soul. She was the only thing keeping him in line for so long."

Winchester's wife, Constance Jane Cobb Wingrove, had been able to keep him in line because, as one of the heirs to the Cobb Steel fortune, she controlled the family purse strings. Strings he had very much been attached to. Everyone knew he'd only married her for her money. When she'd passed away two years ago, she'd left Winchester a very wealthy—and untethered—man.

"If he excavates the starlight crater, all its light will disappear." Aunt Bean shook her head as if she could not conceive of that level of stupidity. "I—*we*—cannot let that happen."

Winchester, who came from a long line of notorious con-men, cardsharps, counterfeiters, pickpockets, gamblers, and thieves, had become captivated with the starlight field as a young man who'd been in and out of trouble with the law. That was when he discovered an old family journal containing a recounting of the night the star fell, one that spun a fanciful story of how the star had shattered into diamonds when it hit the ground.

That same journal also revealed a long-forgotten fact: the starlight field had once belonged to *his* family. The knowledge ignited within him a powerful jealousy, lighting a fire that still burned to this day. He made no secret of wanting the land back, of wanting to explore the diamond legend, and vowed that he wouldn't rest until the field was his.

He'd been a thorn in the side of the Fullbright family for *decades*.

Bean rubbed the face of her watch, her gaze steady on me. "The issue at hand, as you might have surmised, is Tessa Jane."

I dug my nails into my palms. Tessa Jane was Winchester's only granddaughter—and also, thanks to an extramarital relationship the family didn't like to talk about, Aunt Bean's niece. For a while, Tessa Jane and her mother, Henrietta, had lived with Constance Jane and Winchester here in Starlight. But when Tessa Jane was eleven, her mama, for reasons unknown, had packed up their Cadillac and moved them six hours away to Savannah, Georgia.

It was a move that had confused many around here, considering how close Henrietta was with her mama.

But for me, I'd felt nothing but relief that they were gone.

Aunt Bean was worried now because half the starlight field belonged to Tessa Jane. It was currently being held in trust but would be released at the end of February, on her twenty-fifth birthday.

"I hardly imagine Tessa Jane would disregard your recommendations, Aunt Bean," I said carefully, trying to keep my own feelings for Tessa Jane out of my voice. "She adores you. And she loves the field."

Once, when she was all of nine or ten, Tessa Jane had insisted

Aunt Bean buy all the single bananas at Friddle's General Store instead of a complete bunch because she hadn't wanted the single bananas to be lonely. *That* was the kind of person she was. She had always been a soft, gentle soul in a world full of sharp, hurtful edges.

I added, "Has she said anything that would make you question her desire to keep the land?" Tessa Jane certainly hadn't said anything to me, as I hadn't seen or talked to her in more than a dozen years. To say that we had a complicated relationship was putting it mildly.

"Not in the slightest," Aunt Bean said. "She's been rather preoccupied as of late."

I fought through a wave of guilt for not being more involved in Tessa Jane's life and slid a cake pan down the counter. "Then you have nothing to worry about."

"We all know that when it comes to the Wingroves nothing is ever that easy, especially when Winchester holds so much sway with her. But I've done come up with a plan to head him off at the pass. A fair one, I believe."

I suspected she had many plans, all stored up like the alluring jars of colorful sprinkles, dusting sugars, nonpareils, and edible confetti that sat on the long shelves in the cake decorating corner. Enchanting, yes, but also incredibly messy and frustrating if you weren't careful.

Aunt Bean said, "But my plan is complex, which is why I need your help."

Delilah snorted. "Her plan has more layers than an apple stack cake."

Aunt Bean threw her dear friend a droll look, then in a supremely measured tone that set off high-pitched alarm bells in my head, said, "It must be completed in stages. In order to help me with those stages, Addie, you'll need to move back to Starlight for a spell."

My hand froze and cocoa powder drifted like dark snow onto the cement floor. "Move back?"

Emotionally, it had been hard enough *visiting* Aunt Bean

and the Sugarbirds. Every few months, I'd arrive like a whirlwind to catch up with everyone, indulge in the local gossip, visit the shops, and soak up all the love and affection I could, tucking it away for the lonely days ahead. But I never stayed longer than a day or two. And each time I left, it was with tears in my eyes and wishes that I could stay.

Even *thinking* about moving back stirred up all kinds of emotions I'd tamped down for years, making me lightheaded and queasy.

I'd left for a reason. And that reason hadn't changed in all the time I'd been gone.

Bean's gaze held steady. "As much as I feel like I'm Superwoman most days, I know that whatever is ahead for me, healthwise, is best conquered with all the help I can get. I'm going to need extra assistance with the bakery, plus rides to and from doctor's appointments and such."

Knots formed in my stomach as a long-kept secret perched on my lips. I clamped my mouth shut to keep from speaking. I couldn't blow it now, after all this time. It had been kept safe nearly twelve years, ever since the warm summer day Ree had taken her last breath.

But no one knew why I left. So Aunt Bean didn't know what she was asking of me.

"You can work from anywhere, so why *not* move back here?" she asked, calmly, reasonably, as if she had anticipated any potential excuses. "We do have internet. This isn't some backwoods, Podunk, one-stoplight town."

Starlight, Alabama, had all of *two* stoplights. And though it was off the beaten path, it was hardly unimportant like *Podunk* suggested. Tourism was the main industry of this town, drawing crowds from all over the world. It thrived on legend, on folklore, on starshine.

I stood and made my way to a back window. Over a low fence, down the slope of a gentle hill, and beyond a stretch of pasture, there was a grass-covered indent in the earth. It was where, all that time ago, the fallen star had hit the ground.

During the day, there was nothing to suggest this land was special. But at night, when the starlight rose from the crater, swirling and twirling, there was no denying it was pure magic.

The starlight drew dozens of visitors every night. Even on cloudy days when the aurora was lackluster, it was still bright enough to be a guiding light, to provide clarity to those in need.

But I didn't need the starlight to know what I wanted.

I already knew. I'd longed to come home for a good while now.

Yet, how could I possibly keep quiet if I moved back? I couldn't keep a secret to save my life, which was why I'd left in the first place. It had been the only way to safeguard what had been shared with me—information that would destroy the lives of people I cared for. People I *loved*.

With an ache in my chest, I looked upward and saw a flock of silvery starlings flying toward the farmhouse. Usually the birds stayed in the trees that bordered the starlight field, but in times of trouble they flew nearer, as a reminder that they were always keeping watchful eyes over the family. I wasn't surprised to see them now, considering Bean's health worries— and her current request.

"You can set up a sound studio in the storage room upstairs here. Or," Bean said, oozing practicality, "in a closet in the farmhouse."

She was right. I was a voice actor. I owned all the equipment I needed and often worked out of a converted closet in my apartment. But moving here would mean taking time off in order to get a studio set up and ready to record. It would be a headache but doable.

"It's not forever," Aunt Bean added, her tone light in a desperate attempt to brighten the darkness.

The meaning hiding behind *it's not forever* tore open my heart and made me suddenly wonder if she knew more about her condition than she was letting on.

I turned away from the window and glanced at Delilah,

looking for confirmation that Aunt Bean was sicker than she'd told me, but Delilah had her back to me as she placed a pan into one of the ovens.

Aunt Bean tapped her stick again, twice. "What say you, Addie?"

I took deep, even breaths, trying to fight the surge of panic threatening to swallow me whole. My gaze fell on the cake pans lined up on the shelves. It lingered on jars of rainbow sprinkles. I studied the bottles of vanilla extract that Bean had made herself, focusing on the long, dark vanilla beans soaking in bourbon. Then my gaze dropped to the head of my aunt's walking stick, which was shaped like a starling. The carving was intricate and delicate yet somehow able to bear her weight, her troubles.

Moving back to Starlight was going to be challenging, but I couldn't turn down Aunt Bean. Not after all the years she'd held me close, kept me safe, helped me through the darkest times of my life.

No one knew me like she did. My daddy and I had moved in with her when I was just four years old—right after my mama left town. Left us. And after Daddy's death when I was ten, I'd stayed put, my mama too happy living a carefree life by then to return to mothering.

I'd do *anything* for Aunt Bean.

"Of course I'll come back."

She smiled, the melancholy in her eyes shining as bright as the stars she loved so much. "That's my girl."

Outside, car tires crunched on the chipped-slate driveway, and I hoped it was another Sugarbird arriving to assist with the massive workload still to complete. Help was more than welcome to clear the production list and also, hopefully, rid the air of its heaviness. All the talk of Bean's plans and uncertain future could be tucked away for another time, after I let it sink in. Settle.

A moment later the front door creaked open. Warm wind whistled in, and out of the corner of my eye, I caught a flash of light I hadn't seen in years as Tessa Jane tentatively stepped inside.

"Hello," she said, her gaze searching our faces. "I'm not too early for the family meeting, am I?"

I'd have recognized her anywhere with her big blue eyes, pale blond hair, and the dreamy ethereal haze that had surrounded her since the day she'd been born, like she'd been dropped straight out of the heavens and into a bassinet at the Coosa County hospital. I stifled the shock wave at seeing her and threw a look at Aunt Bean, who was already greeting Tessa Jane with an effusive hug.

Slowly, I stepped forward and mentally prepared myself to greet the last person I'd ever expected to see today.

Tessa Jane Cobb Wingrove *Fullbright*.

My half sister.

CHAPTER TWO

Tessa Jane

"Whoo-eee!" Aunt Bean howled with laughter early Monday morning as she swerved around a corner, making the back end of Sweetie, her pea-green 1951 Ford pickup truck, swing into the empty oncoming lane. "Don't you just love this time of day, girls?"

"I'd love it more if I wasn't scared to death," Addie said from her spot in between Aunt Bean and me. "Is there a reason you're driving like a maniac?"

The day had dawned cool and misty, and I sat on my hands so I wouldn't grip the truck's bench seat, or the dashboard—or anything—as Bean sped along the side roads that ran between her farmhouse and the Starling Cake Company on Market Street.

It was a few minutes past seven, and the temperature inside the truck roughly matched what was outside—low forties—since the heater was broken and had been for decades.

"Maniac? Hardly." Bean scoffed. "You're not scared, are you, Tessa Jane?"

"Terrified," I admitted. "I've never wished so hard for airbags in my whole life."

My voice was thick with exhaustion. I was bone-tired. Soul-weary. I hadn't been able to relax since I'd arrived. Beyond what was going on with Bean's health and the uneasiness that came with being around Addie, every time my phone buzzed or rang, I tensed up, sure it was going to be my grandfather.

I'd been in town three days now—long past time that good manners dictated I should pay Winchester Wingrove a visit. But I kept putting it off. Not only because I didn't want to hear, yet again, what was expected of me—as if it hadn't been drilled into me since I'd been born—but also because I didn't trust myself around him right now. He was used to, demanded, even, sweetness and light. With my grim mood these days, I might do or say something I'd come to regret, because upsetting him was like to kicking a fire ant mound.

The truck's gears creaked and groaned as Bean yanked the shifter. "Lordy. When was the last time you girls had a little fun?"

Addie and I glanced at each other, then quickly looked away, neither of us saying anything.

I honestly couldn't remember. *Fun* hadn't been a word in my vocabulary for a long while now.

Bean shook her head and *tsk*ed at our silence. "Oh dear. We'll work on that."

"Can we work on it while driving the speed limit?" Addie pleaded.

Aunt Bean laughed, but she did slow a bit. "I'm just so dang tickled you're both here. Gavin would be, too. Oh, how he loved you girls."

Gavin. My and Addie's father. He'd died when I was only five and a half years old, and I hated that I'd never really had a chance to get to know him. I tamped down a surge of grief and focused on watching water droplets slide down the windshield.

"Are you sure you can't get more time off, Tessa Jane?" Aunt Bean asked. "I know it's greedy of me, but I'd sure love to have you here longer than a month."

"I'd sure love to stay longer than a month, but my boss just about had a conniption fit when I asked for *that* much time off."

Bean nudged Addie with her elbow. "It's a good reminder that we shouldn't take for granted the perks of being our own bosses."

"True," Addie said with a nod, but didn't add anything more.

She sat still as a statue, her knees pushed together. Her right elbow was tucked in close to her side, as if not wanting a single centimeter of her body to accidentally touch mine. I don't think she noticed the quick frown that flashed across Bean's face before she tucked it out of sight.

Bean had been trying all morning to get Addie to talk to me more. Had been trying all my life, really.

To be contrary, I wiggled a tiny bit closer to Addie, letting my arm rest against hers.

To my surprise, she didn't even flinch, like she used to do when we were girls and I wandered too close.

Her chestnut hair was pulled up and coiled into a neat bun, not a flyaway to be seen. She wore hardly any makeup—just mascara and a tinted lip balm. Her hands were clasped tightly in her lap, her nails short, tidy, and unpolished. She wore ankle-length plain blue jeans, a pair of black tennis shoes, and an olive-green utility jacket, snapped clear up to her neck with the drawstring at her waist pulled tight and tied in a neat bow.

Before this visit, the last time I'd actually seen or talked with Addie she'd been eighteen—nearly twelve years ago. She'd hardly changed a bit in all that time—it seemed she was still as buttoned up as a person could be, hardly letting anyone into her life—or her heart. Not that anyone could blame her, considering the way her mama had all but abandoned her, then with Daddy dying. And then her high school best friend, Ree, passed, too. It was a lot of loss. Too much.

With me, Addie had always been extra guarded, keeping
me at a firm distance, blaming me for something that hadn't
been my fault. When we were kids, she had no qualms about
ignoring me, making me feel like I simply wasn't there. She
had been so adept at blocking me out that if not for Aunt
Bean, I might've questioned my own existence.

But now, even though she'd hardly spoken to me since I'd
been back in town, I sensed something had changed *within*
her. Something had softened.

I didn't know what to make of that. At all.

Crackly country music filled all the empty spaces of the
truck's cab as Aunt Bean took a hard left. The force of the turn
plastered me against the door, and I searched high and low for
a bright side to Bean's terrifying driving.

Seeing glimmers of hope and light in a dark situation—
even in a person—had always been the one positive thing that
I could truly count on in my life, filling me with warmth. But
for almost a year now, it had been a struggle to see any brightness. And over the last two months it had been practically
impossible. Now that the ability had all but disappeared, it
made me feel like *I* was lost in the darkness. Lost and cold.

As moisture coated the windshield and twin stubby wipers
whisked it away, I wished I could go back in time. I'd travel to
just before The Great Humiliation, the incident that had cast
me into this bleakness, breaking my spirit. Breaking my heart.
Breaking *me*.

Actually, I wouldn't mind going back six months, maybe even
a year. No, *two* years. That's when I'd stepped into the massive
kitchen of the Southern Oaks Country Club, where I worked as
a pastry chef and had first met Carson DeWitt, who'd just been
hired on as head chef.

Knowing what I knew now, I'd make different choices.
Avoid the pain. The embarrassment.

Some people, like my mother, thought I should have already
put the heartbreak behind me. But then again, she was the same

person who, only a couple of weeks after Carson left me at the altar, took one look at the misery I wore like the old, comfortable robe I'd been living in since being jilted and gave me a big hug, a kiss on my forehead, and told me enough was enough.

Mama had a big heart but little patience.

Then she'd added, "Don't go forgetting who you are and where you come from, Tessa Jane. Cobbs *do not* wallow."

She preferred to think of herself as a Cobb, her mother's family name, rather than a Wingrove. In fact, she'd rather be *anyone* other than a Wingrove. She and Granddaddy had never seen eye to eye, especially when it came to my grandmother, whom I'd always called Gigi.

Mama had adored Gigi.

Granddaddy . . . seemingly had not. They had their own bedrooms in different wings of their enormous house and barely spoke to each other. Not that they were contentious. They hadn't been. It was simply as though they'd led separate lives—while living under the same roof. For forty-some years.

I learned early on the term *marriage of convenience*, though it took me years to understand it fully.

From then on, I'd vowed to marry for love and love alone.

My throat burned with regret as I pictured Carson down on one knee, asking me to marry him. I gave myself a good mental shake to clear the image, wishing it was as easy to get rid of the memories. Wishing I could change the past.

"If you need inspiration to move on," Mama had said to me back in November, "just remember all the people who have it worse than you."

She knew firsthand the many ways in which others had it worse than me. Beyond her high-visibility career as a fundraising consultant, she'd forged a whole life—a secret life very few knew about—helping those people. The pristine, privileged image she insisted we present to the world was to protect *them*.

Wealth had the extraordinary ability to conceal both sins *and* salvation.

But even though, *yes*, I knew others had it worse, that knowledge didn't magically heal me. It only made me feel guilty on top of brokenhearted.

So I took to hiding my pain, stuffing it deep down, out of sight.

I pretended I was *just fine* working in the same kitchen as Carson after it became clear he was only quitting *me*, not his job.

I *volunteered* to help when he moved out of my condo.

I *graciously* offered to return all our wedding gifts, along with a handwritten note, on my own.

I'd handed back my engagement ring without so much as a *sniffle*.

But silently? I'd cursed upon him a million grease burns. Had hoped he'd slip off the condo's second-story balcony. I'd imagined cramming down his throat all the apologetic cards I'd written, thanking people for their gift-giving kindness. And when I'd handed back my engagement ring, I'd have loved to shove it somewhere the sun never shone.

In short, I'd turned into someone I didn't know.

Days seemed dimmer. Nights, darker. The stars stopped twinkling. Bright sides vanished. I couldn't see any inner lights—even my own.

With my nerves stretched wafer-paper thin, I knew I had to do something drastic if I wanted to find my way back to who I'd once been. To the person who *cared*. About myself. About others. I'd been debating on exactly what to do when I'd received the call from Aunt Bean last Friday about an emergency family meeting. At the tail end of our conversation, I'd made the split-second decision to ask if I could stay with her awhile beyond the weekend. Just a month, I'd added, telling her only that I wanted a change of pace, of scenery.

But really, I needed to return to the place where I felt most like *me*.

"Peanut," Bean had said in that booming yet loving tone of hers, "my home *is* your home. Stay as long as you'd like."

The farmhouse *had* felt like home, despite my visits being limited to long weekends, occasional holidays, and a few weeks every summer. It was always filled with a sweet vanilla scent and Bean's unconditional love—which by far overrode Addie's stoniness.

But as I'd gotten older, I realized it wasn't the farmhouse that had felt like home.

It was Aunt Bean.

I glanced at her now, my heart in my throat. It was impossible not to notice the rapid decline in her health since my previous visit at Thanksgiving. As I thought about her damaged heart and what that might mean for the future, I searched for even a *spark* of light. And I found a glimmer in the sound of Bean's delighted laughter as she swung the truck around another corner. I'd take a million death-defying rides with her if it meant I could hear that sound time and again.

Bean picked up the conversation, breaking the growing silence. "I can see why your boss wouldn't want to lose you, Tessa Jane, even if only for a month. Not after you were nominated for fancy pastry award last year. Such an honor for a chef so young. Remember, I told you about that, Addie?"

"Yes, ma'am," she said, her tone neutral.

Aunt Bean had probably called Addie or sent a text message right after hearing the news. She'd always been our go-between when it came to communication, even when we were younger. As we aged, she openly told us that she reported Addie's goings-on to me, and mine to Addie unless we specifically asked her not to. She forwarded photos. Shared conversations and gossip and the everyday little things that only family would care about. *Should* care about.

As surely as I knew that Addie's favorite ice cream was pistachio, she knew mine was mocha chip. And as surely as I knew Addie had broken up with her last boyfriend because he'd been rude to a waitress, she knew how I'd met Carson,

when I got engaged, and the disastrous way in which that relationship ended.

It was Aunt Bean's way of keeping us stitched together even
though the thread binding us was so frayed it might snap at
any moment.

"Did you tell Tessa Jane about the part you recently landed?"
Aunt Bean asked her, trying so very hard to get her to engage.
"A role in an animated movie!"

Everyone in this truck knew Addie most certainly had not
told me. Just as everyone in this truck also knew Aunt Bean
had already shared the news with me months ago.

But because Bean was making such an effort, a painful effort
at that, I spoke up. "Wow! Congratulations!"

I tried to sound like I hadn't already known but somehow
the words came out awkward and stilted.

Addie glanced at me, eyebrows raised.

I pasted on a smile.

If I didn't know better, I would've sworn it was humor that
flickered in her eyes before she said, "Thanks."

Addie's talent for impressions and voices had started young.
All her dolls had their own voices—some of which had been
borrowed from classic TV characters like Bugs Bunny or Smurf-
ette. She could mimic sounds and often used them to make
people—especially Bean—laugh. And she also had unique
voices for each of the household pets.

Addie had been ten when Daddy died and afterward, when
she started to close herself off even more, Aunt Bean all but
marched her over to the local theater group and signed her up.
It's where Addie had met Ree. It's where she allowed herself to
be free from the grief, if only for the little while she pretended
to be someone else. But even on stage, she'd never been truly
comfortable in the spotlight. Which was why voice work was
such a good choice for her. A chance to act without people
watching her every move.

Through the years, she'd voiced commercials, documen-
taries, audiobooks. She had bit roles in many animated TV

shows, video games, and a few movies as well. Currently, she had the lead role in an animated TV show about a precocious southern bunny that had been so successful that a theme park attraction and a Broadway show were in the works.

And, of course, I only knew all this because Aunt Bean had told me.

It was such an odd feeling to know someone without truly knowing them at all.

A mile down the road, Aunt Bean slowed at a stop sign and resolutely steered the dormant conversation in another direction. "Surely y'all remember Tyler Underwood? It's his company that's handling the construction at the bakery."

Addie nodded and I shifted on the seat, saying, "Bug's got his own company?"

Aunt Bean smiled. "After working for years in construction down in Wetumpka, last summer Ty started up his own company and I hired him straight off. And he hasn't gone by Bug since about the time you were in grade school with him, having outgrown his childhood fascination with insects. Thank goodness."

Tyler Underwood. The last time I'd seen him was nearly a year ago while I'd been in Starlight visiting Aunt Bean. When he caught sight of me window-shopping on Market Street, he'd abruptly turned and strode off in the opposite direction so he wouldn't have to fake pleasantries.

His behavior hadn't been a surprise.

He didn't like me. Never had. Because I was a Wingrove.

There was bad blood between our families. More specifically, my grandfather had done the Underwoods horribly wrong.

Which also wasn't a surprise.

My granddaddy seemed to have done *everyone* around here wrong.

Aunt Bean said, "These days, he's a magnet for stray or wounded animals. All kinds. Some just show up at his door out of the blue, some he hears about from others. He always finds help for them, one way or another. Right now at his place he's got a puny possum with an injured arm that's waiting on an opening with a wildlife rehabber, a cat with six kittens, and a turtle or tortoise or some such that's taken up residence in his backyard. It's a protected species, so he can't even build a deck until the critter wanders off. He jokes about having his backyard declared as conservation land."

Once, when Ty and I were in third grade, he'd put a big grasshopper in my desk. One that jumped out and hit my face when I lifted the laminated wooden lid and reached inside for my library book. The class had howled with laughter, and my cheeks had burned while I recaptured the terrified critter. I'd carefully cupped it in my hands and carried it to a window to set it free, thinking the whole time that I'd have liked to stuff Ty in a desk, see how *he* liked it. So a few weeks later when he was locked inside the school gym's equipment closet while returning a basketball, I decided then and there that karma might just be real.

"Is he going to be at the bakery this morning?" I asked warily, scratching a sudden hive on my neck.

Aunt Bean downshifted. "Should be."

How wonderful. His animosity first thing in the morning was going to be great way to start the day. Couldn't wait.

As I felt myself tense with irritation, hopelessness nearly overcame me. Suddenly, it felt like the darkness in my life had made itself comfortable and was here to stay. The old me would never be so blithe, so sarcastic. The old me, the one who trusted blindly, who always believed there was good in people, would have tried *yet again* to convince Ty that *I* wasn't the enemy.

But right now I simply didn't have the energy, or the will, or the *light*, to deal with his bitterness.

"Fair warning, best y'all keep your guard up around him," Aunt Bean said. "He's always trying to pawn off his rescues on the tenderhearted."

I turned her way. "Is *that* where Lucy and Ethel came from?"

Aunt Bean laughed. "Sure is. My heart at the moment is at its most tender. I'm an easy mark."

At the mention of her heart, sadness panged deep in my bones. I sought a glimmer of hope, and when I didn't find one, I pulled a hand out from under my thigh and reached for my star pendant, a matching one to Addie's. Only to quickly remember I wasn't wearing it.

"Who are Lucy and Ethel?" Addie asked.

"They're Pekin ducks," Bean said. "Sassy as can be."

Addie hadn't yet noticed the new additions to Aunt Bean's household because after the family meeting on Friday, she'd driven back to Birmingham to tighten up the loose ends of her life in preparation for moving down here for a while. She'd returned late last night, which was when Aunt Bean told us that at first light we'd be going to see the renovations under way at the Starling Cake Company.

"When did you get ducks, Aunt Bean?" Addie asked, shifting ever so slightly on the bench seat.

Our sides were now fully touching, molding together. It was me, this time, who inched away, seeking to put a smidgen of space between us. Keeping her at a distance felt all kinds of wrong since for most of my life I'd wished that if she couldn't accept me as a sister, she'd at least be a friend. But now that she seemed to be letting me in a tiny bit, I couldn't help thinking it was for show. Surface but no substance. All I could think to do was protect myself. Put up a wall. Push *her* away. I could not deal with more heartache.

The mist turned into a steady drizzle as Aunt Bean said, "Ty came to me last week, all wide brown eyes and manly charm, saying a pair of ducks needed a new home, one with a pond preferably. Next thing I knew, I was hiring him to build me a quack shack."

There was lightness in Addie's voice as she said, "I hope he gave you a discount at least."

Her voice was mesmerizing, even more so when there was

humor in it. It was no wonder she was in high demand for work. To be honest, though, I'd been surprised Addie had pursued voice acting at all. I'd always thought she'd stay in Starlight and become the next Sugarbird. She loved baking cakes.

Unlike me.

Cakes gave me nothing but anxiety, because no matter how hard I tried, they never tasted as good as Aunt Bean's. Despite all my training *and* my lineage, my cakes were simply ordinary instead of magical.

The only thing I truly loved to bake was cookies. Decorated cookies. Something I, as a high-end pastry chef, would never dare admit among my peers. I'd also never confess that I didn't love being a pastry chef. Another job, however, had never been an option. My career had been mapped out for me at a young age, my grandfather intent on me becoming the best baker around. The best *Fullbright*. And once he decided on something, it was best not to argue.

Bean slowed as she turned onto Market Street. "Ty isn't charging a thing except for any extra materials that he doesn't already have on hand. He's planning to start work on it soon, so don't go being surprised if you see him at the farmhouse."

I silently cursed the bad timing. I'd simply try to stay out of his way. I would *not* try to befriend him. Or apologize for my grandfather's behavior. Or even *talk* to him unless absolutely necessary.

Then I sighed, absolutely hating that disconnection was my first line of thought.

I might be having trouble with seeing bright sides at the moment, but I could see my shadow—what we called the dark side to our gift—just fine. It emerged when fear-based emotions, like panic and anxiety and insecurity, ran high.

When hope seemed out of reach.

Addie's shadow was that she had trouble keeping a secret.

Aunt Bean developed insomnia.

And me? My personality flip-flopped. I became unsociable and unfriendly. Cool and distant.

Shadows, in general, were often like passing clouds and didn't linger. But recently mine had taken over. I had hoped that being here with Aunt Bean in Starlight would help me find my way back to the light. Yet, here I was, inching away from my sister. And planning to outright avoid Ty.

Determined to fight for who I used to be, I forced myself to inch closer to Addie once again. And I told myself I'd simply be gracious to Ty. Nothing more, nothing less.

"How's his mama doing?" Addie asked.

The concern in her voice worried me. "Is something going on with Miss Ernie?"

"Bless her heart," Bean said, her voice full and round with affection as the truck ground to a stop at a red light. "Ernie was diagnosed with breast cancer last spring."

I hadn't heard about the diagnosis. But then again, I hadn't visited Starlight as often as I should've after meeting Carson— and certainly not in the final months before the wedding. The planning had taken up my whole world for a while.

"I'm sorry to hear it," I said.

I immediately wanted to send her a note and bake her some sugar cookies, which she'd always claimed to be her favorite. Ernestine Underwood had been a good friend of Bean's for forever—and surprisingly kind to me despite the fact that my grandfather had a hand in destroying her family.

Bean said, "Doctors are optimistic. Ernie just wants the chemo over and done with. She says the only bright side to the situation is that it's helped her overcome her fear of needles. Lately, she's been talking about getting a big ol' tattoo once all is over and done with. Some think she's joking, but I wouldn't be the least bit surprised if she goes through with it."

"Has she been able to keep working?" I asked. Ernie was one of the finest glassblowers in Alabama. Maybe in the whole country.

The truck lurched forward when the light turned green. "She's slowed a bit but still gets into her studio one or two days a week. And because she's not her usual sprightly self, a couple of days a week Luna Gray helps her around the house, dusting and such. Luna, with her youthful energy, lights the place up, and personally I think that's been more beneficial to Ernie than anything."

I smiled, easily picturing the effervescent eleven-year-old with her dark hair and expressive blue eyes, who had also been a guest of Aunt Bean's at this past year's Thanksgiving dinner. But at the mention of the girl's name, Addie stiffened up again, pulling her arms in close to her sides.

It didn't take but a second for me to realize why. Luna's mama had been Addie's high school best friend, Ree, who sadly passed away only days after Luna's birth from a delivery complication. It was obvious Addie still felt the loss sharply. If there had been another snap on her jacket, I was certain she would've fastened it in order to tuck herself further into her protective shell. The one she used to hide her pain and grief.

I wanted to reach out, offer a consoling hand, because I knew how hard it was to keep my own pain hidden. But ultimately I kept my hands to myself and looked out the side window.

The town's main street was lined on both sides by two-story brick buildings of varying heights and rooflines. Awnings shaded windows. Lampposts dotted the sidewalk. Twinkle lights, which stayed lit all day long, sparkled in the trees, lending brightness to the dreary morning.

We drove by the swanky Celestial Hotel, the bank, the pizza place, the gift shop, the hair and nail salon. As we passed Gossamer, the fancy dress shop where I'd bought my wedding dress, the wipers creaked, and my broken heart nearly spilled out of my chest. I hated how the pain snuck up on me sometimes, delivering a sucker punch.

"The renovations at the bakery sure are a sight to behold,"

Aunt Bean said, her voice full of excitement as we passed the Stars Above bookstore, which anchored the east side of the business district. "Be sure you to take a good long look around the place, because it's the last time y'all will see it before the grand reopening. I want the finished result to be a surprise."

As we rolled past a quaint pocket park, I looked over my shoulder to see the mural painted on the side of the bookshop. It depicted the night sky, done in inky blues and blacks and purples, dotted with twinkling stars. Below the sky was a crater with an ethereal pathway that glimmered in blue, yellow, green, and silvery tones—the starlight aurora had been captured perfectly.

As I looked forward once again, I noticed a flock of silvery starlings landing in a crape myrtle on the edge of the bakery's parking lot. In our family folklore, the birds were departed loved ones who now acted as guardians. Mostly of the starlight field, protecting the buried star. Partly of us.

They had started as a flock of one shortly after one of my long-ago grannies, Clara—whose name meant light, bright, and clear—vanished the day the star had crashed into the field she'd been tending. And with each passing of a maternal ancestor, the group grew. Currently it was eighteen strong, and one glance was all it took to know these beautiful birds were far from ordinary. Their iridescent feathers were more silver than black and were able to shimmer even in the dimmest light.

However, seeing them now brought a slight quiver of unease—they only appeared this close when something unsettling was about to happen. Something that might require the reassurance of their presence or their guidance.

Or their intervention.

Like the time they'd saved my mother's life before I was born.

The last time I'd seen them this close was shortly after my grandmother's will had been read. They'd perched outside the lawyer's office window as Mr. Stubblefield informed us that it was true—Gigi had left *nothing* of the Cobb fortune to Mama or me and *everything* to Granddaddy. And that there wasn't anything Mama could do about it.

As we let the news settle, it was hard to ignore the talk going around that Granddaddy had strong-armed Gigi while she'd been unwell to change the terms. Or had even forged her name. I wasn't sure what the truth was. All I knew was that it had been her money to do with what she saw fit—and that I missed her dearly.

As Aunt Bean careened into the Starling Cake Company's parking lot, kicking up crushed stone, I tore my gaze from the birds. Behind two large blue tarps attached to scaffolding, the bakery was all but hidden except for the pitched roofline.

Two men stood on a platform at the top of the scaffolding. One of them was Ty, and at the sight of him I could feel more itchy blotches rise on my skin. Hives had plagued me most of my life, popping up when I was emotional or anxious or nervous or stressed.

As my guilty conscience raised welt after welt, I fidgeted to keep from scratching the wheals and glanced again at the mural. Then at the starlings.

Fullbrights were supposed to use our gift of seeing bright sides to bring light and happiness to others. But because I couldn't see past the darkness of my shadow right now, it made me feel like I failed my family. Failed the stars.

I had to do everything I could to find my way back to the light, even if it was only baby steps I was taking.

Which meant that it might be finally time to confess—and apologize—to Ty for locking him in that closet all those years ago.

CHAPTER THREE

Addie

Steely gray clouds trimmed in black hung low in the sky as Aunt Bean laid on the horn. "Take a gander at this, girls!"

Uneasy, I shifted on the seat. By seeking a bright side, like how we'd made it here alive despite Bean's wild driving, I attempted, once again, to shake the ominous feeling that had been with me since I'd been summoned back to town. But the dark cloud stubbornly remained. I tried to blame its presence on being back in Starlight, to the fear of revealing Ree's secret, of being near Tessa Jane, to everything going on with Bean, but it felt like there was more to it.

As if all that wasn't *enough*.

Tessa Jane unclicked her seatbelt and shimmied forward. "What are we *gandering* exactly?"

Her presence had always been a painful reminder of a heartbreaking time in my life. When she was born, my little world, so familiar and safe, had fallen apart when my mama packed her bags and left town only weeks after Tessa Jane's birth.

Even though I'd only been four years old, nearly five, I still remembered the day Mama drove off, leaving Daddy. Leaving me. And I especially remembered how, before she left, she'd pulled me aside and told me that if I ever wanted her to come back for good, I best not *ever* make nice with Tessa Jane or any of the Wingroves.

So I'd locked Tessa Jane out, plain and simple, pretending I was an only child.

And I'd been an absolute *pill* to Henrietta whenever she was around.

Because I'd wanted more than anything for my mama to come home.

I sighed, pushing thoughts of her aside as Bean honked again. Two impatient bleats.

"Land sake's alive," she muttered, shaking her head.

Ty Underwood held up a wait-a-sec finger. Another man, his face hidden by a ball cap as he looked downward, tugged at a length of rope connected to the tarp.

Aunt Bean's exasperated laugh came out in a steamy puff as she cut the engine. "So much for the grand reveal. When I pulled into this here lot, the tarp was supposed to drop, and it was going to be a dazzling moment." She gave us jazz hands, then a wry smile. "But instead of getting a *ta-da*, we got a *wah-wahn*," she said, mimicking a sad trombone.

Tessa Jane still peered upward. "Oh, I don't know, Aunt Bean. The buildup to the reveal is kind of exciting. How long until the reopening?"

She didn't sound all that excited. Exhausted was more like it. Outwardly, Tessa Jane looked perfectly pulled together. Beautiful as always. She favored her mama, with her creamy fair skin, bold blue eyes, and thick blond hair that was always parted on the side with long swooping bangs. Her makeup, down to the pale-rose lipstick she wore, was flawless. Her painted fingernails didn't have a single chip. Her clothes, a pink cashmere sweater, designer jeans, and a belted coat, had been tailored to perfection. Her leather boots didn't have so much as a scuff mark. Yet, something was off with her.

I'd noticed it on Friday, the minute I looked into her eyes. Her inner light, the one that practically made her sparkle—even in photos—had lost its powerful glow. Now it only flickered dully, as if trying to flare but not quite catching.

Seeing her in person had thrown me for a loop. It had been so long. I'd locked away so much. I wasn't at all sure what to say or how to act around her.

I didn't know where to *begin*.

Aunt Bean fiddled with her watch, rubbing a thumb over its face. "There's a big party planned for Leap Day, and so help me, we'll be celebrating in a construction zone if it's not done by then because the invitations have been printed already with a banner that says we've grown by *leaps* and bounds!" She laughed at her own cleverness. "I'll hand out hardhats as party favors if need be. Addie, remind me later to add hardhats to the event spreadsheet."

"Yes, ma'am," I said, smiling.

I'd seen the spreadsheet at Christmastime. It was extensive, covering food and beverages, decorations, entertainment, and everything in between. I couldn't say I understood the big fuss. Not about the party and not about the renovation, either.

When Aunt Bean had first mentioned the makeover, I thought she'd meant the storefront would have a little nip and tuck, not a full-blown overhaul. I was shocked when she started talking about raising the roofline, adding a stamped concrete parking lot edged with brick, building a porch with fancy millwork. And that was just the exterior design. The plans to rehab the inside were equally as expansive. Vaulted ceilings. Custom paneling. Top-of-the-line appliances.

"Why?" I'd finally asked her after hearing about exposed wooden beams, fancy light fixtures, and blown-glass decorations. "Why spend a fortune to fix what isn't broken?"

She'd taken hold of my hand, held it soothingly, as if knowing

I wasn't going to like what she was going to say. "Truth is, punkin, I was thinking of hanging up my whisk for good when I took a walk in the starlight and had a moment of clarity. Where the star leads, I follow. I always have. Always will."

I wished I had the same faith as Aunt Bean when it came to the starlight—believing that there was only goodness and hope to be found in its guidance.

My skepticism came naturally, through my mama. From early on she had warned me against seeking help from the starlight aurora. She told me its clarity wasn't all good. That it could hurt people. People like her.

Because when my daddy sought clarity about their troubled marriage, he'd somehow ended up having a baby with another woman. And though I knew there was more to that story, eventually I'd learned her lesson about the starlight for myself.

Tessa Jane said, "Something's happening."

Bean and I leaned forward. Ty had pulled out a pocketknife and was now sawing through the rope.

"Should they have harnesses on?" I asked. That scaffolding didn't seem the least bit safe.

"I'm sure they know what they're doing," Bean said, but I heard no confidence in her tone.

As I stared at the wall of blue tarp, all I could picture was the old bakery. Sitting like an outcast just outside the charming main business district, the square, squat, flat-roofed, cement-block structure had once been a laundromat.

The year I started high school, Aunt Bean decided to close up the barn kitchen and open an official retail storefront closer to the center of town, wanting the cake shop to be a bigger part of the community. She bought the no-frills building for a steal from Petie Pottinger, Petal's cousin, after Petie decided to relocate her sudsy business to Orange Beach.

Even after Aunt Bean transformed the laundromat into a bakery, it still held on to its utilitarian feel. She'd scoffed at suggestions by town uppity-ups to beautify the shop in order to draw in customers. Because she knew the only thing the business needed be successful was *her*.

And she'd been right. Once the sign on the metal door had been flipped to OPEN, people—townsfolk and tourists alike—had flocked to the most lackluster of Starlight's shops. The visitors ignored the building's ugly exterior, the deep clay chasms cutting through the gravel parking lot, the rusted window frames, and the missing roof shingles.

All had recognized that there was no need for bells or whistles at the Starling Cake Company. Its magic came from within.

As I waited for the big reveal, from the corner of my eye, I caught a flutter of movement. The stretching of wings. The silvery starlings had gathered in the crape myrtle at the edge of the lot, their feathers appearing almost metallic in the murky, damp morning.

My chest squeezed tight with apprehension. The last time I'd seen them this close was shortly after Winchester Wingrove had inherited his wife's fortune and ramped up his talk about wanting to build a resort alongside the starlight crater. He'd also started playing up his ancestor's diamond tall tale, which had caused curious treasure hunters to sneak onto the land. Fortunately, either the field's caretaker or the starlings always scared the trespassers off before they did any damage to the starlight aurora.

For a brief moment, I allowed myself to think of that caretaker. Sawyer Gray had been eighteen years old when Aunt Bean had offered him the job, which came with a small cabin on the property.

A cabin just big enough for him and his then infant daughter. A child he was raising on his own because sometimes life was nothing but cruel.

I pressed my lips together so tightly they hurt, then glanced again at the starlings, banishing thoughts of Sawyer and old hopes and dreams.

As I watched the birds I wondered if Winchester had something to do with their presence now. Traditionally in our family, the bakery had always been passed along to the oldest woman in the family. And the field and hundreds of acres of surrounding land was given to the oldest male. However, with his death, my daddy had broken the pattern, willing the land to Tessa Jane and me, his only children. It was being held in trust until we *both* reached the age of twenty-five.

That day would come at the end of February on Tessa Jane's birthday. After which, we had one week to decide if we wanted to accept or decline co-ownership of the land. If we declined, all would be sold, the profit divided between us. It had to be a unanimous decision.

All or nothing.

Without a doubt, if we sold, Winchester would find a way to be the highest bidder. Then his development plans would be quickly set into motion.

But even if Tessa Jane believed her grandfather had good in him, somewhere deep down, couldn't she see that what he had planned would damage the field, the starlight? Would she really let that happen by letting the land go?

The thought hurt. Because while I had my own complicated feelings about the field, I wanted it to protect it. And keep it in the family. The *Fullbright* family.

As I tried not to worry about what might happen, a shout rang out. All three of us leaned forward as far as we could. In a blink, half of the tarp fell, and I simply couldn't believe my eyes.

The Starling Cake Company had transformed from frumpy to fairy tale.

"Wow," Tessa Jane whispered.

Before us stood a charming cottage straight out of a children's storybook that had three gables, a stone and stucco exterior, and a wide front porch with dark rustic beams full of knots and enchantment. Warm light glowed in the windows, inviting and welcoming.

It was almost as if you could *feel* the magic housed within long before ever stepping through the door. Long before biting into one of Aunt Bean's extraordinary cakes.

"Come, come, girls. Let's take a closer look, shall we?" Bean rooted around inside her pocketbook and came out with a plastic rain bonnet that she placed gently over her sky-high pompadour.

Once we'd all climbed out, the sound of hammering from the crew inside came from deep within the building. Wonder lifted Tessa Jane's voice as she said to Aunt Bean, "Tell me you're going to be planting trees. Lots of trees. This place needs a forest. There needs to be moss and boulders and toadstools and gnomes."

Bean laughed. "There will be trees, yes, but sadly not a whole forest. I'll show you the landscape design when we get back to the house. Addie, remind me to add gnomes to my bakery renovation spreadsheet."

Drizzle pooled in droplets on my coat as I smiled. "Yes, ma'am."

The scaffolding groaned as Ty Underwood descended, leaping the last three feet to the ground in a move that made my knees ache in sympathy. The other man had crossed the platform and was sawing through another length of rope in order to release the rest of the tarp.

Ty cleared a path to the entrance, then wiped his hands on his jeans and strode toward us, his steps long and sure. "Sorry about the snafu, Miss Verbena. Those knots weren't coming loose no matter what."

"All's well that ends well," Aunt Bean said lightly.

Ty tucked his hands into the pockets of a black fleece jacket. "Good to see you, Addie." Then his gaze flicked toward Tessa Jane. His jaw tightened. "And you, Grasshopper."

"Morning, Stinkbug," she said oh-so-sweetly, crossing her arms tightly over her chest.

The sugariness in her voice was unmistakably fake, like Splenda in sweet tea.

I smiled despite myself, never having heard Tessa Jane be anything other than kindness and light. It was refreshing—and surprising—to hear her sassy undertone. And I was oddly proud of her for returning Ty's volley instead of simply accepting it. After all, it wasn't her fault Ty's father had ended up in prison. That dishonor belonged to Winchester. It turned out he wasn't so different from all the other Wingrove men in his family. He was a swindler at heart. He'd just been better at hiding it, especially once he married Constance Jane.

I could practically hear Ty's teeth grinding as he turned his full attention to Aunt Bean. "Scaffolding is set to come down this afternoon, ma'am. Any word on the sign yet?"

Aunt Bean used both hands to lean on her walking stick. "It's still on back order."

"Might be time to pick another option," he said.

She smiled. "Let's give it a while longer."

A passing truck gave a friendly honk as it drove by, and Ty and Aunt Bean automatically lifted their hands to wave before picking up their conversation about the bakery's sign right where they'd left it.

"You say that as though you haven't already been waiting three months." Ty's heavy work boots crunched against the gravel as he shifted on his feet.

"Hush now. We'll put up a temporary sign if we have to. How's your mama doing this morning?"

He accepted that she was done talking about the sign and said, "Well enough to boss me around. Called me up at dawn to go looking for Hambone. He dug out under the fence. Again."

"Did you find him?" Tessa Jane took the tiniest step forward as concern laced her tone. She looked and sounded as though she was ready to launch a search party right that minute if need be.

As she spoke, Ty's chin jutted. He took a step backward, away from her.

Aunt Bean's keen gaze flickered with irritation as it darted between them. No doubt she knew full well why Ty was acting the way he was, and the look in her eyes told me he was treading on thin ice.

"Surely, he wasn't heading for the barn kitchen that early, was he?" Bean asked, trying to defuse the situation. Then she added for my and Tessa Jane's benefit, "Hambone drops by time to time to say hello."

Ty said, "He stops by for cake scraps, which the Sugarbirds are more than happy to feed him. He's developed quite the sweet tooth."

Aunt Bean shrugged. "Who can blame him?"

Tessa Jane's face was tight with worry. Her neck was flushed and splotchy above the collar of her sweater. "But you found him? This morning?"

Ty looked everywhere but at Tessa Jane when he said, "He was over at the Fife place. He's got himself a crush on Dare's dog, Pepper."

At the mention of Dare, I realized I was clenching my fists. My nails dug into my palms.

By his early teens, through a series of tragedies, Dare had found himself orphaned. A local pastor and his wife had taken him in, giving him a home, and eventually adopted him, even though they'd been well into their eighties at the time. Dare might've gotten a new name, but there was no changing the fact that he was still a Buckley. And Buckleys were trouble.

When Tessa Jane didn't seem as fazed as I was by the mention of Dare, I wondered if she didn't know he'd been a Buckley before he became a Fife. It didn't seem likely. Everyone knew.

Just like everyone knew that way back when, Bryce Buckley, Dare's half brother, older by some twenty years, had once poisoned a watering trough on the Wingrove property, killing a pair of Constance Jane's prized horses. It had all been caught on security cameras and Bryce had been arrested, locked up, and years later, had died during a prison fight.

Buckleys were dangerous, plain and simple, which was why I was surprised to hear Bean say with a tone of affection,

"Dare's done a real good job raising that sweet girl. I can see why Hambone's smitten."

Was it possible Dare had broken the Buckley cycle? That he was a good guy, as Bean had claimed the other day? It was hard to imagine. Too hard. So I decided the affection she voiced had to have been directed only at Pepper. Aunt Bean loved dogs. All animals, really.

"Unfortunately for Hambone, Pepper wasn't out," Ty added. "Even still, I had to lure him back into the truck with one of the donuts I had with me for Mama. With the chemo, anything sweet is what she tolerates best. Says most everything else tastes like metal. Her doctors aren't real pleased with her diet these days, but I'm happy as long as she's eating *something*. She's been looking like a string bean."

"If it's sweet she wants, it's sweet she'll get," Bean declared. "I'll put the word out and also whip her up something extra special, too."

I tucked my hands under my arms to warm them, thinking that as far as comparisons went, a string bean was a good choice. They didn't need much to absolutely thrive. Some sun, some water. Mostly what they needed was support, something to hang on to. Or in Ernie's case, a whole community who loved her and would help hold her up until she had the strength to stand on her own once again.

"She'd love that." Ty motioned toward the building with his chin. "Are you ready to head inside? I can't say it's any warmer, but at least it's dry."

"The heat's still out?" Aunt Bean swept an arm toward Tessa Jane and me as though trying to corral us. She used to do the same when we were little, pulling us both to her, anchoring us against her soft curves. It had always made me feel safe. Loved.

I took a few steps forward and Tessa Jane flinched, seeming alarmed by my nearness. At her reaction, I was suddenly flooded with so much shame and regret that it hurt to breathe deeply.

"The issue was traced to the electrical panel," Ty said. "Should be fixed by the end of the day."

"Who's doing the fixin'? Aren't all the Grays up in Mentone?" Aunt Bean asked as we headed for the porch.

The mention of the Gray family made my chest ache even more. My heart pounded. My palms dampened.

What made me think I could do this? Be here? In Starlight? With Tessa Jane? And the Grays? And even Dare *Buckley* Fife?

Have mercy on my *soul*.

I wanted to go back to Birmingham. Where life was so much easier. Where I didn't have to deal with all these emotions. All this pain. Out of sight, out of mind.

As anxiety thrummed, I took even breaths, ignoring the heartache, trying my best to pretend it wasn't there. Like always.

I inhaled for five seconds, held the breath for five seconds, then released it for five seconds. Box breathing was a technique my therapist had taught me years ago when my worries felt out of control, and I prayed it worked now, because I felt like I was about to break open.

I tried to assure myself that around Alvin Gray, who owned Starlight Electrical, I'd be able to hide the secret I kept behind small talk. It was his son, Sawyer, I had to worry most about. Honestly, it was nothing short of a miracle that I hadn't had to face him during my brief visits over the years.

Aunt Bean glanced between Tessa Jane and me. "A few days ago, Annabelle's baby decided to come a month early. A little girl. The Grays drove straight up to lend a hand."

The last time I'd seen Sawyer's younger sister, Annabelle, she'd been a sophomore in high school. It was hard to believe she had a family of her own now.

Once again I felt like an outsider. I should've been at her wedding. At her baby shower. I'd been close to the family once.

Because I'd been close to Sawyer.

Memories flooded as I recalled all the time Sawyer and I had spent together way back when. In my mind, it was so easy to see his kind hazel eyes. His shy smile. To feel his strong hands. To smell his piney scent. It was heartbreakingly easy to recall the hopes I'd had.

And how the starlight had ruined everything.

I reached into my coat and pulled out my star pendant. I closed my hand over it in the hope that it would help ground me, comfort me.

Ty glanced upward at the man on the scaffolding. "Sawyer came back early to take care of an emergency call that came in yesterday. He probably would've had the work here done by now, except I wrangled him into helping me with the tarp. He'll be down in a second, once he pries the rest of it free."

There was a stabbing pain in my chest, like my heart was breaking all over again. Shattering. Panic set in, rooting deeply, like it was never planning to let go.

Because Sawyer was *here*.

CHAPTER FOUR

Addie

Aunt Bean must have felt my panic, because she put a soothing hand on my arm and said, "Didn't I ever tell you Sawyer works part-time for his daddy?"

No. She certainly had not.

Probably because any time his name had come up in the last twelve years, I excused myself from the conversation.

She knew I didn't want to talk about Sawyer. She just didn't know why. Not the full extent of it anyway. She simply assumed, like the rest of town, that he'd broken my heart by choosing Ree over me.

And he had.

But there was more to it than that.

"Since when?" I managed to say.

She shrugged innocently. "Since Luna started school?"

Luna was in sixth grade now, so what? Five years? Six?

It was just one more thing I hadn't known because I'd moved away.

Squeezing my pendant so tightly my knuckles hurt, I glanced upward, but the scaffolding shielded him from view.

It had been so long since I'd seen him in person.

I wanted to get closer.

I wanted to run.

I took deep breaths and tried to think of everything other than Ree's secret. Silently, I started listing as many colors as I could see. The terra-cotta puddles in the parking lot. The umber wood tone of the porch boards. The streaks of green in the stones stacked on the shop's exterior.

Tessa Jane turned my way, as if sensing my distress. Her pale brows were drawn low and worry floated in her eyes. After a moment, she looked the other way but then abruptly said, "Best we get out of this weather, don't y'all think? We can catch up with Sawyer inside."

Not waiting for anyone to answer, she stepped forward to open the door at the same time Ty reached for the handle. Their hands bumped. They both froze. Then Tessa Jane quickly took a step back and jammed her fists into the deep pockets of her coat.

Ty yanked open the door. Through clenched teeth, he said, "Ladies first."

Aunt Bean's eyebrows were pulled low in consternation as she strode past them, rain droplets sliding off her plastic hood and down her raincoat. Tessa Jane followed, her back ramrod straight.

I hesitated and the starlings trilled. I wasn't sure if they were encouraging me to go inside or urging me to make a run for it.

Aunt Bean gave me a tender smile and there was an understanding glint in her eyes as she said, "Addie?"

Pulled forward by her gentleness, I reluctantly stepped into the bakery.

Once through the door, I was immediately wrapped in a vanilla scent I'd recognize anywhere. It came from Aunt Bean's special extract recipe. My anxiety all but vanished as the air went eerily still. I glanced around in astonishment.

There was nothing left to hint that this space used to be a

laundromat. The cement floors had been covered in reclaimed heart pine boards. Cinder block walls had been Sheetrocked and painted a deep blue subtly flecked with gold. Raised panels, about shoulder high, were topped with a rustic wooden shelf. Worn butcher-block countertops gleamed. Light danced along brass-trimmed menu boards. Display cases sparkled, and I could easily see Bean's cakes sitting in them. Like her Gimme Some Sugar cake—a moist brown sugar, cinnamon, and toasted pecan cake filled and topped with cinnamon frosting. Or her Strawberry Stardust cake, which had three layers of strawberry cake, strawberry and cream filling, and was covered in delightful buttercream made with strawberry puree.

From a wooden beam that ran along the vaulted ceiling hung an iridescent glass starling that held a string of three large silvery glass stars, each piece unique, puffed with enchantment.

The room was cozy and inviting, whimsical and charming.

It felt like a hug.

It felt like love.

It was Aunt Bean, pure and simple.

And maybe, I realized, that had been the intention of the renovation all along.

Tears stung my eyes as I watched her studying the glasswork. Light reflected off the pieces, making them seem like they were somehow moving.

"It's my favorite thing about the whole renovation," she said, noticing me looking at her. "Ernie plumb outdid herself."

Tessa Jane had tears in her eyes as well. "It's beyond perfect."

Down the hall came the sound of a power saw and voices. Without tables and chairs in the space, the sounds echoed, bouncing around.

Smiling, Bean waited for the noise to die down before adding, "Ernie knew exactly what it was I wanted and made it happen."

Ty wore a sad-yet-pleased smile as he, too, gazed upward. "She's right proud of them."

"She should be," Tessa Jane said.

His smile vanished. A vein bulged in his neck. He raked a hand through shaggy brown hair, pushing it off his face.

The man knew how to hold a grudge, that was for sure, and honestly, my heart hurt for him, because I understood that his anger was rooted in years of pain. The endless ache that came with loss was one I knew well.

"You should pay Ernie a visit," Aunt Bean said to Tessa Jane. "Tell her yourself. I know she'd love to see you both. She's always had a soft spot for the two of you."

Ty glared for a second at Tessa Jane before looking away again, and then I heard a quiet snort.

I took a step forward, aiming to place myself between her and him, to block the bitterness, but Tessa Jane was already on the move.

"Oh, *so* sorry," she said, when she stepped on his foot on her way to take a closer look at the bakery case.

Accidentally-on-purpose, I guessed.

He smiled tightly. "Steel-toed boots. Didn't feel a thing."

"Pity," I heard her whisper as she passed by me.

My eyes widened. Where had this sassy side of her come from?

Aunt Bean suddenly banged her walking stick against the floor two times and narrowed her gaze at Ty. "What's got your britches in a wad this morning, Tyler Underwood? Do I need to get your mama on the phone?"

Tessa Jane and I gasped. It didn't matter how old you were, threatening to call someone's mama was the ultimate reprimand.

Ty's cheeks burned red, but he didn't say anything in response.

"I'm guessing you're a mite tired," Bean suggested. "What with taking care of all those animals at your place and looking after your mama. Addie, would you mind rustling us up some coffee? There should be a pot in the kitchen. I'm sure some caffeine will straighten Ty right out. Ain't so, Ty?"

Most people round here would've simply ignored his mood or pulled him aside and told him to quit being ugly. But Aunt Bean wasn't most people. She'd effectively let him know that she'd circled the wagons around Tessa Jane, but cared enough about him to give him a second chance to shape up.

If he had a lick of sense, he'd agree even if he didn't even *like* coffee.

"Yes, ma'am," he mumbled. "Coffee would be great. Thank you."

I started for the kitchen and Tessa Jane fell in step with me. "I'll help."

We walked around the display cases, toward the double swinging doors that led into the kitchen. Behind us, Aunt Bean started talking about the renovation work happening today as if nothing major had just happened.

Once the doors closed behind Tessa Jane and me, we looked at each other, eyes wide in surprise.

After a moment, I said, "He deserved it for being so unkind to you. I've never seen him like that."

"Well, it's nothing new to me."

I thought again about a small boy whose father had been taken away, but knew that if there was ever a time to circle my wagons, too, this was it. "When we go back out there, I can kick him in the shin if you want."

Her eyes lit, then she shook her head. "Probably best to just let it go." She then glanced around. "Whoa, look at this place."

Whoa was right.

High rectangular windows and overhead fixtures flooded the space with light. There were four long worktables, deep sinks, many racks, shelving galore, a giant dishwasher, bakery-depth ovens, a range top, and two industrial reach-in refrigerators. Large ocean-blue hexagon tiles with a worn, rustic finish covered the floor. The walls had been painted in warm orange tones, and the stainless steel counters reflected it, making it look like the color of a sunrise.

If the front of the bakery represented nighttime, the kitchen was daybreak.

It was a bright room. Happy. I could easily picture the Sugarbirds in here, twittering away while creating magic.

Tessa Jane walked into the middle of the room and spun in a slow circle, taking everything in. "The culinary school I went to had a less impressive kitchen."

I knew she had to be exaggerating, but I got the gist. Aunt Bean had clearly spared no expense.

She said, "Has Aunt Bean talked about expanding the business?"

"Not to me. Why?"

"It's excessive, is all."

The whole renovation had been a bit excessive, in my opinion, but I loved seeing Aunt Bean reflected in the space. Even in the commercial kitchen, her love of color shined through. "You know Aunt Bean. If she's in, she's all in."

It felt so strange to be talking *with* Tessa Jane. Strange and not wholly comfortable, if I was being honest.

I sidestepped to a counter near the swinging doors where the coffee maker sat, its pot full. Stacks of paper cups sat alongside it, along with lids, sleeves, stirrer sticks, pods of half-and-half, and sugar packets. I filled four cups nearly to the top and glanced over my shoulder at Tessa Jane.

She was running her palm back and forth across a worktable, a thoughtful look on her face.

Because of the growing silence, I forced myself to say something. "Do the renovations inspire you to bake a cake?" After all, she was a pastry chef. This kitchen had to look like a dream come true to her.

"I think I'll leave the cake making to the Sugarbirds," she said tightly.

Before I could dissect her response, I heard Aunt Bean greet Sawyer with a loud, hearty hello.

He'd finally come inside.

My hand stilled, mid-stir of the sugar I'd added to my coffee.

Tessa Jane stepped up next to me. She added hazelnut half-and-half to one of the cups I'd filled, and her voice held a note of apprehension as she said, "Do you not want to see Sawyer? You two were close once, weren't you?"

Because she was trying to make conversation even though she clearly wasn't comfortable either, part of me wanted to tell her what had happened between Sawyer and me. To share something of myself with her. To see if I could open up just the tiniest bit.

And also to get it off my chest. Out of my heart.

But I couldn't.

"*Once* was a long time ago." I set the stir stick aside and put a lid on my cup.

"Have you seen him at all since you moved away?"

I shook my head.

The power saw whirred again, then quieted.

"How do you think Ty likes his coffee?" I asked, needing to change the subject.

"With a little salt?" Then she gave a small shake of her head. "I meant sugar."

I smiled as I pictured an angel sitting on one of her shoulders, a devil on the other. I dumped four packets of sugar into his cup. "The more sweetness he can get, the better."

She handed me another packet. "One to grow on."

"Good thinking." I poured it in.

She said, "I know why he acts the way he does. I do. But I wish he'd realize that what happened wasn't *my* fault."

I swallowed hard, knowing, *feeling*, that I'd hurt her much the same way he had. Before I could talk myself out of it, I said, "Sometimes it's easier to hide from the truth instead of facing the pain that comes with it."

Our gazes met. This was the longest conversation we'd ever had. My skin prickled. My heart rate skyrocketed. I finally had to look away because I felt stripped bare in that moment, completely exposed.

Which was why I nearly jumped out of my skin when the door swung open. Aunt Bean filled the doorway as she stared at us, an eyebrow raised. "Just checkin' to see if you two had gotten lost back here."

Tessa Jane snapped a lid on a cup. "We've been admiring the renovation."

"It's something, isn't it? Now finish up and come on out and say hello to Sawyer."

"Yes, ma'am," we answered in unison.

The door swung shut behind her, and we quickly finished making the coffees in silence.

Tessa Jane picked up two cups, placed a shoulder against the door and pushed it open—but only an inch or so. She looked directly at me. "If you want to sneak out the back, I'll cover for you."

In her eyes, compassion swam in a sea of blue. Sudden emotion twisted my heart, wringing it out. Her offer might have been the kindest one I'd ever been given.

And it was tempting. *So* tempting.

"Thanks," I finally said, picking up two cups, "but I should probably get it over with. Seeing him, I mean. And it might be easier with people around."

"Girls!" Aunt Bean said. "I *swannee*."

"Coming." Tessa Jane took another step, fully opening the door. Holding it open for me.

Pulling my shoulders back, I stepped forward.

The last time I'd seen Sawyer had been a sunny summer day a lifetime ago in a cemetery not too far from here.

I'd left town the very next day.

I tried to avoid looking at him now, but I couldn't tear my gaze away. He'd always been a big guy—the kind that should play football, but he'd never been interested in the sport. Shy and quiet, he'd preferred books and music and long walks in the woods. He was a gentle kind of giant.

Old wounds ripped open as I studied his face, which had hardened a bit with age. Copper shot through the stubble covering his cheeks, his jaw. Long russet eyelashes framed his hazel eyes, a beautiful mix of pale green with a touch of gold and brown. Freckles dotted his nose, his cheeks. His broad shoulders sagged just a bit, as if he carried the weight of the world, and his soulful eyes reflected it. He'd always felt things deeply, as if life itself depended on him. Seemed that hadn't changed.

"Hi, Sawyer," Tessa Jane said as she handed Bean a cup. "Good to see you again."

I couldn't speak, so I only nodded, hoping it conveyed that I was glad, too.

Though I wasn't. I'd been dreading this day for years.

I stepped in close to Aunt Bean and handed Ty his extra-sweet coffee. He took a sip, winced. But to his credit, he kept drinking it.

"Would you like some coffee, Sawyer?" Tessa Jane asked. "I'd be happy to fix you a cup."

"That's okay, thank you." He hooked a thumb over his shoulder. "I've got a thermos full around here somewhere."

Ty cleared his throat. "Is this a good time for you to look at the suggested changes to the restroom plans, Miss Verbena?"

Aunt Bean looked between me and Sawyer, then said, "All right, but let's make it quick. I'll be right back, girls. Y'all carry on."

I *knew* I should've made a run for it when I'd had the chance.

A hazelnut scent wafted from Tessa Jane's cup as she took a sip of coffee, then said to Sawyer, "How's Luna doing?"

Luna. Oh my heart.

The last time I'd seen her in person, she'd been wrapped like a burrito in a white knit blanket, sleeping peacefully. Her newborn cheeks had been rosy red, her tiny lips pursed, and she had a tiny pink bow clipped to her dark fluffy hair.

She'd be twelve in July.

"Good. Great, even," Sawyer said, rocking on the heels of

his work boots. "She's currently with my folks up in Mentone."

"Aunt Bean mentioned Annabelle had her baby," Tessa Jane said. "Congratulations."

"Thanks. She's a tiny thing with big ol' lungs. Luna's in love, and I'm not sure how I'll convince her to come home without the baby in tow." He pulled out his phone, swiped a few times, and showed us a picture of a young girl with curly dark hair and blue eyes peeking over the edge of a bassinet that held a tiny baby.

"She's beautiful," I forced myself to say, pretending that Aunt Bean hadn't been sending me pictures of Luna all these years. Every time I'd receive one, I'd enlarge the photo to study her. To soak her in, to look for resemblance to her mama, to simply get to know who she'd become.

Tessa Jane smiled. "Is she still on winter break?"

I listened to every word like they were cookies and I was starving. It'd been a long time since I'd heard about Luna without it being filtered through Aunt Bean first.

"Technically," Sawyer said as he tucked his phone into his pocket, "she started back last week, but she's able to do her work online. School's come a long way since we were kids."

He held his damp ball cap in his hands. It looked like as soon as he'd taken it off, he'd run a hand through his gingery-brown hair. It stuck out every which way, reminding me of long-ago summers when we'd splash around in Sassafras Creek, which twined through the woods that bordered the starlight field.

We'd spent a lot of time together as kids, as his family's farmhouse wasn't too far from ours. We went on adventures through the woods, played on his swing set and trampoline, caught lightning bugs. As we got older, we'd go for long hikes, taking lunch with us. We built a treehouse in the woods. We read old comic books, played board games, found shapes in the clouds, wished on shooting stars. When I joined the theater program, so did he. When we met Ree, it felt natural to fold her into our friendship. And for a while it had been the three of us against the world.

Fighting tears, fighting longing for what used to be, I bit the inside of my cheek. I shifted my gaze to look out the front windows.

"Sure has," Tessa Jane said with a laugh. "Did she get the part in the play?"

Play? What play?

"Yeah. She did," Sawyer said, smiling.

My god, his smile. It made my knees weak.

Tessa Jane's eyes were filled with empathy as she said to me, "At Thanksgiving dinner Luna was talking up a storm about trying out for a children's theater production of *Alice in Wonderland*. She was practicing her Frog voice on us. I had no doubt she'd get the role. Best ribbitting I've ever heard."

Thanksgiving. Right. I'd bowed out the minute I knew Tessa Jane was going to be there. Another regret to add to the growing pile.

"If you're still in town in March, I know Luna would love for you to see the performance. Both of you," Sawyer added.

Learning that Luna was a theater kid filled my heart to the tippy top. Ree would be beyond proud. She loved acting more than anything. Well, almost.

Sawyer tucked his hat into his back pocket and added, "But I suspect you'll see her far before then. Once she's back from Mentone I'm afraid she's of a mind to camp out on Miss Verbena's doorstep. So if you open the door and see a tent, don't be alarmed."

Tessa Jane laughed. The sound was light and sparkly. "Why's that?"

"She wants to talk to Addie."

My heart dropped clear to the floor. I shifted my gaze to meet his and it was easy to see his inner light shining in the hazel depths.

"She wants to know more about Ree."

I swallowed hard, thinking of my best friend. Of her quick laugh, her dark eyes, her devilish personality, her determination to be *someone*, do *something*, to get far away from Starlight. Her secret perched on the tip of my tongue, ready to take flight, and the stabbing pain returned to my chest.

I gripped my star pendant for dear life and eyed the front door. Four long strides, maybe five, and I could be out of here. And free of the pain. At least temporarily.

It always came back.

Sawyer's gaze cut toward the hallway, then found its way back to me. "Luna knows why you're here in Starlight. Knows Miss Verbena is feeling poorly. And I told her you might not be in the mood to take a walk down memory lane, but she's stubborn and persistent. What she wants, she goes after until she gets it."

In my head, I could hear Ree's determined voice saying, "Just watch me."

My throat ached as I said, "Sounds a lot like her mama."

He didn't agree or disagree. Only said, "I didn't want Luna to blindside you by showing up out of the blue. Don't feel obligated to talk with her. Just send her on home to me." He glanced toward the hallway again. "I best be getting to work on that electric panel." He started walking off toward the back of the shop. Then he stopped, turned. "It was real good seeing y'all again."

With that, he was gone.

I blew out a breath. I'd done it. I'd kept the secret. But I felt torn to pieces from keeping quiet.

As soon as his footsteps faded, Tessa Jane asked, her voice low, "You okay?"

I wasn't, not really. I gave a halfhearted shrug and walked over to the window and looked out. The starlings, I noticed, were gone.

I took a deep breath, then another, trying to calm the turmoil within me by focusing on the scents around me.

I was amazed that after all its renovations the bakery still held on to the scent of vanilla.

And that after all this time, Sawyer still smelled of pine.

✳

Later that night, I stood inside a room on the second floor of the big red barn, a space no bigger than a decent walk-in closet. It was packed with cleaning supplies, and had a stained ceiling with a single low-wattage lightbulb that cast the room in spooky shadows, a thick wooden door, creaky floorboards, and a small window that was painted shut.

It was going to take a lot of effort to make the room work as a recording studio, but it was doable.

I began a mental checklist of things to be done, starting first with a full cleanout since the shelving and supplies would cause unwanted echoes. I'd also need to add acoustic tiles to the walls, a thick rug, and hang a heavy drape over the window.

I pulled out my phone to start a shopping list when it rang, the ringtone, "Too Good at Goodbyes" by Sam Smith, revealing exactly who was calling.

My mama, Cecelia.

It was almost eleven, and I sighed, debating whether to answer.

She'd been calling multiple times a day since Friday evening, and I'd been ignoring each and every call. Because she didn't leave a voicemail, I knew it wasn't an emergency. Like the time I'd had to bail her out of jail after she was arrested for indecent exposure for bathing nude on what *wasn't* a nude beach.

My mama, I'd come to discover as I aged, was *a lot.*

She was loud, overdramatic, and often acted inappropriately for attention. Even if it got her in legal trouble. Hand in hand with that, however, she could be extremely charming and flirtatious. I suspected that's what my father had been drawn to initially—but knew I was the reason he'd stayed.

I'd been in my early twenties when my mama admitted to

me that they'd only married because I was on the way. She'd told me how he begged her to say yes to his proposal. How he wore her down. How she'd felt trapped.

When I asked if she'd meant trapped by marrying him—or having me—she'd said it didn't much matter now.

But it had explained a lot.

She'd never really wanted to be a mother.

But my daddy had always loved being a father.

The phone kept singing and I took a deep breath and answered. "Hello?"

"Finally!" Mama exclaimed. "You've been harder to catch than a greased-up hog."

"I've been busy."

"I heard tell. Moving in again with Verbena."

I didn't ask how she knew. It didn't matter.

"Feels like a step backward to me," she said, her voice sweet but sharp. "You're twenty-eight now. Too old to be moving back home."

I clenched my teeth. "Twenty-nine."

"I think I would know, Addison."

I breathed in for five counts. I knew better than to try and correct her. In her mind, she was never wrong.

Suddenly feeling like I was suffocating in the small space, I stepped into the hallway, then strode into the large storage room at the rear of the barn. I scooted around sacks of flour and headed straight to a large window that overlooked the backyard.

I put the phone on speaker so I could use both hands to shove the window upward, using more force than necessary.

"It's been a long day. Why're you calling, Mama?" I asked, gulping in the cool breeze and wishing I hadn't answered her call.

It had taken me years and a truckload of therapy to understand the emotional damage she had done to me as a child.

She rarely visited. She didn't call on my birthday, let alone send a present. She hadn't even sent a card when I'd been hospitalized with appendicitis when I was fourteen.

Yet, I couldn't bring myself to fully cut her out of my life. Somewhere in me still was the little girl who hoped her mama would come back. The little girl who never understood why her mama had left her behind.

And . . . I'd seen with my own eyes that she had some good in her. Not a whole lot, but enough to give me hope that one day she'd change.

"You know why," Mama said.

It was impossible not to notice the glow of the starlight aurora in the distance, dimmer than usual because it had been a cloudy day. Some of the scientists who visited at least once a year to study the phenomenon speculated the light was some sort of bioluminescent event, which sort of made sense, since it seemed to be powered by sunlight. Others thought it had to do with mineral deposits left behind by the meteorite. No one knew for sure. However, everyone in Starlight was more than happy to believe it came from bits of broken star.

No matter how cloudy the day, at night the land still glowed weakly, offering a hint of what could be. A gas stove burner on low versus high. Even faint, the light was take-your-breath-away lovely. And finding clarity, certainty, was still possible.

While I wasn't necessarily a fan of the gift the starlight offered, I'd always been able to appreciate its stunning beauty. Ribbons of blue, silver, green, and gold light swayed in the darkness. As it always did, the sight brought tears to my eyes and made my chest expand with an emotion that was hard to identify. There was just something so powerful about the light, a reminder, really, that there was still so much about this world that was mysteriously beautiful.

"Are you wondering about Aunt Bean's health?" I asked, knowing full well that wasn't why she called. She rarely asked after Bean. Heck, she rarely asked after *me*. "Because we don't know much at this point."

She called only when she wanted something from me. Usually money. Or, like today, a renewal of my promise to always pretend I was an only child—using me to nurture her hatred in her absence.

Her voice was calm, even, but it was coated in ice. "I hear *she's* there, too."

By *she*, she meant Tessa Jane. Mama never said her name. Not hers or Henrietta's, whom she only called *that woman*.

By all accounts, my parents had never had a happy marriage. According to Aunt Bean, they'd tried their hardest to make it work in deference to me and had sheltered me from the worst of it. Knowing what I knew now, it was likely my daddy who'd done the sheltering. I was beyond glad I didn't remember the separations, the arguments. My earliest memory had been when my mama left.

"You know how I feel about *her*," Mama said, still talking about Tessa Jane.

I did know.

Because she had always told me that if I loved her I had to feel the same.

I studied the shimmery starlight, captivated and oddly comforted by its familiarity. Soon, though, my gaze drifted to the small cabin near the edge of the woods. Lights glowed in the windows, and I couldn't help picturing Sawyer's face, those hazel eyes. My attention was drawn away from the cabin by the sound of quacking. I shifted a bit to get a better view of the farmhouse's backyard. In the shine of a floodlight, I saw Tessa Jane running around, chasing after the ducks, trying to herd them into the shed that was their temporary home. They were outwitting her at every turn.

I smiled at the antics.

"You know what I *expect* of you," Mama said.

I knew.

But I wasn't a little girl anymore who believed her mother's empty promises.

Back then I didn't really think I had a choice in the matter. Not if I wanted her back.

Now I knew better.

Now I knew she never should've asked such a thing of me in the first place.

Outside, the ducks kept quacking. In the light, I could see Tessa Jane's smile, and could hear the humorous, cajoling tone she was using to convince them to go to bed.

"I have to go now, Mama," I said abruptly.

"But—"

"Bye!"

I hung up, quickly closed the window, and hurried next door to help my sister rustle up some ducks.

CHAPTER FIVE

From the Kitchen of Verbena Fullbright

Cold ingredients will make cake batter dense and lumpy and prone to curdling. Ain't nobody wants that. Letting the ingredients come to room temperature will ensure a smooth mixture with lots of air bubbles that will expand in the oven, making the sponges nice and fluffy with an even texture. Just like cakes, time can also work wonders for warming up to people who might've once been a little cold.

Tessa Jane

On Tuesday afternoon, the big red barn's kitchen was buzzing as all three of the Sugarbirds flitted about the space. I was set up at the frosting station, and the knuckles on my right hand were starting to ache from gripping the electric hand mixer—or whizzer, as Aunt Bean liked to call it. Using a stand mixer for this task, like the Sugarbirds did, made much more sense. Truly. But because Bean preferred to make frosting this way, exactly like her mama had taught her, I did, too.

"There's magic to be found in tradition," she used to tell me when I asked why she didn't make the switch.

I liked being part of that tradition. Very much so.

When she left an hour ago for a doctor's appointment, choosing Addie to drive her, she'd said to me, "It's a great day for you to get caught up with the Sugarbirds, peanut. You'll be in good hands with them as you settle in here."

Settle.

It sounded so appealing. Being with the Sugarbirds, where

there was a sense of friendship, coziness, and sweetness, made me want to stay. Made me want to make another attempt at baking the shop's trademark cakes even though I'd given up trying a long time ago, failing time and again.

As a Bee Gees record played on a turntable in the corner, Willa Jo Digby peeked over my shoulder. She was a tall, broad woman who had a thick brown braid laced with silver strands, kind grayish-brown eyes, and a deep longing to visit her grandchildren in California, who she saw only once a year because travel costs were simply too expensive. The need to see them pulsed off her, rattling the bangle bracelets on her wrists. Sad, silvery jangles.

I wished I could make a donation to her travel fund but any extra money I had at the end of every month was donated to my mother's secret society. Many around here would be quite shocked to see the bottom line of my bank account.

The *most* shocked would probably be my granddaddy. Every month he gave Mama and me generous stipends, using money from the trust account he'd inherited from my grandmother. Although he made it clear he didn't like sharing the money, he was dutifully following Gigi's wishes. She'd been giving Mama and me an allowance for as long as I could remember and requested the practice continue after her death. I was honestly surprised he was complying, though I shouldn't be. Not with the way he wanted my and Addie's land. He knew he had to stay on my good side.

"Absolutely beautiful," Willa Jo said, still peeking in my bowl.

She was one of three Sugarbirds, named for their sweet natures and incessant chatter, chirping, and squawking. Friends since grade school, they were now in their midsixties and had worked in the bakery for what felt like forever. Individually— and especially as a whole—they were the most hardworking, salt-of-the-earth people I'd ever met in my life and truly felt like family.

"Thanks, Willa Jo," I said.

She was talking about the bowl of ermine frosting I was whipping up. Made with a cooked milk and flour base, it was an old-fashioned frosting, light and fluffy, that had the texture of whipped cream. It was less sweet than a classic buttercream and Bean used it—or a variation of it—for a few of her cakes like her Luminous Lemon cake and Red Velvet Delight.

Willa Jo leaned a hip against the worktable. "Not that I expected anything less. Considering that fancy degree of yours."

Though her husky voice was pleasant, cheerful even, I heard an undercurrent of concern. It was as if she worried that while I was here helping out I'd swap out Bean's humble cakes for petit fours or mille-feuille. Or use a Swiss meringue buttercream instead of the ermine.

The Sugarbirds needn't worry. Nothing was going to change.

As the scent of Aunt Bean's vanilla extract swirled in the air, I switched off the whizzer to change out the flat-edged beaters for a whisk attachment. Willa Jo still loomed, and trying to put her mind at ease, I said, "I've had no better teachers than y'all."

A chorus of "awws" drifted through the room, then Willa Jo added, "We're real glad you finally found your way back here, honey. Right where you've always belonged."

Just like that, my shadow darkened. I pasted on a fake smile. "It's like old times." After all, this humble barn kitchen was where I'd learned to bake.

"You took your sweet time getting here," Pinky Doucet, another of the Sugarbirds, said on a laugh. "We expected you years ago."

Something that felt like grief welled up in me, and I forcefully tamped it back down.

"Hush now," Delilah said. "Clearly, Tessa Jane gets her time management skills from her auntie."

Delilah and Bean liked to say they'd been friends since the womb—their mamas had been pregnant at the same time. Delilah was a tiny but solid workhorse of a woman, always moving, always going, always pushing forward. She'd been married for thirty-six years, had raised three boys—and tragically buried one of them—and now had six grandchildren keeping her busy when she wasn't working full-time.

Again, I forced a smile and turned the whizzer back on. It was true Aunt Bean's inner clock tended to run a bit behind, but the reason I hadn't shown up here years ago looking to become a Sugarbird had nothing to do with timing. And everything to do with pain.

It hadn't always been that way. Once, a long time ago, I dreamed about working alongside Bean and the Sugarbirds, and making the cakes—oh, the *delightful* cakes.

Eventually, however, Granddaddy had robbed me of that dream after he'd become fixated on me mastering Aunt Bean's recipes. Every day after school, I'd bake a cake for him. And every day I failed to replicate Aunt Bean's magic.

It was all too easy to recall him saying, "It's not good enough!" before throwing a cake I'd made into the trash.

Aunt Bean had always said that it took only following her recipes for the magic to happen, but no matter how hard I tried, I simply could not infuse my bright side into a cake.

Not back then.

Not now.

At the reminder, it took everything in me not to flee the barn, to escape the vanilla-wrapped reminders that I'd never measure up to what was expected of me.

From either side of the family.

As I worked on the frosting, I thought about the summons I'd received this morning, hand delivered at first light by my granddaddy's assistant, Jenna Elkins. He was throwing a black-tie party at his home on Friday night and I was expected to be there.

I'd known I couldn't avoid him forever, but I'd been hoping for a longer reprieve.

I wished I could ask Aunt Bean—or even Addie—to come along. Someone to act as a buffer. But there was no need for them to be miserable, too.

As music filled the air, my thoughts stayed with Addie. Something had changed between us yesterday at the bakery. Shifted. *Began?*

I wasn't sure. I was still wary of letting her in. Afraid of being hurt yet again. Still, I had to admit it had been nice for a moment there, the two of us feeling like a team. Feeling like we had each other's backs. Feeling like sisters.

Pinky wandered over, sidling up to my workstation. After the briefest pause, she said, "We were real sorry about what happened with Carson, Tessa Jane. The way we see it, he's dumber than a box of rocks."

Pinky's voice was light and breathy, making her outrage toward Carson sound more like indignation. She fully embraced her name by wearing all pink and even dyed her angled bob a shade of fuchsia.

"Dumber than *dirt*," Delilah exclaimed.

Willa Jo crossed her arms. "He's so dumb, he could throw himself at the ground and *miss*."

Honestly, I'd expected the Sugarbirds to say something about my disastrous wedding as soon as I'd walked in the door two hours ago. Their restraint was impressive.

"A right coward." Delilah edged closer to join the conversation. Fire flickered hot and bright in her dark eyes as she *tsk*ed. "We couldn't believe him leaving you standing there like that."

They all stuck their hands in their apron pockets and rocked on their heels, waiting for me to fill in some blanks.

Hives formed on my chest as I tried to banish the image of me waiting behind a floral hedge for Carson to take his place at the end of a flowery aisle. And waiting. And waiting.

"Did he ever explain himself?" Pinky asked.

I switched off the whizzer. I'd known these questions would come, and I'd tried preparing myself by practicing answers on the long ride to town. Things like "some things aren't meant to be" or "it was probably for the best." But standing here, I couldn't quite force the words from my lips.

They felt . . . too little.

And I felt too brittle.

I shrugged. "Not really."

He hadn't needed to. I knew full well why he'd fled.

I forced myself to loosen the death grip I had on the bowl of frosting. Feeling all kinds of anxious, I absently reached for my star pendant, only to realize, yet again, that I wasn't wearing it. Aunt Bean had given the star to me right after my daddy had passed away and each and every time I held it tightly, it calmed my restless soul, giving me the same feeling as one of Aunt Bean's hugs. I suspected it wasn't a coincidence—that somehow, some way, she'd managed to put a little of herself into the gift, so that I would always be able to feel her love. I'd worn the necklace constantly right up until my birthday last February. That was when Carson had presented me with a heart-shaped diamond pendant that he'd expected me to wear instead.

Even though I'd stopped wearing his gift after our breakup, for some reason I hadn't returned to the routine of wearing my star every day, which only showed how out of sorts I'd been. I made a mental note to text my mama and ask her to send it to me, because lately I was feeling the need for its comfort more than ever.

A horn honked, a staccato bleat, and we all turned toward the sound as the Bootsie's Blooms delivery van rolled up to the door.

Delilah's eyebrows lifted. "Anyone's birthday? Anniversary?"

We all murmured no and moved in closer as Stan Reeves sauntered in, carrying a purple cellophane-wrapped basket. He was a big teddy bear of a man who reminded me of Santa Claus, with his white hair, beard, and bushy eyebrows. And, of course, a big belly that jiggled like bowl full of jelly when he laughed.

"Afternoon, ladies. My, don't it smell like heaven in here?"

It truly did. The sponges for the Vanilla Dream Cream cakes, a vanilla cake with a silky custard filling, were currently baking, infusing the air with Aunt Bean's divine vanilla scent.

"I've got a delivery for Miss Tessa Jane." My eyes widened as he stepped up to me, handed over the basket. "Good to see you, sweetie."

My cheeks were hot, and I felt the itch of a hive starting on my arm. Who on earth had sent me a gift basket? "You too, Mister Stan. How're your grands?"

"They're teenaged terrors." He grinned broadly. "But I love every hair on their troublemaking heads."

Delilah slipped him some money from the petty cash tin, and he thanked her. Then he took a good long look around, his smile faltering ever so slightly before saying, "I best be off. Y'all have a good day."

Once he was out the door, Pinky let out a light laugh. "Poor guy."

"What? Why?" I set the basket on the edge of the counter and the Sugarbirds closed in around me.

Delilah said, "He has a crush on Bean, but can't seem to work up the courage to ask her on a date."

Pinky added, "He hasn't been in a relationship since his wife passed six years ago, bless his heart, so he's a bit rusty when it comes to the dating game."

Willa Jo poked her with an elbow. "You should give him tips. You've mastered that game."

Pinky laughed, not offended in the least. She was proud of being a serial dater. "I've offered. He turns red as a ripe cherry tomato and starts stuttering about needin' to fix his carburetor or some such nonsense."

Stan and Bean? Suddenly, I could see them together. I could see it quite well. "How does she feel about him?"

All their faces softened, and I saw the love for my aunt clearly in their expressions. Delilah smiled. "She fancies him. Won't admit it, of course, but she's been sweet on him since high school."

Pinky said, "I've told her a million times she should just ask him out."

"And a million times she's said no," Delilah added.

Aunt Bean was a fascinating mix of old-fashioned and forward-thinking. She loudly and proudly embraced Willa Jo and her lifelong partner, Mary Beth, but asking a man out? No way.

Not that she'd been pining away. She'd been in plenty of relationships through the years, but one by one they always petered out, and she'd simply say, "He's not the one."

Now I wondered if Stan was.

"Enough about all that," Delilah said. "I'm going to bust of curiosity if you don't open up that basket. And you don't want that on your conscience, do you? Me busting open?"

Willa Jo said, "I've seen it happen a time or two before. It's not pretty."

Delilah whapped her with a tea towel. "Hush your mouth. I'm always pretty, even when I'm busted open."

I laughed, loving them, and tugged on the basket's elaborate bow. The cellophane unfolded like petals on a flower. A card was tucked into the assortment of goodies nestled inside the wicker, but at seeing the contents, I knew immediately who had sent the gift.

"What on earth?" Delilah picked up one of three packages of Grasshopper cookies.

Also in the basket were two bags of hazelnut coffee from a local roaster and coffee mug that had an adorable cartoon grasshopper printed on it.

I opened the card anyway.

Grasshopper, my apologies for bugging *you.* —*Stinkbug*

The apology held little water with me, since I knew Ty had sent the basket only because Aunt Bean had scolded him. However, if it meant that he'd be on his best behavior from here on out, I'd accept it.

"Stinkbug?" Willa Jo said as she read over my shoulder. "Who's that?"

There was no point in hiding the truth. All she had to do was place one call to Stan's sister, Bootsie, at the flower shop to get the scoop. Bootsie was a talker. "Ty Underwood."

Delilah's eyes widened, glinting with interest.

Pinky elbowed me playfully. "I can give *you* a few dating pointers as well."

"Seems to me, it's Ty who's needing the pointing. Tessa Jane ain't been in town but a minute and he's already in the doghouse? What'd he do?" Willa Jo asked. "Do we need to have a come-to-Jesus meeting with him? I've got some free time this afternoon."

Smiling, I said, "Aunt Bean already gave him a talking-to." I tucked the card back into the basket and threw the wrapping away. "We're good now."

"All right, but so help us if he *bugs* you again," Willa Jo said, and Delilah and Pinky nodded. "Now, what's the meaning of the nicknames? I know there's a story there."

It was old news, water under the bridge, but I was ready to tell them all about it anyway simply because I was enjoying their friendship. Feeling like I belonged.

It was the sound of a dog barking that stopped me. I tipped my head. "Is that the infamous Hambone?"

Pinky said, "No doubt. He's the best cake-hunting dog around. In fact, it's the only thing he hunts. That dog is a lover, not a fighter."

"Should we call Miss Ernie?" I asked. "To let her know he's loose?"

"I'll send her a text, but usually Hambone wanders on back home after visitin' a spell," Willa Jo said.

I wiped my hands on my apron and walked to the front of the room to look outside. The bare branches of a pecan tree seemed to be shivering on this cold, gray day. Snow was being predicted for the weekend, and it was such a rarity in this area that I was having trouble believing the forecast.

Willa Jo gathered up scraps that had been trimmed off one of the vanilla cakes and squished the pieces into small balls. "He comes by two or three times a week," she told me. "He's going to be right sorry when we move back to Market Street."

Or he'd simply start showing up there. Coonhounds were excellent trackers.

Delilah pointed through the glass door toward the woods on the far side of Aunt Bean's expansive lawn. "See there, that dot of cinnamon? That's Hambone."

The reddish blur seemed to be galloping. The echo of his barks filled the air, faint explosions of sound.

Delilah frowned. "But something don't sound right. Usually he's baying, not barking his dang head off."

He did sound a bit frantic, now that I listened carefully.

As the dog zoomed past the farmhouse, we all hurried outside and gathered on the stone walkway. His big ears flopped with each step he took. His jowls flapped. And as he neared, I noticed a long, broken rope trailing behind him. How it hadn't snagged on anything during his adventure here was beyond me.

But then I saw the starlings. They circled overhead, dipping and rising, gleaming like freshly polished silver against the gray clouds, their iridescence glowing in the dull sky. Their movements were jarring—up, down, left, right—sharp turns, not smooth like usual. Almost . . . desperate.

Goose bumps rose on my arms.

Hambone zoomed past the cars parked on the cement pad next to the barn, hurdled a low hedge, and ran straight to me. The rope, I noticed, was a tie-out—its clasp remained firmly attached to Hambone's collar. The other end was missing its snap hook.

"Here, boy." Three cake balls sat on Willa Jo's palm.

Despite Hambone's sweet tooth, he didn't seem to have any interest in her offerings.

"Well, I'll be." Willa Jo clucked her tongue. "That's a fine how do you do."

I picked up the nylon rope, and once I had it in hand, Hambone jogged off.

Pinky's quiet voice was as crisp as the cold air as she joked, "Looks like he's taken a shine to you, Tessa Jane. He's wanting to take *you* for a walk."

I stayed where I was, and as soon as he felt resistance, he came racing back to me, his long nose in the air as he howled his displeasure. I patted his head, running my fingers over his silky ears. I didn't agree that he'd taken any kind of shine—I thought he'd been *led* to me. By the starlings. Something was very wrong.

Worry lines creased Willa Jo's forehead. "He's sure in quite the tizzy, ain't he?"

I looked upward. The starlings were flying toward the woods where Hambone had emerged. On the other side of those woods stood Ernie Underwood's house.

I said, "I think we should check on Miss Ernie."

Delilah searched my gaze for a long second before pulling a phone from her pocket. "I'll call over there right quick."

We all waited, watching her. Finally, she hung up and shook her head. "Went to voicemail."

My heart was racing. "Someone should drive over. Just to make sure everything is okay."

"I'll go." The words were barely out of Willa Jo's mouth before she was heading for her aging minivan, her long strides and determination making quick work of the short distance.

"I'll go with you," Delilah said.

Pinky looked back at the barn. "I'll stay here. There are cakes in the ovens. I'll get in touch with Ty. Give him a heads-up."

"I'll stay, too." I handed Hambone's rope to Delilah. "Please call when you know something."

"Will do." She started toward the minivan, but instead of trotting off with her, Hambone sat down at my feet, refusing to budge. She tugged on the rope. "Come on, Hammy."

He looked up at me with his big brown eyes and whimpered.

Delilah said, "Best you come along, Tessa Jane."

It wasn't a request. "Yes, ma'am."

Once I started toward the van, Hambone fell in step with me. I checked the sky just before climbing into the back seat. The starlings were circling over the woods.

A minute later, we were flying down Bean's driveway, the balding tires on the van lamely spitting bits of chipped slate behind us.

Hambone kept his nose to the window as we sped along a narrow two-lane road bordered by tall pine trees.

The ride was quiet. No talking. No music. No nothing, except the sound of our breathing and the road beneath the wheels. We passed the local cemetery, then the driveway that led to Sawyer Gray's cabin. Not long after that we crossed the bridge that spanned a thin ribbon of Sassafras Creek and Willa Jo slowed to turn in to Ernie's paved driveway.

Hambone started crying again, and I ran a hand down his back. He was trembling, which made my nerves kick up a notch, even though nothing looked amiss.

The lengthy driveway led to a small bungalow painted a sunny shade of yellow, with trim done in a cheerful purplish-blue. A mud-splattered SUV was parked in a leaning carport. Fenced in behind the house was a barn-style outbuilding painted the same shade of blue as the shutters: Ernie's glass-blowing studio.

In a blink, we were all out of the van and standing in front of the door, where Delilah started alternately knocking loudly and ringing the bell.

Willa Jo reached around her for the doorknob, giving it a turn. "This ain't no time for visiting etiquette, Delilah."

As soon as the door swung open, Hambone howled and raced inside, making a beeline for the kitchen. We quickly followed.

Ernie was unconscious, sprawled on the floor, blood staining the thin silk scarf wrapped around her head. An upper cabinet was open. A step stool was upside down by her feet. As Hambone licked her face, she let out a small moan.

I heaved a sigh of relief that she was alive even as I worried about the head injury.

Willa Jo nudged Hambone out of the way and knelt on the

floor next to Ernie. She picked up one of her hands, and held it tightly. "Ernie, can you hear me? Say something, darlin'."

Ernie moaned again and mumbled something I couldn't quite make out.

"It's not bossiness, woman," Willa Jo said, emotion making her voice shake. "It's *leadership* skills."

Delilah paced as she talked to the 9–1–1 dispatcher by name and asked for an ambulance.

Hambone was crying and wiggling, trying to find a way around Willa Jo to get to Ernie.

"Hambone, come," I said. He threw a look at me, as if debating whether to comply, but finally trotted over to where I stood in the wide opening between the living room and kitchen, out of the way. I bent down and gave him a hug. "Good boy, Hammy. Good boy."

Through the window above the sink I saw the starlings sitting on the studio's roofline. I didn't question how they knew to send Hambone for help. Or why they chose to intervene. I was simply grateful.

When I looked back at Hambone, he was creeping toward Willa Jo, his dark nose pointed at her pocket. He snuffled, then bayed.

Willa Jo laughed. "I suppose you done deserve a treat, being a hero and all." She reached into her pocket and pulled out one of the small cake balls he'd dismissed earlier. His jowls shook as he chewed happily.

Ernie wiggled, like she was planning to sit up, and Willa Jo said, "You stay right there. Banged your head but good when you fell. Help will be here soon enough."

Just as she said it, Delilah called out, "Ty's here."

I turned toward the front door and braced myself as he ran up the front steps and into the house, saying, "I was already on my way here when I got the call about my mama. Is she okay?"

"She's in the kitchen," Delilah said, stepping aside—and sidestepping the question. "An ambulance is on the way."

He barely spared me a look as he ran past me and dropped down at Ernie's side. His hand was shaking as he picked hers up and patted it tenderly. "It's going to be okay, Mama. Everything's going to be okay."

Hambone was doing circle eights, and I was trying not to cry. Because when Ty had looked at me, I hadn't seen his usual disdain. Instead I saw only the shiny love he had for his mother swimming in a pool of anguish and apprehension. In that unguarded moment, I'd caught a glimpse of his heart and his true nature and wished he wasn't so set on hiding it all the time. Because it was utterly beautiful.

Ernie blinked her eyes open. She mumbled something again, but this time I heard her plainly as she said, "About time this hard head of mine came in handy. Don't you worry none. I'm going to be just fine."

Then her gaze slid right past him, to me, her eyes the same color as her son's.

She smiled weakly. "It's real good to see you, Tessa Jane, minus the circumstances and all. Don't suppose you brought those cookies of yours I love so much?"

✳

It was late. And cold. And dark.

The cloud cover hung low in the sky as I crept through the backyard on tiptoes as to not disturb the sleeping ducks, and climbed over the fence, to avoid the creak of the hinges on the back gate. Aunt Bean and Addie were already in bed for the night, and I didn't want to disturb them.

To my left, Sawyer's cabin was a mere silhouette, but I could hear the trill of the starlings in the woods as I made my way through the pasture, heading toward the star crater. The birds were chattering as though talking amongst themselves, probably wondering what I was doing.

I wasn't quite sure myself.

All I knew was that I'd been pulled toward the starlight tonight. Had to see its glow up close and personal, even though at this hour it was well into its waning period. By midnight, the crater would be dark and it would stay that way until the following evening when the aurora would rise again, blooming like a mystical night flower.

I stuffed my hands into the pockets of my coat and hurried along, my steps sure and steady despite the uneven terrain. Although the sky was pitch-black, the faint glow of the starlight nestled inside the crater was enough to guide me along. The night was fairly quiet but for the sound of the birds and the wind. The field had closed to visitors at eleven, nearly half an hour ago, so no one was around.

No one but me.

As I walked, I thought of the journal that Granddaddy had unearthed years ago, the one that had sparked his obsession with this land. It had belonged to Abner Wingrove, who'd been in his late forties when the star fell from the sky. The weathered, faded pages of the journal had been full of Abner's daily thoughts, humorous musings, poems, limericks, and doodles. It also contained the story of how he'd once won a farmhouse and a large plot of land in a back-room card game and decided it might be a good time to give up his gambling lifestyle for good, put down roots, and become a farmer. However, when he quickly discovered the difficulties of farming he sold the land to the highest bidder at an auction and happily went back to his gambling ways.

That bidder had been the teenage son of Clara Fullbright, a hardworking widow and mother of two, who'd been bidding on her behalf.

Little could Clara know that less than three years later, the early-evening sky would suddenly be filled with light as a fiery shooting star fell from the heavens. It landed in one of her fields with a dynamite-like explosion and blast of heat, creating a huge dust cloud. Windows around town had broken. Farm animals had gone wild, escaping their stalls and pens.

Charity, Clara's nineteen-year-old daughter had raced from the family farmhouse to the field to find her mother, who'd been out harvesting cabbage for the night's supper. But there had been no sign of her mama.

According to his journal, Abner had been one of the many townsfolk who'd rushed to the farm to see what all had happened. As night fell and the search for Clara continued, he noticed something glowing near the woods, not too far from the crater. Upon further inspection, he'd found what he believed to be a piece of the broken star and described it as a gemstone that looked like a chunk of grayish glass, about the size of a pecan. Even though it lost its glow as soon as he picked it up, when he held the star in the light of his lantern it sparkled like a diamond. Before he could make sense of what he found, a silvery bird came out of nowhere and plucked the broken star right out of his hand, carrying it away.

No one had seen it happen. And no one believed him when he told the story.

In his journal, he reflected on whether he'd imagined the occurrence until the next night, when the aurora fully appeared, glowing brightly. Glowing like the gemstone he'd found—but on a much grander scale.

Grass crunched as I followed the curve of the crater upward toward its entrance point. When I was younger, I'd read Abner's journal cover to cover many a time. I'd been captivated by his writings. He looked at the world around him, a challenging world to be sure, with humor and grace and kindness. Although he was a gambler, he often gave money away to those in need. He took in an injured bird and nursed it back to health. His doodles were often nature scenes. A caterpillar on a twig. The whiskers of a cat. The veins of a leaf. His poems had been whimsical, almost feeling more like nursery rhymes.

I'd been heartened by the similarities between us. Heartened by the fact that there was a male Wingrove who wasn't cold, distant, and greedy.

A cool wind blew as I paused at the entrance to the star-walk, the wooden walkway that curved around the crater, as I took in the sight before me. The reaction at seeing the light was incredibly emotional. It was as if it reached inside me, making me feel *all* the feels. It was blissful and spellbinding, joyful and overwhelming in the best possible way.

Tears came quickly to my eyes as colors flickered, the green, gold, silver, and blue melding together seamlessly. Even as faint as it was now, the aurora was stunning. Breathtaking. Mesmerizing.

I pressed my hands to my chest as though I could capture these feelings and hold them there forever. This awe. And the knowledge that even on the darkest night, light could still be found. Whether it was here, in a luminous crater, or deep within a heart, a soul.

In the distance, the starlings still chattered as I stepped onto the starwalk and into the light. I was immediately engulfed with a sense of calm, and I soaked in the peace of the moment.

Until I realized I wasn't alone.

Ahead of me on the walkway stood a man, his hands braced on the railings, his head hung low.

I froze, unsure what to do. No one should be out here. Not even me.

Yet, the starlings weren't swooping in, so I knew he didn't pose a threat.

I turned to go, not wanting to intrude, when I heard, "Grasshopper?"

Slowly, I faced him. "Stinkbug?"

"What're you doing out here?" he asked, sticking his hands into his pockets.

"What're *you* doing out here?" I returned.

Light swayed under the walkway, ebbing, as I took a step closer to him. That's when I noticed tears glistening in his eyes, and my breath caught. "Are you okay?"

"Fine."

"Is your mama—"

"She's doing all right. She has to stay in the hospital, though, while they run a bunch of tests."

His voice held no hardness. No derision. Only exhaustion. I could only imagine the day he'd had.

I resisted the urge to give him a hug. "Is there anything I can do to help?"

"No. But thanks. I should get going. I need to collect Hambone and a few things for my mama."

I realized he must've come here on foot. Ernie's house wasn't too far away through the woods.

"You don't have to go just because I'm here. Stay. Especially if you're needing the clarity right now. I'll go."

He dragged a hand down his face and sighed, a deep, soul-weary sigh. When he looked at me, I saw a warmth in his eyes I'd never seen before. "I think I got what I needed. But if you're fixin' to leave, can I walk you back? I don't like the idea of leaving you out here alone."

I held his gaze for a long moment, suddenly questioning if the clarity he'd been seeking here tonight had to do with *me*. As I studied his face, and saw no trace of animosity, deep down I knew it to be true.

Because I fully understood what it must've taken for him to ask to walk me home, for him to even be worried for me, I didn't push back. Instead, I accepted the peace offering for what it was. "All right."

As we headed off into the night, toward the farmhouse, I noticed the starlings had gone quiet. I couldn't stop thinking about how I'd felt compelled to go to the field tonight. Of all nights. And couldn't help wondering if the starlings had played a role in our truce—and in Ty Underwood walking me home in the dark.

CHAPTER SIX

Addie

For as much as Aunt Bean loved baking, she despised cooking. She rarely made any meal that took longer than ten minutes. Her freezer was stocked with store-bought TV dinners. Her pantry was full of cereal and canned soups. It wasn't unheard of for her to eat microwave popcorn for supper.

Everyone knew this about her, too.

That was why most of her meals came from the kitchen of kindness. At least once a week a friend would inevitably drop off a casserole or covered dish, claiming they had extra and wanted to share.

I suspected there was a schedule floating around—a campaign most likely orchestrated by one of the Sugarbirds. Willa Jo, probably. She was a get-it-done kind of woman. Or perhaps Delilah. Small and fierce, she made things happen—sometimes by sheer will. Or even Pinky, who seemed flighty on the surface but often took care of details others overlooked.

All the women were at their best in an emergency—like what had happened with Ernie Underwood earlier this week.

"Ernie's due to be released from the hospital on Saturday,"

Aunt Bean said as she slathered a whole-wheat dinner roll with butter early Thursday evening.

Poor Ernie had lost her balance and fallen off a footstool, hitting her head on the edge of her kitchen countertop on the way down. What was thought to have been a simple head wound that would only require stitches had turned out to be a touch more serious. She had a small brain bleed. But Ernie was fortunate—no surgery had been needed as the doctors predicted the injury would eventually heal itself. However, to be on the safe side, they'd wanted her to remain at the hospital for a while.

"Is someone going to be staying with her when she gets home?" Tessa Jane asked, leaning forward over her bowl of beef stew, looking like she was ready to volunteer for the job if need be.

This morning Tessa Jane had unearthed a Crock-Pot from one of the kitchen cabinets and had made quick use of it. When I came in after working an afternoon shift in the barn kitchen, I'd been greeted by the delightful aroma of simmering stew, and it felt for a moment like I'd walked into the wrong house. I'd found Tessa Jane looking perfectly at home, sleeves pushed up to her elbows, as she kneaded dough on the marble-topped prep table. She'd whispered to me that the stew recipe had come from the American Heart Association's website—but hadn't mentioned that fact to Bean.

We'd been dancing around Bean's condition since we'd heard about it. And so had she. When I drove her to Montgomery on Tuesday for an echocardiogram, I'd had to stay in the waiting room during her appointment. Later, when I asked how it went, she'd said only, "Not too bad, punkin. We'll know more soon."

I had the feeling she knew more than she was letting on. That her condition was worse than she was telling us. It was a fine line to walk, suspecting but not knowing for certain.

Aunt Bean dunked the buttered roll into her bowl. "Ernie's

planning on staying with Ty for a spell, until she's steady on her feet."

Despite the fact that Bean hardly used her kitchen to cook, it was the heart of her big, rambling home, which had seen numerous renovations and additions through the years. Its style, much like her wardrobe, was a mix of old and new with plenty of color. Old white cast-iron farmhouse sink, wood floors, and shiplap walls. Newer sage-green cabinets, granite countertops, and stainless steel appliances. The windows were trimmed with white lace curtains. Various brass and cast-iron pans that had been passed down through the family hung from a pot rack above an antique blue prep table in the middle of the room. Colorful vintage Pyrex bowls sat on open wooden shelves. A large, rusty metal starling hung on the wall—it had been crafted by Granny Fullbright, my daddy and Bean's mother, a long time ago, when Granny had been in her teens.

The woodstove that divided the kitchen from the living room currently had a fire blazing within its box, warming the whole downstairs, chasing away the winter chill. Bean's two tabby cats, Miney and Moe, were stretched languidly on a cat bed set up in front of the stove, clearly loving the heat. As far as I'd seen today, they'd taken fairly well to having a dog in the house.

Of course, it helped that Hambone had practically been glued to Tessa Jane.

"So, Hammy will continue to stay with us?" Tessa Jane asked, her tone light and hopeful.

The dog sat like a perfect gentleman next to Tessa Jane's chair at the round table, watching her intently as she ate. Every once in a while, he'd whimper deep in his throat. A reminder, really, that he was being a good boy and would enjoy a piece of stew meat.

I pretended not to notice when Tessa Jane slipped him a bite.

If I hadn't seen it with my own eyes, I wouldn't have believed it. Once when we were younger and having a backyard tea party with Aunt Bean to celebrate her birthday—which was the only reason I'd agreed to it—Tessa Jane had made sure we packed cloth napkins, held her cup delicately, and when she stirred sugar into her tea, she took extra care to ensure that the spoon didn't clank against the porcelain.

"Granddaddy said stirring shouldn't make a sound," she'd said as she concentrated, her eyes full of bold blue determination.

Looking back now, I realized there had been a bit of fear in her eyes as well. Worry that the spoon would slip. That she'd make a mistake. I'd dismissed it then, because in those days when it came to Tessa Jane I'd dismissed everything, always hearing my own mama's voice in my head, telling me to pretend Tessa Jane didn't exist.

I shoved those painful thoughts aside and glanced at my sister.

Somehow she'd gone from mastering every etiquette rule known to mankind to feeding a dog under the table. She even let him lick her fingers. And I didn't know how she'd gotten from there to here. Because I didn't know my sister well at all.

"Yes, ma'am," Bean said to her. "Hope you don't mind none since you've been doing the lion's share of caring for him."

There was a twinkle in her eye as she said it, as if knowing perfectly well that Tessa Jane didn't mind at all.

Tessa Jane's smile lit her whole face. Lit the whole room, really. It was an angelic glow, one born from pure happiness, and I was glad to see it after noticing how her inner light had dimmed.

She said, "I love having him here, though I do feel for Ernie, having to miss out on his company. Once she's back, maybe we can take him over for a visit. Outside, of course."

Hambone whimpered again and Tessa Jane patted his head. He was here because he'd lost his fool head his first night at Ty's place, what with there being an opossum *inside* the house, never mind the kittens. He'd howled to wake the dead the whole night long. It had been Delilah who suggested *we* care for the dog, since he'd taken a liking to Tessa Jane. I thought that *liking* was putting it mildly.

I broke open a roll, which was somehow light and fluffy and surprisingly delicious for something deemed *healthy*. Then I reached for the butter, which *hadn't* been replaced with a heart-healthy plant-based substitute.

Around here, butter was sacred.

"I'm sure Ernie won't mind a little porch-sittin' at all," Bean said, "but I'll check with her in a few days."

Tessa Jane threw a glance toward the window. "I hope the weather doesn't delay her release."

Measurable snow, a couple of inches, remained stubbornly in the forecast. According to our favorite weatherman, it would fall in bursts, the bands spread out over several days, beginning late tonight. The worst of it was predicted to come down in a twenty-four-hour period starting Friday night.

The town was divided on how to feel about the storm, torn between those excited because snow was a joyful rarity and those worried about the havoc it might wreak. The South, as a whole, was unprepared for snow. Very few owned snow shovels. Or had rock salt on hand. Snow often strained power grids and snapped power lines, causing mass electrical outages. Here in Starlight, there were no salt trucks. No plows. No one knew how to drive in snow or on ice. The last time the town had a snowstorm, nearly ten years back, there had been innumerable fender benders. Cars had been abandoned on roadways for nearly a week.

All day, Aunt Bean been looking out the windows, her eyes full of anticipation, like a little kid searching the skies on Christmas Eve. She was firmly in the *excited* camp.

"Ty will move heaven and earth to get her home. That truck of his has four-wheel drive, so don't you go worrying none, peanut." Bean dragged her spoon around her bowl. "Any word from your granddaddy about canceling his party? I don't like thinking about his guests, especially you, out in a storm."

Winchester was throwing a big to-do tomorrow night. The Sugarbirds told me half the town was invited because rumors were swirling that he was planning on running for mayor. It was a bold, egotistical move. A power move, really, because he knew he could use fear to his favor. Thanks to Constance Jane and her numerous investments, he now owned half the town. People wanted to keep the peace with him, unable to afford rent hikes on their homes and businesses.

At the mention of the party, Tessa Jane went still as a statue. Stone had never looked so pretty. Her blond hair was down tonight, falling in waves over half her face. Emotion filled her blue eyes, making them seem bigger, brighter.

"No, ma'am," she said.

To be fair, a party that large would take months of planning, and Winchester couldn't have known about the storm system when he chose the date. Yet, not postponing now that he knew snow was blowing in was such a Winchester thing to do. One that showed how little he cared about others.

Bean said, "No doubt he's betting the storm peters out, but it's unwise of him to take the risk."

I sighed inwardly, noticing her reach for her watch to smooth its face with her thumb. The gesture told me exactly how worried she was. Rubbing her watch was a soothing technique to ward off her shadow, just like how I grabbed hold of my pendant when stressed. I wouldn't be the least bit surprised if Aunt Bean didn't sleep a wink tonight, since her shadow caused insomnia.

"Any word from Petal Pottinger about postponing her wedding?" Tessa Jane asked.

It was a good question. I thought it equally unwise to hold a wedding in bad weather.

Earlier, none of the Sugarbirds had wanted to talk about the wedding cake scheduled to be delivered on Saturday morning, as though in fear of jinxing the outcome.

"Last I heard," Bean said, reaching for another roll, "she

was considering moving the wedding and reception up a few hours. Late morning for the ceremony, early afternoon for the reception. But I haven't been notified of any official change."

Only in a small town where everyone knew everyone could such a feat occur. A few hours might make a big difference in terms of the weather. Or it could be pointless. Putting the wedding off a week—or maybe forever, since a Buckley was involved—would be a better choice, in my opinion. Not that I had a say-so.

I glanced outside. Floodlights illuminated a wide swath of the backyard. The doors to the shed, the ducks' makeshift home until their coop was built, were closed, keeping Lucy and Ethel warm and dry and safe from any bad weather. Temperatures had hovered just above freezing for most of the day, and the sky had been a solid sheet of gray. Right now it was hard to believe that once this storm system moved through there was sunshine and warmth in the forecast.

"The time change wouldn't make a lick of difference for us anyway," Aunt Bean said. "Willa Jo will still need to drop off Petal's cake at the Celestial Hotel first thing Saturday morning. But if the weather's terrible, I won't open the bakery. An extra day off would be right helpful since I'd like to sort through some closets and such to get an inventory together of what all I've stashed away over the years." Then she casually added, "For insurance purposes."

We both eyed her suspiciously.

I think we both realized she wanted to take inventory not for her insurance agent but for her lawyer. For her *will*. I felt queasy just thinking about it.

Before either of us could say anything, Hambone suddenly started baying. He scrambled to his feet and dashed to the front door. Not a second later, headlights beamed through the front windows.

"Are you expecting someone?" Tessa Jane asked loudly to be heard over the dog as she pushed back her chair. "Hambone, *quiet*."

Miraculously, he obeyed.

"Not me," Aunt Bean said.

I shook my head, praying it wasn't Sawyer and Luna at the door. I didn't know when she was due home from Mentone. And I wasn't at all sure what I was going to do when she returned and wanted to talk about Ree.

At the knock on the front door, Hambone started jumping and barking. Hissing, the cats darted under the couch. Aunt Bean laughed.

Tessa Jane peeked out the sidelight and I noticed her shoulders stiffen. She grabbed hold of Hambone's collar and pulled open the door. "Jenna! What a surprise. Come on in, out of the cold." She backed up a step.

"That's real nice of you," Jenna Elkins, Winchester's assistant, said, "but I need to be getting on home. Mr. Wingrove wanted me to drop this by on my way."

I could easily hear the apology in her voice as she handed over a large brown shopping bag.

Tessa Jane took the bag by its handles and Hambone immediately stuck his nose in it. "Are you sure you can't stay? We have supper on the table. We're happy to have you join us." She looked over at us. "Aren't we?"

The offer was pure politeness on Tessa Jane's part—part of *her* DNA as a southern woman.

"Sure are," Bean said.

I nodded. "There's plenty."

Jenna stuck her head in the door, gave us a tired smile as she patted Hambone's head, and said, "Thank you, it smells delicious, but I need to get on my way. I promised my mama I'd carry her over to Friddle's to load up on groceries before snowmageddon."

"Best you hurry then," Aunt Bean said. "I heard tell the shelves were clearing out fast. But let me know if they don't have what you need. Between here and the barn kitchen I've got plenty to spare."

"Thanks, Miss Verbena. I'll let Mama know. Y'all have

a good night." With one last pet of Hambone's head, Jenna turned and left.

Tessa Jane waited until the headlights were pointing down the driveway before she gave one final wave and closed the door. She let go of Hambone's collar, and he immediately trotted to the couch and stuck his nose under it.

"A gift?" Bean asked, nodding to the bag.

"I'm not sure. It's heavy, whatever it is." Tessa Jane walked over to us, put the bag down on her chair, reached inside, and pulled out a notecard. Her lips thinned as she read silently, then dropped it on the table.

The notecard was monogrammed with WHW at the top. Winchester Henderson Wingrove. His handwriting looked like scribble. Pure chicken scratch scrawl.

Once again, Tessa Jane reached into the bag. "Granddaddy wasn't sure I'd packed anything appropriate to wear to his party, so he took the liberty of sending over two dresses."

As if she couldn't buy something appropriate on her own. Tessa Jane had been raised on a strict diet of *appropriate*.

Aunt Bean lifted an eyebrow. "Well, wasn't that nice of him?"

Her syrupy tone made it clear the gesture was *not* nice. Not at all.

Tessa Jane pulled out a tissue-wrapped bundle and set it on the table, carefully separating the tape from the paper. With a flourish, she unfolded a red mini dress, a one-shoulder number that was covered in eye-catching sequins. She held it against her body as horror shined in her eyes. "He can't be serious."

She threw that dress over her shoulder and pulled out another bundle. In it was a floor-length emerald column dress made of velvet, complete with poofy sleeves, the cuffs of which were trimmed in black feathers.

"It has to weigh five, six pounds," Tessa Jane said, holding it against herself.

Hambone snarled.

"I *swannee*," Bean said. "It's feast or famine."

Both dresses had designer labels and undoubtedly had come

with high price tags. But neither looked like something Tessa Jane would choose. She'd always leaned toward light and floaty. Dreamy. These dresses were the complete opposite.

Bean reached for her glass of wine. "Which one are you leaning toward?"

Tessa Jane sighed as she carefully refolded the dresses and tucked them into the bag, which she then placed on the prep table behind her. "I suppose the green one, since I'd freeze to death in the red. But I don't particularly care for either." She wrinkled her nose. "Maybe I'll drive to Montgomery tomorrow afternoon to find something off the rack. Granddaddy won't be happy, but sometimes you have to draw a line."

"A deep line," I said.

Tessa Jane cracked a smile and tucked her side bangs behind her ear. "A whole chasm."

That smile. It made my chest ache and stirred hopes that we could piece together some sort of relationship.

For a couple of reasons, I didn't let many people into my protected, sheltered life. But the longer I stayed away from Starlight, from Bean, from the Sugarbirds, from Tessa Jane, the lonelier I'd become. A friend my own age would be nice. A real friend, not just the acquaintances I had in Birmingham, like Ellie at the coffee shop, or Dwayne the pizza delivery guy, my weekend hiking group, or Taj, the sound engineer at the studio where I recorded my lines for the animated series I worked on.

Someone . . . like my sister.

Maybe we could use this time here in Starlight to get to know each other. Really know each other—not only what Bean shared with us. Perhaps being here was the fresh start we both needed.

Bean said, "Why Montgomery? With the Valentine's Gala coming up soon, Gossamer's bound to have more dresses on hand than usual."

The dress shop here in town usually carried a varied selection, but between Thanksgiving and Valentine's Day, they catered more toward party dresses and formal gowns. The gala was a huge community affair, so the shop would likely be fully stocked.

"Perhaps so, but the department stores in Montgomery will have more off-the-rack options."

I wondered at the grim tone of my sister's voice until I remembered that last year Bean had told me Tessa Jane had bought the *perfect wedding dress* at Gossamer. No wonder she didn't want to shop there, what with all the memories it would dredge up.

Tessa Jane sat down, picked up a spoon, and dragged it through her stew. "With any luck, Granddaddy will cancel, and I'll be spared from going at all." Her hopefulness rang out like a fragile crystal bell.

Hambone whimpered and put a paw in her lap.

Tessa Jane picked a carrot out of the bowl with her fingers and fed it to him. As he gobbled it up, I glanced at Aunt Bean. She was looking at Tessa Jane with her eyebrows practically raised to her hairline. Tessa Jane's blatant disregard of her table manners hadn't gone unnoticed by Bean, either.

"You don't have to go. Stay home," I suggested, immediately postponing my plans to work on my new sound booth tomorrow night. "We can watch a movie."

Aunt Bean nodded eagerly. "Popcorn. Spiked hot chocolate. George Clooney. Snow falling. A more perfect night there could not be."

Tessa Jane wiped her hands on her napkin. "It's not as easy as that."

"Why?" I asked, truly curious. It was obvious by her body language that she was dreading the party. "You're allowed to say no."

She glanced at me. There was something in her eyes, a heartbreaking peek into the life she'd led, that suggested I might be wrong.

Fidgeting with uneasiness, I revised my question. "What would happen if you said no?"

"It doesn't matter. I need to be there." Pushing her bowl away, she added, "At least for a brief appearance. I certainly don't plan on staying long, so count me in for the movie, as long as you don't mind starting it a bit late."

"We don't mind at all, do we, Addie?" Bean asked.

I shook my head.

Hambone shuffled forward and put his head on Tessa Jane's lap. She gently tugged his long ears through her fingers. She was going to be heartbroken when it came time for him to go home to Ernie. It was clear she'd become as attached to the dog as he had to her.

"Girls, look!" Bean exclaimed. She tossed her napkin on the table and pointed toward the kitchen window.

Snow fell lazily. Gentle flurries of drifting flakes.

"Hurry now," Bean said. "We must try to catch a snowflake before the snow stops."

Bean thought all snow to be magical but held firm that the first snow of the season was especially so, believing that if you caught a flake on your fingertip, it foretold a winter of happiness.

She left her walking stick and coat behind as she hurried toward the back door and yanked it open. Hambone sailed past her into the fenced yard and started howling and jumping, his tongue lolling as he tried to catch falling flakes. Tessa Jane and I quickly followed.

"Isn't it glorious?" Bean said, clouds of steam puffing in the dark night. She stretched her hands out toward us.

I took one. Tessa Jane, the other.

Then I held out my other hand toward my sister.

Surprise flashed in her eyes as she set her hand in mine, completing the circle.

As one, we lifted our faces to the sky.

Snowflakes landed in our hair, melted on our faces.

We stood there like that for a good minute, caught up in the magic of the moment, before realizing that the flakes were slowing.

"Hurry now, girls!" Bean pulled her hands from ours. She held out her index finger, and laughter filled the air as she scurried about, trying to catch a snowflake.

It wasn't as easy as it looked.

Tessa Jane followed her lead, keeping her arm steady as she darted about. "I keep missing!"

"Me, too!" Bean said, jogging right left, then right.

I stood perfectly still with my arm outstretched, watching, waiting, and a large flake soon landed on my fingertip.

Aunt Bean saw it happen and rushed to my side. "Lucky girl! A winter of happiness for you."

I took a second to watch them, tears threatening, knowing my season of happiness had already begun.

Then the snowflake melted on my fingertip, disappearing as if it had never been there at all.

CHAPTER SEVEN

From the Kitchen of Verbena Fullbright
If the butter and sugar for your batter are looking a mite curdled after creaming them together, they just need more time, so keep on mixin'. Trusting the process and staying the course will almost always get you where you're wanting to go.

Tessa Jane

Crisp blades of grass crunched under my feet early the next morning as I stepped off the back patio. By the sound of their excited chatter, Lucy and Ethel likely knew I would be arriving soon with their breakfast. Inside the house, Hambone howled in dismay at being left behind, but it was best to feed the ducks without his eagerness to help them finish their food.

Shimmery frost clung to branches, fence posts, the garden bench. There had been bursts of snow flurries throughout the night, but they'd come and gone without leaving much behind. Still, the forecasters hadn't backed down on their prediction that the area would see a couple of inches of snow on the ground by Sunday.

A pail banged against my thigh as I bypassed the shed and made my way across the backyard. Steam rose from the small pond in opaque wisps, and the tall grasses that surrounded it stood frozen in time, frosted in place. Behind me, the starlings sat on the farmhouse's roofline watching me, their iridescence quivering like an admonition in the dim light.

But that might've just been my imagination.

I'd given up on guessing why they were staying so close lately. It could be any number of things, honestly. Starting with my lingering shadow and Aunt Bean's heart troubles, then moving on to Ernie's fall, and now my grandfather's party, where he would undoubtedly remind me that he expected me to relinquish the starlight field when the time came.

So he could buy it.

Feeling a stab of guilt, I offered a weak hello to the starlings and carried on my way.

As I had every morning since I arrived in Starlight, I walked over to the back fence. I tried not to think about the other night when Ty had walked me to this very spot, gave me a nod, then turned and headed for the woods.

Or how I'd watched him walk away, his shoulders hunched with the weight of his troubles, his memories.

The old me would've stopped him from leaving and tried yet again to start a friendship—because for once, he'd given the impression he might be willing.

The new me, however, hadn't wanted to be hurt again.

So I let him go.

I shook my head, clearing him out of my thoughts. My breath puffed out in small clouds as I set the pail down and pulled myself up onto the lower fence rail to get a better look at the starlight crater in the distance.

I shoved my cold hands into my coat pockets as I scanned left to right, over the field, the pastures, the woods, and along the curve of the crater. Everything I could see was my and Addie's land. Our inheritance. Five hundred acres—a tiny fraction of which held the star wound, which was only a hundred and fifty feet in diameter.

The starlings trilled behind me, and I had the uneasy feeling they knew why I was assessing the land. The crater, especially.

I was looking for something specific. Something Abner Wingrove had written about in a poem all those years ago. In his journal, it had come after mentions of returning to the crater in search of another glowing diamond only to be thwarted by the bird.

> *'tis a spark*
> *a twinkle*
> *at daybreak*
> *at first dark*
> *a wink*
> *a blink*
> *the stone in reach*
> *but for the screech*
> *of the silver bird*
> *'tis a spark*

I interpreted the poem to mean he'd seen glimpses of glowing stones at dawn and dusk. Granddaddy interpreted it as Abner having had too much to drink. He didn't believe in the legend at all, though he liked to pretend he did. Mostly to build the buzz for when he bought the land and partly to annoy Aunt Bean.

In fact, he'd made it clear that he didn't think highly of Abner, either, and often poked fun at me for being intrigued by the journal. For caring about a man I'd never met.

Granddaddy didn't seem to have an empathic, understanding bone in his body. Not that I'd ever seen anyway. And I'd looked.

As I stood on the fence railing, the cool wind whipping my hair across my face, I tried to imagine the aftermath of the star falling. The chaos. The heartache of losing Clara. The wonder of the light. Charity's strength to carry on running the farm and to take care of her younger brother.

When my granddaddy spoke about reclaiming the land for the Wingrove family, he'd often rage about the Fullbrights, calling them brainless for not taking financial advantage of the starlight. I'd known, even from a young age, that the anger came from the fact that the Fullbrights hadn't *needed* to monetize the field to make ends meet. That they hadn't known poverty, like his daddy and most of the Wingroves before him. Like he had. Before Gigi.

I knew he believed that if Abner had kept the farmland in the first place, his own life wouldn't have known a moment's turmoil.

Which just showed how narrow-minded he could be.

As I hopped down from the fence, retrieved the pail, and made my way to the ducks, my thoughts turned to Granddaddy's party and how he was likely going to bring up his plans and what he expected of me.

It seemed like every time he talked about his ideas for the land surrounding the field, his plans expanded. It had started simply with entrance and parking fees. Then a lodge. Then a hotel. A resort. A waterpark.

It was impossible to ignore that all he saw when he looked at the starlight aurora were dollar signs. He cared little about the light and its clarity. Or that the Fullbrights felt like they were the guardians of something magical—something *everyone* should be able to experience for free.

Given Granddaddy's background he should appreciate that more than anyone, but he was too focused on what he coveted to be able to see the bigger picture.

Suddenly, Addie's voice echoed in my thoughts, telling me I could say no. She'd meant in reference to attending Granddaddy's party. But right now, I thought about *all* the times in my life I'd wanted to say no to him. But like I'd told her, it wasn't that easy. My grandfather was a steamroller of a man, always planning, always scheming.

According to my mama, my first words had been "Yes, sir," to him.

It was telling. I'd grown up thinking I'd never had a say-so. Not really. Honestly, I still felt that way most of the time. Mostly because voicing what *I* wanted, choosing what *I* wanted, remained out of my control.

Because of the Starling Society.

It was the secret network founded by my mama to protect victims of domestic violence.

Unknowingly, my grandmother had funded the society with her allowances to Mama and me, and if we wanted that money to keep rolling in by way of checks from my grandfather, I needed to toe the line when it came to appeasing him.

It was something I'd been doing ever since I was old enough to understand what was at stake. In my head, I could hear my mama saying, "Smile, Tessa Jane, and just do as you're told. Think of all the people who need our help."

So I pretended all was okay. That I didn't mind my life being mapped out for me, my career path chosen. That I didn't have an opinion. That I didn't mind giving up the starlight field when I turned twenty-five.

But now, in my current frame of mind, I couldn't help thinking about the person I'd been hurting by doing all that pretending: me.

Feeling all kinds of selfish, I sighed and pulled open the shed doors and Lucy and Ethel greeted me with loud quacks and excited flaps of their wings. They ran circles around me before darting into the yard, heading for the pond. I quickly filled their dishes, swept up, and replenished their straw. Aunt Bean had set up a portable heater in the shed that hung from the ceiling, but I was still chilled as I finished the chores, my grandfather's icy stare looming large in my mind. As I headed to the house, I kept my gaze down, away from the watchful eyes of the starlings.

When I reached the patio, I looked up and saw Addie's face framed in the glass of the back door. For the first time, I saw a light in my sister that I'd never seen before.

A welcoming light.

I wasn't at all sure what to make of the change in her. Or how to feel. The old me would've been jumping for joy at a truce, even an uneasy one, but right now I was more than a little apprehensive.

She opened the door before I reached it, and Hambone raced out and galloped toward the ducks.

"I have an idea," Addie said.

The kitchen smelled of coffee and wood smoke and the egg and hash brown casserole I'd made us for breakfast. I kicked my boots off by the door after I stepped inside, then hung my coat on a peg. It was quiet. Only us and the snoozing cats. Aunt Bean was already working, but our shift in the big red barn didn't start until nine thirty. Today Addie and I would be the faces of the Starling Cake Company, working directly with our customers, taking orders and payments through the barn's take-out window.

"An idea for Aunt Bean?" I asked.

"No, for you."

The sleeves of her sweatshirt were pushed to her elbows and her fingertips were water-wrinkled. Clean dishes drip-dried in the strainer next to the sink.

"About what?"

"About your grandfather's party. You need a fancy dress, right?"

I wasn't sure what I'd been expecting to hear but it wasn't that. I headed to the coffee pot, my emotions warring between wanting to let her into my life and wanting to keep her out. "Right."

"Well, I have a dress," she said. "You're welcome to borrow it if you like it."

Surprised, I nearly spilled coffee as I poured it into a mug. She was offering me something of hers? What was the catch? There had to be one.

Didn't there?

"It's fancy but not too fancy. It's old, but a classic design. It was bought during my Audrey Hepburn phase. It's been hanging in my closet here forever."

I got lost in the melodious sound of her voice for a moment, my heart calming, my body relaxing, as I added cream to the coffee and stirred. I hadn't seen much of my sister during her Audrey phase—which occurred during her senior year of high school—but remembered thinking her pixie haircut had beautifully suited the angles of her face.

Addie tugged down one sleeve, then the other. "I never wore it—so no one will know where you got it."

No one, meaning my grandfather. Obviously, she knew he'd probably keel over if he learned I was wearing a hand-me-down. "Why didn't you ever wear it?"

"It was for the senior homecoming dance, but I had a headache that day and had to skip."

There was pain in her voice. A story untold. For some reason I suspected it had nothing to do with a headache and everything to do with Sawyer and Ree.

Addie narrowed her gaze at my waist. "We might have to take it in a bit. Easy enough."

The darkness that loomed over me forced me to ask suspiciously, "Why?"

She seemed to immediately know what I meant. "Montgomery is nearly an hour away. The weather . . ."

Why did she suddenly *care*?

What had caused this shift? Did she really think we could go from virtual strangers to sisters in a blink of an eye?

At the thought, I felt a tug deep down. A tug of *longing*. What she was offering me now was something I'd always wanted.

"It's midnight blue with a lace bodice. Three-quarter sleeves. Tea length. Do you want to see it?" she asked, folding her arms across her chest, as if bracing herself for rejection.

Seeing her start to close up again so soon after she'd begun to open up pulled at my heartstrings. For whatever reason, she was giving me a piece of herself. Could it really hurt to give a little in return?

With an inward sigh, I nodded.

The wooden stairs, dark with age, creaked as we climbed. At the top of the steps stretched a long hallway lined with a floral runner. Bean's and my bedrooms were on the right.

The hall bath, Addie's bedroom—which looked the same as it had when she lived here—and the guest room were on the left. Family photos lined both sides of the hall. Smiling faces, all watching me much like the starlings had from the rooftop.

I glanced over all the photos, smiling at the image of me in a bassinet at the hospital not long after I was born. Then my gaze landed on one picture in particular and stayed there. It was a photo of my father, me, and Addie that had been taken by the local newspaper photographer at a school carnival when I had been in kindergarten and Addie in the fifth grade. After seeing the black-and-white picture in the paper, Bean had sweet-talked the photographer into giving her a full-color print.

In the photo, Addie and I flanked our father as he stood tall, with one hand resting on my shoulder, the other on Addie's shoulder. She leaned comfortably into him, her head pressed against his side. I stood awkwardly on my tiptoes as if trying to appear taller and my closed-lipped smile was slightly lopsided as I peered up at him instead of looking at the camera.

Daddy had been smiling with pride, the ever-present sparkle in his green eyes glittering. A knot formed in my throat—grief popping up, unwelcome yet familiar. I'd barely had a chance to get to know him. He'd died a few months after this picture was taken.

I studied myself in the photo, the sweet innocent girl who didn't understand the complexities of extramarital affairs and illegitimate children. The little girl who'd only wanted a big, loving, accepting family. Suddenly I wanted to cry, because nothing had changed.

I was still that girl.

"Feels like forever ago, doesn't it?" Addie had doubled back and now stood at my side.

"Yes," I said, my voice catching on all my emotions.

I heard her swallow. "Look how cute you were. I look like I had been rolling around in mud at recess." She leaned in a bit closer to the photo. "And this was taken only a week or two after I cut my own bangs right before one of my mama's rare visits. When she saw what I'd done, she pitched a hissy fit that I can still hear ringing in my ears if I listen hard enough."

Addie didn't usually say so much, so it was obvious she was trying hard to be nice. To be open. To be sisterly.

I still didn't understand why, but as I looked at the girl in the picture, I decided to stop questioning and just accept it for as long as it lasted.

"Your bangs are sweet." I let out a hollow laugh. "After this picture was published in the paper, and my grandfather saw it, Miss Pomona—the prominent pageant coach?—showed up at my house every weekday for four weeks. She schooled me on posture and posing and everything in between, including different ways to smile."

Addie's eyes widened and she gave a small shake of her head. "You were only *five*."

"Never too young to learn," I said, mimicking my grandfather.

Sympathy floated in her eyes. "You lived in a whole other world at that house, didn't you?"

"It definitely feels that way sometimes." All of the time, actually.

She took a deep breath and shook her head. "I had no idea."

My shoulders stiffened, my jaw tightened. Of course she had no idea. She'd done her level best to ignore me for most of her life. And even though I knew why—because of her mama—it still hurt.

"I'm so sorry," she said, her eyes watery.

The apology caught me off guard and for some reason made me want to give *her* a hug. Instead, I wrapped my arms around myself, gave her a nod, and went back to looking at the photos.

We stood so close that our arms were touching yet neither of us stepped away. It felt a bit surreal, if I was being honest, because I could count on one hand how many times we'd actually touched in our lives, this moment included.

After a second of looking at the pictures, she said, "I'm so curious, I have to ask. How, exactly, is smiling taught?"

"Hours in front of a mirror to master a dozen different smiles."

"*No.*"

I nodded, then took a step back and flashed her six of them. Bright, affectionate, charming, mischievous, embarrassed, compassionate. I paused in between each one for dramatic effect.

Addie watched me closely, her sage-green eyes growing wide. "I don't know if I'm impressed or horrified. I'm leaning toward impressed."

She tried to copy the faces I'd made, which made me smile—a real smile. "I had a refresher course with Miss Pomona every spring right up until I moved away, and I have to admit the lessons have come in handy a time or two."

And Miss Pomona had been wonderful—loud and encouraging and colorful—but young children should be full of natural smiles, not practiced ones.

I turned back to the school carnival photo, this time my gaze focused on Addie. She really did look like she'd played in the mud that afternoon. She was absolutely filthy, her hair was a rat's nest, and her bangs *were* too short—though still adorable.

I noticed now, for the first time, that our eyes were the same. Not the appearance, of course, with her shape and color favoring our father, but the sadness in them.

We definitely came from different worlds, but both those worlds had been far from perfect.

"I wish I'd had more time with him," I said, not having to specify who I meant.

"Me, too."

We'd both lost so much when he died.

"Come and see the dress," Addie finally said on a sigh, breaking the thick silence. She faced me, smiled. "I think it'll be perfect for you."

There was something about her smile, about the gentle tone of her voice, that healed a tiny part of my broken heart. I swallowed over that lump in my throat. "Lead the way."

Outside, Hambone bayed. The ducks quacked. The starlings chattered.

And inside, as I followed Addie toward her bedroom, I swore I saw a flicker of light in my darkness.

CHAPTER EIGHT

Tessa Jane

Lifting my wrap against the wind later that night, I stood on the front porch of my grandparents' house, what many around here called the mansion on the hill. It had been in Gigi's family for nearly a century.

Over the past year, Granddaddy had commissioned a complete renovation, and it broke my heart thinking about all the little pieces of Gigi that were now gone. Like her embroidered throw pillows, the oil paintings of her beloved horses, and even the china that had belonged to *her* grandmother. He hadn't even asked Mama or me if we'd wanted anything before turning her possessions over to a Birmingham auction house. Everything had been sold before we even knew it had been removed.

It seemed to me that Granddaddy was trying his hardest to erase Gigi from his life. And from ours, too.

"Tessa Jane, I have a question for you," Gigi had said to me only a few years ago, when I'd visited for her birthday. "Please know you don't have to answer if you don't want to."

We'd been in her suite of rooms on the second floor of the west wing of the house, the patio doors open. She had the perfect view of the starlight crater from her living area, and when I was little and still lived here, we'd often curl up on her couch and watch the light shimmer in the distance. It had been one of our favorite things to do together.

"What's the question?" I'd asked, suddenly worried about her tone of voice.

She'd held my hand tightly, her skin thin and feathery soft, her gentle blue eyes troubled. "Your granddaddy. Do you see any good in him, sweetheart?"

She was one of the few who knew about the Fullbright ability to see the inner light, the goodness, in people. But it was the first time she'd ever asked me about my assessment of a specific person.

As I stood here on the porch, my throat ached with emotion. What I would do to have her back, to hold her hand, to watch the starlight with her once again.

I leaned against one of the columns and looked upward. Tonight, the stars were hidden behind low, thick clouds. A quarter inch of snow had fallen during the afternoon but melted as soon as it had hit the ground. Temperatures were predicted to dip below freezing over the next few hours, which would ice the roads, making travel treacherous. I planned to be back at Bean's long before then, tucked onto the couch with her and Addie and Hambone. I was already dreaming of the sundae I planned to eat, made of smashed Grasshopper cookies, chocolate ice cream, and fudge sauce. Lots of fudge sauce.

Unbidden, a memory of Ty drifted into my head. It was when he'd spotted Miss Ernie on her kitchen floor and I'd been able to see how good a man he was.

It was the first inner light I'd seen in almost a year.

Snowflakes blew about, few and far between. I tried to catch one on my fingertip, but kept missing. Since it wasn't technically the first snow, snagging one wouldn't guarantee happiness, but I didn't think it could hurt to try.

Happiness, like fun, had been sparse lately.

Bundled up against the cold, the parking valet watched me from his post near the porte cochere. He'd assisted me out of my car five minutes ago and was probably wondering why I hadn't yet gone inside.

Or maybe since he worked for my grandfather he understood perfectly.

I would tip him well on my way out—because I knew he wasn't getting paid near enough. Granddaddy was a scrooge. Once when I was younger, I asked my mama about it, questioning why someone with so much could be so stingy to those with so little. She told me she believed it was because when he was a boy he had nothing, so now he wanted to hold on to everything, afraid to lose it all again.

My heart always broke when I thought of my granddaddy as a young boy. His mama had died when he was a toddler, and his daddy had never been around, often floating in and out of jail for one scheme or another. He'd been raised by a cousin, who wasn't really interested in having another mouth to feed but felt duty-bound to care for her kin. It wasn't long before Granddaddy started following his father's footsteps, landing in the county jail several times and gaining a reputation for being trouble.

Finding Abner's journal had given him the purpose he'd been lacking in life. He knew he had to clean up his act, at least outwardly, if he wanted to accomplish his goal of owning the starlight crater one day. He had to be taken seriously. He needed to be rich. Powerful. Because he knew the Fullbrights weren't going to let go of that land willingly.

And he knew exactly how he, with hardly any schooling and a rap sheet, would make that happen.

At twenty-three, he found a job at a local dairy as a farm-hand and started working his way up. By twenty-six, he was delivering milk to customers around town.

It was a job that allowed him direct contact with Gigi, a known recluse. And who, at thirty-eight years old, was the wealthiest person in the county.

After a year of small talk every time he made a delivery, he made her an offer she probably should've refused.

But then again, if she'd refused, I wouldn't be here, standing on this porch delaying the inevitable.

At the end of the long driveway, headlights appeared, glowing bright in the darkness. Another guest arriving. I turned back toward the massive front doors and told myself to ring the bell. Get it over with.

But as I reached for the buzzer, the door swung open. "I didn't think you were ever going to come inside."

"Mama!" I rushed forward, and threw my arms around her. "What are you doing here?"

She despised coming home since Gigi had passed. My grandmother had often been the buffer between Mama and Granddaddy. The soft middle between two hard heads.

"Reinforcement for you, of course." She put her arm around me and ushered me into the house. "You shouldn't have to deal with him alone."

It was impossible not to notice the changes in the entryway from the last time I'd been here. The oak floors were gone, replaced with slate. All the trim was painted black, and the walls were now a deep green. Modern art pieces were scattered about. Large abstract paintings practically covered the wall where family portraits used to hang.

After taking my wrap from my shoulders she handed it to one of the uniformed staff passing by. She lifted an eyebrow as she eyed my dress. "Vintage?"

She wore an exquisite black sheath dress with a sequined bodice. Her blond hair was pulled back in a sleek twist and diamonds hung from her ears. Circling her left wrist was a thin gold bangle she rarely removed. A casual observer might think the band was engraved with a chevron pattern. But if one looked closely, they'd see there were actually eighteen starlings circling the gold bracelet.

"Yes," I lied to save myself from explaining.

She gave a half smile. "It's sweet."

I knew by her reaction she wished I'd chosen something different—something my granddaddy couldn't nitpick—but I couldn't recall the last time I'd felt this comfortable in a dress. I swished the full blue skirt. "I love it."

"Remember that when your grandfather sees it. He's trying to hide a bad mood behind a thin smile and a whiskey neat."

It was rare day when he *wasn't* in a bad mood. Sulky and thunderous were his natural states. He was only charming when he wanted something. Which was why he almost never raised his voice to me. I had something he wanted badly.

"Half the guests have canceled due to the weather," Mama said. "Brave souls. He's probably plotting a way to have their electricity cut."

A jazz trio was set up in the parlor and people milled around. We stood out of the way, not yet ready to join the fray.

She said, "How's your week been? How's Verbena?"

My mama had always had a fondness for Aunt Bean— they'd become close after I was born.

"She's tired—moving a lot more slowly than her usual full steam ahead. Her echocardiogram results haven't come in yet. Or if they have, she hasn't shared them. She's been putting on a brave, happy face around Addie and me."

"And Addie?" My mama lifted an eyebrow. "How is she?"

"Being surprisingly nice."

"Really?"

I heard the tone of distrust in her voice. "I don't know what to make of it either. But it feels . . . genuine."

"Have you considered it's an act to protect the starlight? She has to have considered what's likely to occur on your birthday."

I dug my nails into my palms and felt a splotch of heat on my neck.

Mama noticed the hive immediately and her gaze narrowed. "You will be letting the field go, correct? This was decided a long time ago, Tessa Jane."

I lifted my chin. "*I* never decided anything."

Mama glanced around nervously. "Lower your voice before he hears you talking like that. Have you forgotten what's at stake? This is no time to change your mind."

Both Granddaddy and my mama expected me to let the land go. Granddaddy wanted it for himself. Mama wanted the cash from the sale—which she knew I'd share.

The old me had simply nodded along to their plans, trying to keep the peace, trying to keep everyone happy.

But the new me was sick of people trying to twist my arm.

"Tessa Jane." Her tone made it clear I was displeasing her.

I absently scratched a hive as my temper flared. "Please don't."

I was supremely proud of myself for saying please.

"We've talked about this," Mama argued.

"*You've* talked."

"Think of all the peop—"

"No!" I snapped.

Heads turned our way, and my cheeks burned. More hives formed.

Mama pasted on a fake smile as an old neighbor approached, striking up a conversation about the snow. I checked the time, wondering if it was too soon to leave. I'd been inside less than ten minutes.

After the neighbor moved off to chat up someone else, Mama said, "How about a drink?"

As if we hadn't been arguing a moment ago.

I knew this tactic. Diversion. But I could really use a drink, so I nodded.

We moved as one through the crowd toward the bar set up in the dining room, and I kept a reassuring smile on my face, pretending all was well. Miss Pomona would be proud.

When Mama tipped her head in close to mine, I braced myself for a quiet lecture on helping others, but instead she whispered, "Is your bank deposit late this month?"

It took me a moment to switch my train of thought. Usually, our stipends from Granddaddy were deposited the fifteenth of the month—a week and a half ago. "I haven't seen one, but I also haven't been checking every day." I'd been busy with Aunt Bean. With baking. With the ducks and Hambone. Oh, how I wished Hambone was here with me, zooming through this crowd, poking his nose into everyone's business. "Do you think there was a mix-up because of the New Year?"

She flashed a smile to a passerby, then said, "It's possible." She didn't sound convinced.

"Are you going to ask Granddaddy about it?"

"I'd rather chew broken glass. I'll call our lawyer first thing Monday morning to see if he can find out what's going on. This is a complication I don't need. That money was already earmarked. A roof repair in Charleston. A new air conditioning unit New Orleans. Urgent foundation issues at the newest roost in Biloxi. I'll have to pull from the contingency fund."

A roost, in Mama's vocabulary, was a safe house. There were nearly a dozen roosts all over the South owned by the Starling Society. All were located in bigger cities, where it was easier to hide.

"There's my girl!" Granddaddy suddenly bellowed. The crowd parted as he strode toward me. "A little late, aren't you, Tessa Jane?"

Steeling myself, I said, "Hi, Granddaddy!"

I didn't bother explaining why I was late, like the old me would have.

With a start I realized I was beginning to *like* the new me. That wouldn't do. At all.

Granddaddy gave me a kiss on my cheek and a once-over.

I took a moment to study him as well. He was a stocky man, not particularly tall but strong, even in his midseventies. His expensive suit was cut and pressed to perfection. Wrinkles creased his forehead, his bald head shone, his blue eyes were alert, and his white mustache was perfectly trimmed, curling upward at its ends. When I was younger he'd reminded me of the Monopoly man. As I grew older, I wondered if he'd purposely copied the style. It radiated wealth.

Outwardly, he seemed in fairly good health except for the

purplish hue around a bulbous nose that suggested he drank too much. Which he did. Always had.

A scowl formed as he took in my outfit. "What happened to the dresses I sent over?"

"Too small," I lied.

His thick eyebrows furrowed. "You are lookin' a bit *healthy.* I suppose that's what happens when you sit around and eat cake all day."

I clenched my teeth so hard I about broke a molar.

"*Hmm,*" Mama said loudly, an eyebrow lifted as she pointedly stared at his rounded stomach.

It wasn't like Mama to outright pick a fight, which showed that she was a woman on edge this evening. Money worries, no doubt.

Granddaddy's cheeks bloomed a deep red, and he puffed up like a turkey about to attack.

"Mr. Wingrove? Sir?" someone interrupted from behind him. "Is now a good time?"

Granddaddy schooled his countenance into a semblance of civility, then turned around. As he did, I noticed he had on one black shoe, one blue, both the same style. He was color blind and often had others double-check his outfits to make sure he wasn't making a fashion gaffe. He must've forgotten tonight.

I glanced around for Jenna, his assistant, who was probably the one most often consulted. I found her in a corner looking like she'd rather be anywhere else. Not that I could blame her. I didn't want to be here, either.

Granddaddy threw one arm around my shoulders and the other around Mama's. "It's a grand time, Graham!"

The man who'd interrupted raised a camera and snapped a picture, then another.

Granddaddy said to Mama and me, "Y'all remember Graham Doby? From the newspaper?"

"Of course," Mama said, full of natural charm. "Lovely to see you again."

"Hello," I said, not remembering him at all. And I hoped that in the photos, I would look less deer in headlights than I felt. I wasn't used to this house being filled with people, and I found I didn't like it. Gigi would've hated this party.

For most of her life, she'd battled a panic disorder that prevented her from leaving the house or the grounds. And she let only a few people in.

I once dared to ask my mama why Gigi had said yes to my grandfather's offer of marriage and she told me, "She said yes because she wanted to have a baby, and being in her late thirties, she was running out of time. Your grandfather's proposal made it clear their marriage was a business transaction, but I've always wondered if she hoped there would be more between them. Because with her money, she had other options. For a price, I'm sure a fertility clinic would have paid a visit here."

Granddaddy said, "Graham is writing up a piece about my mayoral run. Ain't that right, son? A win for Winchester. Hoorah!" He laughed, too loudly.

I wondered why now. Why hadn't he run for mayor in his forties, fifties? Had Gigi held him back? Or was this just a recent idea that popped into his head on whim and he was running with it?

Poor Graham gave a closed-lip smile and threw a look of longing at the bar. "That's right, sir."

Mama said, as gracious as always, "Graham, please let me know if I can contribute in any way, but for now, may I get you a cocktail?"

Graham visibly relaxed. "Much appreciated."

I wasn't sure if he was appreciative of Mama's offer of help or for the drink. I suspected the latter.

Granddaddy said, "I could use another drink myself."

It took effort not to roll my eyes. By the scent of him, he'd already had several.

"Tessa Jane?" Mama asked.

Granddaddy's unruly eyebrows furrowed again. He didn't

CERTAIN KIND OF STARLIGHT

like me drinking. Thought it was unbecoming of a young lady. I lifted my chin. "Wine would be lovely."

As I waited for the bartender to pour my glass, in my head, I heard Gigi say yet again, "Your granddaddy. Do you see any good in him, sweetheart?"

I'd stared into her blue eyes, my heart hurting because I didn't want to lie. So I hedged instead. "He's hard to read because his personality obscures the light."

Looking off in the distance, she nodded. "There's a poison deep within him, eating him from the inside out. It feeds off his innate feelings of inferiority and his fear of being poor again." She faced me. "If he could only get rid of that poison, I bet you'd see his light, clear as day. I know it's in there." Then she quietly added, "I *hope* it's in there."

I startled at a hand on my arm. "Tessa Jane?"

I snapped to, focused on my mama. "Yes?"

She whispered, "Are those tears in your eyes?"

I thumbed the moisture away. "Just dust."

Her gaze narrowed with worry.

Graham, I noticed, had slipped away. Lucky guy.

As I picked up the glass the bartender slid over and thanked him, Granddaddy said to Mama and me, "I want to show you something in my library. I think you'll be quite pleased. Come along."

Even though he had calmed, his anger alleviated by the reporter's attention, I had the uneasy feeling I wasn't going to be pleased at all by what he planned to show us.

We followed him past waitstaff carrying trays from the kitchen. At the end of a long hallway, he opened the library's door.

He cut on a light as we went inside. The scent of tobacco and leather filled the massive room that was lined with bookcases and tall windows. One of the leather sofas had been pushed aside, and in its place now stood a square table. On that table sat an architectural model of what looked like a small town.

He gestured toward the three-dimensional piece. "I took the liberty of having my vision for the land surrounding the starlight brought to life. Isn't it magnificent?"

I took a sip of wine, noticed my hand shaking, and set the glass on a side table.

Mama said, "Are those *row houses*?"

"It's an upscale planned community called The Wingrove," he said, his words very slightly slurred. "*Where stars gather.*"

I could barely breathe. Anger crackled in my chest, sharp and painful.

He pointed toward the model. "There will be shops, dining, housing, office space. A theater. A boutique hotel. A waterpark."

I touched the edge of the model, my voice a rasp as I said, "What happened to the woods?"

The woods where the starlings spent most of their time.

Amber liquid sloshed in his cup. "Razed to make way for the golf course. This design utilizes every inch of those five hundred acres."

My stomach rolled, and I pushed a hand against it to quell the nausea.

"And this?" Mama asked, pointing to a building practically built atop the star crater.

"It's the visitor center," he said, "where guests will have a choice of diamond adventure packages and pick up the equipment they'll need for mining."

My head snapped up.

He took a pull from his whiskey glass, then pursed his lips. "Now, Tessa Jane, don't go getting riled up."

Fury flooded my veins, and my hands curled into fists that I hid in the tulle skirt.

Mama lifted her chin, her gaze challenging. "And what happens when there aren't any found? Because we all know stars aren't made of diamonds."

He grinned. "There *will* be diamonds found. I'll make sure of it."

His intention was clear. He was going to plant gemstones for people to find.

I wanted to remind him that digging up the starlight field would make the light disappear, but I knew he didn't care.

There was disgust in my mama's voice as she said, "Mother would be appalled that you're using her money to trick people. Have you no shame?"

Gigi had been as enamored with the field as he was, but for different reasons. She adored the legend behind it, the clarity found in the light, and its sheer beauty. She'd encouraged Granddaddy's plans to bring more attention to the field—but only in a way that wouldn't disturb its magic.

When I was little, she'd whisper, almost reverently, about how lovely it would be if there was a café overlooking the aurora, where people could sit and sip and enjoy and bask in the peace of the starlight. And a gift shop, too, because she'd always had a fondness for the trinkets her parents would bring back to her after they went on vacation.

As she spoke, I'd envisioned those enchanting shops, and began wishing they were real.

It was one of the reasons I'd never shut down my granddaddy's talk about buying the land. Part of me wanted to make Gigi's vision come true.

But what he had planned now . . . She would be horrified.

His face flushed. His chest puffed out. "I'll remind you it's *my* money now, to do with as I see fit."

Gigi's voice suddenly drifted into my thoughts. *If he could only get rid of that poison, I bet you'd see his light, clear as day.*

Suddenly I knew why Gigi had willed all her money to Granddaddy. To rid him of his fears about being poor, to rid him of the poison eating him up. Only, it hadn't worked. Probably because money wasn't the fix.

Granddaddy jabbed a finger in Mama's direction. "And if you want to ever see a cent of that money again you'll keep your mouth shut where your mother is concerned. I'm sure you're already feeling a financial pinch this month. Get used to it. You'll be feeling it again next month, too."

Outrage lit Mama's blue eyes, making them spark. "You're withholding the checks on purpose?"

The darkness that had been surrounding me for so long now swirled like a dust devil, practically lifting me off my feet. "Why would you do that?"

"Consider it an insurance policy in case you go getting second thoughts now that Verbena's playing the sick card. *Bless her enlarged heart*," he said bitterly.

"You can't do that." Panic was written across Mama's face. She needed that money.

He finished off his drink. "I can. I have."

"But, Gigi wanted you to continue—" I started.

"I think I made myself clear, Tessa Jane," he suddenly roared. Then he quieted to a deadly whisper as he leaned in close to me, his sweet whiskey breath whistling between thin lips. "But in case I didn't, I'll lay it out plain as day for you. If you don't decline ownership of that land on your birthday, you and your mama will both get cut off *completely*. You'll never see another damn dime. Not *ever*. Now, if you'll excuse me, I need to be getting back to my guests."

CHAPTER NINE

Addie

"Can you *please* slow down?" I pleaded as the back end of Tessa Jane's car fishtailed when it hit a patch of black ice when we rounded a corner.

A warning beeped from the dashboard, then silenced when the wheels found traction again. The triangular hazards signal glowed as we drove in the dead-center of the road late Saturday morning, hogging both lanes because there wasn't another car in sight and the edges of the roadway were obscured by snow.

Tessa Jane gripped the steering wheel like she was hanging on for dear life. She flashed me an annoyed glance. "I'm only going ten miles per hour."

It was the wintry weather that was keeping people off the roads—and had put us on it. Willa Jo had called this morning to tell Bean that the balding tires on her van were no match for her slick driveway. Which meant someone else had to deliver Petal Pottinger's wedding cake to the hotel ballroom.

That *someone* turned out to be Tessa Jane and me.

"Maybe try eight? Or five?" I suggested. "Just *slower*."

A bundle of anxiety, I sat in the passenger seat, my finger-tips practically indenting the large cardboard box I held on my lap. In the box was Petal's beautiful three-tier wedding cake. Delivering cakes was always nerve-racking business. Deliver-ing cakes on icy roads in a snowstorm? Terrifying. Absolutely, unequivocally petrifying.

In my head, I was cussing up my own kind of storm while trying not to have a panic attack. I took even breaths, searching for something to focus on other than the buzz of my nerves. I started counting the snowflakes that landed on the windshield, adding them up before they melted or were swiped away by the wipers.

"If I go any slower," Tessa Jane said, her words short, stiff, *re-strained*, "we're not going to get there in time for the wedding."

Because of her tone, I didn't point out that I could probably walk to the hotel and still make it on time. The wedding was at eleven. It was currently nine thirty. And the hotel was only three more miles away.

This was a foreign creature, this irritated Tessa Jane. She'd been on edge since returning from her grandfather's party last night and driving in this weather hadn't helped her bad mood any.

The car rolled over a bump, and I clenched my teeth as I tried to absorb the motion and keep the box still. A perfect cake had gone into that box, and I aimed to have a perfect cake come out.

Other than this delivery, the bakery was closed for the day on account of the weather, and I couldn't wait to be done with this errand and get back to the farmhouse. Where it was warm and safe and dry.

Snow fell steadily. I could only see ten to fifteen feet in front of the car and couldn't see the fields that lined the side of the road at all.

I searched for any bright sides to this situation and surpris-ingly found a few.

One, quality time spent with Tessa Jane, even if we both woke up on the cranky side of bed.

Two, at least the wedding party was staying the weekend at the hotel, so there *would* be a ceremony taking place today. No chance of a last-minute cancelation. Well, if the pastor managed to make it there.

Three, the snow was beautiful, in an eerie kind of way.

I took a breath, and felt a twinge of pity for Dare, of all people. The pastor marrying him should've been Pastor Fife, the elderly man who'd taken him in as a teenager. But he and his wife had been gone a few years now. They'd been a lovely couple, and I could only imagine how happy they'd be for Dare today.

A sight happier than me, that was for sure. But only because I worried for Petal's well-being, in light of the Buckleys' violent history. Something I knew about all too well.

Tessa Jane let out a humorless laugh as the wipers whisked rapidly. "If rain on your wedding day is good luck, what's snow mean?"

"I'm not sure."

She pushed a button on her steering wheel and when a tone sounded, she said loudly, clearly, "What does it mean if it snows on your wedding day?"

A computerized voice, connected through the Bluetooth system in her car, answered, "Snow on a wedding day is a sign of fertility and prosperity."

The thought of there being more Buckleys filled me with a sense of dread. Then I felt a stab of guilt, of remorse, of *shame*, and quickly revised my thinking to *male* Buckleys. There were three boys total, all with the same daddy and different mamas: Bryce, Ace, and Dare, with twenty-some years between them. Only Dare, the youngest, had managed to stay out of trouble. Public trouble at least. A lot of the damage Buckley men inflicted happened behind closed doors.

My nerves snapped and crackled, buzzing louder than ever. Ree's secret taunted me, wanting me to spill the beans.

Could Tessa Jane keep a secret? Because if I told her, then the anxiety would go away. It always did, once the words were out of my mouth, even though revealing secrets came with consequences.

But no, I couldn't. The truth would hurt so many if it ever leaked out.

So I clamped my lips together.

Tessa Jane pushed the button again and said, "What does it mean when it's sunny on a wedding day?"

The voice answered. "Sunshine on a wedding day means good luck."

Tessa Jane snorted derisively, then said sweetly, "Thank you."

It said, "You're welcome."

"Do you always say thank you to the voice?" I asked.

"Of course." Her eyebrows snapped downward. "Don't you?"

I was grateful to see the old, familiar Miss Manners side of her hadn't vanished completely, even though it was now served with a side of judgmental attitude. I smiled. "I will now."

The snow lightened a bit and Tessa Jane adjusted the wipers as she crept around a corner, looking every which way twice. "My wedding day was the prettiest sunny day you've ever seen. So much for good luck."

I gripped the box tighter, took a big deep breath, and said, "I'm real sorry about what happened."

"Me, too," she said quietly.

My throat ached with all the things I wanted to say. Of all the apologies I needed to make for treating her so terribly all these years. Just as I opened my mouth, Sam Smith starting singing from my cell phone.

I put my chin on top of the box for extra support and reached for the phone, which I'd placed in the cupholder earlier. I immediately silenced the call. It was as if somehow, wherever she was currently in this world, my mama had known that I was fixin' to make nice with Tessa Jane and wanted to stop me.

"Interesting ringtone," Tessa Jane said. "How's your mama doing these days?"

I practically snapped my neck to look at her. "How'd you know it was her?"

She lifted a shoulder in a half shrug. "I'd like to say it was a lucky guess, considering the song choice, but I saw 'Cecelia' on the screen when you lifted the phone to decline the call."

If she was curious why I'd used my mother's name on my contact list instead of *Mama*, she didn't say. Though considering how much Bean shared our lives with each other, she likely knew all about my troubled relationship with my mother. I was suddenly grateful our aunt had been the bridge between us all these years, because I did not want to explain.

"*My* mama was at the party last night," she said. "I was surprised as all get out to see her open the door at my granddaddy's house."

"That *is* surprising." It was well known that Henrietta didn't like coming back home, especially after Constance Jane had passed away. I put my phone back in the cupholder and resumed my death grip on the cake box. "Is she in town only for the party?"

"More for me than the party. She didn't want me to have to deal with my granddaddy alone."

Before I could ask anything else, she gasped. A black shape in the road caught my eye just as she slammed on the brakes. "Hold on!" she cried as she swerved.

The car slid in what felt like a slow-motion circle—and kept going right off the side of the road and onto the snow-covered berm. I pressed the cake box to my chest and held it up, off my lap, all the while squeezing my eyes shut and praying for all I was worth. Finally, the car came to a thudding stop, complete with a dull crunch, against a post-and-rail fence.

Before I could even think to gather up my scattered wits, she shut off the car, unclicked her seatbelt, and flung open the door, leaving it ajar as she darted into the road.

I took a moment to collect myself. I was shaking but okay.

The cake box—*thanks be*—was unharmed. I wanted to get out, to see what Tessa Jane was doing, but the whole right side of the car butted up against the fence. And there was no way to climb over her seat with the cake box in hand. Not without help.

All was unnervingly silent. The earth strangely quiet. The air felt hollow yet dense. It was a hush like I'd never experienced. It was beautiful but made me uneasy.

"Tessa Jane!" I called out into the storm. Snowflakes drifted into the car, melted on her leather seat.

"Be right there!" she shouted, and I heaved a sigh of relief.

A minute later, she came staggering back, her arms full of black Labrador. She thrust the dog into the car, then pulled the lever that released the trunk. "I thought for sure I was going to hit her." Then she glanced at me, taking stock. "Are you okay?"

"Not a scratch."

"Thank goodness. The cake?"

"I think it's fine. I didn't feel it tip."

Tessa Jane let out a breath of relief. "I'm going to grab a blanket from the trunk." She quickly closed the door.

The dog's tail wagged as she licked my face, then sniffed the box. She didn't look too worse for the wear, other than she was soaking wet and shivering.

A second later, the trunk slammed and Tessa Jane was back in the car, a blanket in hand. She pushed her seat all the way back, then patted her lap. The dog hopped onto it and Tessa Jane wrapped the blanket around her, rubbing the fabric against damp fur. Her face clouded over. "What's a dog doing loose in this storm?"

"Maybe she's an escape artist like Hambone. Someone's probably worried sick."

"It's a good thing we came across her, then." Her face lit. "A bright side."

I smiled. "I suppose so."

"I'm shaking like a leaf. How long does it take adrenaline to wear off?"

"Not sure." I was still shaking, too.

The dog licked Tessa Jane's chin, then gave herself a good shake and hopped into the back seat, her tail wagging. "We'll have to take her with us for now. I'll text a picture to Aunt Bean so she can get a phone chain started."

It was a good plan. We'd know who the dog belonged to before we got back home. I looked at the fence post that was inches away from my window. "What are the chances we can drive away from this?"

Tessa Jane readjusted her seat, turned the key, and started the car. "I'm hopeful. I took a peek at your side of the car when I got the blanket. The doors are dented but that shouldn't be a problem." She put the car in drive. "Here goes."

The car lurched forward, making a sickening noise as it scraped the fence. Then it stayed right where it was, the wheels spinning. Tessa Jane bit her lip, shifted into D2, and tried again. Chunks of mud and snow flew around the car as the wheels spun. She tried putting it into reverse but didn't gain any ground. Finally, she blew out a breath and put it into park. "I'm starting to hate snow."

"Don't let Aunt Bean hear you say that." I loosened my grip on the cake box. Walking to the hotel wasn't really an option, despite what I'd been thinking earlier. Not with the wind and snow and heavy cake. "I'll call Holden's Garage for a tow."

I reached for my phone but froze when I caught sight of the starlings flying by, glittering in the snowfall. They flew upward, disappearing into vast whiteness just as a horn beeped. A big ruby-red pickup truck rolled to a stop on the road next to us, its hazards flashing. The dog barked as a door slammed. A second later, a man came jogging toward us, his hand on his ball cap as he kept his head down against the wind and snow.

I recognized the hat. And the shape of the man. My nerves started buzzing, a million angry bees.

Of all the people in all the world, it had to be Sawyer Gray who'd stopped to help us.

✳

Twenty minutes later, a rosy-cheeked Petal greeted us in the hotel ballroom in a long white satin robe, white marabou high-heeled slippers, full makeup, and Velcro rollers in her hair.

"Lordy, lordy! What a morning y'all had!" she exclaimed. "The cake table is over yonder, Sawyer."

"Yes, ma'am," he said, keeping the box level as he started for the table draped in white and blush linens. I had to admit, I was glad he was the one doing the carrying. Holding that box had felt a little like holding a ticking time bomb.

Petal rushed forward, toward Tessa Jane and me, giving us quick kisses on our cheeks. "It's been an *age*! It's good to see you both. Especially together. Who'd have *thought*?"

In my head, I was singing every lullaby I knew, trying to keep myself from talking. I was walking dangerous ground with Sawyer around. With Sawyer *and* Dare Buckley Fife around. *Mercy.* But I knew I had to say something, so I said, "It's good to see you too, Petal. Happy wedding day."

"You look pretty as picture," Tessa Jane said, smiling tightly. "Rollers and all."

I had to imagine being here among all this wedding frip-pery had to be hard for Tessa Jane. It had only been a few months since her wedding was canceled.

Petal laughed and patted her hair. "If only you could see me in my dress. I'd knock your socks off."

Petal had never lacked for confidence.

"Is there a trick to getting the cake out?" Sawyer called over to us, looking a bit like a fish out of water among all the frilly finery.

Tessa Jane said, "I'll go."

In between the silent lullabies, I was cursing the fates. First, for the snowstorm. Then the accident. Then Sawyer just happening to come across us on his way to pick up Luna in

Mentone—after needing to take a detour due to a blocked road. He believed it had been happenstance. I knew better. The starlings had guided him to Tessa Jane and me.

He'd told us he heard the only tow truck in town was already backlogged with calls and kindly insisted on carrying us to the hotel. Cake, dog, and all. And he'd made a phone call along the way.

Petal wrung her hands, and her gaze darted around. "Where's she at?"

It took me a second to realize she meant the dog. Sawyer had recognized the black lab straight off. She was Pepper—Dare Fife's dog. Sawyer hadn't known Dare's phone number, but he knew Perry Pottinger's—Petal's daddy, who was one of the Starlight Electricals' customers—and had called him up to let him know what had happened. Perry had obviously passed the news to Petal, who'd met us here in the ballroom when we arrived. I'd been surprised to see her, thinking for sure she'd have sent Dare to fetch the dog. Or *someone.* Petal was a delegator.

"She's in the truck. We don't have a leash."

Petal looked over her shoulder, toward the ballroom doors. She tightened the sash on her robe. "Could y'all do me a favor?"

I wasn't sure why it seemed like a loaded question, heavy and dangerous. "What kind of favor?"

"Could you possibly take Pepper home with you?" A noise came from the hallway, and she flinched, then winced and said, "Pretty please, Addie?"

She was suddenly a ball of nervous, worried energy. I wasn't sure what was going on, but something was. "For how long?"

Once again she looked toward the doors. She was making me anxious, which was saying something, because I was already about to snap clean in half.

"I reckon a week or two?"

My eyes widened. I'd been thinking a couple of hours. Just until the ceremony was over. Tomorrow, at the latest.

"I know, I know," she said, "it's a lot, but you'd be doing me a big favor. The biggest. Consider it a wedding gift!"

A gift for a wedding to which I hadn't been invited, for which I'd risked my life delivering the cake. Classic Petal. She'd always been a touch selfish.

I threw a look at Tessa Jane. She was taking pictures of the cake with her phone. Sawyer, I suddenly noticed, was looking at me. I swallowed hard and forced myself to meet Petal's blue gaze.

"And could you keep it real quiet like?" she asked, as if I'd already agreed. "I'll collect her when me and Dare get back from our honeymoon. We're going to the Bahamas tomorrow afternoon if our flights aren't canceled. *So help me* if those flights are canceled."

My brain was having trouble keeping up. "You must've already made plans for someone to keep Pepper. Who was watching her while you've been here?"

She went back to wringing her hands. "The dog sitter we hired fell through. *Please*, Addie? Dare, well, he'll be real up—"

"Sorry to interrupt," Tessa Jane said, stepping up to us, Sawyer right behind her. She motioned toward the cake table. "The cake is set up. Do you want to take a look, Petal?"

Sawyer held the empty cake box. "I'll go put this in the kitchen and check with the front desk to see if they have a rope I can use as a leash to bring Pepper in."

He'd always been this way. He'd see a problem and tackle it. Just dive in headlong. I'd always been more go with the flow.

"No!" Petal cried. "I mean, you don't have to do that. Pepper's going to be staying with Addie for a little while. Ain't so, Addie?"

All of them looked at me.

My stomach churned. What had Petal been about to say? That Dare would be upset? Was that why she was so nervous? Was he a hitter, like his brothers? His father? The thought made me queasy, and I took deep breaths to ease the nausea.

"It's so," I finally said.

Tessa Jane's eyebrows snapped downward, and in her eyes, I saw worry clear as day.

Petal clasped her hands under her chin in a praying gesture. "And if y'all could keep it quiet, I'd appreciate it."

I could feel Sawyer's questioning gaze, heating me from the inside out.

"Now, y'all should probably go." Petal ushered us toward the door we'd come in—the service door that led into the hotel's kitchen.

"But the cake . . ." Tessa Jane said.

Petal threw a glance over her shoulder. "It's perfect. Thank you." She all but shoved us through the door. "Bye, now! Drive safe, y'hear?"

"That was strange, right?" Tessa Jane said as we made our way toward the loading zone after dropping the box in the kitchen so Petal and Dare could use it to tote home the top tier of the cake or any leftovers.

"Really strange," Sawyer said as he opened the heavy outer door for us.

While we were inside, the snow had turned to sleet. Soon it would be rain. By morning, all traces of snow would likely be gone. I wasn't sure why, after all the trouble it had caused, it made me sad that it wasn't sticking around.

"Hey!" Someone shouted from next to Sawyer's truck.

That someone was Dare Fife and he looked none too pleased as we approached. Fisted hands were tucked under his arms. His jaw jutted. Thick, dark eyebrows were drawn low. Steam practically rose from his head.

My heart twisted simply looking at him, at the hard life that radiated from every pore. A scar trailed along his jawline. His nose had been broken at least once, maybe more. His blue eyes were full of confusion. His thick, dark wavy hair had a widow's peak—a trait all the brothers shared—which was damp now from the wintry mix.

He was handsome, I'd give him that. The good looks of Buckley men had blinded many a woman to their faults. Made them weak in the knees. And the brain.

"He's just misunderstood," Ree had said of Ace Buckley when we'd been in high school.

I'd tried to tell her I didn't see much good in him at all, but she wouldn't listen.

"One look in those dreamy blue eyes of his tells me what kind of guy he is," she said. "Give him a chance, Addie."

Turned out, he'd been the kind who'd break her wrist after a month of dating.

I was suddenly queasy from painful memories as I looked over at Sawyer. How could he not see it? The resemblance? How could he not see that his daughter, his curly dark-haired, blue-eyed, widow-peaked daughter, wasn't *his* at all?

I pushed my hand against my mouth to keep Ree's secret in and felt tears sting my eyes.

Dare kicked some snow, stepped toward us, and said, "What're y'all doing with my dog?"

CHAPTER TEN

From the Kitchen of Verbena Fullbright

Stop mixing as soon as your ingredients come together, nice and smooth. If you whip the living tar out of your batter, that pesky gluten will toughen right up, making the cake dense and chewy. A little restraint early on goes a long way toward a sweet reward.

Tessa Jane

"What's cookin', peanut?" Aunt Bean asked early the next morning as she wandered into the kitchen. She leaned her walking stick against the counter, then headed straight for the coffee pot.

"Cookies for Miss Ernie. I'm hoping to bring them round to her tomorrow to brighten her day a bit."

The snow had melted overnight, leaving behind mud, stories that would be shared from front porch rocking chairs for years to come, and for me, a costly car repair. Late yesterday, Holden's Garage had towed my car to the shop, along with a dozen others that had wrecked in the storm. When I would get it back was anyone's guess.

The cloudy morning sky filled the kitchen windows with muted light, hinting that we might see sunshine today. I hoped so. I was eager to catch a glimpse of the starlight aurora at full strength.

It was a little past eight and Addie was still sleeping. Hambone and Pepper were outside. Last I looked, the ducks appeared to be chasing the dogs, rather than the other way around. Clearly, Lucy and Ethel weren't afraid to assert their dominance to keep order.

Yesterday in the hotel parking lot, Dare had been grim faced while we explained how Pepper came to be in the cab of Sawyer's truck. According to him, he'd last seen the dog the day before, leaving her in Petal's care while she waited on the dog sitter she'd hired. He couldn't explain how Pepper could've gotten loose or why she wasn't wearing her collar and tags. He'd been angry. And sad, too, I'd noted. Almost . . . disappointed.

Addie was quick to reassure him that she didn't mind keeping Pepper while he and Petal honeymooned. And I'd piped in that we were already watching Hambone, who'd be overjoyed to have Pepper around. Eventually, if not reluctantly, Dare agreed to leave the dog in our care.

When we brought Pepper home, Bean had welcomed the dog with open arms and plenty of Milk-Bones. Hambone had been ecstatic. The ducks hadn't been quite so friendly, honking and flapping their wings angrily at the sight of her. The cats, so far, had been indifferent. Typical Miney and Moe.

Aunt Bean filled a coffee cup—the grasshopper mug from Ty—and hitched herself onto a stool on the other side of the prep table. She was still in her dressing gown, her hair hidden by a polka dotted silk hair wrap that had a perky, playful bow sitting pretty atop her head. Barefaced, exhaustion showed in the deep circles and dark smudges under her eyes. I suspected she'd had a sleepless night.

She took a sip of coffee, sighed. "She'll be right pleased. Your cookies are something special."

"Thanks, Aunt Bean."

One batch of cookies was already cooling, another was in the oven, and I was currently rolling out the last of the chilled dough. With each push of the rolling pin, I felt a little less tense. And a bit more *me*.

I first attempted decorated cookies the summer I stayed with Aunt Bean when I was sixteen. I wished I could say the first batch I made had been successful, but the cookies had spread into each other, the edges had burned, and the taste wasn't buttery enough for my liking. To add to the disappointment, my icing had been lumpy and dry.

Determined to get it right, I set to work, trying to master the basics like how thick to roll the dough and exactly how long to bake the cookies so they'd be soft yet firm enough to hold their shape. I made minor adjustments to the ingredients. A little more butter. A touch more vanilla. A dash of almond extract for depth of flavor.

When it came to the icing, I scoured websites written by dedicated *cookiers*—bakers who specialized in cookies—looking for inspiration. I'd found a concept I'd never heard of before: one that mixed royal icing *and* vanilla glaze together. Once I gave it a try and fiddled with measurements to better fit my tastes, I knew I'd never need another recipe.

For hours upon hours, days upon days, I practiced piping—outlining, flooding, lettering—until my hands hurt. Aunt Bean bought me dozens of cutters, edible watercolors, and dusting powders. I'd been in creative heaven. At every opportunity, I'd made cookies. For years. Right up until I started work at the country club.

"Will you paint them?" Bean asked.

I nodded. Once the baked cookies were cool, I'd flood them, then create a puffy raised dog design. I'd hand paint the finer details. "I'm going to try to do justice to Hambone's image. My skills are rusty, so he might come out looking like an orange blob by the time I'm done."

"Ernie will get a kick out of that. But why're your skills rusty?" she asked, absently rubbing her watch face. "You love making cookies."

I transferred the cookies to a parchment-lined baking sheet. "Not much call for decorated cookies at Southern Oaks. The menu there leans more toward crème brûlée and soufflés."

"Do crème brûlée and soufflés make you happy like cookies do?"

I was unsure how this conversation had jumped into the

deep end of emotional waters. I treaded carefully. "It pays the bills."

She took a slow sip of her coffee and spoke over the rim of her mug. "Cookies like yours could pay the bills just as well. Maybe better. With cottage food laws, you could work right out of your own kitchen. And it'd make you happy at the same time. Because, peanut, I hate to point out the obvious, but you're clearly not happy these days."

My throat ached and I felt myself starting to sink into murky depths. "It's been a rough few months."

She sipped and nodded. "The roughest."

I wanted to tell her about the darkness, the loss of the bright sides. I longed to ask her advice about what to do about my granddaddy—because I could *not* let him dig up that crater. But if she found out his plans for the land she'd probably have the mother of all conniption fits. With her bad heart, I couldn't risk telling her. I'd just have to figure it out on my own.

As I thought about Grandaddy's threat to cut off Mama and me—to disown us, really—my hands fisted, and I forced myself to flex them. He'd broken something the other night that I didn't think could ever be repaired.

"You can't tell me the cookies aren't helping your mood," Bean added, reaching for one on the cooling rack. "They're sure helping mine."

Full of butter and sugar, they weren't the least bit heart healthy, but every once in a while what filled up a heart took priority over nutrition labels.

I managed a smile. "Cookies always help."

Her phone dinged, and a second later, she made a sympathetic *tsk*ing noise. "Pinky done fell on a patch of ice last night while out with her dog."

"Is she okay?"

"She said it's mostly her pride that's hurting but she banged up her wrist, too. She's icing it."

"I'll make a few cookies to take to her as well."

Aunt Bean texted back, using only the tip of her index finger to punch in the letters. "You're a good egg, Tessa Jane."

The dogs started barking at the back door. "I'll get them," I said, as Aunt Bean made to stand up.

I let them in one at a time so I could dry off their paws with an old towel. Pepper was first, and she immediately dropped to the ground and rolled belly-up for scratches. She was good-natured, playful, and well taken care of. Aunt Bean said Dare had gotten her after his adoptive parents passed away, raising her from just a pup.

I thought about what I knew of the Buckley family, which truthfully wasn't much other than Bryce Buckley's long-ago evil act toward my family.

But Pepper seemed like a happy dog. It was a simple fact that happy dogs were raised by good people. If Dare had raised this sweet girl, then he had to have a good heart. *Had to.* Unfortunately, my ability to see an inner light was still glitchy and I hadn't been able see it for myself yesterday.

I let in Hambone and had to pretty much wrestle him to the ground to wipe his paws. Asking Aunt Bean about Dare's inner light would definitely tip her off about my troubles, so I took the long way around to uncover the answer. "How long did Petal and Dare date? Did they live together before the wedding?"

She let out a hollow laugh. "Where in the tarnation did those questions come from?"

After setting Hambone loose, I washed my hands and went back to rolling dough. "I was wondering if Petal helped Dare raise Pepper."

Bean sipped her coffee. "No, not at all. They only started dating a year ago. And I don't think she's nearly as enamored with Pepper as Dare is. When Petal came in to order her wedding cake, she was complaining that Dare wanted to have Pepper in the ceremony, carrying the rings or some such. She said, and I quote, 'If God had given him a lick of sense, he'd know a wedding wasn't a place for a dog.' Then she went and asked for fondant. Talk about no licks of sense."

I smiled. "You mean *fondon't*?"

I wasn't at all sure why Bean felt the way she did about fondant. Sure, it wasn't the tastiest, but I knew quite a few bakers who worked with fondant to create masterpieces. Absolute works of art. But Bean had made up her mind never to use it and that was that. To each their own, she'd always say.

"Damn straight." She laughed for real this time and the sound of it plunged deep down and wrapped around my heart.

The rolling pin squeaked as I thought about what she'd revealed about Dare and pressed my luck, purposefully keeping my tone light so as not to arouse her suspicions. "So Dare's not like the rest of the Buckleys then?"

"Good heavens no. He's got a good heart, that one. And on top of that the Fifes made sure he had counseling after he moved in with them to help him heal his inner hurts." She sighed, then said, "Now, tell me, will you be working on those cookies all day?"

There was a playful tone to her question, something mischievous, that made me stop what I was doing and look at her. "No. Why?"

She grinned and rubbed her hands together. "How do you feel about helping me sort some closets?"

Yesterday, Pepper's arrival, on top of the car accident, had thrown us all for a loop and the snow-day *sorting* Bean had planned was put on hold.

I'd been hoping it stayed there.

I didn't want to sort anything. Or do any inventory. Or itemization. Or anything that alluded to the fact that Aunt Bean was trying to do what Swedish people called *döstädning*, or death cleaning. Basically, decluttering and organizing your life before it ended.

In theory, I liked the idea.

But in practice, I couldn't bear the thought of it.

"Good morning," Addie said, coming down the stairs in

flannel pajama bottoms and an old oversize Bama sweatshirt that had frayed edges. Her hair was pulled up in a loose topknot and her face had the reddish-pink look of having recently been scrubbed clean. The dogs rushed to greet her as she stopped on the bottom step and looked out the living room windows. "A car just turned up the driveway. Anyone expecting a visitor?"

Both she and Aunt Bean looked pointedly at me.

I wiped my hands on a dish towel. "Don't tell me it's Jenna again. Surely he wouldn't make her work on a Sunday morning."

But even as I said it, I knew it being Sunday wouldn't stop my granddaddy from ordering people to do his bidding. He was ruthless. Even, it seemed, with his own flesh and blood.

Do you see any good in him, sweetheart?

I pushed Gigi's voice firmly out of my head before I started crying.

"We'll see soon enough who it is." Aunt Bean took another bite of cookie and *ahh*ed. "You done good with these, Tessa Jane. Real good. Ernie's going to be mighty grateful."

Addie threw me a look that clearly questioned why I was serving Bean cookies for breakfast but I only shrugged. "Want one?"

"Of course."

I met her halfway and passed it over. She took a bite and did a little shuffle that I took for a happy dance. "*So* good. I hope you made plenty."

"If not, I know where we can get more."

As she walked toward the coffee pot, I headed for the front door, stopping to scratch the top of Miney's head as I peeked out the window. I fully expected to see Jenna, but when the car rolled to a stop in front of the house, I recognized it immediately. "It's my mama."

I spun around, wondering what I could clean in fifteen seconds, and wishing I'd put on lipstick. I scratched at a hive on my neck.

Aunt Bean laughed as I fluffed a pillow. "Well, let her on in, peanut."

What was she doing here? And so early, too? "Do I have any flour on my face?"

"Your face is perfect," Addie said as she sat on a stool next to Aunt Bean.

Taking a deep breath, I pulled open the door, pasted on a smile. "Mama! This is a surprise. Come on in."

She stepped inside, took off a pair of dark sunglasses. "I'm terribly sorry for barging in so early but *hand to God* if I had to stay in that house one more minute, I was going to lose my mind. I had to escape. I wasn't sure where else to go. In the wake of the bad weather, everything's closed up tight, even the churches. Plus, there's something I want to talk to y'all about. Oh! And I brought your necklace, Tessa Jane." She finally took a breath, then kissed my cheeks and studied my face. She gave me a gentle smile and a squeeze. "What smells so delightful?"

I whispered, "Have you been drinking?"

She laughed. "What? No!"

I stared at her. My mother wasn't so chatty. And she hadn't said a word about my nude lips or the fact that I was still in my pajamas. This was strange. Bizarre, even.

"You're always welcome here, Henrietta," Aunt Bean said graciously. "Make yourself at home."

"Can I get you a cup of coffee?" Addie asked.

Another crack deep in my heart healed at her kind tone.

"That would be lovely," Mama said, tipping her head as if also surprised.

As she crossed the room to greet Aunt Bean with a hug and to peck her cheek, Pepper started barking, short happy yips as a truck pulled up in front of the house. Which set off Hambone, who started baying at the top of his lungs.

"Is *that* Jenna?" Aunt Bean asked loudly.

My jaw all but dropped as Dare came around the front of the truck carrying a fabric-wrapped bundle and opened the passenger door for Petal. He offered her a hand to help her down but she didn't take it. The whole time she wore a face like she smelled something foul and didn't say a word to him.

"No, it's Petal and Dare," I said, walking back to the front door, a pit in my stomach.

They hadn't been married but a minute and were already fighting.

"Dare *Buckley*?" my mama asked, her tone apprehensive.

"Dare Fife now, remember?" I nudged Hambone away from the door with my leg. "He and Petal got married yesterday."

"Did they come by for Pepper?" Aunt Bean reached for her walking stick as she stood up.

"Pepper?" Mama sounded all kinds of confused—and also on guard.

"The black lab." Addie nodded toward Pepper, who had started scratching at the door.

I whispered, "I don't know, and I don't want to talk out of turn, but Petal's giving Dare the stink eye. I think they might be fighting."

My mama sighed. "*Buckleys*."

A second later a tentative knock sounded. I pasted on a smile and swung the door open. "Petal, Dare! This is a surprise."

"Sorry to drop by unannounced," Dare said.

Petal stuck out her lower lip, then scooted around him into the house, air kissing my cheeks as she passed me by. "I told him this was a bad idea, but he wouldn't listen to me. Aren't all y'all's pajamas *darling*?"

At the sight of Petal, Pepper tucked her tail between her legs, ran behind me, and whimpered. Hambone bared his teeth in solidarity.

My heart sank straight to my toes.

"Dogs," she muttered.

Dare waited on the doorstep, until I invited him inside. Once he was through the door, he immediately crouched down, set down the cloth bundle, and opened his arms. Pepper whined with pure happiness as she barreled into him, licking his face.

He cracked a smile as he gave her a good belly rub. It was impossible not to notice that he had a small cut on his forehead, the skin around it lightly bruised.

"What happened to your head?" I closed the door behind him, not caring at all that it was rude to ask, which I blamed on my shadow.

It was Petal who answered. "Oh that! So silly. When I was kicking off my heels last night, one of them went sideways, catching him unawares. He shoulda been paying better attention is what I say. Good thing it was after our pictures! Miss Verbena, could I possibly use your little ladies' room to freshen up? We've got a long drive ahead of us."

"Sure thing," Aunt Bean said, her usually airy tone thick. "It's on the other side of the stairs."

As Petal walked off, the room grew heavy with silence. With concern. Puzzles pieces were sliding together, and none of us seemed to like the image that was forming.

Dare kept loving on his dog. The gold on his new wedding band glinted like a big ol' mistake.

Addie finally cleared her throat and said, "Dare, would you like a cup of coffee? A cookie?"

"No thank you, ma'am. We really are sorry to bother you so early." He stood up, lifting the cloth bundle he'd brought inside. He passed it to me. "I wanted to bring by some of Pepper's things. Her leash, collar, a few of her favorite toys. And that there is one of my sweatshirts. She likes to sleep with it."

For some reason, my eyes stung with tears. I blinked them away. "That's real sweet."

"So you found her collar?" Addie asked, and I could tell by her tone that she was fishing.

His Adam's apple bobbed as he glanced toward the powder room. He crouched back down, and put his arms around Pepper, almost protectively. "Yes ma'am. I found it at Petal's place."

He didn't explain further. By the look on everyone's faces in the room, save my mama, I figured he didn't have to. I had the feeling we were all suspecting that Petal had let that dog loose on purpose. In a snowstorm.

Petal came back out, took one look at Dare and Pepper, and let out a mirthless laugh. "I swear he loves that dog more than me! We need to get on our way, honey. Don't want to miss our flight."

Dare stood up, and I noticed he had put himself between Pepper and Petal, keeping them as far apart as he could manage.

As he and his wife stood together, there was no question they were a beautiful couple, and I had to remind myself that for some, beauty only ran skin deep. I hugged the cloth bundle to my chest. "We'll take real good care of Pepper while you're away."

He said, "I appreciate it more than you'll ever know."

Petal rolled her eyes and hooked her arm through his as she pulled open the door. "We'll send a postcard. Bye now!"

Dare gave Pepper one last ear rub, told us thank you again, and followed his wife out the door.

I gave a wave as they drove off, then closed the door and leaned against it.

We all stared at each other, a bit rattled. No one said a word. No one wanted to say what we were thinking out loud.

Pepper had hopped up on the couch to watch the truck drive away and it near to broke my heart. I put the bundle down on the cushion next to her, unwrapped it, and pulled out a well-loved stuffed alligator and a squeaky ball. Her collar and leash were pink.

Bean tapped her walking stick twice on the floor. "Weddings are stressful business. Might could be she's having an off week."

"Maybe so," Addie said, walking over to pat Pepper.

But she sounded like she didn't believe it.

I could practically see my mama's mind racing as she gripped her coffee mug, a frown on her face. Because of her role in the Starling Society, she'd seen this kind of scenario before. Though women by far were often the victims in abusive relationships, sometimes it was the men who suffered. One in nine men, according to the latest statistics. Primarily it was emotional abuse but occasionally it dipped into the physical. Pushing and slapping and throwing things. Like *shoes*. Most men were unwilling to seek help for themselves, gender stereotypes playing a big role in keeping quiet. Ordinarily, this was where Mama would discretely step in, offer guidance. Suggest a counselor, offer to pay for the sessions. But she was only here temporarily and he'd be gone for a while on his honeymoon.

Aunt Bean let out a hearty sigh, and said, "Henrietta? Did you mention there was something you wanted to talk to us about?"

Mama snapped to, pulling her attention away from the window and the retreating truck. She sat on one of the prep counter stools. "Indeed. I went to the starlight field last night, after the weather cleared."

Intrigued, I walked back to the prep island. Addie followed. I had the feeling I knew why Mama was at a crossroads, in need of clarity, direction. But I wasn't at all sure why she was *here*, talking about it.

"Something's been weighing on my mind these last couple of days. My heart," she said. "I was looking for some help with sorting it all out."

Aunt Bean tipped her head and sat down. "Did you find it?"

Mama nodded. "I did. By the time I finished walking the boardwalk, it was clear what I needed to do."

"What's that?" Addie asked, curiosity filling her eyes.

Mama glanced from face to face. "First is that I need to apologize to Tessa Jane. And second, it's time I told y'all the truth. About everything."

CHAPTER ELEVEN

From the Kitchen of Verbena Fullbright
Once your batter is made, don't let it sit around too long before baking or you risk your cake fallin' flat. Nothing is more disappointing than realizing you waited too long and missed a chance at creating something special.

Addie

It had been a *morning*. And it wasn't yet nine A.M. Butter and sugar scented the air as I refilled coffee mugs, then hitched myself onto a stool to hear what Henrietta had to tell us.

Honestly, though, I was still shaken by Dare and Petal's visit. And how, once I'd taken a good look, I'd been able to see a bright inner light in his eyes—but only a faint glow in hers. A dimness that reminded me a little too much of my mama.

I silently sent Dare a million apologies for lumping him in with the rest of his family and tried to focus on Henrietta, who was gazing at Tessa Jane.

"I'm so very sorry, darling," she said.

"For what?" Tessa Jane asked, looking truly baffled.

"Somewhere along the line I lost sight of the fact that my goals are mine. Not yours. That what belongs to you belongs *only* to you. When you told me no the other night, it was the slap in the face I needed to take a good hard look at myself, at what I was doing to you. I didn't like what I saw. It reminded me too much of my father."

I had no idea what they were talking about and was beyond curious.

"Mama, you don't—" Tessa Jane began, tears in her eyes.

"No, no." Henrietta held up her hand. "It's all so clear to me now, and I'm ashamed at how I've pressured you to give, give, give. I couldn't see what it was costing you. Emotionally. And financially, too. It's not your responsibility, it's mine. You need to live life *your* way."

Tessa Jane came around the island and hugged her mother. "You know I've always wanted to help."

Henrietta squeezed her daughter. "I know. You have a big heart. There's no question I've taken advantage of that, even if it was subconsciously. It won't happen again." She let go of Tessa Jane settled back onto her stool. "To tell this story properly, I need to go back a bit. To a time when I was young and foolish. I was twenty-one years old when I fell in love with Bryce Buckley."

Wide-eyed, Tessa Jane inhaled sharply, then pulled over a stool and sat down. If Aunt Bean had given me a nudge, I'd have fallen right off my seat. I could not believe what I was hearing. Henrietta and *Bryce*?

Never in a million years would I have paired the two.

Aunt Bean, I noticed, continued to sip her coffee, not acting the least bit shocked. It was clear to me, as someone who knew her well, that she was already aware of this piece of news.

"It was just one of those things," Henrietta said. "He was tall, dark, and dangerous, and I fell hard and fast, caught up in wanting things I shouldn't have and maybe even wanting to shock my daddy. Rebel a little."

"Gigi and Granddaddy knew about this?" Tessa Jane scratched absently at her neck.

Henrietta said, "Not at first. Not many did. When my mother and father found out, they weren't pleased. But I wasn't to be reasoned with."

"Love," Bean said, shaking her head.

"Exactly," Henrietta agreed. "At first, I was too infatuated to see any of his faults. Then I chose not to see, afraid of losing him. He questioned everything I did, who I saw, what I wore. I made excuses for the bruises, especially to Gavin."

According to Aunt Bean, my daddy and Henrietta had become friends through their jobs at a local retirement village. Daddy had been working as a physical therapist when Henrietta signed on as an event coordinator after she graduated college. They'd bonded over their love of people, the cafeteria's peach cobbler, and the starlight.

Tessa Jane sat frozen in shock on the stool, seemingly not even hearing the buzzer of the oven timer. I got up, took the pan of cookies from the oven, and set it on the counter.

"Gavin didn't buy my excuses and tried endlessly to talk sense into me," Henrietta said. "But I was stubborn. I didn't want to listen."

I wrapped my hands around my mug, feeling a weird sense of déjà vu with this story. My father trying to talk sense into Henrietta mirrored how I'd tried to stop Ree from seeing Ace Buckley.

We'd both failed.

"Bryce and I had been together for seven months when he broke my arm."

A tear slid from Tessa Jane's eye, and my heart about split in half.

Aunt Bean *tsk*ed softly, shaking her head.

"I knew then that I had to end it. I made the mistake of meeting him alone in my mama's horse barn to tell him. I'll spare you the details, but I will say I thought for certain that was the day I was going to die."

Tessa Jane's breath hitched and I rubbed her back, swallowing hard over my own emotions. I could easily picture Ree's battered body as she told me that she tripped and fell. Again.

"But I was saved by the most unlikely heroes," Henrietta said, glancing at Aunt Bean, who had tears in her eyes. She gave a slight nod as if to say *go on*. "I'd just about lost consciousness when I heard a great noise, a battle cry. The most beautiful birds I'd ever seen flew into the barn, dive-bombed, really."

The starlings, I was coming to realize, were not only the guardians of the people in my family, but to anyone nearby who needed help. Like Ernie. Like Henrietta.

"The birds attacked Bryce, pecking and scratching him until he ran from the barn, screaming. Later, I heard he'd needed hundreds of stitches." She arched an eyebrow. "I thought it too few."

Tessa Jane's voice was rough when she asked, "Did you go to the police?"

"I wanted to, but my father preferred to pretend it never happened. He only went to the authorities after Bryce came back to the farm a few months later."

My heart ached. "The watering trough?"

"Yes," Henrietta said quietly. "He needed to hurt something, and since he couldn't get to me inside the house, he took it out elsewhere."

Aunt Bean shuddered. "Lord a mercy."

Henrietta nodded. "My recovery was painfully slow, so I needed to take a leave of absence from work. I spent a lot of time at my window. Every so often, the starlings would line up along the pasture's fence. Eighteen of them. As if they were simply paying me a visit to see how I was doing. Just like Gavin—he came to see me at least once a week, too."

I wondered now if this was when their affair started. Wondered, too, why they'd never married after his divorce was finalized. Suddenly, I had the uneasy feeling it had been because of me.

"I can't say I truly understand why the birds helped me," Henrietta said, "but every time the starlings appeared, I vowed to them that I'd repay their kindness by protecting others. I wanted to show them that I was worthy of their intervention." She twisted a gold bangle on her arm. "As soon as I was well enough, I started the Starling Society."

I grabbed hold of my star pendant as she went on to tell

us about the secret society and how it helped the abused with money, with counseling, with shelter, with *escaping*. It all happened through word of mouth. Secrecy was a must—for the safety of those seeking help.

The *Starling Society*. The name sounded familiar, though I couldn't place how I knew it. I stole a look at Aunt Bean, who once again didn't seem surprised by what Henrietta was saying. She'd known about the society already. Apparently Aunt Bean was an expert at keeping secrets. Unlike me.

Henrietta ran a thumb over the rim of her coffee mug. "The society receives funding from many sources, but over the years the primary benefactor was my mother—not that she knew it."

Henrietta explained how she'd taken the monthly allowance her mother had given her and Tessa Jane and secretly invested it in others. And how Winchester had just cut them off.

She looked at Aunt Bean and me. "You already know my father wants the starlight land. He has grand plans for a big community, using every bit of the acreage he can get his hands on. Plus, he has an inane idea that would allow people to pan for diamonds in the starlight crater."

At this, Bean's eyebrows rose. She pulled her shoulders back. Set her jaw.

Henrietta went on. "He's using money as leverage over Tessa Jane to make sure the property is sold once the inheritance goes through. I've been pressuring her, too. Because the society needs the money. But it was wrong of me. The society is my responsibility, not hers. I will find a way to make it work on my own."

"I *want* to help you," Tessa Jane said, her voice low, weak, as if she was barely holding herself together.

"There are other ways," Henrietta said. "I know letting go of the field isn't what you want. And I daresay, it's not what Verbena and Addie want, either. I think the best step forward when it comes to the society is to create a private nonprofit, where I can hide the organization under its umbrella."

"That is an excellent step forward," Aunt Bean agreed, rubbing her thumb over the face of her watch.

Tessa Jane shifted on her seat, opened her mouth, then closed it again. Opened it once more and then snapped it shut.

"Spit it out, peanut," Aunt Bean said with a smile.

She scratched her neck and looked around the table. "What if we beat Granddaddy at his own game?"

"What do you mean?" Henrietta asked.

Tessa Jane's hands flew about as she said, "We keep the starlight field, protect it at all costs, and keep it free to visit. But what if we built a café and gift shop close by? Maybe on the other side of the parking lot? Since the field is open only at night, it could be a dessert café. We could sell Starling Cake Company cakes there, make it one big family business. We can use a portion of the profits to quietly help the Starling Society."

Aunt Bean tapped her nails on the table and nodded. "Interesting. I have to admit, I like the idea."

Henrietta put her mug down. "You wouldn't have to donate—"

"Mama, hush," Tessa Jane said, her voice tinged with exasperation.

I smiled at her sassiness, then realized everyone was looking at me.

"What do you think, Addie?" Aunt Bean asked.

I started counting the scratches in the wooden countertop. Finally, I said, "I'm not sure. This is a lot to take in all at once."

Aunt Bean patted my hand. "Take your time. No one needs a decision straight away. How long will you be in town, Henrietta?"

"I planned to stay the week, but I had to get out of that house." She glanced at her watch. "I'm hoping the Celestial Hotel has a room available."

Aunt Bean said, "Hotel? Nonsense. Stay here with us."

"I couldn't possibly. I'd never want to intrude."

"It's not an intrusion, is it, girls?" Bean asked.

The look in Aunt Bean's eyes warned us to play nice.

Warned me, at least. I had the feeling my apprehension was stamped all over my face.

"No, ma'am," Tessa Jane and I said at the same time.

"See?" Bean smiled. "It's settled. Tessa Jane, why don't you help your mama bring her things to the guest room?"

Once they were out of earshot, Aunt Bean said, "I know this is a lot to absorb, punkin."

"Winchester's never going to stop trying to get that land, even if we build on it. And if he becomes mayor, he'll have more power than ever. Who knows what he'll do to get revenge?"

Aunt Bean stood, wrapped her arms around me. "This is where we need to take a cue from the starlings."

I rested my head against her chest, heard her heart beating, reassuring me. "How so?"

She kissed my head, took another cookie from the cooling rack, and trundled toward the stairs. She faced me before starting the climb. "Starlings travel in flocks and murmurations because they know there's safety in numbers. And more importantly, they know they're stronger if they stick together rather than try to face hard times alone."

＊

Later that afternoon, Aunt Bean's words were weighing heavy on my mind. I had the feeling her starling analogy wasn't just referring to any future problems we might have with Winchester. She was talking about my past, essentially telling me that I didn't have to shoulder my troubles alone, like I'd been doing for so long now.

It was a little past four, and the three of them had gone to pick up some groceries and a few craft supplies Tessa Jane needed to finish the cookies for Ernie. It was hardly a three-person job, but I suspected they all were trying to give me some space.

I was currently in the storage room on the second floor of the big red barn, trying to put my studio to rights. During the past week, I'd relocated all the cleaning supplies and had given the room a good tidying.

I'd borrowed a folding table from Aunt Bean to use as a desk. I set up my laptop, microphone, and filter. And, of course, I was still waiting on the foam tiles and rug to arrive. I couldn't really do any work without them.

I powered on my laptop, checked my email and schedule. I liked to think it had been fate that had set me on the path of voice work. A consolation gift since I had to leave everyone I loved behind in Starlight and start life over in Birmingham. The mother of one of my roommates in the apartment I rented was a voice coach with connections. The minute she met me, her eyes had lit up. She helped me find a good acting class I could take around working full-time at a local bakery to pay the bills. And within a year, she'd introduced me to the woman who'd become my agent.

Most of those early days had been spent creating audition demos. Then I landed a local radio spot. Then local commercials. Then national commercials. I narrated audiobooks. I voiced a documentary for children about panda bears. And had a few roles in video games. Then I landed a bit role on a long-running animated TV show for young children. Then another. I'd thrown myself into my work, heart and soul, and I loved it.

My big break came when I'd landed the lead role in an animated TV show based on books set here in Alabama. The series featuring Poppy Kay Hoppy, a precocious, adventurous bunny, had been an instant hit. Ratings went through the roof. I'd recently finished recording my lines for the third season and there was no end in sight when it came to the series wrapping.

Its popularity had given me some breathing room, a chance to be a bit pickier with my work. And it had opened other doors. Bigger doors.

Now I was here, knowing exactly how lucky I was because it wasn't an easy industry in which to succeed. But I'd done it. Was doing it.

And yet . . .

Part of me still longed to be a Sugarbird.

Feeling at odds with myself, I walked over to the small window. The sun had come out around noontime and with it had come warmth. As I watched the starlings flit about the pecan tree Sam Smith started singing from my cell phone.

At the sound, I somehow knew my mama had already found out that Henrietta was staying at the farmhouse and was calling to voice her opinion on the matter. Because I didn't want to hear what she had to say, I silenced the call.

I tried to put myself in my mama's shoes, as a young wife who'd discovered her husband had cheated on her and had another child. I could feel her pain, her anger. I could see why she'd want to leave him. But, as hard as I tried, I would never understand how she'd walked away from *me*. Why she kept walking away.

Because my chest was suddenly tight, I tried to open the window to let some air in, but remembered it was painted shut. It was then that I noticed someone walking out of the woods, toward the farmhouse.

My heart started pounding. It was Luna.

The cabin where she lived with Sawyer was located practically in the farmhouse's backyard. It was just a short walk away, through the woods. Honestly, I was surprised they'd never moved. And equally surprised that Sawyer still worked as the field's caretaker after all this time.

It was, after all, a job that was meant to be Ree's.

Bean had created it for her when she found out Ree was pregnant, as a way of giving her a place of her own and a steady income while she figured out what was ahead.

I rubbed an ache in my chest as I watched Luna fast-walk across the property, her short strides sure and steady.

After Ree passed away, Bean offered the same job to Sawyer and he accepted. Back then, along with caring for the field and the crater, he had to open the parking lot gate at seven P.M. and close it at eleven, and tend to the lot, emptying trash bins and the like—which he could do with Luna strapped to his back if he wanted.

These days, however, Sawyer only took care of the field and crater, including the starwalk. The rest was covered by part-time attendants Bean hired about five years ago. Which, I now realized, was right around the time Luna started school full-time and he started working with his dad.

But why stay on at all? He could earn much more money working full-time with his father. And why still live in the tiny cabin?

I turned my attention back to Luna as she neared the front porch. From a distance, she looked surprisingly like her mama. It was the way she moved, I decided. My eyes filled with tears even as I smiled, remembering the way Ree would always lead with her head and chest, as if her feet couldn't quite keep up with her headstrong ways.

Luna quickly climbed the porch steps and knocked on the door. Even from inside the barn I could hear the dogs barking their fool heads off.

I knew she was looking for me. Good manners being what they were suggested I should go down there, invite her in, offer her a cookie. Tell her about her mama.

But I couldn't bring myself to move.

I stayed right where I was, tucked into the shadows, watching her from afar.

Hiding.

Facing my troubles all alone.

CHAPTER TWELVE

Tessa Jane

My hand was cramping.

It'd been a long time since I decorated cookies with such detail. But I was pleasantly surprised to find I still remembered how. I knew when to push the icing, when to pull it. When to squeeze the bag just the slightest bit harder, when to release.

"It's looking like skies will be clear all day," Aunt Bean said as she scrolled through a weather app on her phone. "Which means it'll be a perfect night to do some star walking. It's been a hot minute since I've been to the field."

"Are you needing clarity, Aunt Bean?" I was hunched over the prep table, painting cookies. I dipped a detail brush into rust-colored edible powder and used short strokes on the hardened icing to imitate Hambone's fur.

It was almost noon, and we'd had a quiet morning. When Aunt Bean had gone off to check on the renovation progress over at the Market Street bakery, Addie, Mama, and I split a chore list and tackled cleaning the farmhouse. My mama had been tasked with vacuuming, and an air of peace and contentment seemed to follow her from room to room.

Her life, her *drive* to help others, made so much more sense to me now. I could hardly think about what she'd told us without tearing up. My heart broke for her, what she'd endured. What she'd survived. Knowing what she'd been through, it was impossible not to admire her strength and desire to help others who had been in similar situations.

I glanced at the clock. Right now Mama was meeting with Mr. Stubblefield at his office to see if there was anything to be done about Granddaddy's iron fist where the trust was concerned. It was a long shot but worth a try.

"Not in the least." Bean put her phone down, pulled over her laptop, opened it up. "But don't you agree that there's something special about just walking among the light?"

"Definitely." I straightened, bending slightly backward to stretch my lower spine and wrapped my hand around my star necklace. It was nice to have it back. I'd lit up like a sparkler last night when Mama had pulled it from her jewelry bag, and I would've sworn that the moment I put it on, my world seemed a bit brighter.

"I'll watch from the viewing area," Addie said.

She was curled up on the couch, coffee cup in one hand, her phone in the other. She was scrolling with her thumb. There was a duck feather in her hair—she'd had duck duty this morning and apparently picked up a souvenir. Hambone slept on one side of her, Pepper on the other. Miney and Moe were draped across the top of the cushions near her head, soaking in the sunshine streaming through the windows. I smiled. With her rich brown hair, her sage-green eyes, and her love of nature, she'd always reminded me of a wood nymph I'd seen once in a book when I was a little girl. Now, watching her sitting in a pool of sunlight, surrounded by the animals, I thought maybe I'd been onto something.

But even as much as she loved nature and thought the starlight beautiful, she'd never walked in the midst of it.

Aunt Bean said, "I'm starting a spreadsheet *just in case* y'all decide to build near the starlight." She tapped a few keys, then said, "I have a survey from years ago, but I'm not sure where I filed it away. We'll need to find that, girls. We need to think about zoning. Permits. Utilities. Y'all might want to consider hiring a master planner."

As she talked, all I heard was *ka-ching, ka-ching, ka-ching.* Suddenly, I wondered where we were going to get the money for this build—if we built. Could I get a loan? Why hadn't I thought of this before now? I gripped my pendant, felt my body flood with calm.

Hambone shifted, growling low in his throat as he scrambled to his feet and headed for the front door. Addie twisted to look out the window. "Looks like it's the Bootsie's Blooms van."

Both she and Aunt Bean then looked at me.

I scratched at a hive on my arm. Ty wouldn't have sent something else—would he? No. No way. "I'm sure it's not for me."

Both dogs were full-on barking now as the van rolled to stop at the front walkway.

"*Quiet*," Addie said.

Neither quieted.

Addie threw a helpless glance at me. "You do it."

"Pepper, Hambone, *quiet*," I ordered.

Both stopped barking, and I smiled.

Addie said, "Teach me your ways."

Aunt Bean chuckled and slid off the stool. She grabbed her walking stick and made her way toward the door.

I shared a look with Addie. She wiggled her eyebrows. I'd told her what the Sugarbirds had revealed to me—about Stan's crush—and she'd been just as intrigued as I was about the possible match.

Aunt Bean opened the door with a hearty hello. "Come on in, Stan. Don't mind the dogs. What have you there?"

Stan stepped inside holding a basket of flowers and gave the dogs hellos before saying, "Flowers for a pretty lady." He passed them to Bean.

"For me? Well, me oh my," she said, grinning. "Don't I feel special!"

I wiped my hands on a dishtowel and walked over for a closer look as she set the basket on the coffee table, then plucked a small envelope off the plastic card holder.

Addie leaned in to sniff a rose. "Oh, look, Aunt Bean. There are snowdrops in here."

My eyebrows went up at that. Whoever had sent this arrangement knew Aunt Bean well. Snowdrops were one of her favorite flowers.

Aunt Bean leaned her stick against her hip, opened the envelope, pulled the card free, then frowned.

"What's it say?" I asked.

"All it has is my name and a hand-drawn heart." She turned toward Stan. "Who sent them?"

His forehead furrowed. "I wish I could tell you, but I have no idea."

"Bootsie must know." Bean crossed over to the prep island, where she had left her cell phone. She dialed the florist, putting the call on speakerphone so we could all listen in.

But after only a few minutes' conversation, it became clear that Bootsie didn't know, either.

"How can that be?" Aunt Bean asked her.

Bootsie said, "The order originated from an online site, Bean. I ain't privy to who sent it, unless the sender includes a name on the card."

"But why *wouldn't* they put a name down?" Bean asked, her tone high, as she banged her walking stick two times in exasperation.

Bootsie hooted. "Well, I think that's obvious, honey. You've got yourself a secret admirer."

✳

Bean had begged off going with us to visit Ernie so she could get a head start on making tomorrow's cakes. It was going to be an extra busy week, because two of the Sugarbirds would be missing. Willa Jo had scored a last-minute sale for a flight, leaving tonight, to see her grandbabies. And Pinky would be out as well, as her wrist was still bruised and swollen.

We'd already dropped off a basket of cookies at Pinky's house, leaving them on her porch to find when she returned from getting X-rays, and were on our way to Ty's house.

"I should've brought something to give to Ernie," Addie said.

She drove with her seatback fully upright, both hands on the steering wheel, and she'd checked her seatbelt latch three times before we even left Bean's driveway. Hambone was in the back seat, his wet nose pressed to the window to watch the world go by. We'd left Pepper with Aunt Bean.

"We have cookies."

"Those are from you."

"They're from *us*. As sisters, aren't we a package deal?" I wasn't sure why I'd said it, because I was still wary about our fragile relationship. But somehow the words had tumbled out before I could stop them—and part of me realized I meant it.

She glanced at me quickly, then back at the road. "I want to be. I mean, if you do."

I almost laughed at how she seemed to be torn between looking at me and the road. She was a nervous nelly.

Before I could say anything, she added, "I need you to know that I'm really sorry about . . . well, *everything*. I've been a terrible sister. I hope you'll let me make it up to you."

My throat tightened as emotion welled up. "I mean, I didn't invite you to my wedding, so you're not the only one who's been terrible."

"Do not," she said with a warning in her voice, "try to make me feel better, Tessa Jane. We both know I was just plain awful, and I'm ashamed of myself. I don't know what I was thinking."

"You were trying to please your mama in hopes that she'd stick around for a change," I said, my voice thick. "We're all guilty of doing ridiculous things for the people we love. Take me, for example. I once dyed my hair red because Carson asked me to. He said he liked redheads best of all. It took eight hours at the salon to fix that mess."

"You're doing it again. Trying to make me feel better."

"I can't help it."

"I know. Also, Carson's an idiot."

I laughed.

She spared me another glance. "Do you miss him?"

I scratched my forearm as a hive formed, red and stinging. "I don't know how I feel about him now that I'm out of the furious phase. Mostly I feel . . . a little lost." It was the most honest I'd been with anyone since the breakup, and my heart rate had kicked up a notch at the confession.

"But," I added, "I think being here in Starlight has been helping me find my way. Life has been looking a little bit brighter lately."

She nodded. "I can see a difference. You're starting to glow again. But I'm not sure it has anything to do with Starlight. I think there's another reason."

My breath had caught that she'd noticed my glow. Or lack of one. I hadn't thought it would be that noticeable. "What's that?"

"I think it's Hambone. You've fallen in love again." Hambone heard his name and started baying, then stuck his head into the front seat.

Laughing, I rubbed his ears. "I think you're right."

We turned down the county road Ty lived on, and Addie said, "But there is something special about Aunt Bean's farmhouse. About Aunt Bean, really."

"She feels like home."

Addie glanced at me and nodded. "That's it exactly."

This was the perfect opportunity to talk about Aunt Bean's health—something we'd mostly been avoiding. But I couldn't bring myself to do it, so I stuffed my emotions down. In turn, another hive popped up.

I thought Addie might be thinking along the same lines because I saw moisture welling in her eyes. We drove the rest of the way to Ty Underwood's house in silence.

The car slowed as she turned in to his drive, inched really. A moment later she rolled to a stop behind his truck, put the car in park, then set the parking brake as well.

I wanted to poke fun, but I wouldn't. Couldn't. I suspected I knew why she was always so careful—because our daddy hadn't been. He'd been riding his bike to work, too fast as usual, when he hit a rock in the road and flew over the handlebars. He hadn't been wearing a helmet, and we'd lost him forever.

"Do you want to carry the cookies or take Hambone?" Addie asked.

"Hambone," I managed to say as grief gathered steam, making my heart race, my face flush. I tucked away thoughts of my father, handed her the basket of cookies, and all but flung open the door to get some fresh air. It was a warm afternoon, low sixties, and I inhaled deeply before calling out a hello to Ernie, who sat in a rocking chair on the covered porch of a small country cottage.

Hambone must've realized where we were because suddenly he was racing back and forth along the back seat and howling loud enough for the whole world to hear. It took me three tries to get his leash secured. And when I did, he nearly pulled my arm from its socket in his race to see Ernie. I barely had time to close the car door behind us.

I stumbled along as he pretty much dragged me up the front steps just as Ty came out the front door carrying a pitcher of sweet tea and a stack of colorful cups. His grin at my predicament made me glad I'd locked him in that closet all those years ago. He wouldn't be getting an apology out of me any time soon.

"How y'all doing?" he said to Addie and me, humor in his eyes.

Addie said something I didn't hear as I used all my strength to keep Hambone from jumping all willy-nilly onto Ernie's lap. But much to my surprise, he didn't resist my pull and approached her tentatively. Once he was at her side, he pretty much fell against her, pressing his head into her chest. Crying, he bathed her chin in sloppy kisses. His tail thrashed as he wiggled and jiggled.

I'd never seen a dog so happy.

Ernie beamed at him, cooing and laughing and kissing his head. I would've liked to say she looked good, better than expected, but honestly, she looked like she'd been put through the wringer. She seemed to have shrunk since I'd last seen her, despite wearing layers of clothes. Her head was hidden under a bandana. Her cheeks were sunken, her lips pale. Dark circles colored the skin beneath her eyes. The tops of both hands were bruised.

Addie and I stood off to the side, waiting our turns to show Ernie some love, when she finally laughed and shouted, "Sit, girls, sit! This might take all day."

Four rockers had been arranged in a loose square pattern on the porch. Ty had put the drinks on a side table and seemed to be waiting on us to sit down before he sat as well. I was dismayed to realize he planned to stay.

Once we all sat, Ty held up the pitcher. "Sweet tea?"

Addie and I said, "Yes, please," at the same time, sounding so alike that I was taken aback for a moment.

It was going to take a hot minute before I got used to the sister thing.

After much shushing and soothing, Hambone finally quieted, but he didn't peel himself off Ernie. Just kept leaning against her, his tail whacking the floor.

As Ty passed around cups of tea, Ernie waggled penciled eyebrows at the basket full of cookies, each individually packaged and tied with gingham bow. "Are those there what I think they are?"

Addie lifted one of the cookies and showed it off, making sure to point out that I'd hand-painted Hambone's likeness. "Aren't they the prettiest cookies you ever did see?"

Ernie nodded. "Sure are. Hambone never looked so good."

At the sound of his name, his tail started thumping even harder.

"Almost too pretty to eat," Ty said.

I about got whiplash looking at him. Was that a compliment?

He was watching me, an eyebrow raised. In the shade of the porch, his eyes looked like warm chocolate. His normally disheveled hair was damp and brushed back off his face, where it curled against his neck.

Ernie laughed. "Well, I still plan to gobble it right up. I've been dreaming of those cookies." She held out her palm for Addie to pass one over. "I can't quite match the recipe, that perfect mix of butter and vanilla and bliss."

"I'm happy to share the recipe," I offered.

"I reckon they still won't taste the same," she said, wasting no time unwrapping the cookie. "I've tried to make Bean's cakes a hundred times. They never taste like hers."

I wanted to say, "Me, too!" but only smiled.

Ernie took a bite of the cookie, closed her eyes, and smiled. "Good lord in heaven, child. You've got to start selling these. Y'all have one, too," she graciously offered to us.

Ty was reaching out when I said, "No, no. They're for *you*, Miss Ernie."

He snatched his hand back, picked up his glass of tea, and looked off to the side, pretending interest in birds at a nearby feeder.

For the next half hour, we rocked and talked about the snow and Bean's flower delivery, because it was rare that Addie and I had gossip to share before anyone else heard it. Ty was a perfect gentleman the whole time, nary an eye roll to be seen or an under-the-breath comment to be heard. Hambone's eyes grew heavy and he finally pulled his head off Ernie's lap and put it on her feet instead to take a quick nap.

The breeze blew gently, rustling branches on the evergreens. Soon, crocuses and snowdrops and bluebells would be popping up left and right, declaring springtime, even though the calendar still said winter.

I was being extra chatty, carrying the conversation, not only because Addie was naturally quiet, but because I wanted desperately to make a good impression. I tried telling myself that I was going above and beyond simply out of friendship and support, but I hated lying to myself. I knew, deep down, I was trying to make sure they knew I was nothing like my grandfather. I shouldn't have to try so hard—it should be evident simply from being around me, but I knew it wasn't that easy. Not when pain was involved. Grief.

Ty's father, Clark, had once worked for my grandparents as a bookkeeper. He'd had full access to all their accounts and was the one in charge of paying their bills and also filing their taxes. One year, way back when, the IRS came calling saying there had been irregularities with the taxes. And when my grandmother hired an outside firm for an audit, it was discovered that thousands of dollars had gone missing from one of the household accounts every month *for years*. Clark was fired. Then arrested for skimming the books. Then sentenced to five years in prison on an assortment of charges. It was only after he was in prison a year that he started telling people that it was my grandfather who'd done the skimming. According to Clark, he'd been promised to be paid handsomely to keep his mouth shut and take the fall—except my grandfather never paid up. Although my grandfather denied everything, he did so with an arrogant, *prove-it* grin. Not long afterward, Clark came down with pneumonia and didn't seek proper care until it was too late. Ty had been just a young boy when his daddy died.

I recognized that Clark wasn't completely innocent in what all had happened, but it was hard to deny my grandfather's utter maliciousness and lack of human decency. Years later, my mama told me that not long after Clark had passed, my grandmother had money secretly transferred into Ernie's bank account, with a vague note about it being a settlement from the prison for its irresponsible care. I had the feeling Ernie knew exactly where that money had come from. I had mixed feelings about what Gigi had done. Mostly because I knew money couldn't change what had happened. That it would never bring Clark back to his family.

After Ernie yawned for the third time in a row, Addie and I shared a glance and she stood up. "We should get going. Aunt Bean has plans for us to visit the starlight field tonight, and there are lots of cakes to bake before then."

"The starlight is always something to see," Ernie said. "I wish I could go with you, but I'm not quite up for field trips yet. Maybe soon."

I didn't dare look at Ty as I thought about the tears I'd seen in his eyes not too long ago at the starlight field. I focused on Miss Ernie instead. "When you're ready, just holler," I said, standing. "We'll make a night of it."

"Ty, honey," Ernie said, "grab that bag of dog food, will you, hon?"

"Yes ma'am," Ty said, brushing past as he headed into the house.

Ernie rubbed the dog's ears. "It's Hambone's favorite kind, not that he looks like he's gone hungry. Thank you for taking such good care of him."

"It's our pleasure," I said. "Truly."

Addie said, "Please let us know if there's anything else you need. We're happy to help out where we can."

Ernie stood but used one hand to hold on to the high back of the rocker to steady herself as she wobbled a bit. "Now that you mention it, there is one thing I'd like. Y'all know Luna, right?"

"Of course," I said, pretending not to notice how Addie bristled.

"She's been helping me tidy up my house a few days a week since my diagnosis. At first she wouldn't accept any money for the assistance, but when she mentioned she was saving up for a concert she wants to see next summer in Nashville, I insisted on giving her some cash to help pad the fund. Since I won't be home for a while, I'm hoping y'all could throw a small job her way, a couple days a week? Maybe walk the dogs? Or sweep the barn? Do some dishes? *Something?* It sure would set my mind at ease, knowing I wasn't the one who crushed her dream of seeing Taylor Swift."

I smiled and said, "We'll run it by Aunt Bean and let you know."

"Appreciate it."

We'd just finished giving her gentle hugs when Ty came back out of the house, carrying a big bag of dry food, and I held my hands out to take it.

"It's heavy," he said. "I've got it."

My chin jutted. "I've been lifting fifty-pound sacks of flour for years. I can take it."

I expected him to argue, but he simply lifted an eyebrow and handed over the bag. I sagged a bit against the sudden weight. Addie smiled, most likely knowing why I was being stubborn, and I rolled my eyes. She used her key fob to open the trunk of the car.

"I've got something else," Ty said. "Be right back."

Miss Ernie had a smile on her face as I staggered down the steps to the car and dumped the bag of food in the trunk. Addie tried to get Hambone to go with her, but he stayed rooted at Ernie's side. I walked back to the steps and tried to coax him down as well, but no luck.

Ty came out of the house carrying a laundry basket that looked to have a few towels in it. *That* got Hambone's attention. He started baying.

"Oh lawd," Ernie said. "Here we go."

When Ty headed for the car, Hambone eagerly followed. "Might want to run ahead and get that back door open," he said to Addie.

She sprang into action. When she opened one of the back doors, Ty made like he was going to climb in, and Hambone jumped on the back seat, cutting him off. Ty drew back and

Addie quickly closed the door, trapping the dog inside. She then hopped in the front seat, turned the car on, and put the windows halfway down. Hambone immediately stuck his head out of the opening and barked to let us know he was displeased with being tricked.

I was impressed with Ty's ingenuity but my curiosity was eating at me. "What's in the basket?" It couldn't possibly just be towels.

He motioned with his head for me to come closer. There was a friendly light in his brown eyes I'd never seen before. It made my heart trip up a little. He set the basket on the ground, stuck his hands inside, and rooted around under a towel. When he pulled them back out, in his large palms he held two kittens, both of them pale gray with white patches and yellow-green eyes. My heart jumped out of my chest and flopped around on the ground.

"*Awwww*," Addie said, drawing the single sound out for several long seconds.

"Want to hold one?" he asked me.

I snapped to. I'd been so mesmerized by the way he used his thumbs to lovingly rub the kittens' heads that I'd barely heard what he'd said. I didn't even say yes. Simply reached out and took the smaller of the two kittens, my hand brushing Ty's as I lifted the kitten to my chest. She felt like she was all fluff and no bones, but her tiny claws were sharp as she latched onto my shirt.

Addie jumped out of the car, her hands out as well, as if being pulled by some supernatural force. Kitten magic, pure and simple. Ty smiled as he gently handed over the other kitten.

He grinned. "They're ten weeks old now and the last of the litter. My hands are real full at the moment, so I don't suppose you'd want to foster them until I find them a home? Seems fitting to me, sisters looking after sisters," he added, his voice sugar sweet yet somehow absolutely genuine at the same time.

I cradled the kitten close and let Hambone sniff her so he'd stop making so much dang noise. He slurped at the kitten's face, and the kitten mewed and leaned toward him as if she didn't mind the attention one bit. I looked up at Ty, at his shiny eyes, his self-satisfied smile, and realized he'd known exactly what he was doing by bringing these kittens out here, and it *hadn't* been to lure Hambone to the car.

I couldn't say I hadn't been warned by Aunt Bean, who was surely going to be amused by this turn of events.

I glanced at Addie, who nodded, then met his warm gaze. "We'll do it. We'll foster."

And from the porch, Miss Ernie laughed and laughed.

CHAPTER THIRTEEN

From the Kitchen of Verbena Fullbright

In my kitchen, if I'm using a toothpick to test a cake for done-ness, I want to see a few moist crumbs clinging to it. A dry, clean toothpick means the cake is overdone. There's a fine line between being too early and too late, but all it takes is a little practice to find the sweet spot.

Addie

"May I offer you a seat?"

I startled at the sound of the voice so close to my ear. At the way my body reacted to it, even after all these years. *Sawyer.* I pulled myself together and faced him.

He had two camp chairs slung over his shoulder, and before I could even tell him yes or no, he took one out of its fabric sleeve and set it to rights on the patch of grass that served as a scenic overlook for the starlight field.

It was fully dark and the starlight above was putting on a show tonight, twinkling like a million diamonds in the sky. But the starlight below was even more mesmerizing. The aurora glowed full-force tonight, the blue, gold, green, and silver swaying in a slow, captivating rhythm.

Somewhere in the light was Aunt Bean and Tessa Jane. I'd lost sight of them shortly after they stepped onto the starwalk, but I could easily picture Aunt Bean's smile as she soaked in the beauty around her.

"Thanks," I said to him, not too proud to accept the seat. I was likely going to be here awhile longer.

When Sawyer had approached, I'd been standing, my arms crossed tight, my backside soaked because I'd underestimated how the moisture, left over from the snow, would leach through the blanket I'd brought to sit on.

Behind me, solar path lights illuminated the perimeter of the parking lot, which was near to full. Watching over the crowds that visited the site was the work of four attendants. Throughout the night they manned the parking lot, guided people along starwalk, and regaled tourists with the story of the fallen star.

Before me, colorful waves of light shimmered. I'd seen this starlight hundreds of times. Thousands, even. Yet it was still as wondrous as the first time I'd laid eyes on it. There was something about it that filled the heart, the soul. Something soothing, peaceful.

It was hard to believe that its clarity could ever lead someone astray.

But I knew it had.

Sawyer set up the other chair next to mine, keeping a good foot between us, and sat, stretching his legs out.

Under any other circumstances, his nearness would've sent my stress levels through the roof, but I was full of starlight- and kitten-induced endorphins. Truly, if kitten therapy wasn't a thing, it should be. I'd named the kitten I was caring for Stella, and I was already in love.

It had taken approximately two minutes before deciding to adopt her, but common sense kicked in soon after. Kittens were a big commitment, and I needed to be sure, absolutely sure, before jumping in. Especially since I'd never had a pet of my own before.

I looked to my left, toward Bean's farmhouse. Warm light glowed in the windows, cozy and inviting. Since Henrietta had been to see the starlight recently, she had volunteered to stay behind to keep an eye on all the animals. And again, I wondered if she was giving me space to get used to her presence. Which I appreciated. The weekend had been overwhelming to say the least.

Eventually, my gaze wandered to Sawyer's cabin, only a short distance from the farmhouse, along the tree line. I could see only the porch light on.

"Is Luna here?" I asked, suddenly worried she was going to pop out of the starlight and bombard me with questions about Ree.

"She has play practice until eight." He checked his watch. "She has a ride home, but I'll need to leave soon to meet her at the cabin."

Because it was impossible not to notice how handsome he looked in the glow of the starlight, I forced myself to glance away. "You're not working, are you?"

It didn't seem like it. Plus, I didn't think he worked nights anymore.

He said, "The starlings raised a ruckus about an hour ago, so I drove over to investigate."

The starlings were the best security guards around, hands down.

"Did you find anything?"

"What I found was Bones Ryerson running for his life." He chuckled, and the laugh wrapped around me like a hug from an old friend. "The starlings had put a mighty scare into him. He all but jumped into my moving truck and bawled like a baby, telling me how he'd been looking for diamonds after hearing Winchester talking about them. I carried him home, told him next time I'd turn him in for trespassing. He won't be back. The starlings make quite an impression when they're protecting the land. All the same, I thought I'd stick around for a while just in case someone else came along with the same idea. Then I saw you."

I glanced at him, then quickly away. I zipped my coat up to my neck and tucked my chin into it. I told myself not to think about the sound of his voice when he'd said *then I saw you*. The warmth. The, *oh lord*, the tenderness.

"I came with Tessa Jane and Aunt Bean. They're in there somewhere."

A waist-high rope fence was strung around the edge of the crater—not because there was a steep drop-off but more to keep things orderly. The starwalk had one entrance and one exit and sat low to the ground, supported by cement piers instead of footings that would've had to have been drilled. Along the wooden walkway, rope guardrails prevented people from venturing into the crater. Most respected the rules. The ones that didn't were either escorted away by the attendants or the starlings. One was much more preferable than the other.

He smiled. "Knowing Miss Verbena, she'll be in there awhile."

The starwalk usually took only ten to fifteen minutes to complete start to finish. But with Aunt Bean's mobility issues these days, plus the way she dawdled when surrounded by the light, it would probably take her a half hour or so, maybe more, to walk end to end.

"At least it's a nice night," I said.

"That it is."

I wanted to say so much more. To ask about Luna. And him. And his family. But I didn't want to risk opening old wounds or letting Ree's secret slip.

Because the longer I sat here with him, the more tension built. I practiced my box breathing. He'd be leaving soon. It was fine. I was fine. I could keep a secret for a few more minutes.

"Heard you've got a couple of new furry family members," Sawyer finally said.

"We're just fostering."

He laughed.

The whole town probably knew by now how Ty had pulled a fast one on Tessa Jane and me. I grinned as I pictured the fluffy bundle of joy waiting for me at home as I said, "It's like Ty had Tessa Jane and me under a spell."

"I get it. He's why we have a teddy bear hamster named Melon."

"A *hamster*?"

He shook his head. "Long story."

I wanted to say I had time to hear it, but I didn't exactly want him to stay.

The silence yawned and stretched between us, growing loud and uncomfortable.

A few minutes had passed when he nodded toward the glowing aurora. "You didn't want to walk with Miss Verbena and Tessa Jane? No need for clarity of mind, of heart?" he asked as though he was one of the attendants and I was a tourist.

I was starting to regret accepting the seat. "You know how I've always felt about the starlight."

"I also know people change. I thought time might've given you another perspective on the starlight, other than your mama's."

Even though he spoke with no hint of judgment, I sensed there was more to the statement than he let on. Our conversation had veered into dangerous territory. I tugged my sleeves down over my hands.

I wanted to tell him it wasn't only my mama's perspective— that I'd learned the lesson for myself. Thanks to Ree.

In my head, I heard her telling me, "Luna is Ace's baby, Addie."

In a flash, I was back in the Coosa County hospital, sitting at her bedside. Luna was only an hour old and had been taken by nurses to the special care nursery for some extra suctioning of her tiny lungs. At that point in time, Ree and Ace had been officially broken up for almost a year, but I knew she'd had trouble staying away from him completely, even though he'd been a mess of drugs and anger. She finally quit him cold turkey right before senior homecoming and had enlisted Sawyer to take her to the dance as a ruse to keep Ace away.

After the dance, they kept up the pretend relationship.

But while that phony relationship might've protected Ree from Ace, it had broken something between Sawyer and me.

I couldn't bear seeing them together, even pretending, so I had distanced myself, only hanging out with them every once in a while instead of all the time. I threw myself into working at the bakery, into schoolwork, into anything that would help me ignore my broken heart.

Somewhere along the line, their sham of a relationship had become real, which came to light not long after Christmas that year when Ace had tragically overdosed. At his funeral, Ree had sobbed so hard, she'd made herself so sick she had to be carried off to the urgent care. That was where she found out she was expecting. Everyone assumed, even me, that it was Sawyer's baby.

Tears pooled in my eyes as I had said to her, "Does Sawyer know?"

"Don't go worrying about him." She then winced and rubbed her temples. She'd been fighting a headache since she went into labor. It had been a long, rough delivery. When she had asked me to be there for the birth, I'd been surprised, but I couldn't say no. I still loved her, even though it hurt to be around her and Sawyer.

"How can you say that, Ree? He's down the hall outside the nursery right this minute, proud as a peacock, telling people he's her daddy."

"He *is* her daddy. At least as far as I'm concerned. And as far as the starlight is, too."

"What do you mean, the starlight?"

"I did a starwalk when I found out I was carrying Luna. I had so many decisions, choices weighing on my heart. I came out of there knowing Sawyer was my answer. No matter what happens between us, he'll be good to her."

My voice cracked. "Why're you telling me this?"

It felt like she'd staked a claim on him, when one wasn't really needed. As much as it hurt, I'd already stepped aside, which was why I hadn't known she'd reconnected with Ace at some point.

"I just," she sniffled, "it's just that I was looking at her, all pink and beautiful with that headful of dark hair and adorable widow's peak, and I started thinking about Ace. I was overcome with a need for you to know who she is, who she came from, even if we don't ever talk about it again."

"But Ree, you know how hard it is for me to keep secrets."

She sat up and her eyes went wide as she grabbed my arm. "You cannot tell anyone, Addie! Nobody! We have to protect her from the Buckleys. I will *not* let them hurt my baby. She needs to be raised by people who will love her, cherish her. *This* is how we do it."

Tears ran down my face as I thought about what Ace had done to Ree. I didn't want his daddy or his younger brother to even *look* at that baby.

My throat was so tight with emotion that all I could do was nod.

I would keep this secret if it killed me.

Ree leaned back against the pillows. "It'll be Sawyer's name on her birth certificate, too. He's been so good ab—" The word broke off as she suddenly gasped for air. Her hands flew to her chest. Panic flared in her brown eyes. Alarms started blaring from the machinery at her bedside.

Within seconds the room flooded with nurses, then doctors. I'd been pushed into the hallway, out of the way as they fought to stabilize her, to save her life. Minutes turned to hours. Hours to days. Then she was gone, never having regained consciousness after suffering an amniotic fluid embolism.

A hand on my arm shook me out of my memories.

Sawyer said, "You okay there?"

My heart raced. The ethereal starlight blurred from the tears in my eyes. "Actually, no. Can you tell Aunt Bean and Tessa Jane I went home? I'm not feeling well."

With that, I stood and started jogging, then running, toward

the farmhouse, pretending not to hear Sawyer's voice as he
called after me.

✳

The next afternoon, as I hurried out of the big red barn, I said,
"I'll be back soon."

"Don't go getting lost," Delilah called after me, as if she
knew I didn't want to come back.

Tuesdays were a catch-up, catch-all kind of day that set the
tone for the whole week. And it seemed this week was destined
to be a hot mess.

Pinky's X-rays had revealed that her wrist was broken, so
she wouldn't be able to work for the next six weeks. One of
the refrigerators stopped cooling. A grounded electrical out-
let kept tripping. I'd dropped a jar of sprinkles on the floor,
scattering glass and a rainbow of color. Aunt Bean had taken
Ernie's wishes to heart and had asked Luna Gray if she might
be interested in sweeping up the barn kitchen every now and
again after school, and she'd jumped at the chance. She'd texted
Bean earlier that she had time today. Which meant she'd be
arriving soon.

And if all that wasn't enough, in a long conversation she'd
taken outside, Aunt Bean had spoken with her doctor about
the echocardiogram results. For all that talking, however,
when she came back in, she'd only said that he was calling her
in a new prescription and wanted her to have a cardiac MRI
before he gave an official diagnosis.

My stomach had knotted and hadn't eased up since. She
most definitely was not telling us everything. Probably so we
wouldn't worry. Which only worried me *more*.

By three thirty, I felt like I was about to suffocate. When I
heard the dogs barking in the backyard, I decided they were
the perfect excuse to get some fresh air. An added bonus would
be escaping before Luna arrived. A bright side.

She was expected to arrive at four, and I knew I couldn't
avoid her forever, but I hoped Bean would have her so busy

when I got back that she wouldn't have time to pepper me with questions about Ree.

I wasn't sure I could handle it emotionally. Everything I'd tamped down for the last twelve years was threatening to erupt like a volcano of grief, its lava a fiery flow of anguish and sorrow.

Last night was the first time I'd let myself fully re-live what had happened in the hospital with Ree, and it had left me shaken and vulnerable to memories I'd locked away long ago. Thoughts of her had been intruding all day, making my stomach ache, my chest tighten, my eyes fill with tears. It had been like working alongside a ghost who kept popping up and shouting, "Boo!" in my ear just to see me come undone.

Which she would find hilarious. She loved making a surprise appearance.

Hambone and Pepper trotted ahead of me as we walked through the woods. The Sassafras Creek was full, the water rushing along contentedly. Every so often I'd catch a glimpse of early blooming yarrow, which offered a cheerful flash of color as I led the dogs down a well-worn deer path toward the water, letting them splash and play for a few minutes before moving on. I hadn't set out with a destination in mind, but five minutes into the walk, I realized exactly where I was headed.

At a fork in the path, I steered the dogs down a short trail that led to a small cemetery, tucked into a sunny meadow bordered by a mountain laurel hedge. In a few months the evergreen shrubs would be covered in pink flowers, and I wondered if I would still be here in Starlight when they bloomed.

Today especially, I itched to go back to Birmingham, to my old, lonely life. There, it was easier, so much easier, to keep secrets buried.

But at the same time, the thought of leaving about tore me in two. I adored being here with Aunt Bean and Tessa Jane and the Sugarbirds. It felt like this was where I belonged. But I'd rather sacrifice my happiness than destroy Luna's and Sawyer's by blurting out the truth of her parentage.

The fallout of that situation would be devastating, as I imagined Luna being taken away from him, away from the only home she'd ever known. *I* hurt just thinking about it—I couldn't imagine what a separation would do to her. To him. And then there was Sawyer. He'd rearranged his whole life, abandoned all his dreams, to be her father. How would he react, knowing she wasn't his? Would he be mad at Ree? I couldn't bear the thought. Especially without Ree here to defend herself.

With a shake of my head, I banished the thoughts. I was thinking too hard about something that was not going to happen. Because I was keeping Ree's secret safe and sound.

I drew in a deep breath, held it, and slowly let it out as I walked along rows of headstones, toward one on the far side of the cemetery, thinking for the millionth time that Ree would hate that she was buried here.

I'd lost count of how many times she'd said, "I can't wait to get out of here, move to New York City, become a somebody."

In her bedroom in the doublewide she shared with her granny, she'd tacked pieces of cardboard to the wall to create as a vision board, adding new sections as her hopes and dreams expanded. Every time I visited, there were more pictures—usually ones ripped straight out of library magazines. Skyscrapers and fancy dresses and Broadway billboards. Expensive apartments, champagne flutes, limousines.

"You're already a somebody," I'd always say to her.

She'd laugh and jump to her feet, tossing her head back and throwing her arms wide as if embracing an audience. "No, somebody famous! Beloved by all."

After she'd died, I'd begged her granny to let me scatter Ree's ashes in New York City, sprinkling them here and there and everywhere I could. I'd wanted to take her where she most wanted to go—to make sure her dreams came true, even in a small, bittersweet way. But her brokenhearted granny had overridden my pleas, insisting Ree stay right here in Starlight near her, and I had no recourse but to accept the decision since I wasn't family and had no official say-so.

The dogs stretched their leashes to explore as I stepped up to her headstone, pulled in a deep breath. *Reeanna Finn Oakes.*

I ran my fingers over the word etched into the stone under her name, a request of mine her granny *had* allowed. *Beloved.*

Hambone wandered over to me, nudging my hand. I patted his silky head, trying to assure him that I was okay. "I just miss her," I told him.

I would've sworn there was understanding in his eyes, before his head came up suddenly and he stiffened. Pepper started barking happily, jumping around.

I turned and saw a young girl striding down the grassy aisle toward me. Luna.

I don't know why I'd expected her to get a ride to the big red barn. Of course she had walked—the distance was so short from her home, the path cutting straight through the cemetery. I could've kicked myself.

She wore cuffed jeans, a dark T-shirt with a white flower printed on it, an unbuttoned flannel shacket, and a giant smile.

Ree's smile.

My knees went a bit weak at the sight of it—sheer happiness at seeing a little of my friend once again.

"Howdy, Miss Addie!" Luna said cheerfully, making it clear she knew exactly who I was and saving me the misery of having to make proper introductions. Undoubtedly she'd seen the pictures of me that Bean had scattered around the farmhouse.

"Hi, Luna," I said, forcing a smile as my heart jackhammered in my chest.

Both Pepper and Hambone wiggled with happiness as she came near enough to pat them. She dropped to her knees and let the dogs slobber her face with kisses. "I've missed you, too!" she said to them, giving both their heads noisy kisses.

"You know Pepper?" I asked.

Luna looked at me, her blue eyes shining. "I've had to drag Hambone back from Dare's house a time or two for Miss Ernie. He likes Pepper. Hambone, I mean. Well, Dare does, too." She laughed, the sound as bright as the stars in the sky.

Ree's laugh.

I breathed deeply and fought tears all the while wanting to make Luna laugh again, simply so I could hear a sound I'd long forgotten. No, not forgotten. *Blocked.*

I started counting headstones. "That makes sense."

"I heard you rescued Pepper in the storm." Sun glinted off her braided raven hair, revealing a natural blueish undertone as she gently cupped the dog's face in her hands. She used a funny, singsong voice to say, "That must've been *sooooo* scary for you."

Pepper's tail couldn't possibly wag any harder.

And I couldn't hold back a smile.

Luna also had Ree's big personality.

"And Dare, too, probably," she added. "He loves Pepper more than anything. Well, maybe not more than Petal." She wrinkled her nose as if giving the statement more thought, then shrugged her slim shoulders and stood up. "I went by Miss Verbena's house to see you the other day."

I feigned surprise as my pulse pounded in my ears. "Oh really?"

"But you weren't home."

I brushed a bug off my sleeve. "It's been a busy week."

"I never thought to look for you here. Were you visiting Mom?"

My throat was so tight I couldn't get a word out, so I nodded.

"I do that sometimes, too. Are you going back to Miss Verbena's now? I can walk with you."

I tried to think of a way to get out of it, but she had such hope in her eyes, I couldn't bring myself to let her down. I nodded again.

She held out her hand. "I can take one of the leashes."

I gave her Hambone's and we started back toward the woods, the dogs leading the way.

"Hey, Miss Addie, can I ask you something?"

I clutched my star necklace. "Sure," I squeaked.

"Can you do the Poppy Kay voice for me? I just love it. You're so great in that show. Did Miss Verbena tell you I want to be an actress one day?" She skipped every few steps as she walked, like her energy couldn't be held back any longer. "Did you know I'm in a play? I'm Frog in *Alice in Wonderland*." She *ribbitted*. "It's not a big part, but that's okay. Oh! I heard you got a kitten from Mister Ty. Can I hold it later on, after I'm done helping Miss Verbena? And oh! Did you know . . ."

We walked through the woods toward the barn, the sound of the creek a backdrop to Luna's steady voice. I'd been so nervous about being able to hide the truth around her. Now I started to wonder if I'd been worried for nothing. Because it seemed Luna was perfectly happy to be the one doing all the talking.

CHAPTER FOURTEEN

From the Kitchen of Verbena Fullbright

If you want a good rise and even layers on your cake, be sure to preheat the oven at least half an hour before baking. And don't even dare think about opening that oven door while the cake is baking. Nothing will sink a cake faster than fluctuating temperatures. All good things are worth the wait.

Tessa Jane

"Good heavens," my mama exclaimed, flipping the sign on the barn's take-out window to CLOSED early Saturday afternoon. Our last customer had just driven off, a Strawberry Stardust cake and a dozen cupcakes safely secured in the passenger seat. "I'm worn out."

With all three of the Sugarbirds off work—Delilah had come down with a stomach bug on Wednesday—my mama had volunteered to help with the shop, and ended up shocking us all with how seamlessly she'd eased into working retail.

"Now you know why we take Sunday and Monday off. To recover." Aunt Bean smiled as she parked herself on a stool to reconcile the cash register.

Mama laughed and pressed her hands to her lower back as if it ached. "Makes perfect sense now."

Out the window, I saw Addie walking down the long driveway headed toward the street, carrying the SORRY, SOLD OUT sandwich board, moseying along. I didn't blame her for taking her sweet time. It had been a long week.

I wasn't sure I'd ever worked harder, which was saying

something, since I was used to working twelve-hour shifts for days on end. All I wanted to do for the next two days was put my feet up and play with kittens.

But unfortunately I wouldn't have much time to relax. Tomorrow and Monday, I'd be baking and decorating cookies. Another dozen for Miss Ernie, but also a paying order from Pinky for her granddaughter's first birthday party, done in wild animal designs. Giraffes, elephants, monkeys, lions. I was excited to get started, already imagining what the finished cookies would look like.

"You keep working as hard as you did today, Henrie," Aunt Bean said, "and I'm going to have to make you an official Sugarbird."

Mama had been all smiles today, effortlessly upselling the cupcakes at the take-out window like she'd been doing it all her life. She grinned. "After the fun I had today, I might be tempted to take that offer. Tell me what else needs to be done. Are there cakes to bake?"

Aunt Bean shook her head. "Not tonight. All we need to do is clean up and restock. But don't you need to get going?"

She had a meeting with Graham Doby—the reporter writing an article about my granddaddy.

I didn't want her to go. After meeting with Mr. Stubblefield earlier this week, she was in the frame of mind to throw Granddaddy under the proverbial bus.

Although Mr. Stubblefield promised to go over the trust with a fine-tooth comb to look for loopholes, he informed Mama that because Gigi hadn't put her wishes about the stipends into writing, there wasn't likely anything that could be done. As it was, Granddaddy had full discretion over the funds—to give and revoke as he saw fit.

At the news I felt terribly for Mama, who would've made good use of the money, but I felt even worse for Gigi and her misplaced faith in Granddaddy. She'd had such high hopes that the inheritance would bring out the good in him. Instead it had brought out the worst.

Mama looked at her watch. "I suppose I should go freshen up, though I'm thinking of trading out my regular perfume for vanilla extract. The scent is divine."

"Aunt Bean makes it herself," I said, reminding her. "With bourbon instead of vodka."

"Don't go sounding like it's a big deal," Aunt Bean said. "It's easy as pie. Just takes time. The longer the beans steep, the better the flavor."

I started clearing the workbenches. "Don't let her downplay it. I'm convinced there's a secret ingredient. Unicorn tears, maybe."

Aunt Bean edged off the stool, and while leaning heavily on her walking stick she made her way to the dark corner where she stored the extract on deep shelving, out of the sunlight. I watched her, worried that she seemed to be moving slower and slower these days.

Bean pulled an amber bottle down from the shelf, checked the date on its tag, and carried it over to my mama. In a loud whisper, she said, "They're dragon's tears. Don't tell anyone."

I could only shake my head and smile.

Mama accepted the bottle, hugging it to her chest. "This is the nicest gift I've received in quite some time. Thank you."

She gave Aunt Bean a kiss on her cheek, then kissed mine as well. "I'll see y'all later."

Not a minute after she left, the door swung open again and Addie stuck her head inside. "Ty Underwood's on his way up the driveway, a load of lumber hanging off the bed of his truck. I'm going to put up the dogs and watch the ducks so they don't get loose while he gets set up."

With that, she was gone again.

"I plumb forgot Ty was coming by to work on the quack shack." Aunt Bean tapped her walking stick two times as she glanced around. "Let's break for lunch and finish up here later. I'm near to famished and the mess will keep."

With a good bit of surprise, I realized I wasn't dreading Ty's visit. I'd come a long way since that day at the Market Street bakery, nearly two weeks ago.

In fact, I was seeing a lot of things with a little more clarity, a little more light, since then. What had happened with Carson, while still painful, was beginning to feel like a blessing in disguise. Addie and I had formed a tenuous friendship. I was starting to wonder if I *could* make a living as a cookie artist. And there was hope that mine and Addie's inheritance could be used to help the Starling Society. Being here in Starlight was doing exactly what I wished for—leading me out of the darkness.

I smiled at Aunt Bean. "Sounds good to me."

Tipping her head, she studied me as if sensing a shift, then grinned with a devilish glint in her eyes. "It's such a nice day, we should eat outside. I'll ask Ty to join us. Come along, peanut."

I narrowed my gaze at her retreating back as she speedily headed for the door. It didn't escape my notice that she could rush when she wanted to. Like when she knew I was going to accuse of her something. Like matchmaking.

Ty and me? It was laughable.

But suddenly, I didn't find it so funny.

I didn't take the time to dissect why as I followed her.

Ty's truck was backed up to the gate, and a gentle breeze blew as Aunt Bean veered off toward the backyard. I headed for the front porch, finding utter chaos when I opened the door to the house. The dogs were in the kitchen, on hind legs at the back door, tails wagging, barking up a storm as they watched Ty in the backyard. My mama was sitting on the bottom step of the staircase, holding an angry, writhing duck—Ethel—while Addie chased Lucy around the living room. Miney and Moe were on the back of the couch, their ears flattened, their backs arched. The kittens, thank goodness, were safe in a pet playpen in the corner of the room, sleeping through the commotion.

"The ducks followed the dogs straight into the house," Addie said loudly, to be heard over the barking and quacking.

Mama's eyes were wide with panic as she stood and thrust Ethel at me, then stared at her hands with something akin to horror. "I'm late! Bye!"

The door slammed behind her as she ran out of the house faster than I'd ever seen her move before in my life.

"Aha!" Addie said, scooping Lucy into her arms, being careful of her wings. "Gotcha!" Lucy pecked her arm. "Hey, that's not nice!"

Aunt Bean stepped up to the back door, took in the mayhem with a widening gaze, then turned right around again.

Addie and I looked at each other, then started laughing as we struggled to hold on to the ducks. Finally, I motioned for her to follow me to the powder room, where we turned the ducks loose. When Ty finished unloading, we'd take them back outside.

Once we washed up, Addie started pulling sandwich fixins from the fridge, which redirected the dogs' attention, pulling them away from the back door. They stopped their barking and started licking their lips as they followed her around the kitchen. I patted Miney and Moe then checked on the kittens. My little one was peering up at me. She mewed and I picked her up, holding her to my chest. She pushed herself against my body and started rubbing her cheek against my shirt. She was a cuddler, whereas Addie's kitty seemed to be more of a climber.

I saw Aunt Bean peek through the back door again to see if the coast was clear before coming inside. Ty followed her, practically filling the whole doorway. His gaze landed on me, and he gave me a nod of greeting before turning his attention to the dogs who'd veered off from Addie long enough to get pats.

Bean headed for the powder room. "I'm going to freshen u—"

"No!" Addie and I shouted.

"The ducks are in there," Addie added. "You'll have to go upstairs."

Bean laughed as she climbed the steps. "Lordy mercy. It's been a day. The gate's closed so you can let them out now."

"I'll get them," I volunteered.

Ty stepped forward. "I can help."

I was happy to note I had no compulsion to argue that I could do it on my own. Then over Ty's shoulder, I saw Addie waggle her eyebrows and felt my arms itching as hives formed.

"But first, may I?" Ty asked, and it took me a second to realize he was gesturing to the kitten.

I handed her over, and our hands tangled up for a moment. I told myself I felt nothing in the touch. Certainly no skin-tingling sparks.

He held her against his broad chest as he walked her back to the playpen. "What's her name?"

"I haven't given her one yet. I'm having trouble coming up with one that fits." I scratched my arm and watched carefully how gently he rubbed under her chin. "She's just such a love bug I want the name to be perfect."

He carefully lowered her into the playpen, then pushed a crinkle ball in front of her. She batted it and he said, "Seems to me Lovebug *is* the perfect name. You can call her Bug for short, and then you'll always think of me. You know, if you end up keeping her." He straightened and gave me a grin, a full thousand-watt smile. His eyes twinkled.

As my heart jumped around, I mustered up my best scowl. "That name doesn't fit her at all."

"You'll come around," he said, walking toward the powder room, his laughter trailing playfully behind him.

And for some reason, in that moment, I believed him.

✳

"So, you and Ty?" Addie said later on as she dragged a box across the attic floor. "Is it my imagination, or is something there?"

It was late afternoon, and sunlight spilled in from two small square windows, one set into the gable at the front of the house, and a matching one at the back.

Our luck had run out when it came to avoiding Aunt Bean's big inventory plans.

Addie and I had been in the attic for an hour and had barely made a dent in sorting—and we definitely hadn't discussed the *itemization* of it all. I could hardly allow myself to think about Aunt Bean's estate planning. And why she was adamant about completing it as soon as possible.

I thought about dodging Addie's question, but decided to answer as honestly as I could. "I don't know what's happening. I thought he didn't like me."

I used Aunt Bean's iPad to snap a photo of a plate with a cabbage rose pattern, then wrapped it back up and tucked it back into its box. I added a short description to the inventory spreadsheet she'd created just for this purpose.

Addie sat on her haunches, pulled open a box, and looked inside. "I suspect Aunt Bean's talk with Ty made him take a hard look in the mirror. He obviously didn't like what he saw."

"Maybe so," I said, thinking the starlight might've played a role as well. "I'd be happy if we could be friends."

I counted it a bright side that I had healed enough to even be open to the possibility.

"Only friends?" she asked, eyebrow raised.

In my mind, I kept seeing that twinkle in his eyes. But then, I recalled all the times he'd been rude. "I think it's best that way. The change in him was so abrupt I don't quite trust it."

"I get that. But sometimes we catch a glimpse of ourselves through someone else's eyes and it's a bit of a rude awakening. It creates a great big need to do everything possible to make up for any terrible, no-good behavior." She sat, pulling her knees to her chest. "It's a snap-to kind of moment. Shape up or ship out. Turn over a new leaf. Make a fresh start."

For each of the last three sentences, she'd used a different voice, varying from high and playful to low and droll, and I smiled so wide my cheeks hurt. Her talent was truly extraordinary. And I was thrilled she was finally talking more, speaking in whole paragraphs instead of single sentences.

She laughed. "My brain is too tired to think of any other idioms that fit."

"It's been a long week."

"The longest."

As I studied her, all curled into herself, tucked up protectively, I suddenly noted that despite her laughter, she was uncomfortable with the conversation. With a start, I realized it wasn't just Ty she'd been talking about taking a hard look in the mirror.

She was also talking about *herself.*

She was all but confessing what had happened with her, with *us,* even though she'd already apologized. She was laying her heart bare, opening up like this.

Wait. Was that why she'd used the voices? To lighten the conversation, steering us away from the dark and back into the light?

"What?" she asked, tipping her head. "Do I have cobwebs in my hair?"

I stared as if seeing her for the first time, seeing the *real* her.

How long had she been doing it? Using this coping mechanism? I tried to remember when she'd first started doing impressions. Or giving her toys their own voices—creating characters. Or mimicking sounds to change the mood in a room, like the time Aunt Bean had burned dinner and was working herself into a fine tizzy. Addie, about twelve or thirteen at that point, had started whooping like some sort of air-raid siren, a dead-on imitation. The sound had dissolved the tension instantly.

She'd dissolved the tension.

Looking back, I realized she'd been using her voice as a distraction for as long as I could remember. She'd been avoiding heavy feelings, distancing emotion—especially negative emotions—since she was a tiny girl.

And as soon as I recognized it, my heart broke for her. Her

mama had walked out. Our daddy died. She'd lost her best friend. Of course she wanted, *needed*, a distraction from the pain.

I longed to hug her, and just about laughed with happiness at the thought, because it was something the *old* me would want to do.

Her hands flew over her hair, over the tight bun. "Seriously, Tessa Jane, are there cobwebs?"

"No, you're good. I just got lost in a memory for a second."

"Thank goodness. Spiders. Ugh." She shuddered as if shaking off invisible bugs and pulled another box over to her. As she looked inside, she said, "Oh."

At her sad tone, I peeked in the box. It was full of old albums. Our father's collection. He'd been a big fan of seventies and eighties rock—the music of his childhood. And because of his love of it, it then became the music of our childhoods.

I said, "I can hardly listen to Bob Dylan without tearing up."

"I once heard a Bruce Springsteen song in the grocery store and about fell to pieces. I had to abandon my buggy and make a run for it."

The album covers were worn, torn. The records had been well used and well loved. "He'd hate that these were up here, packed away."

Her green eyes were wet. "I'm not sure I can listen to them."

"Me either."

Grief was timeless. Limitless. Endless.

"Let's bring them downstairs at least," I said. "Baby steps."

She nodded.

I glanced around, wondering if any more of his belongings were up here. If so, I wasn't sure, emotionally, I could handle coming across them tonight. "I vote we call it a day, order in dinner, play with some kittens, and watch a movie with Aunt Bean."

"Seconded."

We quickly put the boxes we'd sorted in order, double-checked the spreadsheet, and stood up, stretching out the kinks and knots.

As we walked toward the stairs, above us came a series of thumps and loud scratching noises.

The starlings had landed on the rooftop.

Addie lowered her voice as if they could hear us and said, "I've never seen them hang around this long so close to the house."

"Me either."

We stood still for a moment, listening as the starlings shuffled about.

Addie shuddered again and started down the narrow staircase, the box of albums in hand. I followed, but at the top of the steps, I glanced over my shoulder when I heard the starlings cry out. There was a great rustling as they flew off, and I walked over to the square window that overlooked the backyard to see what had raised the alarm.

The starlings, silvery-black dots in the dusky sky, were headed toward the starlight crater—where I saw a light glittering in the distance, near the edge of the grassy bowl.

I squinted, trying to see better. The light, a pinpoint really, twinkled in the twilight.

> *'tis a spark*
> *a twinkle*
> *at daybreak*
> *at first dark*
> *a wink*
> *a blink*

"What was that about? Is anything out there?" Addie asked from the stairs.

"I'm not sure," I said, not mentioning the light.

And how it sparkled just like a diamond.

CHAPTER FIFTEEN

From the Kitchen of Verbena Fullbright
When making cupcakes, I use an ice cream scoop to make
quick work of filling the tins. It ensures each cupcake will
be the same size so they bake evenly. In a busy kitchen, it's
best to work smarter, not harder. That way there's still time
to dance.

Addie

"Good morning, punkin!" Aunt Bean said, waving me into the
kitchen in the big red barn.

It was a cool Monday morning filled with early light and
cheerful birdsong. I'd been surprised to find her here when I
opened the door, thinking she was still tucked into bed, getting some much-needed rest. The farmhouse had been quiet
when I crept down the stairs, trying not to stir the dogs, who
were sleeping with Tessa Jane.

Here in the barn, music blared from the record player, and
as the Bee Gees sang a disco ballad about emotion taking
over, being tied up in sorrow, Aunt Bean danced over to me,
leaving her walking stick leaning against the counter. "Come
on in, come dance with me."

She reached out, and I didn't hesitate to place my hand in
hers. I held on tightly and twirled her slowly. She laughed, the
sound lifting my spirits like nothing else. Smiling like fools,
we danced, lost in the moment, lost in the melody of the song,
lost in memories of when we used to do this kind of thing all
the time.

She was already dressed for the day, and I wasn't sure how I hadn't heard her moving about in the early hours, since I hadn't slept much at all. A long, flowy dress patterned in a design that reminded me of stained glass swirled around her ankles. White tennis shoes completed the outfit—her usual work footwear. Her burgundy hair was styled about as high as it could be, reminding me this morning of the cartoon character Jimmy Neutron. She wore a full face of makeup, including deep red lipstick.

As the song ended, she sashayed toward the record player, to lower the volume. "I sure am glad you came by when you did. Dancing is always better with two."

How a song about heartbreak could fill me with happiness was beyond me, but Aunt Bean had made it happen.

She gave me a good once-over as she headed back to a workbench. "What're you doing up and about so early?"

On the stainless steel surface was a stand mixer, two sticks of softened butter, three eggs, flour, sugar, oil, buttermilk, baking powder, salt, and a bottle of vanilla extract. Just enough ingredients for a single cake.

"I came to work on my studio." I planned to hang the acoustic tiles so I could record tonight.

"I hope you weren't planning to record."

"Why?" I asked warily as I sat on a stool.

Her hair flopped a bit as she sighed. "The electricity is on the fritz again—quite a few of the outlets aren't working. I've already texted Sawyer. If it isn't fixed by tomorrow, it's going to be another hellacious week, and we don't be needing that, do we?"

No. No, we didn't.

We also didn't need the barn burning down, so I was glad she called to have it checked.

She glanced at her watch. "He'll be here as soon as Luna's off to school."

At least I didn't have to worry about Luna tagging along with him. Not that I didn't enjoy her company. I did—she was funny and sassy and a ball of energy. But with her around I was always on edge, trying to keep Ree's secret while fielding questions like, "Did my mom like cake?" "Did my mom ever work at the bakery?" "Did my mom stop liking the Bee Gees after listening to them *all the time* when she was working?"

They were easy questions to answer. Yes, yes, and actually, once Aunt Bean showed Ree an online image of Andy Gibb, she'd hung a picture of him on her vision board.

So far, Luna's questions had led only to fond memories being pulled out, dusted off. On her first day of helping in the barn, Delilah had been more than happy to talk about the time, early in my Audrey Hepburn phase, that Pinky had caught Ree and me behind the bakery sneaking a cigarette. In effort to help me replicate Audrey's classic look in *Breakfast at Tiffany's*, Ree had fashioned a two-foot-long twig into a cigarette holder, but unfortunately, as neither of us were smokers, we'd ended up having coughing fits—which was what had drawn Pinky's attention.

Delilah's retelling led me to finish the story by sharing with everyone that after Pinky had lectured Ree and me on the dangers of smoking, she then confiscated the cigarette and finished it. She'd smiled the whole time she puffed away, saying, "Do as I say, not as I do, girls."

Luna had laughed with pure delight at the story, making it feel like Ree was right there in the kitchen with us. Which, it turned out, was more comforting than distressing. A nice surprise.

"Will Sawyer need to go upstairs?" I asked.

"Can't see why he would."

I breathed a sigh of relief as she cracked an egg into a small bowl. "Are you making a cake for someone?" It was unusual for her to bake on her days off unless it was a special occasion.

"I'm experimenting." There was a glint in her eye as she leaned forward, toward me, as if we were in a crowded room and not the only ones in the barn. "A new recipe for the bakery. I'm feeling the need to give back. To be appreciative for the life I've been given, the life I've led. All proceeds from this cake will be diverted for charity. I'm actually a mite shamed I never thought of it before now."

I lifted an eyebrow. "Charities like the Starling Society?"

She smiled, nodded. "Now, picture this if you will," she said, her voice rising dramatically. "Fluffy vanilla sponge with a hint of almond. A thin layer of raspberry jam. Pillowy whipped cream filling and frosting."

I could picture it quite well and suddenly I was hungry. "It sounds amazing. I volunteer to be a taste-tester."

"I'll hold you to that."

Rubbing a thumb along the edge of the counter, I said, "Can you think of a reason why I'd have heard about the Starling Society before Henrietta told us about it? It sounds so familiar. Do you think it's possible I overheard Henrietta and my daddy talking about it at some point when I was little?"

"Perhaps. But there's another possibility." She lowered herself onto a stool, rubbed the face of her watch, and said, "Ree."

Almost immediately I saw a business card in my mind's eye. One for the Starling Society with a 1-800 phone number. It had been in Ree's bedroom, and I remember it had caught my eye among all the crafting supplies because of the bird silhouette on the card. She'd brushed aside my question about it, saying only that she'd picked it up because she liked the design.

"Henrietta knew Ree?" I asked, my chest heavy.

"I believe she paid Ree a visit a time or two."

"But how?"

Aunt Bean tipped her head, gave a slight shrug of her shoulders. "I may have put them in touch when I saw bruises on Ree's arms after she started dating Ace Buckley. Thank the heavens Henrietta, with all her experience, eventually managed to get through to her."

I hadn't thought it possible for anyone to get through to her. I'd tried. Sawyer. Her granny. I needed to give Henrietta a big hug, not only for helping Ree but for her work in general. I held Aunt Bean's gaze. "Thank you."

She nodded but I saw the tears in her eyes. She'd loved Ree as much as I had, and right now we were both very much aware that we'd lost her all the same.

Outside came the sound of wheels on the driveway. I looked out, saw Sawyer's ruby-red truck. I wiped my eyes and hopped off my stool. "I should get upstairs."

She gave me a gentle smile. "Punkin, aren't you tired of runnin'? It's got to be exhausting. Might could be the perfect time for you step out of that shadow and stand your ground."

The truck door slammed.

The word *shadow* echoed in my head, and I suddenly knew Aunt Bean was aware I was keeping a secret. A big one.

The star pendant warmed in my hands as I squeezed it.

"You know you can tell me anything, Addie. I'll take your secrets to the grave."

She would. I knew she would. I'd always known. But if I told her, then I'd have to finally admit the real reason I'd run away, and I couldn't quite bring myself to do that.

As Sawyer passed by the take-out window, my heart skipped a beat.

"I need to go," I said, my voice cracking, my emotion taking over, tying me up in sorrow.

And with that I bolted for the stairs.

Running away.

Again.

*

Upstairs, I'd put in earbuds and went to work, attaching the acoustic panels to the walls of the storage room. I'd turned up the volume for the soundtrack to *Wicked* to ensure I couldn't hear anything going on downstairs. No mixing, no whizzing, no Bee Gees. And especially not the sound of Sawyer's voice. Or, *lordy be*, his laugh.

His laugh might do me right in.

But about an hour in, I stopped what I was doing, realizing I was wasting my time.

Because I wouldn't need a studio here after all. I had to leave. Leave Starlight.

It turned out my season of happiness hadn't lasted very long at all.

It was proving impossible to avoid Luna and Sawyer. And, after almost telling Bean everything earlier, it had become clear I was losing the battle of keeping Ree's secret. My defenses were in tatters.

Now, I sat on the floor of the studio, my arms wrapped around my knees, plotting my escape. My plan was one that leaned heavily on Tessa Jane taking up my slack, which I realized wasn't fair, but I was desperate.

I rocked a bit as I thought about leaving, about excluding myself once again. I was going to miss sleepy breakfasts with Tessa Jane and Aunt Bean, where I'd make them laugh by giving the bear-shaped honey container a high-pitched British aristocratic voice to issue the weather forecast for the day. I'd miss the crazy fun, like when the ducks ran wild in the house. I'd miss impromptu dance parties. And late nights on the couch, the scent of popcorn in the air as Aunt Bean sighed over George Clooney. I'd miss everyday moments with Tessa Jane, like washing dishes together. Or how we'd both reach for our pendants at the same time. Such a sisterly thing to do.

I'd miss belonging.

But it was the price I was willing to pay for Luna to have stability, dependability, security, serenity.

Birmingham was less than two hours away. I could drive here on days when I was most needed. Like when Bean had a doctor's appointment. Or one of the Sugarbirds was out of town. It wasn't the easiest commute, but it was doable. I just had to figure out how to tell Aunt Bean. And could only hope she'd understand.

When someone tapped me on my shoulder, I let out a yip

and nearly jumped clear out of my skin. Pressing one hand to my pounding heart, I used the other to pull out my earbuds.

Sawyer stood there, a plate in his hand. The door behind him stood wide open. "Sorry. I knocked and called out your name. When you didn't answer, I got worried."

I scrambled to my feet, trying to pretend that he hadn't found me practically curled into a ball on the floor. "I guess the music was louder than I thought."

"That's not good for your hearing, you know." His voice was kind, concerned.

I almost laughed, because it was something I'd say, but I wasn't really in the laughing mood.

The room suddenly seemed extra small, filled now with his piney scent, with his big heart.

He held out the plate. On it was a fork and piece of vanilla cake with whipped cream frosting. "Apparently, you volunteered to taste test?"

I set my jaw. Knowing Aunt Bean, she'd had ulterior motives with this delivery.

Unfortunately, I'd lost my appetite, but I took the plate from him anyway. "Thanks."

He glanced around the room, at the few wall tiles I'd secured, at my microphone and pop filter. "Do you need any help in here?"

"Nope. I'm good."

"Have you noticed any electrical issues up here?"

"None so far." The scent of him was calling up old memories. Of us walking the train tracks for miles, laughing over silly TV shows, of looking for treasure in the woods, like pinecones and acorns and feathers and hedge apples. I shoved the images away and forced myself to ask, "Did you figure out what's going on downstairs?"

"No. I triple-checked the panel and all the outlets. Everything looks good."

"Strange."

"Very."

I wished there was more space between us and less awkwardness. I wished a lot of things, actually. Mostly, to change the past. I sought out things to count, but the room was pretty much a blank slate. And I would not count his freckles. I *wouldn't*.

"How's work going?" he asked.

Lord have mercy. "Fine. Good."

"Luna's a big fan."

I started counting the bumps in the acoustic foam and wished the window opened so I could jump out of it. "She's sweet."

"I'm a big fan, too," he added before I could respond. "But then again, I always have been."

My eyebrows snapped down and my grip tightened on the plate.

"What?" he laughed lightly, noticing my reaction. "You don't believe me?"

I tried to calm a rising storm by focusing on the cake. I used the fork to break off a small bite, capturing all the components. A bit of sponge, of cream, of raspberry jam. Then I stuffed it in my mouth. Oh, sweet heaven. The cake was good. Better than good. The sponge was delicate velvet. The whipped cream was silky and smooth with a tangy undertone. The sweet raspberry jam had just enough tartness to balance it all. These cakes were going to fly out the door.

"You should try this," I said, feeling oddly brave as I moved toward the door, my only escape route. "Let's go get you a piece."

He touched my arm, freezing me in place. "Addie."

"It's really good," I told him, unable to look him in the eyes.

"We need to talk."

"No, we don't. We really don't."

He stood firm. "I'm not letting this go. I'm not going to let you shut me out again. This is too important."

What? "Shut *you* out? You're the one who tossed *me* aside."

"No."

"Yes."

This was old, painful news, and I hated revisiting it. I stared at the ceiling as if I could find a bucketful of patience in the cracked, stained plaster. I was suddenly reminded of when we were kids, arguing over who won a race through the woods or some other silly competition. Which made me resort to a trick Aunt Bean employed on the rare times Sawyer and I were at odds. A way that would make us listen to one another without interruption.

"Ten seconds," I said. "Go."

Surprise flared in his hazel eyes. "If you didn't want Ree and me to go to homecoming together, you should have said so. Instead you closed yourself off and never let us back in. Not fully."

Ree had devised the plan to go to the dance with Sawyer because she wanted to show Ace she'd moved on. So he'd leave her alone. Simple smoke and mirrors. Only, she hadn't asked Sawyer or me how we felt about it. Just jumped right in, head-long, like she always did.

Until that point, Sawyer and I had always gone to dances together. As friends. But the summer before our senior year, something had changed between us. Since Ree was busy with Ace, Sawyer and I spent almost every free minute together. Alone. We hiked and explored and swam. All things we'd done a million times before. But that summer, an awareness grew. A realization that there was more between us than friendship. I didn't tell anyone how I felt, not even Ree, because it was too delicate, too fragile, too precious.

What grew between Sawyer and me had felt like a waiting game. That if I simply stayed the course, trusted him, I'd eventually get what I was hoping for once he gathered up enough courage to overcome his shyness. Because like Aunt Bean, I was just old-fashioned enough to need him to be the one to make the first move.

So when Ree voiced her homecoming idea, I thought for sure it was the tipping point. I had already told Sawyer about the dress I'd found, and he'd bought blue suede shoes to complement it. We'd talked endlessly about dancing the night away under the October stars—and had even practiced the slow dances, our bodies pressed up against each other, our heartbeats practically audible, our longing gazes saying things with our eyes that we didn't have the nerve yet to say out loud.

I waited for Sawyer to speak up, to tell Ree that she'd have to find someone else to fill in. That he wanted to go to the dance with me, that he wanted to spend the whole night holding me in his arms.

Only he didn't.

The two of them carried on as if fooling everyone at the dance was yet another grand adventure, unable to hear my heart breaking as they practiced waltzing across the room.

I held his gaze now, wondering how it had come to this. We'd once been so close. I'd loved him. There was a chance—a good chance—I still did. Maybe it was that small flame fueling the sudden need to share my feelings, after so many years of keeping them tucked safely inside. So protected I'd never been able to heal.

His jaw jutted. "Ten seconds. Go."

I took a deep breath. "Maybe I should have said something, but I'm not that kind of person. I've never been that kind of person. You knew that. *You* should've been the one to speak up. And when you didn't, it broke my heart. Of course I retreated. I felt utterly foolish. Clearly I'd read more into our feelings for each other than what was actually there."

He dragged a hand down his face, swore under his breath, and said again, "You should've said something."

"And then," I said, gathering steam, holding on to the cake plate for dear life, "as if going to the dance together wasn't bad enough, you two kept on pretending. Holding hands walking down the halls at school. Snuggling in the cafeteria. I couldn't stand seeing you two together, even if it was just *pretend*. It physically hurt me to see you love on someone else. Every time we hung out together, it was like picking at an open wound."

"It wasn't real, Addie. You knew that. Mostly, when Ree and I met up, we were trying to figure out how to get you to come back out of your shell. You shut us down at every turn."

He sounded frustrated with me and it was *infuriating.* "Sure. If it was never real, how do you explain Luna?"

If he thought she was his daughter, then there had to have been an intimate relationship between him and Ree. Did he think I was an idiot?

He took a step back, his face a mask of puzzlement. "You know Luna's not mine, right? Right?" he repeated, almost desperately. "Ree and I were never *together.*"

I staggered backward, bumped against the wall. My heart raced as I stared at him, looking for lies I couldn't find. Still, I couldn't believe what I was hearing. *Never together?* It didn't make sense. Not after what Ree had told me in the hospital. My mind whirled, trying to remember what she'd said, wondering if I'd somehow misunderstood.

Oh, lord, had this all been one big misunderstanding?

No. *No!* She'd grabbed my arm and begged me not to tell anyone. Even now I could see the fear in her eyes.

But she *had* downplayed my concern about Sawyer believing he was Luna's father, hadn't she? She'd easily brushed it aside. Because Sawyer had known Ace was Luna's father? If so, I couldn't fathom why she wouldn't have just told me he knew straight off, except now I realized she was probably already three steps ahead of me in the conversation—trying to get it all out before I found an excuse to leave.

And I would have found one.

Because I hadn't wanted to be in that room when Sawyer came back in, glowing with pride from seeing his new baby.

Ree hadn't known she wouldn't have time to clarify.

None of us could've known how little time we had left with her.

My voice was strained, weak, as I said, "Ree told me about Luna in the hospital after she was born and begged me not to say anything to anyone—to protect Luna." Grief sat heavy on my chest, pushing the air out of my lungs. "Until then, I was under the impression you were her father. Ree didn't—" I took a deep breath. "There wasn't time enough for her to tell me you knew the truth before . . . Well, before."

His jaw clenched as pain flashed in his eyes.

Before he could say anything, I rushed on. "And because I'd rather die than let one of the Buckleys hurt that baby, I left town before I could let the secret slip."

He knew. All this time and he knew he wasn't her father.

I wanted to scream at the injustice of it all. I wanted to cry, to sob with everything I'd been keeping in for the last twelve years. I wanted to run, because *this* truth hurt like nothing I'd ever felt before. But I kept standing there, knowing it was time to face the past.

Sawyer's voice was rough as he said, "After Ace died and Ree found out she was pregnant, she was in a panic. She didn't want the Buckleys to know about Luna. She was afraid of Luna being hurt, abused. We knew people assumed the baby was mine at that point, so it was easy to keep on pretending. I'd have laid my life down for that baby, to protect her. I still would. I *am* her father. I learned real quick that it's not blood that makes a family. It's love. Only one thing has changed."

"What's that?"

"Addie, *everyone* knows she's Ace's biologically."

It took me a moment to process what he was saying. *Everyone?*

I shook my head. It wasn't possible.

"It's not a secret. Not for a long time now, anyhow. There was really no use in pretending after Luna was born. She's his spitting image. But since I signed paperwork at the hospital acknowledging paternity and my name is on her birth certificate, in the eyes of the law, she's mine. The Buckleys never challenged it. I don't know why. Could be it was the cost of a lawyer. Or maybe in a moment of decency, they realized she was better off with me. Whatever the reason, I'm glad they never did, because I'd have fought tooth and nail for her."

I thought I might be sick. I oh-so-carefully set the dessert plate on the edge of the table, then covered my mouth. My hand trembled.

Everyone *knew*.

For twelve years, I'd been missing birthdays and engagements and town festivals. Missing Aunt Bean. And Delilah, Willa Jo, and Pinky. Missing Sawyer and Luna.

Missing life.

"Luna is even friendly with Dare," he added. "I'm still a bit wary about her getting too close, even though it seems like he's not like the others."

The words *not a secret* played in my head on repeat. All these years I'd locked myself away. Cut myself off.

And I hadn't needed to.

My lower lip trembled. Aunt Bean probably thought I already knew the truth. And because she and the Sugarbirds never really talked about Sawyer around me, to protect my feelings, I never heard any gossip, either.

If I hadn't run, I'd have known. Maybe I could have patched things up with Sawyer. Helped him raise Luna.

But I *had* run.

To protect Luna.

I squeezed my eyes shut and made myself finally face the truth.

I hadn't left only because of Luna.

I'd run away to escape the pain. Of heartbreak. Of grief.

I'd run so I wouldn't have to see Ree's granny around town.

I'd run so I wouldn't have to face Sawyer in a grocery aisle.

Or see him and his sweet baby girl on a hike. Or *anywhere*.

I'd run because I'd loved him, and I didn't know how to deal with him not loving me back.

So I'd borrowed a page from my mama's book and hit the road. If anyone in this world should've known that running wasn't the answer, it was me. I knew firsthand the damage it caused.

Yet I'd done it anyway. And look where it had gotten me.

I'd lost *twelve* years of being here, close to everyone and everything I loved.

"And you're right," he said. "I should have spoken up, especially after you didn't go to the dance, which was when I realized how upset you were."

A tear ran down my face as I looked at him.

"But I didn't, because I was scared."

My voice cracked as I said, "Of what?"

"Of my feelings for you. How big they were. It crushed me when you shut down, locked me out. Your heart wasn't the only one that was broken, Addie. And I thought if it hurt that bad when we weren't even officially dating, maybe it was a good thing we never got together. Then next thing I knew I didn't recognize my own life. I'd lost my best friends in the world. But I gained a beautiful, smart, funny little girl who makes my world go round."

I swallowed hard, thinking about the choices we make in life. About regrets. About not speaking up, about not talking problems out. About owning fault. And about forgiveness.

Mostly about forgiveness. Sawyer and I had both made mistakes.

We could leave here right now knowing we'd stuck a piece of tape on what we'd broken. We could be friendly, if not friends. But if there's anything I'd learned from my relationship with Tessa Jane and from finally admitting some hard truths to myself, it's that I don't want a patch. I wanted to heal. I wanted true friendship. I wanted to plant my feet and be firmly *here*. I wanted the life I should've had if only I'd been brave enough to stick around.

As I counted his freckles, I gathered my courage. "You didn't lose me."

He locked his gaze on mine, gold flecks glinting like treasure in his eyes, his beautiful inner light shining bright. "No?"

"I wasn't lost. I just took a detour. It took me a while to circle back."

He hung his head, his jaw bobbing as he let my words sink in. When he finally looked at me again, there was no denying the hope in his gaze. "So you're staying? In Starlight?"

Was I?

I had no reason to go back to Birmingham. No secrets to hide, no lies to keep telling myself. There was no reason to *run*. I could finally come home for good.

"I guess I am."

"Luna will be glad to hear that." He smiled and it practically made him glow. "I'm glad, too."

We grinned at each other for a long moment before I said, "Let's get you some cake. You're going to need a sugar boost to help me attach all these tiles to the wall."

As we headed out the door, I felt shy and awkward all of a sudden but determined to not let it stop me from opening up more, to fully share my life. Share who I was. And to embrace all I had.

I was done keeping secrets.

Forever.

CHAPTER SIXTEEN

From the Kitchen of Verbena Fullbright

Did you forget to grease your pans before baking your cake? Don't go worrying. Tip the warm pan upside down and place a hot, damp towel on top of it for five minutes or so. The steamy reaction should have that cake sliding right out when you lift the pan and give it a little jiggle. Remember, hard rarely means impossible.

Tessa Jane

"There it is! Right there. Do you see it?" Addie let out a squeal and pulled her feet up onto the kitchen chair early Thursday morning.

She'd tucked the kittens, Stella and Lovebug, whom I'd nicknamed Lovey, into her chunky cardigan, as though protecting them from a giant beast and not a tiny house spider.

I had a paper cup in one hand, a take-out menu in the other as I stalked the tiny creature, grateful the dogs were outside and Miney and Moe were too lazy to hunt.

Definitely a bright side.

They were coming more and more frequently.

Like when Holden's Garage had called to tell me they noticed I had a small transmission fluid leak, and did I want them to fix it while they did the rest of the repairs on my car? If they hadn't found the leak, it could have resulted in a much bigger problem.

Another bright side was that if my granddaddy hadn't been so *him*, I'd never have gotten to see another side of my mama, a softer side, while she'd been here with us. To my great surprise, she'd stayed in her pajamas most of Sunday, before finally getting dressed in the late afternoon to head back to Savannah. Her terrible hangover probably had something to do with wardrobe choice, but still, it was remarkable.

The hangover was a result of meeting with Graham Doby, who'd driven her back here after she'd had a bit too much to drink during lunch. When she'd sobered up some, she spoke only a little about the interview, mostly saying she hoped in her tipsiness she hadn't revealed anything she shouldn't have.

Usually, Mama was a vault, but between her anger at Granddaddy and the alcohol, I was worried she might've kicked the fire ant mound, so to speak.

Granddaddy, for his part, had been quiet since the blowup at his party. Too quiet. His silence was unnerving.

"I'm not going to hurt you," I told the spider as I chased it across the kitchen.

"How is it so fast?" Addie asked, still perched on the chair.

"Probably because it has eight legs."

"That's it. I'm going to have nightmares."

Yet another bright side had come through Miss Ernie. If I hadn't been making cookies for her, she never would've told her dear friend Randie Beth Robinson about them. In turn, Randie Beth, who was the director for Hand to Heart, a local charitable foundation that focused on neighbors helping neighbors, ordered two hundred heart-shaped cookies to be included in gift bags for attendees of the group's Valentine's gala at the Celestial Hotel.

Though I'd been more than happy to take the order, there was no denying it's been challenging. I'd been working on cookies all week, staying up until the wee hours, and I still wasn't near done. At this point, I was glad the gala tickets were sold out, so I had an excuse not to go.

Addie wasn't going either. We were both looking forward to a quiet night at home—and lots of sleep. She'd also been working nights this past week, recording in the studio she'd set up in the barn, and we were both bone-tired.

Aunt Bean, who was never one to miss a party, had bought a ticket ages ago and already had her outfit pressed. I honestly didn't know where she found her energy.

"Please tell me you didn't lose sight of it," Addie said. "We'll have to burn the house down."

"Hold your matches, firebug. I see it. I just didn't want to startle him by approaching too quickly."

Addie laughed, bold and rich and velvety. "It's lucky you and your soft heart are here because it would've gotten the broom from me. And that probably would've been quite *startling*."

My soft heart.

I'd healed so much during the time I'd spent here with Aunt Bean. With Addie. The Sugarbirds. But I wasn't fully back to where I wanted to be. I still felt the hardness every so often. Mostly when I thought of my grandfather—and also my work at the country club.

I had a little more than a week left before I had to return to Savannah, and I was kicking myself for not asking for *two* months off. Or at least until my birthday, at the end of the month. I'd been ignoring calls from my boss for days now—he wanted me to come back early. The old me would've jumped in the car after hearing the first voicemail. But the part of me still lingering in my shadow simply deleted the messages.

"Mind your legs now," I said to the spider as I dropped the cup over it. I carefully slid the menu underneath the cup, inch by cautious inch, trapping the spider safely inside. "You're going to be just fine."

Addie jumped up and opened the back door. She shivered as I passed by. "Please take him far away. Minnesota, maybe."

Laughing, I stepped outside. The dogs galloped over to sniff the cup, and I held it away from them. The ducks quacked from the pond, probably asking if I was bringing them a snack. I'd quickly learned that a couple of raspberries could get them where I needed them to go. Bribery, pure and simple. When I didn't head toward the pond, they spun their white bodies around, shook their tail feathers, and swam off.

I threw a glance at the quack shack. It still needed roofing tiles, a door, and some trim, so I knew Ty would be back soon. Despite him being extra busy these days, between running Ernie to doctor's visits and finishing up work on the bakery renovation, I'd somehow been seeing a lot of him lately. Limited snatches of time when he was working here or when I took Hambone over to visit Ernie. Just enough for small talk. For us to get to know each other as adults. For me to see that goodness glowing in him.

I carried the cup trap over to the forsythia bush in the side yard and let the spider loose among the tiny yellow buds. Music drifted from the big red barn, but I couldn't make out the song from this distance. I imagined Bean and Delilah and Willa Jo—who was full of grandchildren stories since returning from her vacation—frosting and decorating and boxing, getting ready for the stream of customers sure to arrive later this morning. Addie and I had an afternoon shift today, and I was hoping to find a way, yet again, to wiggle out of cake duty.

As I turned back around, my gaze went immediately to the starlight crater in the distance. Since I'd seen that sparkle from the attic window, I hadn't seen another.

The dogs ran around my feet as I went back inside the house, and I gave them lots of pets. Extra ones for Pepper, because she was going home today. Dare and Petal had returned from their honeymoon late last night, and he would be here this afternoon to collect Pepper. I tried to ignore the pit in my stomach at the thought of her leaving.

They followed me into the house and ran straight to Addie, who was back at the kitchen table, scrolling through her phone. They eagerly sniffed her sweater, then galloped into the living room after she showed them the sleeping kittens and patted their heads.

With thoughts of sparkly diamonds foremost in my mind,

I sat and started a conversation I never thought I'd be having with Addie. "You know how Aunt Bean has always said the starlight will disappear if it's dug up? Do you know why she thinks that? Is its origin based on a specific incident? Or just family lore?"

She put her phone down as if sensing these weren't random questions. "Is this about building the gift shop and café? Because I thought the construction would be a good distance from the crater. Besides, I haven't decided yet if it's something I want to take on."

"No, no," I assured. "It's only that as far as I know, no one's ever done any real digging. Sure, a few shallow holes here and there by people who've sneaked onto the land, and of course, the soil samples taken by researchers. But not anything deep. How are we so sure the light will disappear?"

"I've only ever heard the same as you. I've never questioned it." She tipped her head. "*Why* are you questioning it?"

I wanted to tell her the truth about seeing the sparkle but didn't want to burden her with a secret. Especially after what she'd gone through with Sawyer, which had just about broken my heart to hear about.

I kept rubbing the edge of the table, and she tipped her head, an eyebrow raised as she waited for me to answer. Taking hold of my star pendant, I said, "I'm curious is all. Aunt Bean wants us to learn everything about the family businesses, right? I feel like this is something we should know. It's part of the starlight's history."

She reached for her pendant, too, clasping it tightly. After a moment, she said, "Do you think it's time we talk about why she wants us to learn everything? And why she has us taking *inventory*? And why she's been rubbing her watch so much?" Her voice dropped low, real low, like she could barely say the words out loud. "How worried do you think we need to be about her health?"

I scratched my neck. Hives were popping up all over. We both knew why Aunt Bean was doing what she was doing.

Addie and I were her next of kin. If something happened to
Bean, it was likely we'd inherit her estate, including the bakery
and the farmhouse—along with its entire *inventory*.

She wanted us to know what we'd be dealing with if she
wasn't here. What decisions and choices would need to be
made. But my brain simply refused to think about a time when
she might be gone.

"Let's wait until after we get the results of tomorrow's MRI
before we really start to worry, okay?" I said, wanting to live
in the happy land of denial a little while longer.

"Okay." One of the kittens wiggled inside her sweater, and
she let go of her pendant to readjust them. "But now you've
made me curious about the starlight and digging, so I guess
there's really only one thing for us to do."

"Grab a shovel?" I joked.

She laughed. "No. Ask Aunt Bean."

✳

"Truth be told," Aunt Bean said, gently tapping her walking stick twice on the cement floor of the barn's kitchen later
that afternoon, "I'm not sure if the story I've been told is fact
or folklore. You know how tall tales grow in families." She
wiped her hands on a tea towel and hitched a hip onto a stool.
"Are y'all sure I've never told it to you?"

Addie, Delilah, Willa Jo, and I shook our heads as we moved
in close to her, like we were gathering around a campfire for
story time instead of circling a flour-dusted prep table.

Willa Jo said, "I know the birds will attack anyone who
tries to dig, but I don't recollect ever hearing that the starlight
went out."

"Same here," Delilah added.

Outside, Hambone let out a mournful howl. Dare had come
by a couple of hours ago to pick up Pepper, and Hambone was
already mooning. We'd been taking turns going out to the
fence to give him love and cake balls.

Inside the barn, the Bee Gees sang about mending broken

hearts, and a warm breeze blew through the open windows. The ever-present vanilla scent swirled around us, wrapping us in sweetness.

"It was my granny who told me all the tales of the olden days," Bean said.

Delilah sighed. "No one told stories like your granny. May she be resting in peace with a big ol' glass of bourbon on the rocks in hand."

There was a round of clucking and murmuring and smiles among the older women. Addie and I had never met our great-granny—she'd passed before we were born. And I was suddenly taken aback by the loss. I wished I had known her and her big personality, though I supposed in a way, I did. It shined through Aunt Bean.

She rubbed her watch face, then said, "With the starlight, the best days to get Granny talking was on warm summer evenings, long after all the baking was done. We'd sit out on the front porch, snapping beans, and all I'd have to say was, 'Granny, tell me about the time the star fell.' And then there'd be no stopping her, the heat loosening her tongue, her memory, until the lightning bugs started sparking and we realized how late it was."

A timer buzzed and Delilah grabbed a pair of oven mitts. "Go on, go on. I'm listening."

Aunt Bean carried on. "Granny said her mama told her that back after the star fell and the light started glimmering people came from all over to see it. Soon, people started realizing that they were finding clarity in the light when they walked through it, suddenly having an answer to something that had been plaguing them. Word of mouth spread real quick after that, about this mystical place that had been hit by a falling star. Charity Fullbright, all of nineteen at that point, had been wise enough to walk about the crowd with a donation box and tea cakes for sale. With her parents both gone, she was the one running the farm and taking care of her younger brother, and doing her best to make ends meet."

Those tea cakes had been the foundation of the Starling Cake Company.

"Well," Aunt Bean huffed, "it didn't take but a minute for some fool-headed idiot to declare some sort of trickery was going on, and that Charity was a swindler. So, he decided to prove she was a fraud by taking a shovel to the ground where light was swirling around his feet." Bean smiled, a big toothy grin. "This is the part where my granny would always tell me, 'Iff'n I'd a been there, I'd a taken that shovel straight to his head.'"

Bean spoke that last part in a deep southern drawl, and I could easily imagine her and her granny sitting in rocking chairs on the front porch, snapping beans, musing about justice being properly served.

"Now if you recollect," Aunt Bean said, "this is 1833. I don't rightly know what that man expected to find that would produce the light he was seeing. It's not like any of them even knew what electricity was back then. But the halfwit started digging anyway. Got about two shovelfuls in when the light around him cut out. Just flat disappeared, like someone had pulled a plug. So, this man falls to the ground, and starts pawing at the dirt looking for a gimmick or gadget. That's when a silvery starling done came out of nowhere and chased him off. Charity happened to be nearby, and she quickly set the dirt to rights, and the light came up once again. After that, digging was forbidden, and those who tried were quickly run off by the bird. Or birds, as the case may be these days."

Through the years there had been *many* stories of the starlings scaring people off. And even some tales of those who'd tried hunting the birds, only to become the prey. Not many realized they weren't your garden-variety starlings that were simply territorial.

At the sound of a car approaching outside, we all turned toward the window. It was Stan in the Bootsie's Blooms delivery van.

Willa Jo said, "Well, well, well, what do we have here?"

Everyone turned and looked at Bean. She slid off the stool. "Why're y'all looking at me like that? Might could be another delivery for Tessa Jane from Ty Underwood."

Now all the eyes were on me. "What? Nope! He's been a perfect gentleman lately."

"Or maybe they're for Addie," Delilah said. "I heard tell she and Sawyer kissed and made up."

Willa Jo made loud kissy noises as we all swung our attention toward my sister.

Addie laughed. "Sorry to burst any bubbles, but there was no kissing to be had. No kissing, no hugging, no hand-holding."

I was real proud of her for not tugging her sleeves down or shying away from the teasing.

"Dang it," Delilah muttered, then she tipped her head. "Any plans for kissing?"

Addie said, "You're a hopeless romantic, you know that?"

I couldn't help noticing she'd dodged the question.

There was a knock on the door before it swung open. "Afternoon, ladies!"

Stan received a chorus of hellos in reply. All of us were wide-eyed as he entered the barn, holding three boxes of chocolates and three pink heart-shaped balloons.

Not a minute later, he was followed inside by Luna, who came bursting through the open door, out of breath, as though she'd sprinted the whole way here. Her gaze immediately landed on Stan's delivery, her big blue eyes full of curiosity and delight. "Who are *those* for?"

The way Addie smiled at her pulled at my heartstrings. It was a luminous mix of amusement and love darkened by the tiniest smudge of remorse, which no doubt came from having cut herself out of Luna's life for so long.

Delilah put her arm around Luna's shoulders. "I was about to ask the same thing."

"These goodies are for the lovely Fullbright ladies." Stan handed me, Addie, and Aunt Bean a balloon and a box that was wrapped in pink ribbon. A pink envelope was nestled under the bow.

My envelope had a small heart drawn next to my name. Addie's had the same design but with her name.

Aunt Bean tugged the envelope free and quickly tore into it. She pulled out what looked like a fancy bookmark. "What in the world?"

Luna squeaked. "Someone sent you a ticket to the Valentine's Day dance! My grandpa's company got a deal on a bunch of tickets to give to everyone who works for him, so my dad's making me go. Something about family and community." She rolled her eyes.

I smiled.

"You don't want to go?" Willa Jo asked her. "It's always so fun."

"All the people there are old," Luna said. Then quickly added, "No offense."

Aunt Bean laughed, the sound filling the room to the rafters. "None taken, darlin', but I've already got a ticket, so this don't make much sense."

Addie and I opened our envelopes. We'd also been given a ticket.

"Who sent these over?" Aunt Bean asked Stan.

He shrugged. "I don't know, Verbena. I only make deliveries."

"Land's sakes," she muttered, pulling out her cell phone. A moment later, she had Bootsie on speakerphone. "Enough's enough. Spill it, Boots. Who's sending these things?"

Bootsie seemed to be expecting the call. "Wish I could tell you, but it's a right mystery. Found a box on my doorstep with the chocolates, the tickets, and a request to add balloons to the delivery along with a hand-drawn heart on the cards just like last time. Also a wad of cash that more than covered everything. I'm as intrigued as all y'all."

"Did you check security footage?" Bean asked.

With a big booming laugh, Bootsie said, "What am I? NASA?

I don't have any of that fanciness. Cameras. Ha! Now, listen, if you're needing any flowers for the dance, corsages or boutonnieres, you know where to find me. Take care now and eat up one of those chocolates for me. Just not one of the cherry-filled ones. *Blech*."

Bean grudgingly said, "You take care, too," and hung up. "Well, if that don't beat all."

Delilah's eyes gleamed behind her glasses. "Your admirer must be Mr. Moneybags, Bean. Those tickets aren't cheap!"

"We don't know all this came from *my* admirer," she said.

"Don't we?" Willa Jo asked. "Bootsie herself said they asked for a heart *just like last time*."

My mind was spinning with who it could be. The tickets alone cost fifty dollars apiece. "Why give a ticket to us, too?" I asked.

Willa Jo said, "My guess is the admirer didn't realize Bean had a ticket already and didn't want you girls to feel left out. Your admirer has got manners, Bean. That gets a bonus point from me."

I glanced at Addie. Were we really going to go? She shrugged in answer, as though reading my mind.

Delilah pulled the lid off the coffee can where we kept the petty cash, pulled out a ten-dollar bill and handed it over to Stan. "There's more of that to be had if you can tell us who Bean's secret admirer is."

"I'll throw in my allowance, too," Luna said, completely serious.

Grinning, Stan stuffed the bill into his shirt pocket and gave us an apologetic smile. "As much as I'd love to tell you, I don't know. But I will say whoever it is has excellent taste in women. I do hope he won't mind none if you save me a dance or two at the gala, Verbena." With that, he nodded and walked out.

We all turned toward Bean wearing the same gleeful expressions.

Luna sang, "He likes youuuu!"

Bean wagged a finger at us. "Don't go getting ideas. None of y'all. Now let's get back to work."

But I noticed as she turned away that she was grinning.

"All right, all right," Luna said as she stalked toward a broom. "No ideas. Gotcha. But for the love of Taylor Swift, can we *please* listen to a different record?"

CHAPTER SEVENTEEN

From the Kitchen of Verbena Fullbright

Making white buttercream can be a tricky business. Being that butter has a natural yellow tint, it tends to give the frosting a sallow appearance. To create a vibrant white, add a drop or two of purple food coloring into the bowl and watch the magic happen. Sometimes the most unexpected things bring about the brightness we're looking for.

Addie

"It'll be here when it gets here. Ain't much we can do about it, so don't go spending another minute worrying," Aunt Bean said into her cell phone as I pulled into the parking lot of Friddle's Market on Friday afternoon. "We'll reopen without the sign if we have to. Now, I'm fixin' to visit your mama in just a little bit. Do y'all need anything? Milk, bread, squirrel food? I'm about to run into Friddle's."

She was talking to Ty Underwood about the bakery sign that was still on back order. And apparently, groceries. Yesterday he'd found a tiny, dazed squirrel sitting on the hood of his truck before heading off to work and was taking care of it until tomorrow when he planned to run it to a rehabber down in Auburn. Ernie had texted pictures of the critter to Aunt Bean and we'd all *ooh*ed and *aah*ed over the cute baby.

I parked the car, cut the engine. As I waited for Bean to finish her call, I turned my face toward the sky and watched the clouds drift by. For the past week, I'd noticed that colors seemed brighter. My mood lighter. Lighter than air.

My shadow had lifted.

Even still, there had been moments, many moments, since my conversation with Sawyer that I'd found myself in tears. From anger. From sadness. From relief. I was trying not to beat myself up over closing myself off for so long, but I'd be lying if I said it had been easy. It was going to take time to sort through all my feelings.

Staying busy helped keep my emotions from becoming overwhelming. The bakery was as hectic as ever, I'd been helping Tessa Jane with her cookies, and I'd been working at night, recording auditions and several commercials for a national cereal campaign. I'd also started planning my move back to Starlight. For now, I was going to continue living with Aunt Bean.

In the rearview mirror I noticed Tessa Jane frowning as she stared out the window. I followed her gaze and saw the starlings perched on top of the market. They'd been staying close for weeks now, and it was impossible not to wonder why. Impossible not to worry.

Bean laughed at something Ty must've said. "All righty, but if you think of anything, give me a call. See you soon." She hung up, dropped her phone into her pocketbook, and then glanced at us. "Ready, girls?"

As if *she'd* been the one kept waiting.

"Yes, ma'am," we answered, sharing a smile as we climbed out of the car.

It had already been a long day, even though it was barely half over. Tessa Jane and I had both gone with Bean to her cardiac MRI appointment, hoping to hear news on the test directly afterward. Something along the lines of the tech proclaiming that Bean's heart looked perfect, but we had no such luck. Everyone had been friendly and professional and disappointingly tight-lipped. It would likely be days before the doctor called with the results.

Tessa Jane and I dutifully followed Aunt Bean into the store. She'd left her walking stick in the car and leaned heavily on the shopping buggy as we navigated aisles. She drove it much like she drove her truck on empty roads: wild and reckless. We were lucky to get out of the pet food aisle without a major catastrophe. And when she swung into the produce section, she nearly crashed into a display of oranges, just barely missing.

I was filling a bag with apples when I heard her call out a great big hello. When I turned, I saw it was Dare and Petal she'd been greeting.

Petal wore a frown as she clung to Dare's arm. The wound on his head had healed but a faint yellow tint still marked the spot where Petal's shoe had hit him. His cheeks were flushed and he didn't look like he had an ounce of energy.

"It was rather disappointing if I'm being honest," Petal was saying to Aunt Bean as I placed the apples in the buggy. "It rained most of the time we were there. The food wasn't that great. The bed wasn't as soft as I'd like. And the birds were so loud in the morning I could hardly sleep in."

Petal appeared bright-eyed and bushy-tailed. The tan she'd somehow acquired despite the rain brought out the blue in her eyes. She wore a flattering dress that emphasized her narrow waist, high heels, and her silky blond hair cascaded down her back.

Aunt Bean tut-tutted appropriately as Petal finished talking while Tessa Jane wandered over and added a bag of raw peanuts to our order.

"It sure is a good thing honeymoons aren't meant for sleeping." Bean gave a big wink and waggled her eyebrows.

Petal's voice was sickly sweet as she said, "Some honeymoons, perhaps." She didn't see Dare take a deep breath, but she must've felt it, because she leaned into him extra and added, "Dare was feeling puny on the trip."

"Food poisoning, I think," he said, sounding utterly miserable.

"Oh, I'm right sorry to hear that," Aunt Bean said. "You still look a little peaked if you don't mind me saying. Have you seen a doctor since you've been back?"

"No, ma'am."

Petal said, "You ain't seen someone with a weaker constitution. I had to go on our snorkel excursion by myself since he couldn't man up enough to make the trip."

Next to me, I felt Tessa Jane stiffen. She crossed her arms and tucked fisted hands under her elbows.

"I insisted she go," Dare said weakly. He was hunched over the buggy much like Aunt Bean was. Using it for support.

"Though without him there, I did get extra attention from the snorkel instructor, who was as cute as a button. I have a picture, let me show y'all!"

I saw Dare take another deep breath as she rooted through her bag.

"How's Pepper doing?" Tessa Jane asked suddenly. "We sure do miss her."

Petal snorted as she pulled out her phone. "Do you want her?"

"She's kidding," Dare said.

Petal's mouth pursed as she continued to scroll through her phone. "But seriously."

Not liking the direction this conversation was going, I looked for an escape route. "We should let—"

"Oh, here it is!" Petal held out her phone.

We leaned in. The picture was of Petal in a teeny tiny bikini on a boat. A muscled blond man who looked straight out of a Marvel movie had his hand on the small of her back. She was all smiles and googly eyes as she looked up at him.

"Well, look at how beautiful . . . that water is," Aunt Bean said, slowly, purposefully.

Tessa Jane nodded. "And look at the way the *sun* is sparkling on the water. Is it really as crystal clear as it looks?"

Obviously Tessa Jane had overheard Petal complaining about the rain.

I had to bite the inside of my cheek to keep from smiling.

Petal tucked her phone away, her brows knitted in irritation that she hadn't gotten the reaction she'd wanted from us.

"Absolutely. I never did know how much I loved the ocean until this trip. Now I want to move to the beach. My cousin Petie lives down in Orange Beach and says there's a condo for sale not too far from her." She elbowed Dare sharply near his ribs. "But he's being a party pooper."

Dare tensed up. His grip tightened on the buggy. "I just don't think it's the right time to move."

"He'll come around." Petal smiled as she looped her arm around him once again and gave a tight squeeze.

He flinched.

"Are you okay, darlin'?" Aunt Bean asked him, her eyebrows pulled together in concern.

He'd broken out in a sweat. "Mostly, ma'am. My stomach still isn't quite right, but I'm sure it'll be fine in another day or two."

"Men," Petal muttered. "I had to drag this lazybones out of bed today just to do some shopping." She rolled her eyes. "He's takin' the man flu to a whole new level. It's downright embarrassing."

Dare shot her a look.

She shrugged. "Well, it is."

Aunt Bean's nostrils flared but she kept her voice even as she said, "Considering that he hasn't gotten better in what, a week now, perhaps a visit to the doctor would've been a better suggestion than shopping."

Petal's chin lifted. "It's a *stomachache*. He'll live. Tell them, Dare."

Before he could say anything, Bean asked him, "Does it hurt to touch? Your stomach?"

He glanced at Petal, then back at Bean and nodded.

"He's *fine*," Petal said, pulling her hand away from him. "Really, Miss Ver—"

Bean glared at her. "Hush up, Petal."

Petal's mouth fell open, and she crossed her arms.

"Only on your right side? Or is there pain all over?" Bean asked him.

He fidgeted. "Mostly my right side. Some toward the middle."

Bean reached over and placed her hand on his forehead. "My word! You're burning up." Suddenly she rose to her full height of five foot three, drew her shoulders back, and used her most no-nonsense tone of voice to say, "You best take yourself straight over to the emergency room to get checked out. It might could be your appendix acting up. I've seen this before with Addie."

I glanced at him, full of sympathy. I'd been fourteen when my appendix nearly ruptured because I ignored the pain for a week. It had been sheer misery. "Queasy? Can't eat much? Hurts to walk? Hurts to even breathe?"

Subtly, he nodded.

Petal shook her head. "Y'all are making a mountain out of a—"

Bean's fiery glare silenced her. Petal's jaw clenched.

Tessa Jane was shifting foot to foot and eyeing the door like she was fixin' to grab Dare and take him to a doctor herself.

"If it is your appendix," Bean said, "you're risking a rupture if you don't get it fixed. And if it's not your appendix, it's *something*. You need to get it looked at." She held Dare's gaze for a long moment, then added, "I'll take you if you want, darlin'. I'm real good at navigating hospitals these days."

Before he could answer, Petal snapped to. "I'll take him. I'm his wife."

"I'm real glad you remembered, sweetie. For a moment there I thought you'd plumb forgotten your vow of in sickness and in health." Bean's perfectly pleasant tone only served to highlight the rebuke instead of downplaying it.

Petal fluttered her eyelashes and cocked a hip. "What would *you* know about wedding vows, Miss Verbena?"

I gasped. Tessa Jane pulled her fists out from underneath her arms as though she was getting ready to throw one. Dare straightened and looked absolutely mortified.

With the spiteful question Petal had all but declared war

between her and Aunt Bean, and it seemed to me she'd under-estimated her opponent, heart ailment or no.

Bean smiled thinly. "Apparently a sight more than you, dear, considering how unwell your husband appears to be. *Bless your heart.*"

They stared at each other for a long second before Petal turned to Dare, her face pinched. "I'm ready to go now."

Bean patted Dare's hand. "I'll check in with y'all later to see what all the doctor had to say."

With his eyebrows drawn low, he nodded, and Petal didn't even spare us another glance as she latched onto his arm and steered him toward the front doors. As they walked off, she said in that syrupy voice I was coming to loathe, "You should've told me how bad it was, honey. I had *no* idea."

"Lord have mercy," Aunt Bean said under her breath.

My stomach churned.

Tears brimmed in Tessa Jane's eyes as she watched them go. "Do you think she loves him at all?"

Aunt Bean sighed deeply. "Peanut, I think Petal has made it perfectly clear that the only person she loves is herself."

Tessa Jane

"Are you sure you're ready to do this?" Addie asked me.

We stood on the sidewalk outside Gossamer, our reflections staring back at us from the wide storefront window. On display was a mannequin wearing a big floofy fairy-tale wedding gown with a sweetheart neckline, a darling satin belt, and a billowy tulle skirt.

I held on to my pendant, the sapphires warming in my hand. "Mostly sure."

Addie gently steered me toward a bench under a tree draped in twinkle lights. "There's no need to go in right this minute. Let's sit for a while."

We sat, and she said, "We can drive down to Montgomery, check out the boutiques there."

Before coming here we'd searched the farmhouse for dresses to wear to the Valentine's gala, but had come up empty-handed. It was probably a sign we should stay home, like we'd originally planned, but we were hoping Aunt Bean's admirer would be revealed and that alone made it worth going.

"We don't have time. I'll be okay in another few minutes. I promise," I added.

Addie had two commercials to record tonight and I had three dozen cookies to decorate. Tomorrow, the bakery schedule was jam-packed between normal operations and finishing up two wedding cakes and the cupcake tower for the gala. We were going to be lucky if we got more than a few hours' sleep tonight.

As the sun sank behind the buildings on Market Street, casting tall shadows, my gaze kept wandering back to the mannequin.

I said, "Carson would've loved the dress in the window. He'd encouraged me to choose a princess gown, but when I tried one on, it swallowed me whole. Think marshmallow with stick arms. I looked ridiculous."

She smiled. "Impossible."

"Trust me, it wasn't a good look. When I told him I'd chosen a more form-fitting lace dress, he gave me sad puppy dog eyes and said, 'I'm sure you'll still be beautiful.'"

Addie winced.

"Yeah. His comment made me run back to the dress shop to try on another ten gowns before my mama talked some sense into me, reminding me that the choice was *mine*. And then, once I calmed down, she asked if I'd considered how manipulative his response had been. She called it a red flag."

Addie shifted, turning her body toward me. "Wow. I mean, she's right, but still."

"I know. Suddenly, all I could see were his red flags."

Like how when we went to a restaurant, he always ordered for me without asking me what I wanted. And how on our rare days off, we had to do what he wanted or he pouted the whole time, ruining the outing. Or the way he questioned how I spent my money. And how he'd critique my pastries— especially if I'd received compliments on them from guests. Or how he talked and talked about his day but rarely asked about mine. And how he would never admit when he was wrong. Not ever. Not even about the silliest things, like the time he argued for an entire shift that a red panda was a bear, even when an online search confirmed it wasn't. The name was a misnomer. The list went on and on.

The awning above the dress shop flapped in the wind, as if encouraging me to finish the story, to tell her the worst of it. "That was also when Mama suggested that before we got married we visit a counselor who could help us *mesh our communication styles.*"

Addie tucked a flyaway hair behind her ear. "Did he agree to go?"

I nodded and gave her a wry smile. "After six sessions, the counselor gently recommended that we consider postponing the wedding in favor of more therapy."

She gasped. "No!"

"Oh yes. Somehow the sessions, which were meant to bring us closer together, had only showcased our differences. And deep down, I knew the therapist was right—that she was trying to warn us that we were incompatible, but I simply couldn't bear the thought of postponing. The wedding was only three weeks away at that point. The venue had been booked, the menu chosen, the invitations sent. Changing the date would have meant forfeiting thousands of dollars in deposits. More importantly, it would've meant disappointing so many people. People who love and care for us. The thought of notifying everyone made me sick to my stomach. I couldn't do it. I just couldn't."

Addie blew out a breath and compassion filled her eyes. "Oh, Tessa Jane."

"So I talked myself out of how bad things really were between us. I purposefully chose to see things the way I *wanted* them to be. Instead of the way they were. And Carson did, too, right up until it was time to walk down the aisle."

Addie lifted an eyebrow. "When he bailed without warning."

I nodded again. "And over these last few months when everyone would tell me he was a fool for what he'd done, I agreed, because I couldn't accept the truth."

"What truth is that?"

"He wasn't the fool. *I* was. I should've called everything off the minute I saw those red flags."

"Hindsight is a messy business, Tessa Jane. Trust me, I know. You can't take full blame for this. Nope. Not happening. I won't let you."

"It's okay, it really is. It's about time I stop being so angry and embarrassed and accept that I blew my chance to back out with only minimal embarrassment and emotional damage."

"It's hard to back out when love's involved."

I rubbed a finger over my pendant. "That's one of the hardest parts to accept. To *admit*. I didn't love him. Well, at some point I did, certainly. A long time ago when I built up a store of dreams about a house with a picket fence and lots of babies because I wanted a big family. A big, happy, *loving* family. But by the end of those therapy sessions I had to convince myself that the love was still there. Somewhere. I was in denial. Which was why I'd been devastated when he wasn't standing alongside the pastor on my wedding day."

I suddenly wondered about that denial. And how it had been in the early days of the therapy sessions that my shadow had fully enveloped me.

For the first time, I considered that I hadn't been lost in the dark.

I'd been hiding.

Hiding from the truth. Hiding from speaking out and acknowledging my true feelings. Now that I was stepping back into the light, I could see the past so much more clearly.

"The truth is," I said, "we're better off apart. Much better off."

After all, the breakup with Carson had led me here, where my aunt's laughter filled me with joy, where I was happy baking cookies, walking dogs, playing with cats. Where I'd reconnected with my sister.

Addie surprised me by throwing an arm around my shoulder, tugging me in close to her side. "Maybe so. But he *is* a fool. And an idiot. And a host of other words that would make Aunt Bean blush. Okay, maybe not Aunt Bean. But you know what I mean. What he did to you on your wedding day was unconscionable. Indefensible. You might have regrets, yes, but the blame for what happened *that day* sits squarely on his shoulders. He could've come to you before the ceremony. You could've faced your guests together. Instead, he took the easy way out. The coward's way out."

Truly, it was yet another example of his self-centered attitude. It made me want to smack him upside his head, honestly, which told me I still had a little more healing to do.

"Thanks, Addie." I allowed myself to lean against her. After a minute or two of watching tourists drift by, shopping bags in hand, I said, "I worry, though."

"About?"

"Dare. I see some of myself in him. I think he's seeing things the way he wants them to be. Instead of the way they are."

"I'm worried, too," she said quietly.

As we sat there, huddled together, I imagined Dare becoming lost in the dark, hiding from the truth of his situation. I knew I had to do something to help him. Because if I'd learned anything since coming back to Starlight, it was that the more people there were to lean on, the easier it was going to be to find the way back to the light.

And that the support might come from the most unexpected people.

CHAPTER EIGHTEEN

From the Kitchen of Verbena Fullbright

Has your buttercream gone all kinds of wrong after storing it in the fridge? First things first, let it come to room temperature before trying to use it. If it's still not coming together quite right, add in a little bit of melted butter and give it a good mixin'. In my opinion, when it comes to butter, more of it is always a good thing.

Addie

As Freddie Mercury crooned about finding somebody to love, light drizzle drifted lazily from the skies outside the big red barn. It was a cool and cloudy morning and the sky seemed to be growing grayer by the minute. Sitting among the branches of the pecan tree, eighteen silver starlings fluffed and preened.

At seeing them, my thoughts went straight to Dare Fife. He'd sent a text message to Aunt Bean late yesterday afternoon saying the doctors had confirmed it was his appendix and he was being prepped for laparoscopic surgery. There'd been no updates since. Bean had plans to pay him a visit after work, and once Luna heard, she'd begged to go with her. Sawyer had volunteered to drive them and would be here in a half hour to collect them both and carry them off.

It was almost two in the afternoon, and Willa Jo was still out making deliveries. Delilah had headed out the door a few minutes ago with the SOLD OUT sign and hadn't yet made her way back up the long driveway.

Aunt Bean walked to the window and looked out. I noticed

she was rubbing her watch face, which made me immediately grab hold of my pendant, my thumb bumping over the five blue stones that made up the star.

"Anyone hear an update about this weather clearing up before the gala tonight?" she asked.

"My dad said it's going to rain all day," Luna said.

She'd taken to coming by the kitchen even when she wasn't there to tidy up. It reminded me of when I was little, always wanting to be here with Bean and the Sugarbirds. Among their warmth. Their love.

"I might have to swap out the heels I'd planned to wear tonight for rain boots," Bean said, turning away from the window, the birds, the weather.

"It's a fashion statement to be sure," Henrietta said.

She'd returned to attend the gala this weekend—using Bean's extra ticket—and we'd immediately roped her into helping out today since Pinky was still nursing her broken wrist.

"I'll do it if you do, Aunt Bean," Tessa Jane said from her spot at the decorating station, where she'd spent most of the day piping intricate designs onto heart-shaped cookies. Every so often, she'd straighten up, tip her head side to side to stretch her neck, and shake out her hands. Once she finished, and the icing fully dried, she needed to package and deliver the cookies to the hotel so they could be added to tonight's goody bags.

"Me, too," I added.

"Not me," Luna said, grinning. "I'm wearing tennis shoes."

Henrietta's eyebrows rose, and I smiled. Ree used to wear tennis shoes—Converse, specifically—with dresses all the time and it made me wonder if Luna had seen a picture.

I fought a yawn as I wiped down a worktop. I wasn't a napper usually, but I could use one today. I'd been up since five this morning had been on my feet most of that time. After finishing up here, I had to edit an audition tape and send it to my agent. The job was for a lead role in a major, big-budget animated film, and if I landed it, it would give me the freedom to cut back on voice work. Way back.

Which would then give me the freedom to also work at the bakery.

At least part-time. Which should be enough to fill the empty spot in my heart where the longing to be a Sugarbird has lived for so long.

I tried not to get my hopes too high as I continued down my mental to-do list. After editing the tape, I had minor alterations to do on the dresses Tessa Jane and I found at Gossamer last night. Hers needed taking in at the waist, and I needed to shorten the straps on mine. On top of all that, the ducks needed tending, the indoor pets needed to be fed, and Hambone also needed to be walked. And of course, I had to get ready for the dance and the possible reveal of Bean's admirer.

"Done!" Tessa Jane exclaimed, tossing a piping bag aside. Her bangs flopped around as she did a little dance, half jig, half cha-cha, as we all clapped for her.

"They're gorgeous," Henrietta said, taking a moment to inspect Tessa Jane's work. "I'd never have the patience for such intricacy."

"Thanks, Mama. I'm not sure how I have the patience, either. But when I'm working on them, time seems to fly by."

"That's what happens when you love what you're doing," Aunt Bean said. "Might be time to think about starting an official company."

"The Starling Cookie Company," Tessa Jane said dreamily, clearly joking.

Aunt Bean smiled. "A more perfect name I've never heard. Has quite the ring to it. I'm just sayin'."

"I say, too," I piped up.

"Me three!" Luna added.

Henrietta nodded but didn't say anything, which told me she might have some reservations about the idea.

Tessa Jane laughed and shook her head as though she thought we were in on her joke—instead of being perfectly serious—then set about packaging the cookies that had already dried. I hoped once she had a free minute that she'd give the idea more thought.

The record skipped, and Aunt Bean said, "I can't even tell you how many times Gavin listened to this record in high school. Had to be in the hundreds. I'm surprised the grooves aren't worn clean through."

"Really?" Tessa Jane asked.

"Lord have mercy, peanut. After a while, it was like those guitar solos were jackhammering my brain. I contemplated cuttin' the power a time or two."

Luna laughed as she carried cupcake tins and cake pans to the sink—as if she couldn't help herself from lending a hand. "Couldn't you just ask him to turn it down, Miss Verbena?"

"I'd ask, darlin', and he'd start acting like he couldn't hear a word I said. Cupping his ear and whatnot. It should go without saying that one of his favorite things to do was work my last nerve." She tried to sound peeved, but fondness filled her voice instead. Then she gave a gentle shake to her head and said, "Oh, how I miss him."

I swallowed over the lump in my throat and saw Henrietta thumb a tear from the corner of her eye.

She said, "I can't say I shared his taste in music but I always loved how it made him light right up, his smile the glow of a thousand stars. Once, we went to a concert in Atlanta and I spent the whole show watching him instead of the stage." She sighed heavily and went back to wiping counters.

I'd spent so much of my life *trying* to forget how close she'd been to my father, but now I realized that she probably had dozens of stories about him I'd never heard before. And I wanted to know each and every one.

Suddenly I was angry at myself for what had been lost by nurturing my mama's hatred all this time when deep down, I knew better. *I knew better* and still I hoped that if I took my mama's side, she'd come back. She'd stay. Especially after my daddy died. But she never did.

I took deep breaths. I couldn't change the past. Or my

mama's choices. But I could focus on the people who were here with me now. Who'd always been here for me, really.

Crackles came from the record player as one song ended and another began.

Luna slipped on a pair of dish gloves that practically went up to her shoulders. "My dad said my mom loved Queen, too. It's why I picked this record."

When Luna had discovered my dad's box of records while visiting the kittens, she'd begged to bring a few of the albums to the kitchen in the big red barn. We relented with the stipulation that the Bee Gees also be played to appease the Sugarbirds, who'd been obsessed with the group since the late eighties when they'd road-tripped to New York City to see the band in person.

Earlier, when Luna had first put the Queen record on the turntable, I'd held my breath. At hearing the first scratch and those punchy opening guitar notes, my heart had skipped a beat, my eyes filled with tears, and I thought for sure the grief floodgates were about to open.

It was then that Aunt Bean took my hand and twirled me around as a cymbal crashed, exactly like my dad used to do. Tessa Jane jumped up to join us and before we knew it there was a dance party going on, right up until one of the oven buzzers dinged, bringing us back to reality.

"I wouldn't say your mama loved Queen so much as she loved *Bohemian Rhapsody*," I said to Luna. "She loved anything dramatic and theatrical and that song, and the way Freddie Mercury sang it, ticked all her boxes. She had a CD of her favorite songs and when that one came on, she'd immediately hop up on her bed with hairbrush in hand and start singing along. I'd sit on the floor and pretend I was in an audience, waving my hands and acting a fool. About halfway through, right as she was belting the song out at the top of her lungs, was almost always when her granny would start banging on the wall, hollering for Ree to pipe down so as not to wake the dead with all the caterwauling. Ree and I would laugh and laugh, and because we knew her granny loved her more than life itself, we'd restart the song at the beginning and do it all over again."

The skies opened and rain poured down as I finished talking, snapping me out of the past, and I glanced around. Everyone was staring at me—even Tessa Jane had turned around. She was smiling.

"What?" I asked. "Why're y'all looking at me like that?"

"Lordy, punkin," Aunt Bean said with a sigh. "There's just something so captivating about you when you start telling a story about someone you love."

"Can I record you talking about my mom, Miss Addie? Please?" Luna asked, bouncing lightly. "I want to keep these stories forever."

Before I could answer, Delilah threw open the door. She was soaked to the bone and water droplets covered her glasses. "Are y'all keeping Pepper again while Dare's in the hospital?"

Tessa Jane was already halfway across the room with a towel for her. "No, why?"

Delilah said, "I thought I just saw her near the woods."

We all hurried to the door. Sure enough, on the far side of the lawn, Pepper was running along the fence line. She wasn't barking, and after a moment of watching her, it was clear she was limping.

Tessa Jane was the first out the door, quickly followed by Luna and Henrietta. They all called Pepper's name loudly as they ran toward her, but I wasn't sure the dog could even hear them with the way the rain coming down. It sounded like the sky was falling.

Aunt Bean muttered cuss words under her breath and pulled out her phone. "I'll give Petal a call."

With my chin down, I rushed out the door, heading for the farmhouse, deciding to take a different tactic. If anything could lure Pepper to safety, it was Hambone.

I startled him awake when I threw open the front door. Miney and Moe, too. They bolted for the stairs as Hambone scrambled to his feet, his tail wagging, always up for adventure.

I closed the door so he wouldn't slip out and hurried to grab his leash from the hooks by the back door. But no sooner had I taken a few steps did he hop up on the sofa to look out the window, as if suddenly aware that something of interest was happening outside. He went stiff, his ears twitching. I snapped the leash on his collar, and led him outside.

He barked loudly and pulled me along. I had to use both hands just to keep any semblance of control over him. "Steady now, Ham!"

Across the yard, Luna, Tessa Jane, and Henrietta were closing in on Pepper, but as soon as she heard Hambone, she darted our way. It was heartbreaking to see the way she ran awkwardly, favoring a front leg.

Hambone rushed toward her, and when they met up, they bumped against each other, barking and wiggling, full of joy.

I noticed straight off that Pepper wasn't wearing her collar.

Anger brewed, and I wished I'd offered to dog sit while Dare was in the hospital, especially knowing how desperate Petal was to get rid of her. Then I took a deep breath and told myself not to jump to conclusions. Maybe Pepper had simply slipped out of her collar. Maybe. But doubtful.

As rain poured down, I started walking Hambone slowly back toward the house, and Pepper followed willingly. Luna reached us just as we'd made it to the porch steps, breathing hard from the exertion of running back and forth across the wide lawn. Tessa Jane and Henrietta weren't far behind. They had their heads bent together, and Henrietta was saying something I wished I could hear, because if her heated expression was any indication, she was all fired about it.

Inside the house, Aunt Bean and Delilah were waiting on us. A stack of fluffy towels sat on the coffee table. I took one, wiped my eyes, then sat down on the floor for a closer look at Pepper, who had rolled onto her back at the sight of the towel, her tail wagging. I wasn't sure how she'd found her way to us, but it was clear she was happy to be here.

Luna was doing her best to keep Hambone away from

Pepper while I checked her out, but he was too excited. Delilah finally grabbed hold of his collar and told him, "Sit!" in such a forceful tone that I'd have sat immediately if I wasn't already on the floor.

Hambone reluctantly lowered himself down and Luna pounced, wrapping him in a towel and holding him tight.

When Tessa Jane and Henrietta came inside, Henrietta grabbed a towel for herself and handed another to her daughter. She wiped her face dry and said, "I'll put the kettle on. Hot tea will warm us right up."

Tessa Jane dripped water on the floor as she knelt next to me. Her hair was plastered to her head, her shirt to her body. "Do you see any injuries?"

"Nothing yet," I said, "but I haven't been able to get a real good look at her paw."

"I'll hold her." She gently gathered Pepper, pulling her partly onto her lap.

I used my phone's flashlight to get a better look at the hurt paw. When I touched a spot near one of her toe beans, Pepper let out a yelp and pulled her paw out of my hand. "It's okay," I soothed, giving her belly a rub to show I meant no hard feelings.

To everyone else, I said, "There's something stuck in her paw. Maybe a splinter? I can't really tell."

Tessa Jane scratched at a welt on her neck as she looked at Delilah. "Is the vet clinic open on weekends?"

She'd asked Delilah because her oldest son, Ross, was the local vet. Delilah said, "They closed at one today, but let me call Ross and tell him what all's going on." She pulled a phone from her pocket and stepped into the kitchen to make the call.

I glanced at Aunt Bean. "What did Petal have to say?"

Aunt Bean's eyes were hard as rock and her voice was strung tight as she said, "My call went straight to Petal's voicemail. She either has her phone off or she's done blocked my number."

I suspected the latter, considering their confrontation at Friddle's.

"Why would she block your number, Miss Verbena?" Luna finger-combed her hair off her face but one strand stubbornly stuck to her cheek.

She looked like a drowned rat. We all did, except Aunt Bean, whose hair still looked perfectly perky and whose clothes were mostly dry except for the hem of her dress. I wasn't quite sure how she'd pulled that off.

"Probably because she didn't want to hear what I had to say to her, darlin'. I did leave her a message that we had Pepper and left it at that. For now."

Oh Lord.

Luna's brow wrinkled as she took in this information, recognizing that Bean was furious. She glanced at me, and I tried to tell her with my gaze to let it go for the time being.

Henrietta came back into the living room, using the towel to dry the ends of her hair. "Verbena, do you mind if I go with you to visit Dare?"

I spared a look at Tessa Jane, who didn't seem surprised by the offer. If Henrietta was wanting to talk with him, then she'd obviously recognized his relationship with Petal was far from healthy.

"Don't mind at all," Aunt Bean said. "It'll be good to have you there."

"I'll just run and change real quick." She headed for the stairs.

"Should we call Dare?" Luna asked. "He'd want to know if Pepper's hurt."

Aunt Bean gently put her hand on Luna's head. "Let's hold off on that for now, sweetheart. We'll tell him when we see him. Your daddy will be here soon. You ought to try to catch him before he leaves to ask him to bring you some dry clothes."

"Yes, ma'am." She took one of the clean towels, wiped her face, and bent over. She wrapped the towel around her head, twisting it to hold all her hair, then straightened again, tucking in the tail of the towel so it would stay put on her head. Then she pulled her phone from her back pocket and typed a message, her fingers flying across the screen.

Hambone inched over to Pepper and I unclipped his leash. The two dogs danced around each other, sniffing to their hearts' content.

I half listened to Delilah talking to her son in low tones, then glanced at a seething Aunt Bean, who was setting out teacups. I turned to look out the window. Through a sheet of pouring rain, I saw the starlings perched in the pecan tree. Their lingering presence was a warning that we weren't through the worst of the storm quite yet.

Moments later, Henrietta gracefully came down the steps in dark jeans and a royal blue cashmere sweater. Her damp hair had been slicked back and knotted at her neck in an elegant style. Her face had been powdered, her lips glossed. The kettle whistled and she headed straight into the kitchen. "The tea will be ready in a minute."

Delilah finished her call and tucked the phone in her pocket. "I'm going to run Pepper over to the clinic right quick. Ross is going to meet me there." She faced Tessa Jane and me as the kettle quieted. "Do y'all want to come along? Pepper will be more at ease with you there."

Tessa Jane stood up and wrapped her hair in a towel exactly like Luna had. "Definitely." Then she threw a look at the clock and winced. "Actually—"

"You go," I told her. "I'll finish up your cookies. It's just the packaging, so there's not much I can mess up. They'll be boxed and ready to deliver by the time you get back."

She threw her arms around me. "Thanks, Addie."

It was, I realized, our first full hug.

I squeezed her tightly and then held up Hambone's leash. "Do you want to use this to create a makeshift collar for Pepper or simply carry her to the car?"

Hambone heard the word *car* and started racing this way and that, barking excitedly. I tried to grab him, but he expertly evaded my reach, jumping away, and I about fell over. Henrietta grabbed my arm to steady me. Hambone knocked into Luna, who stumbled into Tessa Jane. They latched onto each other for balance and laughed, their voices blending harmoniously.

Their laughter was infectious and I was smiling until the sight of them all tangled up made me freeze. My breath caught. My knees went weak. Henrietta tightened her hold on my arm and gave me an odd look.

"Have mercy!" Aunt Bean shouted, throwing her hands in the air. "This place is a madhouse. I'm going to freshen up."

Delilah howled with laughter. The chaos *would* be hilarious if I didn't feel like I was free-falling.

I blinked away tears, realization hitting me like an arrow aimed straight at my heart.

Henrietta held on tight as if sensing that my world had slipped a little. I looked at her, silently asking a question that I already knew the answer to. Moisture filled her eyes, and her pleading gaze begged me not to say anything.

I glanced back at Tessa Jane and Luna just to double-check that I hadn't been seeing things. Hoping I was wrong. But I wasn't.

"Help me with the tea, will you, Addie?" Henrietta gently tugged my arm.

I had a hard time following her, because I couldn't take my eyes off Luna and Tessa Jane.

And their matching blue eyes, big smiles, and widow's peaks.

*

I leaned against the counter, my palms face down on the cool countertop. I started counting veins in the marble.

How had I never noticed Tessa Jane's widow's peak? I thought back, way back, trying to conjure her face with her hair pulled completely back but right now my thoughts were too jumbled.

Henrietta's hands were shaking as she poured hot water from the kettle, splashing it on the counter. "She doesn't know. Please don't tell her," she whispered. "*Please.*"

I took deep breaths. Tears filled my eyes, rolled down my cheeks.

Tessa Jane didn't know that her father was Bryce Buckley.

She wasn't my sister.

She was Luna's cousin. And Dare's niece. But she wasn't my sister.

My voice cracked. "Did my father know?"

She held my gaze, and I saw her bright inner light clear as day as she nodded. "It was his idea. To protect her. He was—" she shook her head as tears spilled from her eyes, "an incredible friend and an even better man."

I used the heels of my hands to wipe my tears. My pulse pounded in my ears, drowning out the voices in the living room. Blocking out the dogs. I couldn't even hear the rain as it slapped the windows. It was as though Henrietta and I were the only two in the house, trapped in a bubble of deception, hiding this devastating news.

Oh, lord, the thought of Tessa Jane learning this secret broke my heart because I knew it would break hers.

Henrietta touched my arm. "*Please*, Addie."

My stomach twisted at the thought of keeping another secret. Of how I'd need to leave town again. Of how I'd have to abandon myself, and everything I wanted and needed and dreamed of, so Tessa Jane would never know the truth.

So she wouldn't be hurt.

Because I loved her enough to want to protect her from that pain.

But no. *No.*

I knew, I'd learned, that the longer this was kept from her, the *more* it would hurt.

I loved her so much that I knew she needed to know the truth. She had the right to know.

I loved her, because she was my sister, plain and simple.

Before I could say anything to Henrietta, she said, "I'll tell her, I promise. It's long past time she knows the truth, and she needs to hear it from me. Just give me a little time."

I swallowed hard. "How long?"

"I'll tell her tonight, after the gala. Let her enjoy the evening."

I truly wanted her to pull Tessa Jane aside right that minute, because the secret was already pulsing within me, begging to be spoken. And I hated, absolutely *despised* the thought of keeping something from Tessa Jane after we'd only just patched up our relationship. But as I watched my sister hurrying up the stairs to change, I realized that now probably wasn't the best time.

"All right," I reluctantly agreed.

Later tonight, Aunt Bean and I would be here, to help pick up the pieces. To hug and hold Tessa Jane and help her through it. And, most importantly, to remind her that what Sawyer had told me earlier this week was one hundred percent true.

It was *love* that made a family.

CHAPTER NINETEEN

From the Kitchen of Verbena Fullbright
Crumb-coating a cake is a messy and time-consuming business, but the results are always worth the extra work. Like anything in life, the effort you put in influences what you get in return.

Addie

"It looks a picture!" Aunt Bean said, glancing around in delight at the Celestial Hotel's dimly lit ballroom, trying to take in every last detail.

"It does," I agreed, scanning the room as the band played "This Magic Moment" from a stage that hadn't been there the last time I'd been in this space.

Gradations of pink faintly illuminated the ceiling and floor from lights placed strategically around the room, creating a romantic atmosphere. Tea lights flickered playfully from the tables, inviting people to sit a spell.

Cattywampus to the dance floor was the dessert bar, where the cupcake tower stood proudly, showing off swirls of fluffy frosting topped with twin delicate pink hearts made of white chocolate.

Tessa Jane had been snagged by Randie Beth Robinson on our way in, and Henrietta had headed for the bar the moment she stepped into the room to order her and Bean glasses of wine and me a club soda with lime. I was too nervous to drink, afraid I'd say something I shouldn't.

"Oh, there's Ernie," Bean said.

As I followed her toward the table where Ernie sat, it felt like I was walking behind a vanilla-scented floral cloud. Aunt Bean wore a collared white silk blouse and a floor-length rose-patterned skirt that billowed as she walked.

We'd arrived late. It was already thirty minutes into the pre-dinner cocktail hour. The afternoon had been a blur of emotion as I raced to get everything done before the gala and to keep my lips zipped. I'd powered through packaging cookies and cleaning the bakery kitchen—the Bee Gees my only company because I'd been too fragile to listen to my father's records.

I'd taken care of the ducks, having to use Tessa Jane's method of bribing them with raspberries to get them into the shed because apparently they'd been living their best lives playing in the rain. I'd cleaned litter boxes and mended dresses.

I'd also taken a moment to study the photos in the upstairs hallway, searching for Tessa Jane's widow's peak. But in all the pictures, her bangs had hidden the trait she'd inherited from Bryce. And even though I knew the truth now and saw that she had likely gotten her eyes and smile from her father, in those images, she still looked like Henrietta's mini me. No wonder people had been none the wiser.

And as I'd stood in that hallway, staring at the photo of my daddy and me and Tessa Jane, his arms around our shoulders, his eyes shining with love and happiness, I was surprised by how glad I was that he'd made the choice he had. That he'd chosen to protect her.

Ernie beamed when she spotted us and noisily kissed our cheeks in greeting. She was looking better, healthier, each time I saw her. Her head was covered tonight in a silk wrap, but I knew she had baby-fine silver hair growing beneath it. The injury she'd received when she'd fallen in the kitchen had healed nicely, and tonight she'd disguised any lingering bruising with makeup.

"I heard you've been to see Dare," she immediately said to Aunt Bean. "How is he?"

"Damn lucky," Bean said. "His appendix was fixin' to burst. I don't even want to think about what might've happened if we hadn't crossed paths with him yesterday at Friddle's and made him listen about seeing a doctor. Because heaven knows, Petal was going to let that poor boy suffer. He still looks pitiful, but as it is, he'll only have to stay in the hospital for a couple more days and should be able to return to his normal routines in a week or two."

Petal hadn't been at the hospital when Bean had visited, so my aunt had been denied the come-to-Jesus meeting she'd had planned, but I had the feeling one way or another it would be delivered.

Ernie leaned in, her eyes wide. "What's this about Petal now?"

Bean settled herself into a chair and fluffed her skirt. "Oh, wait till you hear. She called him lazy because he was sick in bed."

"No!" Ernie gasped.

Bean nodded. "And that's just the start."

I didn't think I could bear a full rehashing, so I said, "I'm going to help Henrietta with the drinks. Do you care for anything, Miss Ernie?"

She glanced over her shoulder to a corner of the room, where I saw Ty talking with someone I didn't know. She dropped her voice as though he might hear her, and said, "Why don't you get a glass of white wine for *yourself* and come sit next to me, real close?" She winked theatrically.

I smiled. "Good thing I just had a mighty hankering for a glass of wine." I certainly wasn't going to deny her a sip or two of wine after all she'd been through. "I'll be right back."

I weaved my way through the crowd, skirting the dance floor. The band was now playing "My Girl" and when I spotted Luna and Sawyer on the dance floor, my heart melted into a sentimental puddle.

"Miss Addie!" she shouted, catching sight of me.

She broke free from Sawyer and raced over to me, the skirt

of her dress swaying. On her feet were a pair of pink Converse and seeing them nearly brought a tear to my eye.

"How's Pepper doing?" she asked, her eyes bright, completely oblivious to Sawyer being humorously dramatic behind her, throwing his hands up in the air and muttering about being abandoned.

I knew full well Tessa Jane had sent Luna a message along with pictures not two hours ago, so I said, "Last I saw her, she was cuddled up with Hambone on the couch, sleeping." I added, "You look lovely."

Tessa Jane said it had taken nearly ninety minutes for Ross Peebles to do a full workup on Pepper earlier this afternoon. The thorn he'd pulled from her paw had been embedded so deeply between her toes that he'd needed to use two stitches to close the wound. She was now on antibiotics and her paw was wrapped in a bandage she would surely remove if not for the neck cone she had to wear for the next week or so.

According to Aunt Bean, when she'd told Dare about Pepper, he'd gone ghostly white—which apparently was quite something considering he was already sickly pale. After a minute, he asked if Pepper could stay with us until he was back home.

It told me bucketloads about what *he* suspected had happened to the dog.

Luna rolled her eyes. "Dresses, ugh. Dad had to order this one online. The only dresses around here are all so frilly. Not that your dress isn't pretty! It is. It's perfect for *you*. Oh, there's Tessa Jane!" She skipped off.

Sawyer laughed as he walked over to me. "One day she'll stand still."

"Don't count on it."

He smiled. "She was right—your dress is pretty."

I glanced down at the tiered, ruffled dress. It was a deep teal green color, which didn't quite go with the Valentine's theme, but beggars who shop the night before the dance couldn't be choosers. I fought the urge to fuss with the thin straps I'd shortened earlier so the V-neck wasn't quite so deep and said, "Thank you. I heard it was perfect for me."

There was a smattering of applause as the song ended, and the band immediately started another. I recognized the notes of "When the Stars Go Blue" right away, and waited for the usual wave of grief, because it had been one of Ree's favorites. But it didn't come. Instead, I was filled only with a warmth that came from loving her and wishing she could be here.

Light played in Sawyer's eyes as he held out his hand. "Care to dance?"

I looked toward the table where Bean and Ernie sat, only to find that Henrietta had already joined them. All three were giving me thumbs up. Bean used both hands.

"I haven't danced in a long time," I said, trying to come up with some semblance of a reasonable excuse not to.

"It's like riding a bike."

"I haven't done that in a long time, either."

"We'll tackle that another day." He looked at his hand and made small encouraging nods toward it.

Little bubbles of happiness rose in me at his playful antics, which I thought was a miracle considering the day I had. I took a deep breath and put my hand in his.

I swore I heard clapping from Ernie's's table but didn't dare look.

Sawyer put his arm around my back. "Luna's been talking nonstop about the day she had with y'all."

I settled into his arms awkwardly, as if he were a stranger. As if we hadn't danced a hundred times before. "Well, it *was* quite the day."

Furrow lines creased his forehead. "You should probably know that Petal's been asking everyone here if they've seen Pepper, saying she slipped out the door earlier while Petal was bringing groceries into the house."

I felt my body tense with anger. Why hadn't Pepper been wearing her collar, then? "Wait a second. Petal's *here*? At the gala?"

He nodded. "Sure is."

I glanced around but didn't see her. I wasn't sure whether it was brave or stupid of her to show up tonight with Aunt Bean on the warpath, never mind that she was living it up while her husband was in the hospital. With Petal, I was starting to think they weren't mutually exclusive traits.

Sawyer said, "Or she *was* here, I should say. No one was buying her story, knowing how she feels about Pepper. She was getting some pushback and not taking it too well."

Good. She deserved every bit of it. More, even.

His heat seeped through his shirt and into my hand that rested on his shoulder. His piney scent drifted around us as we swayed, and I inched a tiny bit closer to him. I wanted to press my head to his chest and forget all my worries. Which was impossible, so I said, "Honestly, I could use a distraction from everything that happened today. Any good trespassing stories lately?"

"None today, but something interesting has been happening. A few nights this week, I've seen someone sitting on the edge of the crater at dusk. Different guy each time."

"Sitting? Not digging?" That was new.

His hand burned through my dress at the small of my back, and I swore I could feel every single twitch of his fingertips. My heart was doing all kinds of strange things as he looked into my eyes.

"No shovel in sight. Dressed in full camo, they sit still as a stone, holding a dental mirror, trying to catch the light with it. If the starlings hadn't raised an alarm each time, I probably wouldn't have noticed at all. Even with binoculars, it was hard to spot them from my place."

I was having trouble concentrating, too entranced by the play of light in his hazel eyes. "Why a mirror?"

"Beats me. The starlings run them off before I can even get my shoes on."

I longed to touch his face, run my fingers along his strong jaw. My voice crackled as I said, "How bizarre."

He was staring at my lips.

Lord have *mercy*.

"It really is," he said, resting his cheek against my hair.

I finally gave in and cuddled close, breathing in the scent of him. Safe in his arms, I relaxed as we swayed, and I was already dreading the song coming to an end. Because suddenly I couldn't help feeling that in his arms was where I was always meant to be.

Tessa Jane

"Tessa Jane! Just the person I was hoping to see. Do you have a minute?"

Randie Beth Robinson, the director of Hand to Heart, wore a wide smile, which immediately calmed the sudden jolt of nerves at seeing her, fearing there had been an issue with the cookies I'd delivered earlier.

The lights were low, and music filled the air along with the scent of roses from a series of floral arches that lined a red-carpet pathway into the ballroom. Twinkle lights were tucked into the greenery, making it feel like a scene straight out of an enchanted forest.

Since I'd sent Addie, Aunt Bean, and my mama ahead, saying they didn't need to wait for me, I faced Randie Beth and smiled. She wore a red strapless dress that showed off dark, toned shoulders that appeared to have been dusted with shimmer powder— they sparkled. "It looks like a fairy tale in here, Randie Beth. It's absolutely beautiful."

We stood outside the ballroom, next to a small table that was tucked out of the way. A young woman was busy tapping on a laptop, and I was surprised to see it was Jenna Elkins.

"Oh hey, Tessa Jane," she said, glancing up at me and smiling. She sat tall, as though the weight of the world had been lifted off her shoulders. "You probably didn't expect to be seeing me here."

Randie Beth said, "Jenna started her job with us this week.

We threw her straight into the deep end, but she's swimming just fine."

Jenna looked a sight happier than the last time I'd seen her, that was for sure. "It seems like it's suiting you well."

"Sure is." A walkie-talkie crackled, and Jenna bounced up, her pink gown swirling around her legs. "If y'all will excuse me?"

She stepped away and Randie Beth said, "I won't keep you, Tessa Jane, but I wanted to let you know I'm getting raves about your cookies from people who've already tucked into their goody bags and are interested in placing orders. A birthday, a wedding shower, and a St. Patrick's Day party. I wasn't sure what to tell them. I know you're fixin' to leave town in a few days. Does your cookie business offer shipping?"

"Actually—" I began, then stopped. I'd been about to tell her that it wasn't a business, that cookie decorating was only a hobby. But hadn't I practically been working nonstop on those cookies this past week? The cookies hadn't been a gift for a friend or just because. Randie Beth had placed an order and paid me in full.

That was a job.

A rewarding, creative job, yes, but still hard work. Could I manage it on top of my work at the country club? Probably. It would mean late nights, but I was okay with that. Then I thought about my mama's reaction earlier today when I'd been joking about a cookie company. I'd noticed that she hadn't been as excited as everyone else at the idea.

But wasn't she the one who said I should live my own life, make my own choices? I couldn't keep trying to make everyone else happy. I'd done that and all I'd gotten for it was a broken heart and a heap of embarrassment.

I took a deep breath and jumped into a deep end of my own. "Actually, my cookie business does ship. Go ahead and tell people to email or call and we'll work something out."

My cookie business.

The Starling Cookie Company.

Aunt Bean had said it had a nice ring to it and I agreed. Wholeheartedly.

"Wonderful!" Randie Beth exclaimed. "I'll let people know. Now could you do me a favor?"

"Absolutely. What do you need?"

She stepped over to the table, rifled through a stack of printouts. Finally, she pulled one free. "Could you give this to Verbena for me? She mentioned there was no need for a receipt, but I'm sure she'll want it for her records. A portion of the tickets are tax deductible after all. When she called earlier this week about getting additional tickets, I was so glad I'd held few in reserve. She's been such a generous donor all these years."

It was a receipt for three gala tickets, which had been paid for in cash earlier this week. Specifically, the day before Stan had delivered the tickets to the bakery. As I stared at the paper, I couldn't stop smiling.

Discovering that Aunt Bean was her own secret admirer was a bright side to this night I'd never expected. And as a bonus, she'd managed to get Addie and me to attend tonight— something she'd wanted all along. It had been a brilliant plan. "I'll make sure she gets this. Thanks."

Luna found me as soon as I walked into the ballroom, looking as sweet as could be in her party dress. In a minute's span she asked a million questions about Pepper's vet visit, one after another, rapid-fire, before she gasped as she spotted a friend, a girl who appeared to be around her age, and ran off to look at the desserts.

I made my way to the bar, secured my place in the long line, and took a deep breath. I noticed my mama looking at the silent auction items. Her back was to me, but I could easily imagine the worried look on her face. Her eyebrows pulled down low, her lips pressed together. She'd been wearing the expression ever since she'd volunteered to go see Dare this afternoon. It hadn't changed since she'd been back. If Gigi had seen it, she'd have pointedly warned Mama that if she wasn't careful, her face would freeze that way.

Gigi. I wondered what she'd think about my cookie business and decided she'd be cheering for me.

"My darling girl," she'd said to me the Christmas before she'd passed away, "why are you so sad?"

She'd been in failing health and my heart had hurt at how she seemed to be shrinking. She was but a tiny shell of her former self. Still, she'd insisted we sit on the sofa in her suite, sharing a blanket, watching the starlight in the distance glow through the patio doors.

"I'm not," I'd lied, giving her fragile hand a squeeze.

She'd cupped my cheek. "Lies don't become you, Tessa Jane."

I'd sighed and watched the starlight. "It's just that sometimes I feel as though I'm living a life not my own. The expectations of others are weighing me down."

"It weighs you down only if you allow it."

"It's not that easy, Gigi. The starlight land for example."

She'd watched me carefully, her blue eyes watery but still as perceptive as ever. "You don't want your grandfather to own it."

I'd shrugged, trying to play it off. "It doesn't feel right."

"Then keep it, sweetheart."

"You know he's not going to allow that."

"Tessa Jane," she'd said, her quivery voice somehow firm. "Do not underestimate the strength of a Cobb backbone. Above all else, you must stay true to yourself. Promise me you won't allow others to dull your beautiful shine. Not your grandfather. Not your mama. Not anyone. Embracing who *you* are and what *you* want is the only path to happiness, I promise you."

For a while, I *had* let others dull that shine. I had even done it to myself. But not now. Not ever again. Gigi would be thrilled with my new business venture—because it made me happy.

As I finally ordered a drink, I wished my grandmother were here. I wished a lot of things these days. Today, my wishes had been focused mostly on Dare. According to Mama, he'd "yes, ma'amed" her to death while she talked with him at the hospital and seemed embarrassed when she'd delicately spoke about the warning signs of abuse. She said she wasn't even sure if he was truly listening but left him with a counseling brochure and her phone number in case he ever wanted to talk.

I turned and caught sight of Addie dancing with Sawyer. I gave her a big, cheesy smile and made a heart shape with my hands when she saw me watching her. I couldn't swear to it, because of the dim lighting, but I thought she rolled her eyes.

I startled a bit when my gaze happened to land on my grandfather, who was staring at me from a table near the stage. He lifted his whiskey glass in a mock toast, and I offered a smile and a wave, even though I didn't like the way he glowered.

Uncomfortable, I picked up my drink and studiously avoided looking his way as I headed toward Aunt Bean. When she saw me coming, she patted the empty seat next to her.

I eyed the chair, which happened to be in between her and Ty Underwood, and reluctantly sat. I smiled as I said hello to him and Ernie and the all the Sugarbirds, who were also seated at the table.

I was about to slip Aunt Bean the receipt Randie Beth had given me, but quickly tucked it into my clutch as Stan Reeves stepped up to the table. He gave hearty hellos to everyone, then said, "Verbena, would you care to dance? That is if you don't think your secret admirer will mind." He diligently looked around, studying the face of every man nearby with a healthy dose of suspicion.

And suddenly I knew the true reason why Aunt Bean had orchestrated her own admirer. It was to give Stan the kick in the pants he needed to make the first move.

"A dance? Why that would be lovely," she said as if she'd never even considered the idea.

Now I also knew where Addie had inherited her acting skills.

She rose, leaving her walking stick leaning against the table. Stan gently placed his hand on her elbow to guide her along, and as they headed for the dance floor, she glanced over her shoulder and waggled her eyebrows.

Every last one of us sitting round that table gave her a thumbs up. Even Ty, which tickled me to death.

Pinky started laughing. Her cast was the color of a ballet slipper and had at least a dozen signatures on it. "Do y'all think *Stan* is Bean's secret admirer?"

"I thought it was all y'all." Ernie pointedly looked at the Sugarbirds.

"I wish I'd thought of it," Delilah said. "It sure kicked him into gear."

As they fell into a lively conversation about the identity of the admirer, I excused myself for a moment, making a beeline for a trashcan. There, I crumpled up the receipt Randie Beth had given me and tossed it in the container. I'd let Bean keep her secret, and let everyone else keep wondering.

When I returned to my seat, I accidentally bumped Ty's elbow. "Sorry," I said.

"No harm done."

I took a sip of my drink and told myself I didn't need to make small talk with him. I was perfectly fine sitting here, watching the Sugarbirds and Ernie talk about Bean's love life.

But I found I *wanted* to talk to him.

"How'd the squirrel transfer go this morning?" I asked.

"No problems other than convincing my mama that squirrels aren't meant to be pets. She got attached mighty quick. Thanks for the peanut donation, by the way."

"You're welcome."

I glanced at Ernie and caught her staring at Ty, while jerking her head toward me. When she noticed me looking, she coughed and dove straight back into the conversation with the Sugarbirds as though nothing out of the ordinary had happened.

"What was that about?" I asked him.

Ty gritted his teeth. "Would you like to dance, Grasshopper?" He leaned in close to me, putting his mouth near my ear. I ignored all the tiny flutters in my stomach as he whispered, "If you say no, you're going to break my mama's heart."

I pressed my lips together to keep from laughing, and then I leaned in and whispered in his ear. "My mama would call that a manipulative tactic, Bug."

He laughed a genuine laugh and, still talking into my ear, said, "My mama would call it parenting. It'll be easier for the both of us if you just play along."

I stole a peek across the table. The conversation about Bean and Stan had been paused so everyone could stare at Ty and me.

I whispered, "I'll do it only if you never tell my mama how easily I gave in."

"Deal." He pushed back his chair and held out his left hand.

Across the table came a chorus of *aww*s. I couldn't even bring myself to look that way as I left my evening bag on my seat and placed my hand in his.

His skin was rough but the way he held my hand was gentle as he led me to the dance floor. I looked for Addie for moral support, but she and Sawyer were now standing at the bar. Bean and Stan were lost somewhere in the crowd of couples swaying to Elvis's "Can't Help Falling in Love." Ty put one arm around my waist and the other hand held mine against his chest. I was grateful there was a good ten inches between us.

"I appreciate this," he said.

"It's no big deal," I answered.

He closed the distance between us an inch, and my heart rate skyrocketed. I fought the urge to scratch at the hive that appeared on my arm.

"It is to me. I really am sorry, Tessa Jane. For everything."

Him calling me by name did something strange to my heart. "Me, too. I'm sorry, too."

"For what? You didn't do anything."

"I'm just sorry. I know what it's like to lose a daddy. And, you know, I'm sorry for locking you in the closet that one time." I might as well lay it all out there.

He tipped his head back and laughed. "I didn't think you'd ever confess."

I looked up at him, got caught up in the different shades of brown in his eyes, and said, "You knew I'd done it?"

"I suspected. I'd caught a whiff of vanilla right before it happened. You always smelled like vanilla. Still do." He pulled me a bit closer. "I'll forgive you if you forgive me."

I smiled. "Deal."

We swayed for a while in silence before I caught sight of Addie, who was now making a heart with her hands. I definitely rolled my eyes.

Ty said, "It's nice that you two patched up your relationship. I heard y'all are even going to team up and build near the starlight crater. Let me know if you need any help with that."

I stiffened and stopped moving. "Where'd you hear that? About building? Did Aunt Bean say something?"

He stopped moving, too, but still held on to me. "No, I heard it in line at Friddle's this morning from Sissy Danes, who'd heard it from Bubba Coldwell, who'd heard it from Graham Doby."

My mind spun. Graham Doby. The newspaper reporter who'd had lunch with my mama last weekend.

The lunch where Mama got tipsy and hoped she hadn't said anything stupid.

Ty added, "He's writing an article about it that's going in tomorrow's paper."

"Oh no." This was bad. Real bad.

"Tessa Jane, is there someth—"

He was interrupted by a tap on his shoulder. "Mind if I cut in, son?"

My granddaddy's voice boomed loudly enough for the couples around us to turn and stare.

Ty jumped as if he'd been burned.

"I don't think—" I began.

"That's the problem, ain't it?" Granddaddy said, grabbing my hand.

When he tried to put his arm around my back, as if we were going to dance, I stepped back. I tried to pull my hand free, but he held tight.

His whiskey breath made my stomach turn as he said, "You ain't *thinking*, Tessa Jane. I done heard about your plan to steal my ideas for that land. If you think I'm going to let that happen, you have another think coming."

I tried again to free myself, but he squeezed my hand like a vise.

Ty stepped in, real close, fury in his eyes. In a deadly low voice, he said, "Sir, if you don't let go of her, I'm going to make you let go. Understand me?"

Granddaddy must've seen that Ty wasn't bluffing, because he dropped my hand. Ty immediately put his arm around me. "You okay?"

My palm ached. But it was my heart that hurt the most as I studied my grandfather's face, looking for even the slightest spark of something decent. Something good. But it wasn't there. It had never been there. He was never going to be the man I—or Gigi—wanted him to be.

The only cure for his poison was love. Love for himself, for others. But right now I wasn't sure he even knew what love was.

Mama swooped in out of nowhere, putting herself between Granddaddy and me. She faced him. "What is going on? You're making a scene."

I blinked away tears. Around us, people had stopped dancing even though music still played.

Jabbing a finger, Granddaddy said, "I should've known y'all would betray me the minute I stopped padding your bank accounts. Ungrateful little—"

"Enough!" Mama said sharply, cutting him off. "That's enough."

Hives broke out on my arms, my neck, and I felt nauseous.

Veins pulsed in Granddaddy's forehead and spittle flew as he said, "Good luck getting permits for *your* project once I'm mayor. And don't come crying to me when the land becomes town property through eminent domain. *Boo-hoo.*"

My jaw dropped. Of course he had a backup plan in place if I held on to the land. This was why he was running for mayor *now*. Mind whirling, I could see his scheme so clearly. As mayor, he would have the power to cause all kinds of trouble for us. And yes, he could probably even spearhead a case for eminent domain, nitpicking about traffic and crowd control. But once the town took over the land, I imagined he'd then mastermind a reason for the land to be sold. In a private deal. To him.

Mama stood tall against his wrath. "All you want is more money. Money, money, money. But you know what? You could be the wealthiest man in the world and you'd still be dirt poor, because you haven't realized that it's not money that will fill that needy, greedy hole in your soul."

I noticed Addie and Aunt Bean move in closer, their eyes wide with shock, horror.

Granddaddy laughed, a heartless sound that sent chills down my spine. "I never heard you complaining about my money before I cut you off, Henrietta. Funny, the timing of it all." He stepped to the side and leveled a malicious gaze on me. "That land was payment for my silence. I've been waiting for it ever since the day your ungrateful mama tried to pass off her bastard child as a Fullbright. I should've known you'd double-cross me considering the likes of your daddy. That no-account Buckley boy got what was coming to him, and his daughter will, too."

A gasp rippled through the crowd as he stormed away, stopping briefly in front of Addie, saying, "Now might be a good time for you to consider contesting your daddy's will, little girl. Not that it's going to help in the long run because that land *will* be mine."

Then he strode off, barreling through anyone who stood in his way.

His words were a jumble, tumbling through my mind. At first, I couldn't make sense of what he'd said. Then it hit me all at once, and I staggered a step backward, stopping only because of Ty's firm hand on my back.

There was sympathy in his eyes.

Sympathy for me.

Pity.

Because I was a *Buckley*.

I sagged under the weight of it all, and it was Ty who caught me. I was a Buckley. Bryce Buckley was my father. *Oh lord, oh lord, oh lord.*

Blood thundered in my ears. My heart hammered. I couldn't seem to pull in a deep breath as I struggled to stand tall.

"Tessa Jane," my mama said, her voice cracking.

I couldn't even look at her. Couldn't bear it.

Feeling like I was going to be sick, I ran for the door, stumbling a bit at first as I ignored Mama calling my name.

I kept running, through the flower arches, toward the front of the hotel, the scent of roses racing after me.

Once I made it out into the cool, foggy night, I doubled over, my breathing ragged. A second later, I felt a hand on my arm.

"Tessa Jane . . ." It was Ty.

Tears spilled from my eyes as I shook off his arm and rasped, "I just need to be alone."

"All right," he said after a long second, "but take my coat. It's cold out here."

He settled his suit coat over my bare shoulders, and I clutched the coat's lapels as I ran down the street, through the pocket park, and into the dark woods behind Market Street as fast as I could go. Trying my hardest to outrun the truth.

CHAPTER TWENTY

Addie

"She's probably at home, snuggled up in a pile of dogs and cats," Aunt Bean said from the passenger seat of the car, her tone deceptively light to hide the fact that she was sick with worry.

Henrietta sniffled from the back seat. "She's never going to forgive me."

Fog had moved in while we'd been inside the hotel. A silvery pea soup kind of fog, so thick I could barely see the roadway. As much as I wanted to speed toward the farmhouse, to reach Tessa Jane as quickly as I could, I drove painfully slowly.

"Yes she will," Bean said. "She loves you."

On Bean's lap was Tessa Jane's coat and evening bag, which contained her phone, cash, and a tube of lipstick. Unless she found a phone somewhere else, she couldn't call to tell us where she was. If she was safe.

My fingers ached but I didn't dare flex them, too afraid to loosen my grip on the steering wheel. I couldn't keep my mind from drifting to the look on Tessa Jane's face when Winchester had so callously revealed she was Bryce Buckley's biological daughter. That mix of shock, confusion, and betrayal would stay with me forever.

I just wanted to give Tessa Jane a big hug, but we needed to find her first. It had been an hour and a half since she'd run out of the ballroom.

"I didn't realize my father had figured out the truth," Henrietta said, her voice thin and reedy. "As far as I was aware, only Gavin and you knew, Verbena."

"You *knew*, Aunt Bean?" I asked, glancing at her.

"Of course," she said simply. "Gavin told me everything."

I turned my attention back to the road, my mind whirling. "Why didn't he tell my mama?"

"At that point in time your mama and daddy were separated but he was doing everything he could to try to save the relationship. When he learned Henrie was pregnant, he knew that if he offered to be Tessa Jane's daddy it would be the end of his marriage—unless he told Cecelia the truth: that he and Henrie were only friends."

My gaze jumped to the rearview mirror. "*Only* friends?"

Henrietta nodded. "We actually didn't start a dating until years later."

I opened my mouth then closed it again. This information was a lot to absorb. Almost too much.

Aunt Bean said, "Gavin wanted to tell your mama, but because she's a bit of a loose cannon, he was afraid she couldn't keep the secret. A starwalk confirmed it."

Loose cannon, I believed, was putting it mildly. "Is that why she blames the starlight for the end of her marriage?"

Bean said, "In a way. He let her believe the starlight had guided him to toward Henrie, which was the truth, of a sort. Oh my word, she let him have it and he almost gave in and told her everything. But then she went and told him she'd already filed for divorce the week before, and he realized their marriage was beyond salvageable. Then a while later, when Bryce targeted the horses, your daddy knew he'd made all the right decisions."

My head was aching. I wanted to rub my temples but didn't dare let go of the steering wheel.

Henrietta said, "Bryce was livid when he found out I was pregnant, fully believing the baby was Gavin's. He wanted revenge and took it out on innocent animals. The retaliation only affirmed why I hadn't told him he was the father. I'd have done anything—*anything*—to make sure Tessa Jane was raised up by people who loved her, cherished her."

I stiffened. Something she'd said rang a distant bell. I glanced in the rearview mirror again, met Henrietta's gaze. "Ree once told me that she wanted Luna to be raised by people who would love her, cherish her. It's why she asked Sawyer to pretend to be her father. Did you tell her to do that? Was she copying what *you'd* done?"

Henrietta sighed. "I only advised her on what I'd known *others* to do in her situation. I didn't tell her my story specifically. She never knew my connection to the Buckleys, but I felt a powerful need to protect her from that family. I never would've imagined how that advice would hurt you."

I fought tears, unwilling to let them fall while I was driving. I'd been hurt, yes, but not necessarily by the advice. And my pain was nothing compared to the traumatic life Luna would've had if the Buckleys had a hand in raising her.

As I slowly turned a corner, I said, "I'm grateful Ree had you to talk to. About everything."

We drove in silence for a stretch. The headlights did little to illuminate the road as fog hugged the car. I was concentrating on staying on the pavement, keenly aware of how slow I was going.

We were about a mile from the farmhouse when Henrietta said, "I can't help thinking about all the sacrifices that were made to protect Tessa Jane from the Buckleys, yet I never quite realized the danger lurking in my own family. My daddy is why we moved away, you know."

"I didn't, no," Bean said, rubbing her thumb over the clasp on Tessa Jane's evening bag.

"It was bad enough she had to hear day after day that the starlight land should be his, but it escalated to a whole other level when he started pressuring her to bake cakes every day. At eleven years old! Who does that?"

Aunt Bean shifted, looking into the back seat. "What's this now? Cake?"

"He was obsessed with Tessa Jane making cakes that tasted like yours—no, better. Back then I didn't know why he pushed and pushed her to bake, but now I have a feeling it was his way of convincing others she was a Fullbright. So no one would ever question it and put his goal of acquiring the starlight land in jeopardy." She was quiet for a moment. "That must've been it. Oh my lord, it explains so much. All the etiquette lessons, the pageant coach, everything. He was bound and determined to make sure her Buckley didn't show."

In my head, I could see Tessa Jane flashing me different kinds of smiles, and I could barely breathe. I finally found enough air to say, "Is that why Tessa Jane doesn't like to make cakes?"

"It absolutely is. When she couldn't master the flavor of your cakes, Verbena, my father belittled her. I told Tessa Jane she didn't have to bake. Mama told her, too. But she only wanted to please him, to make him happy, always hoping it would bring out some good in him. And he'd just smile—gloat, really—and tell us she *enjoyed* baking and to leave her be." She sighed, shook her head. "Mama didn't let him get away with it though. She put a freeze on his credit cards and told him they wouldn't be unfrozen until the baking stopped. She was never afraid to stand up to him when it mattered, or to hit him where it hurt him the most—financially. But the whole situation was like a wakeup call to me, a blaring siren

I couldn't possibly ignore. I knew I had to get Tessa Jane out of that house and far away, even if it meant taking her away from my mama and from you. It about broke my heart, but I had to protect my girl."

She spoke directly to Bean because back then I'd been just one more person that Tessa Jane needed to be protected from. My heart ached with shame.

I had to remind myself that I wasn't that person anymore. All Tessa Jane would know from me now was love and acceptance for exactly who she was—and who she wasn't.

"When we did come back to town, it was for short visits to see Mama and y'all, and I did my best to shelter her from him. It's why when she spent vacations with you, I made sure my parents knew not to expect a visit. She was rarely alone with him." Her breath hitched and when she spoke again, the words came out in a tumble. "I knew he could be cold and nasty and spiteful, but I can't believe how utterly cruel he was to her tonight. How could he do such a thing to his own flesh and blood? Does he have no heart at all?"

The air in the car was thick with pain, with grief, and I could barely stand it. I started counting by twos in my head to distract myself from crying.

"I've been wondering the same thing myself," Bean said quietly.

I also recognized something Henrietta hadn't yet, because she was too worried for Tessa Jane. Winchester's cruelty extended to her as well. He'd shared something Henrietta had hidden for decades. Everyone in town was going to be gossiping during the coffee hour at church tomorrow morning. I could only hope she was ready to face the looks, the questions, the *tsks* and *bless her hearts* headed her way.

I carefully turned in to the farmhouse's driveway, the fog so dense I couldn't see the house or even the glow of the porch lights from the street.

I slowed as we neared the big red barn, shining my high beams on its adjacent parking pad, which highlighted the fact that Tessa Jane must've been home at some point since she'd run off.

Because her car was gone.

Tessa Jane

The only thing I remembered about the drive here was that it seemed as though a silver fog had pushed me the whole way.

Which was all kinds of disturbing now, as I walked down a brightly lit hallway, my tennis shoes squeaking on the shiny floor. Once I reached room 223, I paused outside the doorway. Took a deep breath. I knocked as I slowly pushed open the door and stuck my head inside the room.

Dare glanced over at me, did a double take, and shut off the TV show he'd been watching.

It was closing in on nine P.M., and the fact that the hospital had unrestricted visiting hours was definitely a bright side.

But as soon as I had the thought, I felt a sharp pain in my chest.

Bright sides, with their glimmers of warmth and hope, were a Fullbright family trait.

And I wasn't a Fullbright.

"Hey," I said, my voice raw. "Mind if I come in?"

"Not at all."

I stepped inside, suddenly unsure why I'd come here.

He craned his neck to look behind me. "Don't suppose you smuggled Pepper in? She'd be the best medicine for me right about now."

The hospital bed next to his was empty, and fog obscured any view of the night sky outside the wide window. I pulled up a chair next him and sat. "Wish I'd thought of it."

When I'd gotten back to the farmhouse earlier, both Pepper and Hambone had glued themselves to my side, as if sensing my distress. They watched my every move as I changed clothes and started packing, intent on going back to Savannah then and there.

I'd only thrown one or two things in my suitcase, however, when I started thinking about Dare. Before I knew it, I was in the car on the way here.

"Hopefully you should be able to see her soon," I said, taking stock of him. "Does the doctor still think you'll be released in a few days?"

There was an IV in his right hand. His left wrist sported two plastic medical bracelets. He wore a hospital-issued gown that had cords coming out the opening of his sleeve. His black hair stuck out every which way. Dark circles curved under his eyes and seemed extra pronounced because his color had yet to come back. He was pale as a ghostie, as Aunt Bean would say.

Aunt Bean.

Who wasn't my aunt.

Which made me think of Addie, who wasn't my sister.

My lower lip trembled, and I looked all around the room until I felt as though I could talk without bawling my eyes out. A machine kept track of Dare's vital signs, and two bags hung from his IV pole. On his bedside table was a pink plastic pitcher, a cup, a pack of crackers, the TV remote, and his cell phone.

"Hopefully," he said.

I shifted my gaze to study his face, looking for myself in him. He had a widow's peak, the same as me. And our eye color was similar, though my mama also had blue eyes. That was about all I saw. If you saw us side by side, you wouldn't necessarily think we were family.

I'd certainly never thought it. Never for one moment even considered it.

But he was my uncle. My younger uncle, yes, but still.

And Luna. Sweet, vivacious Luna was my cousin.

Without a doubt, it was going to take me a while to wrap my head around this bombshell.

I fussed with the zipper on my jacket before finally saying, "I'm sure you're wondering why I'm here."

"Not really. Petal called from the gala, wanting to know if what Winchester said was true."

I raised my eyebrows. "Why don't you sound—wait. Petal *was at the gala?*"

"You didn't see her?"

I hadn't. "No. And it was probably a good thing."

He tipped his head. "Why's that?"

"I'm not sure I would've been nice."

Chuckling, he said, "I don't believe that."

I tried hard to find the right words. "Going to that dance while you're laid up in the hospital recovering from surgery isn't right in my book. It's just not. And it shouldn't be right in yours either. Did she visit today at all?"

He looked toward the darkened window. "No."

"But she had time to call you to gossip." I sighed and shook my head, thoroughly disgusted with her, and I didn't care if he knew it.

Immediately, I thought that not caring was a product of my lingering shadow, but then I had to check myself. If bright sides weren't in my lineage, neither were shadows.

I scratched a hive and said, "You didn't sound shocked just now. About what Petal said. Did you already know?"

He lifted a shoulder in a half shrug. "I figured it out on my own when I was a teenager. When I was packing to move in with the Fife family, I found a picture behind an old dresser of Bryce and your mama being all lovey-dovey. It got me looking into the timeline of things. I thought you knew but didn't talk openly about it. I reckoned it was why you'd always been nice to me."

Tears filled my eyes. "I didn't know."

"I'm real sorry about what happened with Winchester. What he did ain't right in *my* book."

I wiped my eyes. "That's because you're a good person, Dare."

Whereas my granddaddy was not.

There was no good in him. There was only greed.

It was hard truth to accept, but I had to. I *had* to.

Dare dropped his head back against his pillow. "I never knew Bryce—I hadn't even been born when he went to prison, but I heard plenty of stories about him, and all of them made me want to hide under my bed. It's my thinking you were better off growing up not knowing he was your daddy."

What an ever-loving mess of a situation. My head hurt, trying to sort through it. I rubbed my temples.

"I imagine you're probably real confused right now," he said. "I would be, in your shoes."

I cracked a grim smile. "I've had better nights."

"I know this is new to you and all, but you've got people who love you. They'll help you through this."

I smiled at him counseling me in his current state. I thought it proved his inherent goodness. "But Addie and Aunt Bean didn't even know until tonight that I'm not related." I couldn't let myself think of their reactions right now. I just couldn't.

"Them finding out ain't going to change anything."

"You don't know that."

"I do know. And you will, too, once the shock wears off. You might not be a Fullbright any more than Luna's a Gray or I'm a Fife, but we've been loved like we are, plain and simple."

Was it so simple, though?

I suddenly had an image of Aunt Bean turning me away from her front door and nearly laughed, it was so preposterous. Dare was right. She'd love me no matter what.

But Addie? I wasn't as sure. For most of her life she hadn't wanted me as a sister, and now it was like her childhood wishes had come true.

And I couldn't forget how Granddaddy, as a parting shot tonight, had told Addie to think about contesting my daddy's will.

My daddy.

I blew out a breath. Good heavens. I didn't know how to process all this, how to switch from believing I knew exactly who I was to being someone who had to start rewriting her life, her history.

"Have you talked to your mama yet?" Dare asked. "Petal said you ran out of the dance like your britches were on fire, ignoring everyone calling after you."

I decided I might have to snatch her fully bald the next time I saw her.

But no. That would be stooping to her level, wouldn't it? Maybe only a little bald.

"Not yet," I said. "I just wanted to be alone."

A question floated in his blue eyes. "But you're here."

"I can't rightly explain why. It was the strangest feeling, like I was being pulled here by something I couldn't see."

"Maybe you were feeling the tug of family ties."

I held his gaze, saw hope floating there. "Maybe so."

He picked up the pitcher on the table, tipped it toward the cup, and frowned when hardly any liquid came out.

Bouncing up, I said, "Do you need a refill?"

"Nah. I don't want to put you out none."

I took the pitcher from his hand. "Don't start talking nonsense or I'll get the doctor in here to check your head. He'll have to listen to me, seeing as how I'm family and all."

He cracked a smile. "Okay then."

I hurried into the hallway and found someone who directed me to the nourishment room on the floor, where I could refill the pitcher.

By the time I returned, a nurse was with him, checking his vitals. I set the pitcher on the tray. I looked out the window. The fog had fully cleared, revealing a starry night.

After the nurse left, Dare refilled his cup and said, "Petal didn't only call tonight to talk about you."

There was something in his tone that made me sit down and give him my full attention. "What else did she have to say?"

"She gave me an ultimatum. Pepper goes or she does."

I winced. And knew without a doubt if I was him, I'd have

picked Pepper before Petal even hung up the phone. But I wasn't him. I wasn't the one who loved her.

"I don't understand any of this," he said. "She liked Pepper at first. Played with her. Took her for walks. Dragged her, actually. Pepper never took a shine to Petal."

If that hadn't been a clue, I wasn't sure what was. But love had a way of masking the things we didn't want to see. I knew that better than most.

I said, "I wonder if Petal only wanted you to think she liked Pepper. What would've happened if she told you straight off that she didn't like dogs?"

"I wouldn't have dated her. It's a deal-breaker."

I tipped my head. "There you go. She probably thought she could change your mind, over time. It seems to me Petal is used to getting what she wants. And I suspect she pitches fits when she doesn't."

Fits that ended up hurting others.

He raked a hand over his face. "I don't know what to do."

I swallowed down my vote to ditch her. It wouldn't help him right now. "I'm not sure I'm the right person to ask. I hope you'll give counseling some thought. It's probably best to get someone else's perspective. Someone impartial." Because that person wasn't me. Or anyone who cared about him. Then I took a breath and added, "Did you know I was supposed to get married last November?"

"I heard some talk about it."

I was certain he was being diplomatic. There'd probably been weeks of gossip. "My situation isn't exactly like yours, but I do know what it's like to stay in a relationship for all the wrong reasons. I'd have saved myself a heap of heartache if I hadn't ignored red flags because I was afraid of disappointing people. If I wasn't so afraid of letting go of the picture I'd painted in my head of picket fences and babies and a happily ever after."

After a long moment, he said, "A heap of heartache, you say?"

"It was like a giant landfill. I'm not going to lie, there was a stench."

He laughed, then winced, pushing a hand to stomach. "I'll keep that in mind."

It was nice to see, if only for moment, that he hadn't lost his sense of humor. That he wasn't completely lost in his darkness.

His eyes drifted shut, as if he simply didn't have the strength to keep them open any longer. "Can you keep Pepper till I figure out what I'm going to do? I know she's safe with you."

My heart about broke, because with those words, he'd all but told me he knew Pepper wasn't safe with his wife.

"I need to go back to work in Savannah in a couple of days, but I'll definitely keep her until then. And I'm sure Addie or Aunt Bean will be happy to pick up where I leave off. She's really the sweetest dog."

He nodded, and I pretended not to see the tears gathered in the corners his eyes.

Seeing his emotion made me tear up as well. I hurt for him. *With* him.

After a few minutes of quiet, just when I thought he'd slipped into sleep, he said, "Hey, Tessa Jane?"

"Yeah?"

"Thanks for being nice to me when you didn't even know we were related."

Oh my heart. I reached over and took hold of his hand, gave his fingers a gentle squeeze.

His eyes were still closed when he said, "I wish you weren't leaving so soon. I feel like I'm just getting to know you."

And as he drifted off to sleep, I sat by his side, and wished it, too.

I settled into the chair, letting my thoughts wander, not wanting to leave him alone. When there was a tap on the door a half hour later, I thought it was going to be a nurse. But it wasn't.

It was my mama who stood in the doorway. In that split second, I realized Dare must've reached out to her when I went for water, because there was no other way to explain how she'd known I was here.

At the sight of her, at the anguish etched into her face, tears filled my eyes, and I jumped up. She stepped inside and I rushed across the room, flinging myself into her embrace.

"Before anything else, Tessa Jane," she said, her voice a crackly whisper, "I want you to know that Gavin loved you with his whole heart. He was so proud, so very proud, to be your daddy."

I nodded and kept holding on to her—and to person who I used to be—for just a while longer.

Because after tonight, I knew I'd never be the same again.

And I was starting to realize that might not be a bad thing.

CHAPTER TWENTY-ONE

Addie

Early the next morning, I was making my bed when my phone started singing about goodbyes, and I immediately regretted switching off the Do Not Disturb mode when I woke up.

It was a little past six and I'd obviously underestimated my mother's need to talk about what had happened with Tessa Jane, though the dozens of overnight messages and calls I'd found waiting for me this morning should've been a clue. The dizzying speed in which small-town gossip was dispersed would never cease to amaze me.

I had my finger poised to decline the call but then had the unsettling thought that she might show up on the doorstep if I kept putting her off. Taking a deep breath, I said, "Hello?"

At the sound of my voice, Stella lifted her head from a pillow, blinked sleepy eyes, stretched her tiny arms, then rolled onto her back and closed her eyes once again.

It had been a late night for all of us.

Henrietta and Tessa Jane had gotten back around midnight. I'd only seen my sister for a minute before she went up to bed. Just enough time to give her a big hug and tell her that I loved her.

"You need to get yourself a good lawyer, y'hear? Not that old geezer Stubblefield," my mother said, not even bothering to say hello. "That land is yours and yours alone. I should've known *that woman* was conning your daddy."

I sat down on the edge of the bed and started counting the polka dots on the sheet set, waiting her out.

"He wasn't the sharpest tool in the shed, I'm sorry to say. Ripe for the plucking. And pluck she did, didn't she? Near to picked him clean. You're welcome, by the way. If not for me sensing that she and that girl of hers were up to no good, the Wingroves might've had you in their clutches, too."

I rolled my eyes at her ability to rewrite history to fit her narrative.

"I hope Verbena kicked them to the curb last night. It burns me up to think of the way they've been playing big happy house with y'all, taking advantage of Verbena's good nature and bad heart. It's sickening to think that—"

"Stop!" I couldn't take it anymore.

I blinked away tears remembering how Tessa Jane had clung to me last night—as if she'd been afraid of losing me again—and how she'd told me in a shaky voice, "Love you, too, Addie."

"Don't you dare sass me, young lady," my mama snapped. "You best listen to me—"

"No," I said calmly but firmly, then continued in a rush so she wouldn't interrupt. "You need to listen to me for a change. I'm not doing this with you anymore. As far as I'm concerned, Tessa Jane *is* my sister, and I love her. So you're either going to have accept that and be civil or take yourself out of my life for good. Those are the only options, but the choice is yours. Now, I'm going to go hang up, make some coffee, and when my sister wakes up, I'm going to give her a big hug. Goodbye, Mama."

With that, I put my phone back into Do Not Disturb, scooped up Stella to hug to my chest, and noticed that I was breathing easier, as though a great big weight had finally been lifted off my heart.

✳

With the rain yesterday, the Sassafras Creek had jumped its bed and washed into the woods. Soon enough, it would be tucked back in where it belonged, because the sun was out and there were clear skies in the foreseeable forecast.

Ahead of me on the trail, Luna and Hambone splashed through mud puddles, the dog leading the way.

Next to me, Sawyer said, "I feel guilty for leaving Pepper behind."

I hadn't planned to walk Hambone this morning, thinking he probably preferred to stay with Pepper anyway, but Aunt Bean had suggested a stroll shortly after Luna showed up at the door bright and early, hoping to see Tessa Jane, who was deservedly sleeping in.

When I opened the door for Luna, I'd been mildly surprised to see the starlings on the roof of the big red barn. I thought after yesterday's revelations I wouldn't see them close to the house for a while and couldn't imagine why they were still nearby.

Sawyer had shown up not long after Luna to collect his daughter after finding her note on the kitchen table when he'd come back from the donut shop with their usual Sunday breakfast. He'd texted me to let me know he was on his way, and I could practically hear his exasperation in the message. Apparently he'd told her last night to give us time before barging on in.

But like her mama, she'd been too full of excitement to sit still. All she'd been talking about this morning was about how she and Tessa Jane were cousins. Family.

Sawyer had wanted to take Luna straight home, but I'd suggested we stick to the plan of taking a walk.

"I feel bad, too," I said, "but Ross said no walks for Pepper for a while. Don't worry too much, though. Aunt Bean will spoil her while we're out. She's probably feeding her bacon under the table right now. Maybe not even under the table."

Hambone stopped, glancing back at hearing the word *bacon*. His ears perked, and we laughed.

Luna was singing the line in "Bohemian Rhapsody" about a poor boy from a poor family, and I would've sworn that it sounded like the birds were chirping along to the melody.

I nudged Sawyer with my elbow. "How long before you never want to hear that song again?"

"Already there. But it makes her happy, so I'll deal."

"You're a good dad."

He smiled shyly. "I try."

We walked for a bit, enjoying Luna's concert, before Sawyer asked, "How's Tessa Jane doing?"

He already knew Tessa Jane had gone to see Dare last night—Aunt Bean had been working a phone chain like she was one of those old-fashioned switchboard operators, continuously updating all the people who'd been worried sick since Tessa Jane ran off.

"She's shaken," I said. "I think it's going to take some time for her to sort it through."

"And how're *you* doing?" he asked.

"I'm okay. Sorting emotions, too. Mostly I just want her to know how much I care about her. It took so long for me to learn how to be a good sister that I'm not going to let anything as trivial as DNA stop me now."

"Between you and Verbena and Luna, she's going to be smothered in love."

I could think of a few other people to add to that list as well, like the Sugarbirds and Ernie. They'd always loved her for who *she* was, not who she came from.

Hambone started baying as Luna launched into a repeat performance of the song. The way he towed her along gave the impression that he was trying to outrun her, so I assumed he was as sick of the song as Sawyer was.

"This is nice, walking in the woods with you," he said.

"Feels like old times."

Old times when we'd been each other's whole worlds. The love I had for him then was still there, under the surface, waiting to see what the future held.

As we passed the path that led to his cabin, I said, "I'm surprised you never moved away."

He kicked a rock. "Are you? Don't you think some things are worth sticking around for?"

I got lost looking in his eyes, all warm and tender, so it took me a moment to realize he was talking about me.

All these years that I'd been running, he'd stayed, hoping I'd come back.

My eyes filled with tears, and I nodded. "I learned that lesson a little late, but now it's one I plan to keep close to my heart."

"That's a good place for it."

I smiled and bravely reached for his hand.

His fingers immediately entwined with mine as though it was second nature. "Don't suppose you'd like to go up to Mentone next weekend with Luna and me? Annabelle would love to see you."

"I'd like that."

Whether what was happening between us was simply friendship or something more, time would tell. Either way, I was looking forward to finding out.

The creek splashed and burbled as he said, "Heard some interesting news at the donut shop this morning. About Winchester."

I didn't like wishing ill will on anyone, but Winchester was seriously pushing my resolve. "Is it something to do with Tessa Jane? Because I'm not sure I can stomach it."

"Not about her—or any of you. It has more to do with him digging his own grave."

I faced him. There was a devious sparkle in his eye. "Okay, spill."

"Apparently Winchester had a bit of an altercation with the editor of the paper last night towards the tail end of the gala and was arrested on a drunk and disorderly charge. He tried to buy his way out of it, offering the arresting officer a thousand bucks, so then he was also charged with trying to bribe a public servant."

"No!"

"He was cuffed right in the hotel lobby and hauled off to jail."

"Please tell me someone got pictures."

"Not that I know of but supposedly there were plenty of witnesses."

I stepped over an exposed tree root. "But wait. I thought he was friends with the sheriff?"

"From the talk at the donut shop, Winchester treatin' Tessa Jane the way he did last night was one sin too many for folks to stomach. The tide decided it was time to turn."

"I can't believe it."

"It gets better."

"How could it possibly?"

"Winchester is still sittin' in jail right now. Because it's Sunday, he can't get bail until tomorrow, after his arraignment. And do you want to hear the best kicker of all?" His eyes glinted, the gold flecks glimmering. "If Winchester gets convicted, which I don't know how he wouldn't, considering all the eyewitnesses, he'd be disqualified from holding public office. Meaning that even if by some miracle he won the mayoral election, he *can't* be mayor."

I was practically walking on air. This was the best possible news.

"He can't do *anything* to stop you and Tessa Jane from building near the starlight crater."

I wasn't so sure about that. Winchester was a vindictive man, and if we built, I knew he'd be out for revenge.

If we built.

I was still on the fence, unsure if it was the right thing to do.

It had become obvious that my feelings for the starlight had been tainted by my mother's anger and my grief over Ree's death. The clarity my daddy and Ree had found in the starlight hadn't truly been the things that hurt my mama and me.

It had been our reactions to those choices.

Mama had chosen anger.

I'd closed myself off.

I realized now that the only way to judge the clarity fairly—and maybe get some guidance on the decision that needed to be made—was to experience it firsthand.

It was finally time to walk among the starlight.

Tessa Jane

I was awoken by the gentle shake of a hand on my arm. "Come take a walk with me, peanut."

The words were quickly followed by the jingle of dog tags and a wet slurp on my hand. I wasn't sure which of the dogs had given me the kiss, because my eyes were so gritty that I could barely open them.

Wiping my face, I cracked open an eye and squinted at Aunt Bean, who stood at my bedside. "What time is it?"

My voice was raspy. Mama and I had gotten back to the farmhouse at midnight and thankfully, after giving me hugs and kisses, Aunt Bean and Addie had accepted my plea to talk in the morning about my grandfather's revelation. I'd gone straight up to bed but had barely slept at all, the long conversation I'd had with my mama rolling around in my head. That and how Addie had said she loved me. Thinking about it now immediately brought tears to my eyes. But blinking them away eased the grittiness, so there was that.

A bright side.

And thinking *that* brought a stab of pain.

What a roller coaster I was on.

"Eight thirty," Aunt Bean said.

"Is everyone else already up?"

"Your mama's still sleeping. Addie, Luna, and Sawyer took Hambone for a walk in the woods."

Ah, so the doggy kiss had come from Pepper. A fluff ball wiggled near my shoulder, and I sat up, pulling Lovey to my chest for cuddles. I didn't need to ask why Luna and Sawyer were here so early. I'd found at least two dozen messages from Luna on my phone last night after I got home. Her joy at being related to me had managed to bring a smile to my face. But the thought of facing them all right now, answering a million questions, made me want to hide under my covers. "Is that where we're going? To join them?"

"No, ma'am. I have another destination in mind. Wear your rain boots. It's a good distance and it'll be muddy."

"Are you *trying* to talk me out of going?"

She patted my cheek. "The journey will be worth it. Trust me. And it'll also buy you some time to shore up your emotions before facing everyone."

It amazed me how well she knew what I needed right now, but then again, she'd always been the one who most saw me for who I was. When Mama had shared with me last night that Aunt Bean had always known I wasn't a Fullbright, it had knocked the fear right out of me that things would be different between us.

"Can I at least bring coffee with me?"

She laughed, then noisily kissed my forehead before heading to the door. "I've already got a fresh pot brewing."

Pepper looked torn about whether to stay with me or go with her but ultimately trotted out the door.

"Aunt Bean?"

She paused in the doorway, looked back. "Yes?"

"I love you."

Her smile stretched across her whole face, ear to ear. She came back to the bed, sat on the edge, and wrapped me in her arms, taking care not to squish Lovey. "I love you, too, Tessa Jane. More than you could ever know." She let go of me, nudged my chin, and used her thumb to swipe my tears. "Now get a move on or Luna's going to hold you hostage for the next hour and a half, and so help me if I have to hear her sing that song one more time. I almost threw myself out of the truck yesterday on the way to see Dare."

I smiled and she lifted off the bed. A second later, she and Pepper were down the stairs.

My heart was heavy as I thought about Petal's ultimatum. If Dare chose to surrender Pepper, I had the feeling I was going to be adopting a dog along with this kitten. Which meant I was going to have to cut back on my work hours.

Or find a new job.

A job like making cookies full-time.

I let that thought simmer as I gave Lovey kisses before dragging myself out of bed. I was still thinking about it when Aunt Bean and I walked out the back door ten minutes later, both of us with travel mugs in hand. Mine filled with hazelnut coffee, hers with cold water.

The ducks waddled quickly over to us, looking for treats, and squawked loudly when they didn't receive any.

Aunt Bean patted their heads as they used their beaks to peck at the pockets of her coat. She said to them, "Y'all will survive without a treat. I *swannee.*" To me, she added, "We've done spoiled them rotten and now they're bossy as all get out."

As soon as she started off toward the back of the yard, I pulled a handful of raspberries from my coat pocket, dropped them on the ground, and hurried to catch up to her.

The sun was shining and there wasn't a cloud in the sky. We'd left Pepper with a new chew toy and she seemed perfectly content to be left behind in the care of Miney and Moe. We also stuck a sticky note on the coffee pot to let everyone know we'd gone for a walk.

Aunt Bean had done her hair more in a sweeping pixie style today instead of the sky-high hairdo she usually preferred. Dark jeans were tucked into rain boots patterned with lady bugs. Instead of her walking stick she used a four-footed cane, industrial gray in color, and I wished she'd spray-painted it hot pink or bright yellow. Something that better fit her spunky nature.

I wanted to ask if she was sure she was up for the exertion of a long walk but held my tongue knowing it was pointless. She was a woman on a mission. I just wasn't sure what mission yet.

She swung open the back gate, held it for me, then made sure it was closed securely behind us.

She squinted at the ducks pecking furiously at the raspberries, then turned her head ever so slightly to look at me.

I smiled innocently.

She snorted and led the way into the pasture behind the house, seemingly heading for the starlight crater, which made no sense because it would've been quicker to drive than walk.

I kept a close eye on her as we moved along, watching her breathing. The MRI results should be ready in the next couple of days, and I was hoping and praying and wishing for good news.

But halfway to the starlight field, when we stopped to rest and take a drink, agitated chirps came from the trees that lined the field as the starlings landed in high branches, their silver wings glistening in sunlight. As I watched them, I somehow knew, down deep in my soul, that their close presence lately had to do with Aunt Bean and her health troubles. I couldn't explain how I knew—just like I didn't know why I'd felt the need to see Dare last night or why I'd been determined to see the starlight the night Ty had been there.

She followed my gaze, raised an eyebrow. "At least they're not circling above us like vultures. Then I'd be really worried about my old ticker calling it quits right here and now." She looked around. "Not that it's a bad place to go."

I scratched at a hive on my neck. "You're not *going* anywhere. Not today. Or tomorrow. Or *ever* if I have a say so."

She smiled at me, love shining in her eyes. "Oh sweet darlin'. None of us gets a say-so. When it's our time, it's our time."

A tear spilled down my face. "I don't want you to go."

Her gaze slid back to the birds. "I won't ever be far, peanut. I promise you. One day I'll be watching over you same as them. And I want you to remember that I love you and your sister more than anything in the world. Even more than all the stars in the sky."

I just kept shaking my head.

"I reckon the birds are making a fuss because I'm going to show you something that you're not supposed to know until after I'm gone. I'm bending the family rules, and I don't care a whit if it ruffles their feathers," she said loudly, banging the cane twice against the ground for good measure.

When she started walking again, I followed, wiping my eyes. "Showing me something at the crater?"

"*Near* the crater."

We walked in silence for a stretch. I was having trouble catching my breath, all tangled up in grief. I tried telling myself over and over that she was still here, but it seemed like my heart wouldn't listen to reason.

"Here we are," she said ten minutes later, coming to a stop a stone's throw from where the star had fallen so long ago.

I glanced around expecting some sort of aha moment. But all I saw was tall grass, weeds, and an old hand-cranked water pump.

Bean said, "Last night your mama shared with Addie and me that your granddaddy pressured you to bake cakes like mine and you failed time and again. I hadn't known. So today, we're going to bake a cake *together*."

The thought alone made my stomach hurt. "I don't think that—"

"Hush now. Did you use one of my bottles of vanilla extract when you made your cakes?"

"No, ma'am. But I used a similar kind my mama ordered in special. It didn't make any difference."

"That's what I figured. Well, today I'll show you why those cakes never tasted the same as mine. It starts with me teaching you how to collect a special ingredient, the one you didn't use in the cakes you made for your granddaddy."

I smiled despite myself. "Unicorn tears?"

She laughed, and I lost myself in the sound for a moment. "Not quite. It's the taste of magic." She beamed. "Starry magic."

I was intrigued by her tone, a mix of wonder and delight.

She slipped a silver hip flask from her coat pocket and handed it over. "Hold this."

I took it from her and watched her every move. But as she strode toward the pump, something in the tall grass distracted her and she took a detour. "What's this now?" She bent down and picked up what looked like a silver stick. "Well, I declare!"

"Is that a mouth mirror? Like a dentist uses? How'd it get out here?"

"It is indeed. And I know exactly where it came from. Last night, when Addie was trying to keep my mind off . . . *things*, she shared that Sawyer told her how the starlings had scared off several men this week sitting on the edge of the starlight crater at twilight, all of them holding one of these doohickeys. One of the trespassers must've dropped it when he ran off."

As she tucked the mirror into her coat pocket, a shaft of sunlight hit the glass and flashed back at me. I blinked against the light and nearly gasped as the truth hit me.

A flash of light at twilight. A wink. A blink.

The reflection of light off the mirror had to have been the sparkle I'd seen from the attic window. I felt so foolish that I hadn't questioned the timing of seeing a glint after all these years. I should've known my granddaddy would do and say anything to get his hands on this land. Including using my fascination with Abner's journal against me.

I couldn't help wondering why he'd go to the trouble. Did he think that if I saw a sparkle, I'd be eager to dig for diamonds? Or be willing to let others pay to do it?

Most likely, which showed how little he truly knew me.

I hadn't been looking for a twinkle because I wanted to sell the stones. I'd been looking because I'd felt as though Abner had been a kindred spirit. A kind soul in a hard world.

Because no one else did, I'd chosen to believe him when he said there were diamonds.

And now I wasn't sure what to believe.

Bean said, "What I don't rightly understand is why Winchester would be sending men out here to sit and play with a mirror. Because you know this had to have been one of his schemes."

"I'm done trying to figure him out," I said, too embarrassed to admit that I knew the reason why.

"Rightly so," she said after a moment that stretched, as though she wanted to say more. Then she walked over to the pump. "Now, this is easy as pie to operate, peanut." Aunt Bean pushed down the lever, then lifted it back up. After a few pumps, water started trickling out, and she motioned to the flask in my hand with her chin. "Fill 'er up, Tessa Jane!"

I twisted the cap off the flask and held it out, angling the mouth under the spout. When water started to overflow onto my hands, Aunt Bean stopped pumping. "Whoo-ee. It's been a long time since I've done that. Usually Sawyer collects the star water when I need it."

I capped the flask. "Star water?"

She kicked the stem of the pump, which sat on a cement ring. "This here is the head of an old well, hand dug after one of your ancestors realized that when they drank runoff water from the starlight field, life seemed a whole lot brighter."

My eyes widened. "You use this well water in the cakes?"

"I use it in the vanilla extract—after filtering and boiling of course. No need for anyone to get any stomach nasties. And I'll let you in on another secret as well." She slid a glance toward the starlings, then dropped her voice. "Suppose when you were just a wee baby, a teeny tiny thing with delicate pink lips and big blue eyes, someone maybe, might've, *possibly* bathed you in the star water, downy head to tiny toe, a Fullbright custom that goes *way* back. And perhaps that bath is what's believed to give the women in our family the ability to see bright sides." As the starlings started trilling, she added loudly, "Hypothetically, of course."

It took me a moment to fully understand what she was saying. All our gifts were from the water. No. From the *star* that had fallen so long ago.

Bean reached over and lifted my pendant, balancing it on her fingertip. "And because sometimes the dark side of life can overwhelm us, we're given extra help to see the light. Yours and Addie's necklaces have been soaked in the water, the same way my mama dipped my watchband in it."

My eyes widened, and I latched onto my pendant. No wonder my ability to see bright sides had waned after I stopped wearing it. Without it, my shadow truly had taken over, only allowing me brief glimpses of brightness.

"How come I've never heard all this before? About the power of the star water? Does Addie know?"

She looped her arm around mine and we started back to the farmhouse, the wind blowing gently, the flask of water in my pocket.

"She doesn't yet. Traditionally, this is information that's passed down in death from one generation to the next, but I decided today's the day we break the rules. You needed to know, to set your heart at ease about those cakes."

Learning about the water had already helped, but I knew it was going to take time, and a whole lot of cake baking, to remove my granddaddy's derisive comments from my memory.

"But we'll tell Addie, too?" I asked.

"Of course, peanut. As soon as we get back."

We walked for a while in companionable silence before I said, "Do you—" I cut myself off, not sure what I was doing. I hadn't thought this through enough. Or the impact of it, or the ripple effect it would have on others. Then I gave myself a good mental scolding. For so long I'd put myself last. It was time I put myself first and hold true to what I wanted. "Do you think I could use the big red barn's kitchen for a cookie business once the cake company moves back to Market Street?"

"Do I mind?" She whooped. "I thought you'd never ask! But I'd like to make you a counter offer."

"What's that?"

"I'd love for you to join us at the Market Street location. Become a partner. The kitchen's plenty big enough to make cakes *and* cookies."

I squinted at her, wondering if she'd made the kitchen extra large on purpose, somehow knowing this day would come.

She lifted her eyebrows innocently.

But no. How could she have known? The plans for the renovation had been in the works for a long time now.

I scratched a hive on my neck. "Would I have to bake cakes?"

She smiled. "Only if you wanted to."

Working alongside her and the Sugarbirds every day was a tempting offer, but right now it felt a little overwhelming. "Let me think about it a bit."

"You just let me know."

As we approached the back fence, Hambone and Pepper saw us coming and started barking hellos. We gave them love and pats as Addie came out the back door, holding a mug. "Where'd you two go off to?"

"Secret mission," Bean said.

Addie held up a hand. In a voice that sounded a lot like Eliza Doolittle before she met Henry Higgins, she said, "Pardon me, but I'm going to stop you right there. I love you both dearly, but I don't want to hear about anything secret. Lalalala!" And she turned around and rushed back into the house.

Aunt Bean and I looked at each other and started laughing at her delivery.

But as we followed her inside, it wasn't her humor that was filling me with warmth and happiness.

It was the part where she said she'd loved us dearly.

CHAPTER TWENTY-TWO

From the Kitchen of Verbena Fullbright

Baking is a messy business, no two ways around that fact, especially if flour, powdered sugar, and cocoa powder are involved. Lordy mercy. Best way to clean those spills is keeping them dry. Resist using a vacuum—it'll clog its filter right up. Instead, use a bench scraper or hand broom for a quick clean up. A tidy kitchen is a happy kitchen.

Tessa Jane

As I walked a piece of cake and a cold drink from the patio to the duck coop, I heard Ernie Underwood say, "If I had my druthers, I'd send her packing. Don't let the door hit ya where the good lord split ya!" She sat at the outdoor table, the open umbrella shading her thin face.

The sentence was punctuated by hammering, as if Ty was driving home the statement rather than simply shingling the roof of Lucy and Ethel's coop, one of the last steps before the pair of ducks could move in.

From around the table, Bean and the Sugarbirds murmured their agreement.

I was certain Addie would've agreed, too, but she was in her studio trying to catch up on auditions. Tonight, she had plans to walk in the starlight since she was still conflicted about building near the site, and I'd volunteered to go with her, since I was looking for some clarity myself about my new bakery business. Did I want to start small? Or jump into the deep end with Aunt Bean?

"Who asks a man to give up the dog he raised from puppy-hood? It ain't right," Pinky said, her high-pitched voice carrying easily.

I wished my mama was here to weigh in, too, but she'd had to leave this morning—there was a fundraising event tonight in Savannah that she couldn't miss. But she promised to be back for my birthday.

The Sugarbirds, Ernie, and Aunt Bean were, of course, talking about Petal's ultimatum. As was most everyone in Starlight, because apparently at the gala, Petal had gotten tipsy and talked an ear off Graham Doby, telling him about the demand she'd made of her new husband. With him being a blabbermouth and all, it hadn't taken long for word to spread. People were taking sides, but it seemed to me that most of those sides belonged to Dare.

Between that gossip, my paternity shocker, and Granddaddy's arrest, the town was in a tizzy. I'd been grateful the bakery had been closed yesterday and today. A brief respite from the onslaught of busybodies about to descend on me under the pretense of buying cakes.

As I made my way toward Ty, I looked back at the ducks and the dogs as they trailed after me, wanting to see what I held. "This isn't for you," I said to them.

None of them seemed particularly convinced.

The cake slice I carried came from the cake I'd baked yesterday with Aunt Bean. The recipe was the one she had created to benefit the Starling Society. She called it the Darling Starling cake, which I adored.

Much to my surprise, baking the cake had been comforting—because being alongside Addie and Bean in the kitchen, laughing and listening to my daddy's records and reminiscing about him, had been exactly what my soul needed to accept that they were my family, always and forever.

As soon as the cake was done, Bean, Addie, and I had shared a slice. They both declared that it tasted just like Aunt Bean's had. Their compliments hadn't been overly effusive, which I appreciated, because then it would've seemed like fake praise. Empty words spoken to try to quickly rebuild what my grandfather had broken.

Instead, it was as if they understood that rebuilding would come slowly, one compliment at a time. And when I took a bite of the cake for myself, that mix of raspberry and cream and Aunt Bean's special vanilla, I knew my shadow had finally given way to the light.

No, I hadn't quite found my way back to who I used to be like I'd originally wanted when I came to Starlight. But now I was someone better. Because I knew exactly who I was. I was a mix of the dark and the light. I'd learned that my shadow was what helped me to shine brighter.

As I approached the coop, Ty looked down at me from the top of a ladder. I said, "Your mama says it's time to take a break."

We both glanced toward the patio.

Ernie finger-waved, a grin on her face.

Ty shook his head. "There's probably no use in arguing."

I squinted against the sun. "It'll be easier for the both of us if you just play along."

He cracked a smile and slid the hammer into a loop on his tool belt. He came down the ladder, skipping the last few rungs as he jumped to the ground. It reminded me of a misty day at the Market Street bakery nearly a month ago. We'd come a long way since then.

"Thank you," he said, taking the plate and drink from my hands. He threw a look toward the patio, as if weighing whether he should eat at the table, then turned and walked behind the coop to sit on one of two sawhorses.

I sat on the second one to keep him company. The ducks waddled around us, and Hambone and Pepper sat at Ty's feet, blatantly begging, tails wagging.

Ty set his glass down next to him on the sawhorse and nodded at Pepper, who was still wearing a cone. "She seems to be doing well."

This spot behind the coop had the added benefit of being out of sight of the patio. It was nice not to have all those eyes on us. "Just a bit of a limp still. She took to the cone a lot better than I thought she would. Hambone probably would've eaten straight through it to get it off."

Hambone looked over at me, his eyes full of outrage that I'd think such a thing.

"I've seen him try to eat rocks, so yeah, he probably would." Ty smiled, and it lit his brown eyes, making them look like warm honey. "Once he ate a whole box of earplugs. Those squishy orange ones? And Mama hadn't realized it until all these orange dots started showing up in the yard."

Hambone bayed and trotted off.

I laughed, watching him go. "None of us like our most embarrassing stories told, I suppose."

Pepper wandered over to me, licked my hand when I patted her head, then followed Hambone. Then the ducks chased after them both, trying to start trouble.

I was going to miss the dogs when they went back home. Well, in Pepper's case, *if*. But for Hambone, I suspected it wouldn't be long. Ernie was gaining back her strength by leaps and bounds.

"What'd you end up naming your kitten?" Ty asked, watching me watch the pets.

I picked a feather off my jeans. "Her name is Lovey." I mumbled the rest of the sentence under my breath.

"What was that?" He leaned forward carefully, as to not tip the sawhorse.

"I said, her name is Lovey."

"The part after that."

"Short for Lovebug."

He laughed and I rolled my eyes. Which only made him laugh louder.

"What's so funny?" Willa Jo shouted.

"Lovebugs!" I yelled back.

"Oh! Okay then."

Ty and I shared a smile. He said, "I'm going to get the third degree on the way home."

"You might get it before you leave. We both might."

The dogs started barking, then the ducks quacking. There was a loud splash, then they all quieted. Ty used the side of his fork to cut a bite off the cake. "So, do I need to start looking for a forever home for Lovebug?"

"Start?" I asked. "I thought you already were."

He shrugged. "Had a gut feeling I might not have to look far."

"You know a sucker when you see one?"

"I know a gentle soul when I see one."

My eyebrows went up. "Do you now?"

With a guilty smile, he nodded. "But sometimes it takes a while. I'm a slow learner."

I could only shake my head at that and wonder if he had any clue I could see the good in him.

He took a bite of the cake, closed his eyes, and sighed. I could practically see the glimmers of hope and optimism working their magic. "Miss Verbena's outdone herself with this cake."

Inwardly, I did a little jig. "She sure has."

He didn't need to know I'd been the one who made it. It was enough for me to see his reaction. It healed another piece of my heart.

"I overheard everyone talking earlier about you quitting your job," he said, shoveling another bite of cake into his mouth. "That's a big change."

I dug my toe into the ground, made a small hole. "There's something terrifying about starting over, but it's time."

I'd called my boss this morning to let him know. Then, I'd called a real estate friend to get the ball rolling on listing my condo.

It was time to come home for good.

The Sugarbirds had been all aflutter with the news, encasing me in a group hug that nearly suffocated me with the love they gave so freely.

He polished off the rest of the cake slice, then dragged the fork over the plate to catch any crumbs. "It's not starting over. It's starting from experience."

"I like that better."

"I saw it once in a fortune cookie. It stuck."

I laughed, not sure I believed him. "Fair enough."

He took a sip of the sweet tea, then lifted an eyebrow. "Is this spiked?"

"That's something you're going to have to ask Pinky and her flask."

He glanced over his shoulder, as if he could see the patio through the duck coop. "How many glasses has my mama had?"

"I lost count."

He made to stand up, and I grinned. "I'm kidding! She's only had one." That I'd seen at least.

"She's going to be the death of me." He took another sip of the tea and held up the glass. "It's not half bad."

"That's because the first sip numbs your taste buds."

"That makes more sense." He licked his fork clean, then kicked at the ground. Finally, he said, "I'm glad you're moving back. The town needs more good-hearted folk like you."

I lifted an eyebrow, eyed his glass.

He laughed. "It's not the liquor talking, I swear. Might be helping me say it, though."

"Then, thanks."

"You know, I'm ashamed to admit that in all the time I've known you, I never once thought about what it must've been like to live under the same roof as Winchester. I got a good glimpse of it Saturday night, and it made me sick to my stomach. I'm real sorry, Tessa Jane. For not ever noticing, and for what you went through."

I looked away, not wanting him to see the tears in my eyes. "It's okay."

"It's not, actually. But there's that good heart showing itself again."

I took a deep breath. "I wanted to thank you for standing up for me at the dance. I really appreciated it."

He shook his head. "That man . . ."

"I know," I said sadly. I blew out a breath and eyed the duck house. "Looks like you're just about done here."

He accepted the change of subject. "It'll be finished today. Unless Miss Verbena wants it painted. I can do that next weekend."

Before I could think twice about it, I said, "She was already making noise about painting it but hasn't decided on a color."

Truth be told, she hadn't said a peep about paint, so I was going to have to plant that seed right quick.

"Then I guess I'll be coming back."

"I guess so." We locked gazes for a long minute before I stood up. "Let me take those dishes for you."

"I can bring them inside," he said, standing, too. "I wanted to say hello to my namesake anyway."

As we walked toward the patio I tried to act like I didn't notice all the eyes on us. "Are you going to be insufferable about her name from here on out?"

He grinned. "Forever and ever."

Aunt Bean was in the middle of waggling her eyebrows at me when her phone rang. She'd been keeping it nearby all day, waiting on her doctor to call.

We all froze as she picked the phone, squinted at the caller ID.

Then she looked at all of us. "It's the cardiology office."

"Don't just sit there like a bump on a log," Delilah said. "Put it on speakerphone!"

As Bean swiped to answer the call, I think I was the only one to notice that as she said hello, the starlings flew in and landed on the fence, as if they, too, wanted to hear what was about to be said.

Addie

The stars were out, shining bright. The ones in the sky. And the one in the ground.

It was a rare night that we closed the gates to visitors, but Aunt Bean insisted I have time to experience the starlight without a crowd. Once I was done, then we'd open the gates so others could experience the enchanting light as well.

It was just past full dark as Aunt Bean, Tessa Jane, and I stood at the entrance of the starwalk, watching the light dance, caught up in the beauty. Caught up in wondering what lay ahead for Aunt Bean.

Earlier, I'd arrived at the patio right in time to hear the tail end of Aunt Bean's conversation with her doctor. Her official diagnosis was congestive heart failure caused by viral cardio-myopathy, stage 3. She had an appointment to see the cardiol-ogist later this week to talk more in depth about the diagnosis and possible treatments. Quick searches via Dr. Google were enough to make us shut down the laptop and cling to hope that with treatment and a whole lot of wishing and praying we'd get more time with her than the prognosis suggested.

But there was no denying her life was about to change. Diet, exercise, medication, possibly surgery for a pacemaker or even a transplant. Only time would tell how she'd weather it all, but I knew for certain that Tessa Jane and I would be by her side each step of the way.

"Ready?" Tessa Jane asked me.

The light danced, twisting and twirling. "As I'll ever be."

"I'll be right here waiting when you get out," Aunt Bean said, heading toward the lawn chair set up in the viewing area.

Tessa Jane held out her hand. I slipped mine into hers. To-gether we stepped into the light.

As we walked, side by side, I found myself smiling. The way the light played was absolutely entrancing. As it swirled, I felt lighter, like I was walking on air. My heart lifted, my mind cleared, and I lost myself, utterly charmed and captivated. The light was pure, beautiful, spiritual, *magical*.

By the time we exited the starwalk, I knew exactly how wrong I'd been about that light my whole life long.

And exactly what Tessa Jane and I needed to do to stop Winchester for good.

CHAPTER TWENTY-THREE

From the Kitchen of Verbena Fullbright

It's not only cakes, or cookies, or vanilla extract (unicorn or dragon tears optional), or anything you *make* that I consider homemade. Homemade comes from what's inside of you. Because life isn't what you make of it. It's what you give of it. So give openly, love always, and happiness will shine through you, bright as can be.

Addie

The sun was shining, glistening on the morning dew in the fields that lined the road as Aunt Bean drove like her hair was on fire. The tail end of Sweetie swerved into the oncoming lane as she swung around a corner.

I thought, perhaps, her driving was going to do her in—all three of us in, really—long before her heart ever did.

With the force of the turn, I fell heavily against Tessa Jane, who was plastered against the door.

"Whoo-ee!" Bean hooted, yanking the gearshift.

"Seriously, have you considered adding airbags?" Tessa Jane asked. "Surely they can be retrofitted."

"I'll add them to a spreadsheet," I offered.

"Fuddy-duddies," Bean chirped. "Just sit back and enjoy the ride."

"It's worse than a roller coaster," I said to Tessa Jane, sure I was as green as the truck itself.

She nodded. "I'm wishing I'd taken a dose of Dramamine with breakfast."

Aunt Bean glanced over at us and rolled her eyes.

It was coming up on seven thirty in the morning. The roads were empty, not a car in sight, not a person, not even a cow, and Bean was taking full advantage of it to appease her inner race car driver.

It had been a little more than two weeks since Bean's diagnosis. Last weekend, she had thrown a potluck indulgence party. Her last hurrah before she made the enormous change to her lifestyle. The farmhouse had been packed with friends and neighbors who'd come bearing fried chicken and catfish, onion rings, honey hams, tacos, Chinese food, gumbo, biscuits and gravy, pizza, sausage and peppers, chips, dips, salsa, and chicken and dumplings. Willa Jo and Delilah brought the booze. Pinky provided a carton of cigarettes. Ernie had brought ideas for matching tattoos. Stan had brought Bean a bouquet of wildflowers, which rekindled the debate that he'd been her admirer all along. There had been dancing until the wee hours, the record player put to constant use.

When Bean woke up the next day, she declared it the first day of the rest of her healthy life, punctuating the sentence with two raps of her walking stick. The declaration had been of the whispered variety, in which the quiet thudding of her walking stick, with its rubber tip, seemed wholly sympathetic.

Because she had an enormous hangover.

For breakfast, she drank a cup of black coffee and ate cantaloupe, scrambled eggs with only pepper, and low-carb toast with just a smear of butter.

Because butter was the one thing she refused to give up.

Then she went for a walk with Tessa Jane and me into the woods.

Because the doctor said regular exercise could only help her damaged heart.

That night she'd sipped herbal tea instead of spiked hot chocolate.

Because cutting back on alcohol was important for regulating heart rhythms.

But only one cup.

Because too much liquid intake could start causing trouble with her kidneys.

There were already whispers of a pacemaker, but it was talk pushed off to another day. It had become clear after visiting her cardiologist that she had just started out on what was going to be a lengthy road. Bean already had spreadsheets. For medications. For doctors. For her new diet. No one was more determined to live as long as possible than she was.

After the phone call had come with the results of her MRI, the starlings had been keeping to the wood line near the starlight crater. Their distance meant there wouldn't be any more upheavals in our lives. Not anytime soon, at least. Now we just had to focus on leveling out again. Learning to live with all that had been revealed. Continuing to find the bright side of life.

Bean slowed down as we neared Market Street. There wasn't so much as a wiggle from the back end of the truck as she made the turn.

"Get ready to have your socks knocked clean off," Bean said as we rolled toward the bakery, the trees twinkling.

The sign that had been on back order for what felt like years was finally in and Bean wanted us to be the first to see it.

"We're not going to be gandering another tarp, are we?" Tessa Jane asked.

"Such sass." Bean *tsk*ed loudly, shaking her head, which made her hair wobble to and fro. Then in an offhanded manner she added, "Last I heard, Ty was going to use a drop cloth for the grand reveal."

Tessa Jane and I laughed and as the sound bounced around the cab of the truck, I realized how happy I was. I'd just been booked for the movie I'd auditioned for, I'd accepted a part-time job as a Sugarbird—just twelve hours a week—and I was sitting next to the two people I loved most in the world.

Oh, and Sawyer and I had a date tomorrow night and plans to see Luna's play on Sunday.

Life could only be better if Bean was fully healthy, but as

she'd taught me when I was girl, light needed darkness to make you appreciate its brightness.

The radio played a jaunty classic country tune that had a lyric about a mule and a grasshopper eating ice cream, and I noticed Tessa Jane smiling. No doubt she'd caught the grasshopper reference as well, and it had made her think of Ty. He, who was coming up with every excuse under the sun to stop by the farmhouse for a visit. I didn't think it was only because he wanted to help Aunt Bean paint the quack shack or clean gutters or to replenish Hambone's kibble supply.

Aunt Bean rolled to a stop at a red light. In the pizzeria's storefront window hung a mayoral campaign poster, covered in stars and stripes. Mostly stars. On it read: VOTE STAN REEVES FOR MAYOR. Most of the shops along Market Street had similar posters in their windows.

Despite Winchester's criminal charges, he'd refused to withdraw from the election. That's when Stan had stepped up, deciding to throw his hat into the ring.

The town quickly chose sides, as it tended to do, and by all the posters and yard signs, it had become clear the town was backing Stan. What was to become of Winchester was still to be determined by the courts, but I breathed easier knowing he'd never be able to damage the starlight.

Mr. Stubblefield had fast-tracked our request to conserve the starlight crater. Once the crater and several acres of land surrounding it—including the woods where the starlings lived—was put into a land trust, the starlight would always be protected. And we were free to build on the remaining acreage.

As the light turned green, the truck jolted forward. "Now close your eyes, girls," Bean instructed as we neared the end of the business district.

It seemed like forever ago that we'd taken this same drive to see the bakery, while it had still been a work in progress. But today was Leap Day and the bakery's grand reopening celebration.

The party started this afternoon and would undoubtedly

run well past dark, but Aunt Bean insisted on giving Tessa Jane and me a sneak peek at the finished result.

I heard the click of the blinker, then I swayed slightly as the truck turned. We bobbled over what I knew to be the stamped concrete parking lot, and Aunt Bean brought the truck to a stop.

She cut the engine and said, "Okay, on the count of three, open your eyes but only look straight ahead. One, two, three!"

I cracked open my eyes and was disoriented for a second, because we were parked parallel to the bakery, the nose of the truck facing the pocket park.

It took everything in me not to look to my right, at the bakery. Instead, I focused on the two men standing in a landscape island, one on each side of a wooden sign draped in two paint-stained drop cloths.

Tessa Jane leaned forward, squinted, and smiled. "Is that a *gnome* next to that shrub?"

Bean laughed. "Sure is. One of the games on tap for today is Gnome Quest, which is kind of like an Easter egg hunt but with gnomes. Whoever finds one wins a prize. Whoever finds the *most* wins the grand prize."

Tessa Jane rubbed her hands together, looking like she was ready to hop out of the car and start searching right that minute. "What's the grand prize?"

With her eagerness, she looked much younger than her twenty-five years. Her birthday had been a few days ago, and it had been a quiet celebration, just the way she wanted it. We'd had a heart-healthy dinner with Henrie and Dare, Ernie and Ty, Luna and Sawyer. I'd made berry tarts for dessert and stuck a single candle in Tessa Jane's as we sang the birthday song. When she made her wish, she'd hesitated for only a moment before glancing at Aunt Bean, then blew out the flame.

"To be determined," Bean said with an air that declared she knew full well but was choosing to be secretive. "Now, are y'all ready? Ty looks like he's about to pop with impatience."

"Yes, ma'am," we said.

She gave Ty a grin and a thumbs up.

He took hold of one drop cloth, and Dare Fife, who stood on the opposite side of the sign, took hold of the other. They yanked the cloths away, revealing the new sign, a masterpiece done in silver and blue that had an iridescent starling flying along with a string of three stars in its beak. The sign read THE STARLING CAKE AND COOKIE COMPANY.

Tessa Jane's breath caught, and I automatically reached for her hand, holding it tightly.

"This sign has been on order for months. How did you know I'd say yes, Aunt Bean?" she asked.

Aunt Bean smiled at Tessa Jane. "I was working with nothing but glimmers of hope, peanut."

Tessa Jane had accepted Aunt Bean's offer to share bakery space right after our starwalk. A few days later, I'd asked Aunt Bean if getting Tessa Jane to work at the bakery had been her grand plan all along.

Gently, she'd cupped my cheeks, and said, "My plan had nothing to do with the bakery or the starlight field or anything other than hoping you two would realized that you're stronger together. I love you both so very much."

It was then I realized that when she'd called the emergency family meeting last month she hadn't really needed Tessa Jane's and my help, no matter what she'd claimed. She'd wanted us to reconnect, to bond, to find each other again, and she'd known we weren't likely to do it without her. After all, she'd always been the bridge between us.

It was a plan that had worked out beautifully despite some bumps in the road.

"Can we look around now?" I asked, my curiosity getting the better of me.

Aunt Bean laughed as she pushed open the door. "Absolutely."

As soon as Tessa Jane climbed out of the truck, she made a beeline for Dare's truck, which was parked close by. Pepper's head hung out the window.

I followed her out and took a moment to soak in all the changes. The new parking lot, the gas lamplights, the rockers on the porch, the lettering in the window that matched the sign out front. Flowers filled window boxes and the branches of the new trees rustled in the breeze.

And it hit me then why Bean had really taken on this renovation.

She'd done it for Tessa Jane and me.

It was a reflection of our fresh start. Of working together.

Suddenly, I realized that the three stars the starling carried represented Bean, Tessa Jane, and me.

Family.

"You like it?" Bean asked, stepping up next to me.

I blinked away the tears in my eyes. "I love it."

"Me, too, punkin. Me, too."

While Ty deposited the drop cloths in the bed of his truck, Dare let Pepper out of his. On the day he'd been released from the hospital, he contacted a divorce lawyer, saying he couldn't abide being married to someone who could be so cruel and callous to an animal . . . or to him. Not even a week later, Petal packed up and moved to the beach.

We'd all rallied around him, trying to fill up the empty space, but he still carried an air of sadness that I suspected would hover for a while. He'd shared with us that he'd started seeing one of the therapists Henrietta had recommended, and I had the feeling that given time he'd realize he was better off alone than with someone who seemed to care about only herself.

Because Dare had some lingering weakness from his illness and operation, he was on what would hopefully be a brief unpaid leave of absence from his job at the flour mill, where he usually did heavy lifting his whole shift. Ty had stepped up to fill that particular emptiness with an offer to temporarily work with him doing odds and ends, light duty. The bright side to that, of course, was that at most of the sites Pepper, who was now fully healed from the thorn incident, could go along with him.

Once Pepper was out of the truck, she didn't hesitate to throw her front paws on Tessa Jane's chest and start licking her face. Hambone had taken to moping without Pepper at the farmhouse until we finally let the kittens have the run of the place. Then he took to herding them all day long. It wouldn't be long now before he was home with Ernie, though. She was no longer having dizzy spells and planned to make the move back home within the month. Luna had promised that when she walked him for Miss Ernie, she'd bring him by to see us.

As the sun glistened on the morning dew, Tessa Jane said something to Dare and he laughed. The way the two of them—three of them, really, because Luna wasn't to be left out—had bonded was truly special to witness.

Aunt Bean's phone trilled. She fished it from her bag and her eyebrows dipped as she looked at the screen. "It's Henrietta. Hello, darlin'," she answered. "What's that now? She sure is. Her phone's probably in the truck. One second." She lowered the phone and said, "Tessa Jane, your mama's on the line. She wants to talk to you. Says it's urgent."

Concern flared in Tessa Jane's eyes as she rushed over to take the call, scratching at a hive on her neck as she did so. "Mama? Is everything okay?" There was a beat of silence before she said, "This afternoon? But why? I don't under-stand." Then her eyes grew round and her mouth dropped open. "I can't believe it. Right, right. Okay. I'll see you soon." She hung up the phone and looked at us. "Y'all are *not* going to believe what's happened."

CHAPTER TWENTY-FOUR

From the Kitchen of Tessa Jane Fullbright

If the ingredients for a sugar cookie were in a play, the butter would be the star of the show. Butter is what helps the cookie spread, gives it a soft bite, and fills it with flavor. I never skimp when buying butter, because the better the butter quality, the better the cookie. And also because someone near and dear to my heart taught me that butter is sacred.

Tessa Jane

Addie had told me once she believed that rooted in every woman's DNA was the right to pick and choose the traditions and societal conventions she followed. That it was especially true for southern matriarchs, who, after years of living, of giving, of conforming, now played by a set of rules carefully crafted from experience.

This theory had proven true when it came to my grandmother. And Gigi had taken it a step further by twisting those rules even after she was gone.

It had been seven months since the bakery's reopening and that fateful phone call from my mama. The day Mr. Stubblefield informed us that he had discovered that the trust my grandfather had inherited was revocable if he cut off Mama and me, something my grandmother had buried in the provisions my grandfather hadn't bothered to read.

The trust that had once been Granddaddy's—which included the mansion on the hill—now belonged to my mama. Granddaddy was now the one who would receive a stipend, a modest one at that, but only if he abided by a strict set of rules set forth by the terms of the trust.

It was also disclosed that Gigi had set up separate trust—a secret one—for me. One that would be revealed only if I *kept* the starlight field on my twenty-fifth birthday. If I had let the land go, allowing my grandfather to buy it, the windfall would've gone to charity.

I wasn't at all sure why she'd set up her estate the way she had but thought it had something to do with her wanting to believe Granddaddy would change—and hoping I'd use the backbone she'd passed on to me.

And once again, I wished she were here to see me being true to myself. Because she'd been right. It truly had brought happiness.

Addie and I were currently sitting on the starwalk, atop a blanket, sharing a picnic lunch on a sunny Monday afternoon. It was the end of September, and the land was awash in late-season wildflowers, pollen-drunk bees, and dust from the tractors working behind us.

We'd broken ground on the café and gift shop last week.

Addie was watching the starlings, who were watching us, from the rope railing near the entrance to the starwalk. They'd been creeping closer and closer all week. "I wish I could tell who was who," she said. "Which one is Charity? Clara? Granny?"

"I think about that sometimes, too." But it was enough for me to know who they were, as a whole.

Family.

We were avoiding talking about their nearness. I suspected it was because we both knew why they'd begun creeping in, toward us, as if trying to prepare our hearts for what was ahead.

Aunt Bean's pacemaker had been implanted a few months ago, and there had been complication after complication. We were taking every day we had with her as the gift that it was.

We weren't the only ones.

She was currently in Alaska with Stan, where she'd been

hoping to see the northern lights—and finally had, last night. She'd texted pictures, plenty of which were of her with a big ol' smile on her face. It filled my heart right up to think about her and Mayor Stan, and I wondered if she'd ever told him the truth about her admirer. Somehow I doubted it—she was living life her own way now.

Addie tucked her sandwich wrapper back into the basket and pulled out her phone. "How about another picture for the hallway wall?"

Months ago, we'd hired Ty to convert the upstairs of the big red barn into a two-bedroom apartment and we'd been busy filling the hallway with family pictures now that we'd finally moved in. I wasn't sure how long we'd be living together, though. On our date last night, Ty shared a secret with me—Sawyer had been looking at engagement rings.

I had to wonder if news of an engagement would finally elicit a phone call from Addie's mama—there had been no contact between them since February. Addie seemed at peace with the estrangement, but I knew way deep down she still wished her mama would come around.

Addie scooted next to me, swiped her phone screen, and tipped her head next to mine.

I said, "Try to get the tractors."

She captured two shots, then held up her phone so we could decide which one was better.

However, as soon as we looked at the first photo, we both shifted to look behind us.

In the shot, there was a wave of blue light along the curve of the crater, halfway up the bowl, between the starwalk and the entrance.

But I didn't see anything there now.

Addie swiped the screen to look at the other picture. Sure enough, there was a shimmer. It looked like the starlight aurora but on a smaller scale. A much smaller scale.

"You don't see anything, do you?" she asked, glancing over her shoulder again.

I was already standing up. I held out a hand to her. "No."

We backtracked to the entrance, where I ventured off the walkway.

"Are you sure you should be doing that?" she asked.

The starlings watched our every move. "This isn't the time to be a nervous nelly. Get down here."

Her eyebrows dropped low, narrowed in concern, but she carefully stepped down and made her way to me.

"I still don't see anything. Do you?" I asked.

"No. But hold on." She took a picture of the area where we'd seen the shimmer, and it glowed on her screen, clear as day. I bent down, brushed aside a clump of clover, and picked up a small blue stone.

As I did, the starlings silently swooped in even closer, landing on the rope right next to us. This close, they were a sight to behold, with their glittering feathers and kind eyes.

Addie nodded to my hand. "What is that?"

I rubbed it on my shirt, taking off the haze of dirt, and held it up to the sunlight. It sparkled and glinted. I held the stone out to her. "I'm not sure."

She lifted her phone to take a picture and the birds trilled a warning.

"I'll delete it as soon as we're done," she said to them. "I promise."

The birds quieted.

She took the picture and did an image search. The results came in instantly. My jaw dropped as I read.

Blue rough diamond.

Natural blue diamond.

Rough uncut blue diamond.

Sell diamonds online!

She quickly deleted the picture from her camera roll, and her eyes were wide as she looked at me.

I was shaking my head, disbelieving, as I recited part of Abner's poem. "The stone in reach, but for the screech, of the silver bird."

Addie recognized the words immediately—I'd told her all about Abner's journal and the poem. "But the stone he'd described wasn't *blue*. It was gray."

Suddenly I grabbed her arm—mostly to steady myself because I was woozy from my thoughts spinning round and round. "A lot of the Wingrove men are color-blind, Addie. I bet Abner was, too."

"This is, it's . . . What does all this *mean*? The glow, the diamond. Obviously they're connected."

I was at a loss, too. "I don't know." Then I recalled something buried deep in my memory. "Wait, wait. My mama and I went to the Smithsonian once when I was a teenager and they had a blue diamond on display." I racked my brain trying to think of its official name. "The Portuguese Diamond. One of the reasons why it's famous is because it glows bright blue under ultraviolet light. It's some sort of fluorescence or phosphorescence. I can't remember which."

Addie looked upward. "UV light like the sun has?" She gasped. "Do you think the diamonds were here all along and the force of the star hitting the ground brought them up to the surface? That must've been what happened, Tessa Jane. Closer to sunshine, they were then able to start glowing. But what gives the clarity? Is that from the star?"

She was talking so fast that I could hardly keep up. "I mean, the clarity has to come from the star. It's why the star water makes the cakes magical. It's what gives us our ability to see bright sides and inner light."

Addie nodded. "They work together."

One of starlings trilled and suddenly the field lit up with the aurora. I looked all around and realized that there was a break in the light, like a section was missing—right where I'd picked up the stone. I also noticed the rest of the light was dim. It had lost some of its luster.

I glanced at Addie. "They're *stronger* together."

"Like the starlings," she whispered.

"Like us."

Addie nodded. "We need to put the stone back."

Of course we did. It had never been about keeping the diamonds for ourselves. Not now and not back when the star had first fallen.

The beautiful light from the diamonds combined with the clarity from the fallen star was *priceless*. The value much greater than what the stones could ever sell for.

I closed my hand over the stone, tears in my eyes, realizing that the diamond tale had been true. Abner hadn't imagined what happened, and I was flooded with a sense of relief that I'd believed him.

I bent down and using my fingers, I dug a hole as deep as I could, then dropped the stone back into the earth. Once I patted the dirt down, colorful light bloomed, linking seamlessly to the rest of the aurora, which glowed brightly like nothing had ever dimmed its shine.

Then the birds squawked and all the light disappeared completely.

I dusted off my hands, glanced around. "I didn't see anything, did you? Nothing to see here at all!"

Addie's eyes were wide with alarm. "How am I ever supposed to keep this secret?"

I put my arm around her. "It's only a secret if two people know. And by my count there's a good twenty of us here."

She glanced at the birds on the rope, eighteen in all.

"You're right," she said, nodding. "Plus Aunt Bean knows, too."

"How do you know that?"

She smiled and held up her star pendant. "I bet you anything these stones aren't sapphire at all. Or the blue stone in her watch, either."

I sat down on the grass. "But how? There would be a section of light missing if our stone had come from the crater. Unless . . ."

I tried to recall Abner's words about finding the stone the

night the star had fallen. He'd written that he'd discovered it just beyond the crater. Near the woods.

"Unless the stone had been an outlier, never part of the aurora." I told her what I was thinking. "What if that starling took the stone out of Abner's hands and gave it to Charity? Her daughter?"

Addie sat down next to me, her eyes wide, as she followed my line of thinking. "And eventually the raw diamond was cut into many gemstones and passed along to the women in the family to help them see light when life was at its darkest."

Aunt Bean had told me it was the star water on our jewelry that provided that assistance, but now I suspected it wasn't the whole story. The water gave clarity. The stones gave light. Together, they gave comfort, warmth, peace, calmness. The same feeling I had every time I stepped into the starlight. The same feeling I had every time Aunt Bean gave me a hug.

The birds trilled, a beautiful melody.

"You know," Addie said, "there have been times I could've sworn this pendant glowed."

"Me, too! I always thought I was seeing things, though."

"But why didn't Aunt Bean just tell us about the diamonds?" Addie asked.

I glanced at her. "I bet it's one of those family secrets that she mentioned to me the day she showed me the star water. One that's passed down in death from one generation to the next."

Then I'd realized what I said, and my heart started pounding.

The birds chattered, then went quiet.

We both looked at them, still lined up on the rope railing.

She quietly said, "Does it feel like they showed us the diamond on purpose?"

I nodded, a lump lodged in my throat.

Suddenly, I heard a loud trilling coming from above. We both looked upward as another starling came swooping in, its feathers glinting as it landed on the rope next to the others. Number nineteen. As silvery and beautiful as the others but whose poofy head feathers seemed to have a burgundy tint.

My breath caught. A tear slid down Addie's cheek.

The new bird chirped at Addie and me and stamped a small foot twice on the railing, two short raps.

Then in a great commotion, the flock flapped their wings and took flight, heading back to the woods. I reached for Addie's hand, and our fingers twined together, holding on tight.

Tears flooded my eyes as I heard Aunt Bean telling me to remember that one day she'd be one of the birds watching over us, and that she loved Addie and me more than anything in the whole world.

Even more than all the stars in the sky.

ACKNOWLEDGMENTS

I'm often asked where I get the inspiration for my novels. Truly, it comes from everywhere. For this story, I was heavily influenced by my father's heart attack and quadruple bypass, which occurred shortly before I started writing this book. He's doing well now—thank goodness—but during those weeks he was in the hospital, when the outcome was up in the air, I couldn't help thinking about the what-ifs.

What if you received a terrifying diagnosis? Would you bury your head in the sand? Or start making lists? And what if someone you loved received this diagnosis? From there, this story was born. A story about mending what you can, making peace with the rest, and living—and loving—life to its fullest.

I'm so grateful to Jessica Faust and BookEnds, Kristin Sevick, and the entire team at Forge Books and Macmillan Audio, who breathe life into my stories. You all are simply amazing.

An extra big thank-you to Stephanie Willis and Hallie Ricardo, who've done such incredible work narrating my novels. That you can make me forget that I wrote the words you're speaking—that's true magic.

Speaking of magic, thank you to all the bakers out there who put your heart and soul into what you do. You're an inspiration.

Thank you to Sheri P., Stacy W.H., Liz C., and Erin S., who helped me name some of the cakes in this book. I can't help wishing the Starling Cake Company was a real place where we could sit and chat and eat the cakes you imagined.

To all the readers who choose to spend time with my stories, thank you so very much!

A special thank-you goes to my mom, who's dedicated to making sure my dad eats as healthy as possible, but is willing to look the other way when it comes to his love of butter.

And, as always, a big thank-you to my family. Much love.

ABOUT THE AUTHOR

HEATHER WEBBER is the national bestselling author of more than thirty novels and has been twice nominated for an Agatha Award. She loves to spend time with her family, read, drink too much coffee and tea, bird-watch, crochet, watch cooking competition and home improvement shows, and bake. Webber lives in southwestern Ohio and is hard at work on her next book.